BLOOD CRESCENDO

BLOOD CRESCENDO

DEREK ERICKSON

BOOK 2 OF THE SYMPHONY SAGA

Interior Design and Formatting by

www.emtippettsbookdesigns.com

The Top Hat Bet

Like every young, hopeful writer, I dreamed of writing a bestselling book one day. I always enjoyed writing adventure, fantasy, science-fiction, but my friend Cameron told me the only way to become a successful author was to make a teen paranormal romance. He then made me a bet.

If I could write a teen paranormal romance that became a bestseller, he would eat his top hat (it's a very nice hat).

I'm holding you to this promise Cameron. Here's book two in the Symphony Saga, Blood Crescendo.

ABOUT THE AUTHOR

Derek originally wrote Howling Symphony as a joke bet that he never expected to go anywhere. The first book started as an almost cliché paranormal romance, as the bet demanded, but there were no rules when it came to Blood Crescendo. After requests for a second book, he decided to write a sequel with a bit of flare and madness thrown into the romance. It was after he completed this book that he realized he'd found his style and knew he had to publish his work. Unfortunately his own life went to hell, and he joined the Army to get a new start. His writing continued, but the thought of publishing was severely delayed.

Since then he's moved all over the United States serving in the Army, going on to finish his Master of Public Health, and is currently living in Florida working to battle the Covid19 pandemic as an epidemiologist. In the past eight years he's lived in California, Florida, Hawaii, New Mexico, and Washington. He's hoping to stay in one place for a change. Between work, research, writing, and trying his best to maintain a real life, he's very busy. One day he'll get enough sleep.

TABLE OF CONTENTS

Chapter 1: An Early Start 1

Chapter 2: Riding Snow 8

Chapter 3: Maiden of War 23

Chapter 4: A Dangerous Ally 39

Chapter 5: Tools of the Trade 55

Chapter 6: Brilliant Snow 64

Chapter 7: Ghouls 84

Chapter 8: Shadows Hunting Shadows 93

Chapter 9: We Run Alone 117

Chapter 10: Scouting the Future 131

Chapter 11: Swirling Dresses 139

Chapter 12: A Miraculous May 157

Chapter 13: From Predator to Prey 165

Chapter 14: An Invitation 178

Chapter 15: Different Mountain, Same Crowd 185

Chapter 16: Resurrection 199

Chapter 17: The Premarital Run 204

Chapter 18: Battles in Celebration 227

Chapter 19: Acceptance 241

Chapter 20: True Dance of the Night.................................... 251

Chapter 21: Interrogation.. 259

Chapter 22: Going to War 265

Chapter 23: The Sinner and the Saint 275

Chapter 24: Chaos is Upon Us.. 289

Chapter 25: Endless Hunger 300

Chapter 26: Walking Plague.. 309

Chapter 27: Lady Death... 318

Chapter 28: War is Merciless... 335

Chapter 29: It's all over.. 344

Chapter 30: Collateral Damage... 349

CHAPTER 1

AN EARLY START

"Ashley, wake up."

Ashley groaned and rolled over in bed. Someone was prodding her, but she didn't want to wake up yet. It was another freezing night, and she was too warm to want to move. It didn't matter if the heater was on and her winter blanket was twice as thick as any blanket she'd ever owned before, it was still cold.

"Come on, wake up."

Ashley opened a bleary eye and saw only darkness. She'd developed a technique of curling in her blankets like a cocoon. Not even her head was exposed to the cool air and if she could have, she would've stayed that way all winter. She felt tugging on her blanket and then heard her dad.

"Honestly where are you in all this mess?" Ashley grumbled and untangled her upper half from the blankets and peered out at him.

"There you are," said Alex with a smile. He was fully dressed and leaning over her bed. Her dad was far too happy and awake for how early it must've been. Ashley couldn't see the clock but knew it was way too early. The room was almost pitch black and the only light came from the hallway.

"What dad?" she muttered, half asleep and half annoyed.

"I've got a surprise for you. Get ready." Ashley sighed and rolled onto her back.

"Why…"

"Just get up."

Ashley nodded and just laid there. She didn't know what her dad had planned and at this hour, honestly didn't care. She rolled her head to the other side and looked at the clock. It was 4:32AM on Saturday, February the 5th.

"Ashley! Get up!" She looked back at her dad bitterly.

"I am up."

"No, you've been asleep for ten minutes."

Ashley glanced back at her clock and saw she had indeed slept for ten more minutes. She didn't even remember falling asleep again. It didn't feel like it. It felt more like someone had magically stolen ten minutes from her. "Alright, I'm getting up."

"I'm staying until you are actually up this time."

Ashley glared at her dad and rolled slowly out of bed. Her blankets took on a life of their own and pulled on her to stay in their warmth. She felt like she was denying a lover as she parted from them and placed her feet on the floor. She winced as she stood up and felt the cooler room. Ashley longed for her bed as much as it longed for her.

"There, I'm up," she said with a flap of her arms. Her dad grinned and flicked on the light. The sudden brightness in the room almost shocked her back to bed. Her eyes burned and an uncontrollable angry moan left her.

"Good, get ready. I'll get breakfast started." Ashley nodded and stumbled into the bathroom. She flicked the weaker of the two lights on and looked at herself. She was a taller girl with long black hair. Her hair was one of the things she was almost always proud of, but not right then. It was filled with tangles and knots, and overall looked gross. Almost instantly she had her comb and began running it through her hair instinctively.

Her lean body was covered much more than it usually was. This winter she'd donated all of her old pajamas and had had to buy completely new ones. She was in heavy long johns, a sweater, and thick socks. Like her friend Liz had said, it wasn't pretty, but neither was freezing to death. Despite the amount of exercise she'd gotten in the snowy mountains, Ashley swore she'd put on weight. It happened to everyone in the deep cold. The little extra weight was the body's way of keeping a little warmer.

Ashley put on heavier clothes and brushed her teeth. Her eyes were barely staying open as she got ready. She was pretty sure she'd fallen asleep on her feet more than once. After brushing her teeth an ingenious idea came to her tired brain. She left the sink running for noise and kept her light on as she collapsed back to bed. Her loving blankets covered her eyes and sleep took her almost immediately. It would take her dad a while to realize this time.

The door quietly creaking open told her her time was already up. She didn't know how much time had passed, but it wasn't enough. Muffled noises were coming up the stairs and Ashley realized something was wrong. People were talking. The only people who lived here were her and her dad.

"WAKE UP!" shrieked a shrill voice. Ashley's eyes shot wide open. Either her dad had turned into a little girl or else…

"I said WAKE UP!" Something heavy dropped onto the bed and started bouncing around. "Get up! Get up! Get up!" Ashley rolled as feet came down randomly. They landed on her stomach and all the air left her lungs. Angry and hurt, she pulled on all of her blankets and pitched them all off the bed in one throw. There was a squeak of surprise and Ashley grinned in revenge.

Then a shadow came over her and Ashley's grin vanished. Lidia had somehow avoided coming off with the blankets and was sailing back down. Ashley brought her limbs in to protect herself, but Lidia landed where her legs had just been. She leapt to Ashley's side and smiled at her.

"Get up."

Ashley wanted to yell at her, but she was too confused and the air was still returning to her lungs. Lidia cartwheeled out the door and giggled all the way down the stairs. Ashley got out of bed, half in surprise, half hoping to see the little troll rolling down the stairs. She jumped as someone else came through the door.

"Good morning," whispered Nathaniel. He hugged her and placed his warm lips to her cheek. Ashley sighed in confusion, embracing that this must all be a dream, and let her arms slide around him. Nathaniel was always so warm, even in the cold. He nuzzled his head against hers and she knew she wasn't dreaming. This was most definitely her boyfriend.

"What are you doing here?" she asked.

"We're all here. We came to get you obviously."

"Why?"

"Get ready and come downstairs. You'll see." Nathaniel gave her a quick kiss and left the room.

Ashley shook her head, but started getting ready again. She was awake now and curious as to what was going on. On came the long socks, the multiple layered pants and shirts, the scarf, and she was down the stairs. The noise definitely sounded like Nathaniel's family. She started to head downstairs but there was something too big to avoid in the doorway.

"There she is," said Morgan cheerfully. He pulled Ashley into a hug just as she got down the stairs. With arms bigger than her torso, Ashley thought he was about to squeeze the life out of her.

"About time you woke up," said Alex.

"I'm so confused," she said as she looked about. Nathaniel's entire family was either standing about in the living room or eating in the kitchen. Nathaniel put an arm around her and smiled.

"We're going on a little adventure today."

"We thought it'd be funner to keep it a secret," said Kevin.

"YAAAA…" Lidia started before she was muffled by Mary.

"Shush," said Mary.

The only two not talking were Samuel and Melissa. Samuel was just reaching his teenage years and had hit the bottomless pit of stomach point of puberty. He might've waved between bites, but it was hard to tell. Melissa just stood facing the window, eyes reflecting the frozen bleak world outside. The glance she gave suggested the woman would like to see Ashley out in the dark cold.

"So what's going on?" asked Ashley, trying to keep away from Melissa.

"Didn't we just say we were keeping it a secret?" laughed Nathaniel. "Get some breakfast before it disappears down Samuel's endless gullet."

"So hungry," joked Samuel as he reached for another piece of French toast. Ashley sat down next to him at the table and started getting some food.

"We're going to have fun!" giggled Lidia.

"Look Lidia!" said Nathaniel suddenly. "Poor Roland looks lonely." Lidia's head snapped to the side as quickly as a distracted squirrel. The huskie puppy was tapping the outside door furiously. Her dad must've put him outside while company was over. He was mewing pathetically, chewing on the handle to get back to the people.

"Poor puppy!" Lidia shouted and practically flew outside. Seconds later she was chasing Roland around the yard.

"So easily distracted," muttered Kevin.

"A good thing too," said Morgan. "Is Ashley's bag all packed up?" Ashley stopped eating, but Alex nodded.

"Everything is ready, snacks included. All she needs is a lift. I'm surprised you came down in two cars."

"Adding Ashley to our group makes eight," said Morgan. "We could manage it, but some of us boys are a little bigger." Morgan patted his belly happily. "Could get a little crowded." Ashley didn't know why he patted his belly. None of Nathaniel's family was fat, they were just extraordinarily large.

"Two cars would be easier I guess," laughed Alex.

Ashley finished her breakfast quickly and was handed a large bag to take with her. Inside was all of her snow gear. This didn't really give her a clue as to what they were doing. It was February in Montana after a harsh winter. It was hard to find a place in the state not covered by snow.

At 5:30AM she climbed into Morgan's truck with Nathaniel and Samuel. All the girls and Kevin went into the other truck. She waved goodbye to her dad who said he'd see her tonight. When they started out of town she asked where they were going again. All of the boys just grinned.

"Today, we're going to teach you how to ride snow," said Nathaniel.

CHAPTER 2

RIDING SNOW

The whole journey out of town, Nathaniel didn't tell her what he meant by riding the snow. He said she'd understand when they got there and she should save her energy until they did. She would've dug for a better answer, but it was still 5:30AM, and she was exhausted. She nuzzled up close to Nathaniel and used him as a pillow for the next couple of hours.

When Ashley woke up, she didn't recognize where they were. All she could see outside were snow covered trees and streets. Morgan could've been going in circles and she probably wouldn't have known the difference. Nathaniel was still asleep with his head against the window. Samuel was slumped over in the front seat while Morgan drove listening quietly to the radio.

She could see Melissa driving the other truck behind them and winced. She knew it was no mistake that they'd taken two cars for this trip. Melissa wanted nothing to do with Ashley and neither did Kevin if he could help it.

Ashley could've imagined dating a werewolf wouldn't be easy, but she'd never imagined the kind of trouble it'd put her in. A group of monsters called jackals had attacked her and Nathaniel just before Thanksgiving last year and it had ended badly. As sweet as Nathaniel looked sleeping, he'd lost his boyish innocence that day when he'd been forced to kill. Four jackals, all boys themselves, had lost their lives to him.

Ashley had also lost her naivety about the world that day. She'd thought her boyfriend was a monster and a murderer and had wanted nothing to do with him. Only time and loneliness had taught her the error in her ways. Nathaniel was not a monster; he'd fought back to save their lives. Yes, he'd been forced to kill, but sometimes that's how the world is. She'd be dead without Nathaniel. And she would never forget what he'd done for her.

Melissa didn't find their reunion very romantic. She thought Ashley was a foolish girl who would get her son killed. Kevin felt Ashley would betray his brother a second time and abandon him when things became dangerous again. Ashley held Nathaniel's hand tightly and promised herself that wouldn't happen.

The car slowed, breaking her out of her reverie. They were driving up to some sort of rental station in a small town. Nathaniel shook awake when the car stopped.

"We here?" he yawned.

"Yup. Time to work," said Morgan. The boys yawned and followed their father out of the truck.

"This is what we're here for," said Nathaniel as he took her hand. Ashley looked at the machines, confused. They looked like jet skis people used on the lake.

"What are they?"

"They're snowmobiles. Think of them as motorcycles made for snow and ice." Ashley grinned and tightened her hold on him.

"Why am I not surprised?"

"We're getting four of them," he said happily. "We're going to go zooming around the mountains today." Ashley shook her head with a smile.

"What is it about you and going fast?"

"It's in my blood," he said before he kissed her cheek. They all stepped inside the rental station and enjoyed its heater as Morgan finished the paperwork. When everything was finalized, the man at the desk led them out back. He had a number of snowmobiles and trailers for them.

"We'll just get these attached and you'll be on your way," said the man cheerfully.

"Let's turn the trucks around for the man," Morgan said to his wife. "Boys, you get the honors of pushing." A small grumble came up from the boys as they pushed the first two snowmobiles onto the first trailer. The owner just guided them and let them do all the work. Nathaniel and Kevin took the front of the trailer and dragged it forward as Samuel pushed. Mary stood next to Ashley with Lidia sitting on her shoulders and they just watched.

"You could help us Mary," said Samuel bitterly.

"My hands are full with this one." Lidia cheered. She was a bit old to be sitting on Mary's shoulders, but Mary didn't seem to mind. "They all wonder why I offer to watch Lidia," Mary said slyly to Ashley. Ashley couldn't help but laugh as the boys grunted past them.

They hooked a trailer up to each vehicle and all climbed back inside. Even when Morgan was free, he didn't help the boys. He laughed when they asked for help and merely replied. "Why do you think I had kids?"

They drove out a bit further and this time Ashley was awake. Morgan and Nathaniel were explaining everything there was to know about snowmobiles to both Ashley and Samuel. Samuel had never driven one before, but he'd been on the back plenty of times. This year he might be old enough to learn.

They pulled off the road and entered a large open field. Ashley had no idea where they were, but she decided after hours of driving, they could be a lot of places. There seemed to be nothing around for miles except the occasional bunch of trees. She smiled in the cool air of the day and slipped on the rest of her snow gear.

The boys pulled all the snowmobiles out and checked them over. Ashley had to admire the sleek machines. They really did look like jet skis with skis attached. Kevin was the first to rev his engine to life. It roared like a motorcycle before dropping to a comfortable purr. Morgan and Nathaniel did the same while Melissa grabbed the last one. With four snowmobiles there would be two people to a snowmobile. Not bad thought Ashley, considering she, Lidia, and Samuel couldn't drive them.

"Come on Ashley," said Nathaniel as he sat on his snowmobile. Ashley nestled herself behind Nathaniel and looked around for anything to hold onto. Nathaniel saw her puzzled expression and laughed. "You can either try holding onto the seat or me."

Ashley leaned forward and wrapped her arms around him. He was much comfier than the seat and she was sure if it came down to it, he'd probably hold on better.

"Isn't there some type of safety gear?" she asked. Off to their left, Kevin's snowmobile sped away with Samuel sitting on the back cheering.

"You can wear a helmet, but I just suggest you don't fall off."

Unlike his brother, Nathaniel started the snowmobile forward slowly. It jerked at first as he played with the throttle, but he kept it slow. "Riding a snowmobile is kind of like riding me. When it turns, you need to turn with it. You always have to balance yourself." Nathaniel sped up a little bit more and began a slight turn. Ashley saw him leaning with the snowmobile and tried to mimic him. She realized she was already leaning as well. All the times she'd ridden Nathaniel in the mountain had paid off.

The other two snowmobiles fired off past them. Ashley didn't see who was driving, but she did see Lidia waving frantically as they passed. Nathaniel turned the snowmobile around and brought it to a halt. He pulled his goggles down over his eyes and his mouth slid into a dangerous grin. "We can't just let them get away from us, can we?"

Ashley didn't even respond. She knew her boyfriend and that look all too well. Nathaniel was about to sprint and she had two choices, jump off or hold on. She pulled her goggles down and squeezed her hands around him.

This time the snowmobile really jumped. It made one heavy lurch before it launched itself forward. Ashley wasn't as startled as she'd expected though. Nathaniel ran much rougher than this as a werewolf. She leaned away from him and watched as they began to gain on his family. Her eyes strayed down and she saw the snow shooting up all around them as they cut through. She laughed at how easily they moved across the icy fields.

The family split up on paths they must've already known. There were a few cases where Ashley screamed as she thought they were about to hit a tree only to have Nathaniel veer past it at the last second. He laughed joyfully as Ashley hit him on the back. Ashley knew he was showing off and enjoying every second of it.

After about twenty minutes of driving around, he slowed onto the open field again. He brought his goggles up as he swiveled around. "So what do you think?"

"It's fun," said Ashley as she raised her goggles. She was less covered in snow than she'd imagined, but she was still cold. Wind was already bad enough over the ice, but driving through it with only Nathaniel to break it was murder.

"Do you want to try?" he asked and leaned away from the controls.

"I don't know how," she said fearfully.

"Let me show you," he said as he stood up. "You can't come out all this way and just sit on the back."

"Why not?"

"Because that's boring," he smirked as he sat behind her. He nudged her towards the front and placed her hands on the handlebars. "The snowmobile is already on and warmed up. All you need to worry about is the throttle and the brake." He patted each with her hand as he spoke. "You want to curl your hand over the throttle so you're a bit overextended. That way when you're driving your hand is back and comfortable." Ashley nodded and moved her hand a bit over the throttle. Nathaniel rubbed her brake hand gently. "Don't be so tense or you'll just be squeezing the brake. Keep your fingers ready, but stay relaxed. Now take a deep breath and go whenever you're ready."

Ashley did take that deep breath and looked ahead. This couldn't be any worse than driving her jeep. Just keep your eyes forward and don't hit anyone she thought. She pulled back on the throttle slowly and felt the snowmobile jerk below her. It started as slow as she liked and waited for her to add more gas. She pulled back more until they were driving forward at a steady pace.

"You got it," said Nathaniel. "Now try some small turns."

Ashley slowed down and turned. The snowmobile responded fluidly to her commands. She understood now why Nathaniel went faster on turns. The snowmobile couldn't pull sharp turns without the extra boost. She moved the snowmobile up and down the field with Nathaniel's encouragement.

Ashley had to admit there was a certain rush when she squeezed the throttle and shot across the snowy plains. Nathaniel sat behind her cheering as she drove them around. She wasn't going half the speed he was, but she was learning. She leaned in with the corners and laughed as the snowmobile moved with her. Nathaniel motioned for her to turn to the long stretch of snow they'd been going up and down. Then he held his fist up for her to stop.

"Ready for some real speed?" he asked. Ashley took a deep breath and grinned.

"I think so. As long as we don't do any sharp turns."

"You won't," he said as he got off the snowmobile and stretched. "You just have to keep up." Nathaniel started to walk away and waved for her to follow.

"Why aren't you getting back on?" she yelled.

"Because I want to see if you can keep up for once." Nathaniel turned and started to jog down the path without her.

"Nathaniel," she cried. "Come back."

"You better chase me!"

Nathaniel started to pick up his pace. Ashley looked at the snowmobile hesitantly. She knew how it worked, but she was afraid to squeeze the throttle. She didn't want to jump forward without Nathaniel's strong hand there to keep her safe.

Ashley suddenly shrieked as something cold and heavy hit her chest. Snow splashed across her jacket and sprayed her exposed face.

She looked up to see Nathaniel rolling in the snow just ahead of her, laughing. She pointed at him and laughed. "You!" Nathaniel sat up suddenly and resembled a rabbit who'd just been spotted. Ashley revved the engine.

"Wu-oh!" he shouted and was on his feet. Even without turning into a wolf, Nathaniel was insanely fast. No human could ever keep up with him in a race if he really wanted to move. Ashley knew she was no match against him, but today she wasn't running.

She let the throttle fly and the snowmobile pounced forward. Nathaniel was spitting up snow behind him as he soared across the open plain, but Ashley was gaining on him. She could hear Nathaniel laughing up ahead as he ran.

Ashley screamed with joy as she pulled ahead of him. Nathaniel put his head down and started running faster, but he wasn't the beauty of a machine that Ashley had. The more he tried to close the distance, the further she was able to pull away. She kept her head low and felt her pounding heart. She understood the thrill of speed now.

Nathaniel leapt across the snow and landed near her before he began sprinting again. He moved closer to her and motioned for her to keep going straight. She laughed and watched him line up with the snowmobile. His hand took hold of the back end and he leapt onto the snowmobile gracefully. Ashley felt the slight jolt of his weight and cheered as his hands went around her. She leaned into a turn and didn't even bother slowing her speed. Nathaniel pointed to the speedometer and Ashley gasped.

She was going twice as fast as before. She'd enjoyed the thrill of the chase so much that she hadn't even realized how fast she was going. Keeping control or taking turns wasn't hard anymore. It wasn't just easy, it was exhilarating. After a few more minutes she stopped and lifted her goggles to look Nathaniel in the eye.

"Now that is what I call riding the snow," he said. Ashley kissed him so fiercely they fell off the snowmobile. She landed on Nathaniel and didn't let go. After a minute she let released him and rolled into the snow.

"Now that is a rush," she said loudly. Nathaniel chuckled and leaned over and kissed her.

"We better get up," he said sweetly.

"Why?" She wrapped her arms around him and smiled. "I'm comfy here."

"Yeah but we're about to be interrupted." He looked up and she looked back to see two snowmobiles coming towards them.

"Who is it?" she asked.

"My dad and Samuel on one, Mary and Lidia on the other." Ashley sighed.

"I guess we have to get up."

"Probably."

Nathaniel went in for one last kiss. Instead he received a mouth full of snow as Ashley hit him with a snowball point blank. Laughing hysterically, she pushed him away and jumped on as driver. She started it up quickly when Nathaniel hopped on the back.

"Go, go, go!" The other two snowmobiles were closing on them and Ashley started away. "Oh and I got you a present." Ashley felt the back of her coat come out and a handful of snow drop down her bare back. She gasped in anger as Nathaniel patted it against her skin. Her hands were firmly on the handlebars and she couldn't stop him.

"Nothing you can do!" shouted Nathaniel. Ashley saw Morgan pointing back the way they came and nodded.

She threw the snowmobile as hard as she could to the left. Nathaniel squeaked in surprise as he tumbled off the back. Ashley started laughing as she continued away without him. It only took him a few seconds to recover and run back to the snowmobile.

"You are evil," he said as he hopped on the back.

"Let's just say I won," she shouted back. Nathaniel hugged her tightly to secure himself and squeeze the snow against Ashley once more.

They pulled alongside Mary and followed Morgan back. Lidia was cheering from her seat upon seeing Ashley was the one driving. Ashley just smiled and kept her head low as Morgan picked up his speed. After a few turns Samuel wheeled around in his seat and began waving at them all. His arms changed from mad waving to a weird dance. He stuck out his tongue and shouted taunts at them.

"Come on little girls! Keep up."

"Go to the left," Nathaniel commanded.

Ashley veered away from the group for a second. Nathaniel leaned down and ran his hand through the snow. He came back up a second later and pointed back to Samuel. "Get him!" Ashley brought the snowmobile up alongside Morgan and pretended to wave to him. Morgan waved cheerfully back.

"WOOOOOOHOOOO!" shouted Morgan.

Ashley gave him a thumbs up and immediately began laughing. Samuel started to dance at them again, but Nathaniel had packed the snow he'd gathered into a hardball and pelted Samuel in the chest. Samuel began shouting angrily at them. Morgan just laughed and pulled ahead of them.

They went back and had sandwiches for lunch. They laughed about their adventures and many congratulations were given to Ashley. Not wanting to be outdone, Samuel asked to learn to drive after lunch. He picked it up even faster than Ashley and pretty soon they were all flying across the snow. After a few hours though, Ashley was beginning to feel like she'd been riding a horse all day. Her butt and legs had never been this sore before in her life.

Morgan was ready to pack things up, but Kevin proposed a final race. There were eight people and four snowmobiles. Ashley found herself driving with Nathaniel on the back. Morgan was next to them with Lidia squeezing his back. Kevin had Samuel which left Mary driving with her mother behind her.

"THREE!" shouted Melissa.

"TWO!" shouted Morgan.

"ONE!" shouted Kevin.

All the engines revved and dangerous looks were shared. Nathaniel was baring his teeth and Ashley realized his family were all doing the same. The cold wind on her teeth told her she was doing it too.

"GO!" they all screamed and the roar of the engines filled the air. Snow blasted up behind them as they shot forward. Ashley had half expected them to try and smash into each other to get the chance to go ahead, but nobody tried. They weren't wolves right now and these were expensive. Today's race would be determined by skill, not brute force.

They were all neck and neck for the first half. The course was a straight forward and back and it would all be determined on the turn around. All of them knew how to squeeze the throttle and go forward, but keeping that speed when they turned was a different matter. Ashley started to slow down as they came to their flag, but Nathaniel pushed her to keep going.

"I can't turn at that speed!" she countered.

"I'll help you! Just do what I say!"

Ashley nodded and kept the speed up. Morgan was slowing down, but the rest kept their speeds high. They were nearing the flag when Nathaniel told her to let go of the throttle. Ashley took her hand off and the snowmobile immediately began to slow.

"Now turn! Hard as you can!" Ashley yanked the snowmobile around as hard as she could. "Hit it!" Ashley closed her eyes and opened up the engine again. The snowmobile lurched forward and to the side at the same time. She felt it tilt slightly and she was afraid it was about to flip.

When she opened her eyes again she saw Nathaniel leaning off the snowmobile with one hand buried in the snow. He was pitting his strength against the snowmobile, stabilizing it and forcing it to turn at the same time. Ashley relaxed the throttle quickly to stop it in the direction she wanted and then pulled it back as hard as she could.

Turned out many of the family knew this trick and they were sailing forward just as quickly. Morgan was in the rear as he tried to pick up maximum speed again. Kevin and Mary were fighting for the lead, but Ashley wasn't too far behind. She didn't know why, but she suddenly understood the competitiveness of the family.

"Snowball them!" she shouted to Nathaniel. He looked at her surprised.

"What?"

"You heard me."

Nathaniel snickered evilly and stuck his hand in the rushing snow. He packed a ball like lightning before flinging it at his brother. He had more snow and was creating a new ball before the first one hit. Ashley saw a number of them going wild, but Nathaniel put a few into his brother and his snowmobile. Kevin started shouting something at them, but they were too far away to hear. Ashley and Nathaniel just laughed as more volleys were launched.

Mary took advantage of her brother's distraction and pulled ahead. Ashley pointed out her as the next target and Nathaniel turned his sights obediently. He had the first snowball in his hand when Melissa turned on them with a stern glare. It was like she sensed the attack coming and met them with a look colder than ice. Nathaniel dropped the snowball as if he'd never had it. Ashley silently agreed his mom was a bad target.

Mary held up her hands in joy as they crossed the finish line. Kevin met them only moments later and Ashley moments after them. Morgan brought up the rear laughing.

"I'm too heavy for these kinds of races. I can't get the thing moving!" Morgan shouted.

"I would've won if not for them," complained Kevin. Nathaniel grinned.

"I don't know what you're talking about."

"I beat you at least," said Kevin.

Nathaniel wheeled up from the ground and threw an underhanded snowball straight into Kevin's chest. Ashley laughed, but Kevin had had enough. He snarled and leapt at Nathaniel. Ashley shrieked and rolled away before Kevin fell on his brother. Nathaniel caught Kevin and together they rolled into the snow. Ashley couldn't tell if they were actually fighting or just playing. She just saw limbs come up and clouds of snow when they went down.

"Come on boys we're leaving," said Morgan. "Help me put the snowmobiles back on their trailers." The brothers didn't appear to hear their dad and continued their vicious assault on each other. "Now."

Ashley heard a lot of snaps and growls amongst the snow and neither one appeared.

"Your father said…" started Melissa sweetly before she turned on the boys, "**NOW!**" The whole family seemed to shake at the sudden earthquake. Nathaniel and Kevin both popped out of the snow and quickly brushed themselves off. There was a small bruise on Nathaniel's cheek and one on Kevin's forehead.

"We're just playing mom," said Nathaniel calmly.

"Friendly snow fight is all," continued Kevin. Melissa stared at both of them.

"Ah-huh," she said slowly before she turned to the truck. Ashley tried not to laugh as the brothers shared worried looks before snickering. A snowball flashed between them and smacked Melissa in the back of the head. Everyone tensed as Melissa turned around with an evil smile on her lips.

"Who…" she started.

"Boys!" shouted Morgan with an enormous smile on his face. "Be more mature and leave your mother alone!" Nathaniel and Kevin's jaws dropped and Morgan tried hard not to laugh. Melissa dragged her boot through the snow and sent a wave at her husband. She laughed manically and raced into the truck to avoid retaliation. Morgan laughed in the hail of snow. He gasped suddenly as his legs buckled as Samuel took him from behind.

"Get him!"

Morgan turned on Samuel laughing just as Nathaniel and Kevin leapt in to help. They tried to pin their father's arms as Samuel wrestled down his legs. Ashley just laughed and helped Mary grab a few bags to take into the truck. The boys kept at it for a full minute before they were suddenly covered in snow. They all ducked away as snowballs came on furiously. Lidia threw the last of her pile before throwing her hands up in the air.

"Winner goes to the lone wolf! Oh yeah!" She started dancing victoriously back to the truck. The boys all started to reach for snow and Lidia immediately squealed and ran to get inside. The boys dropped the snow and moved the snowmobiles back onto their trailers. Ashley helped Mary get any remaining supplies before stripping off her heavy coat and hat and throwing them in the truck.

Once they started away Ashley fell into Nathaniel's arms and practically fell asleep. As much fun as the snow was, it always sapped her. Her whole body felt worked and sore. She just wanted to close her eyes and take a nap on her warm boyfriend's shoulder. Morgan turned the heater on and she instantly felt ten times sleepier.

"How was riding the snow?" asked Nathaniel. Ashley held her thumb up in approval.

"It was awesome."

"You enjoyed the snowmobiles then?" asked Morgan.

"Think it's possible for me to trade my jeep in for a motorcycle in the spring?" Nathaniel laughed and squeezed Ashley.

"Remind me to take you out when the snow melts." Ashley tried to say more, but all she could do was snore on Nathaniel's sleeve. She'd had enough excitement for one day.

CHAPTER 3

MAIDEN OF WAR

It'd been nearly a month since the snowmobiles, but they'd changed Ashley forever. She understood now why Nathaniel enjoyed speed so much and she'd become far more reckless after that day. She drove her jeep faster and took turns harder. While most drivers would be terrified to drive as she did in the snow, she loved it. Her jeep had been designed to ignore the worst of conditions and plow on through, and that's exactly what she did.

She did learn quickly that while her jeep could take a lot, it couldn't beat the worst storms. She had snow tires and four-wheel drive and none of it mattered if the ice became thick enough. She'd taken a corner hard one day and found her jeep turning, but she kept going forward. Panic had set in as she slid sideways down a street for twenty feet before sliding to a halt. Her mother must've been looking down on her that day as there was no one else on the road.

She thought about her mother as she took the mountain road up to Nathaniel's. It'd been almost a year since she'd passed away. It wasn't so long ago but living with her and her life in California seemed like another life completely. She still had her mother's picture by her bedside, but she didn't miss her as much as she used to. Her mom would've wanted her to live her life happily. Ashley looked out the snowy windows and hoped her mom really was watching over her. Instead of seeing the beautiful forest though, she saw something dark rushing at her.

Ashley screamed as something heavy collided with the side of her jeep. The windows exploded, covering her in a hail of glass. She saw a large, furry backside smashed up against her door. She tried to turn to get away but combined with the hit and the slick roads, it only made it worse. She gave one last scream as her jeep rammed into a tree off the road. Ashley's head bounced off the airbag and then off of the back of her seat.

The blow to her head was hard and her body instantly felt tired and heavy. She wanted nothing more than to close her eyes and fall asleep, but the snarling form of the jackal outside of her door compelled her to stay awake.

Jackals. She'd encountered them last year as they tried to fight Nathaniel. They were cousins to werewolves, smaller and mangier by comparison. They were more scavengers than hunters. A small band had tried to make a push for the mountain before, but Nathaniel had forced them away. She'd thought they'd left the mountainside for good. Whatever she thought didn't matter however, all thanks to the snarling beast outside.

She tried to get out of her seat as the beast tried to tear the door off her jeep. She started to scoot to the other side when a second jackal appeared at that door. Panic started to overwhelm her as she realized there was nowhere to go. The safest place she had was where she was sitting and very soon that wouldn't be safe at all.

The jackal on her left suddenly howled in pain and dropped out of view. Ashley looked back just in time to see something fly past her head. It came so close to her that she felt the flying knife cut her hair. It went straight into the second jackal's eye and it dropped into the snowbank without a sound. Ashley looked for her savior.

A woman was standing in the middle of the street. She wasn't dressed in winter clothing and didn't appear to have a car. It looked like she'd come out of the forests just as the jackals had. She had long blonde hair and a lithe, beautiful body. Her strong curves were visible since she was only in a long sleeve shirt and tight pants. Ashley started to ask who she was when a third jackal burst out of the forest.

Ashley screamed for the woman, but the woman didn't even appear to be concerned. The woman stepped aside and kicked the jackal in mid leap. To Ashley's and the jackal's surprise, the woman's kick knocked the jackal over. It hit the ground hard but was on its feet in seconds. It slashed and bit but never came close. She dodged it left and right and for every swing it took, she hit it back. Ashley knew this woman could not be normal and the jackal seemed to be thinking the same thing. It started to step away from her.

The woman's face hardened and she started to advance. The jackal fled on all fours and for a wonder, the woman turned into a blur for how fast she moved. The jackal still might have gotten away but the woman pulled two knives from behind her and sent them hurtling towards her prey. One hit the jackal in the back and the other caught one of its hind legs. It stumbled to the ground and the woman stepped over it with all the confidence of an apex predator. Ashley looked away as the woman raised another knife above the jackal. The jackal let loose a high pitched howl and then all went silent.

A moment later Ashley opened her eyes to see the woman walking towards her. The woman's hard look hadn't disappeared and she was holding a pair of bloody knives. Panic returned to Ashley as she realized she may not be safe still. She moved for the other door and tried to kick it open, but it was no good. The jackal had mangled the door and it wasn't going anywhere.

"Ashley Lebell?" Ashley turned to the woman who was now at the driver's side. The woman had put away her knives but Ashley still had a feeling she was no friend. "Are you Ashley Lebell?"

"Yes," Ashley said slowly. The woman smiled.

"Good, I got here in time. Can you get out?" Ashley looked at the doors and shook her head. "Stupid beasts…" The woman took hold of the driver's door and grunted. Ashley heard the jeep groan and then it shook as the woman's ripped the door off completely. The woman threw the door aside casually and waved to her.

"You can come out now." Ashley stayed where she was. The woman had killed three jackals and pulled her door off as easily as popping open a soda.

"What are you?" The woman laughed in response.

"Not your enemy, not yet anyway. I suppose you don't have to get out." The woman reached inside her pocket and pulled out a folded envelope. "In exchange for saving your life, you have to be sure to give this to Morgan." Ashley cocked her head in curiosity as she was handed the envelope. "Do you promise to do that?"

"Yes."

"Good. I imagine he'll be here soon. I'll see you again." The woman patted her jeep and walked out of sight. Ashley crawled out to see where she was going, but the woman was already gone. She looked at the envelope again. On the back, the letter was sealed with a red lipstick kiss. Ashley pulled out her phone.

"I think you need to get here Nathaniel." She called his phone and didn't get a response. She called again and this time it was picked up by Mary.

"Hey Ashley. Nathaniel's not in right now."

"I need him. I just got attacked on the road to your house."

"Are you okay? Where are you?"

"I'm about fifteen minutes away. The jackals are dead, I was saved by someone I don't know."

"That's where Nathaniel went was to the jackals. Make some noise and my brother should get you." Ashley nodded and said goodbye. She should've figured Nathaniel's family would've heard the noise. The jackal's howl was pretty loud.

She held her head back and let out a long howl. It wasn't anything like a true wolf's howl, but Nathaniel would know it was her. She howled a few more times before she started to call out his name.

"Nathaniel!" She started to pace a bit on the road and away from her jeep. She felt uncomfortable near the dead jackals. She heard barking nearby and looked up expectantly.

Another jackal wandered into the street a way down from her. It was sniffing the dead jackal and nuzzling it. Ashley started to move slowly for the side of the road to hide when the jackal turned to her. She gulped as its ears went down and it started to snarl. She really hoped Nathaniel was close by. She heard metal creak and turned to see more jackals appearing around her jeep. Ashley had only ever seen a few jackals at a time before. Now there were so many coming out of the woods she could only assume multiple families had arrived. They were examining their dead and many were eyeing her dangerously.

She jumped at the sudden roars next to her and she thought the jackals had surrounded her. The sound of heavy pounding behind her made her turn in fear. Her pounding heart calmed itself as she saw Morgan, Nathaniel, and Kevin all charging towards her. She turned back to the jackals and considered their numbers. If a fight broke out here it would turn very nasty and very bloody. The jackals had superior numbers by far, but Nathaniel's family was much bigger physically. Nathaniel and Kevin stopped in front of her and started barking furiously at the jackals. Morgan rose to his hind feet and showed off his incredible size.

Ashley waited for the inevitable fight, but it didn't seem to want to come. The jackals stayed where they were and Nathaniel's family didn't advance. A large jackal came out of the back of the group and started calmly walking towards them. Morgan dropped to all fours again and moved to meet it. Ashley dropped close to Nathaniel's side.

"Are they going to fight?" she whispered. Nathaniel shook his head. "Talk?" He nodded. The alpha jackal and Morgan barked at each other for a short while and everyone stayed tense. Ashley couldn't understand them, but understood it could still end violently if the wrong words were said. After a few moments, the jackal barked to its followers and walked away from Morgan. Nathaniel nudged Ashley and laid down. She got on his back quickly and they started forward. The jackals were retreating into the forest, taking their dead with them as they left. Once the road was clear of them, Morgan led the way back into the forest.

It was at times like this that Ashley truly hated not being able to understand what had happened. She could only watch for a few little signs and just wait until they were human again. All she knew was when Nathaniel's ears went down that they were going to go faster. The ride back to their house went uninterrupted. Ashley was surprised when they crossed the jackals again in the woods, but the two groups didn't bother each other. Some form of agreement must've passed.

Melissa was waiting for them outside when they arrived at the house. Ashley hopped off of Nathaniel and went over to her. Melissa wasn't smiling or appeared happy to see her.

"I see you've brought more trouble with you," she said cruelly. Ashley frowned, but didn't say anything. To her surprise, Morgan barked loudly at her. Melissa looked at her husband angrily and then back to Ashley. "Well then, perhaps there's more to the story. Come inside and get warm. The boys will be in in a minute." Melissa led the way and held the door open for her. Ashley wondered what Morgan had said that had shocked Melissa into acting a little nicer. She forgot about it as the dogs charged her and almost knocked her to the floor. It took a minute of Melissa and Mary shouting at them to get back before they could get inside. Lidia appeared in the middle of the excited dogs.

"Hello. Did you get in trouble again?" Ashley smiled.

"Not quite."

"Everyone into the dining room," said Melissa forcefully. "We need to have a family talk."

"But those are boring…" whined Lidia. Melissa turned a look so dark upon Lidia that the girl went instantly quiet. Ashley cringed as she knew how those looks felt. Lidia lost the skip to her step and proceeded straight to the dining room table. They all took their seats just as the boys came back in.

"Are you okay?" asked Nathaniel as he hugged her.

"I'm fine. Just a little shaken up."

"So what happened out there?" asked Melissa to her husband. Morgan gave out a heavy sigh and sat down.

"The jackals in the forest were here for revenge. They were upset over the boys they lost last year. A few families came in to take the mountain from us. A small group saw Ashley going up the road and figured out who she was. They meant to kill her as a warning to the rest of us. They got her off the road and almost had her when something else came." Morgan looked at Ashley. "Ashley, you're the only one who saw what happened out there. What kills three jackals and doesn't leave a scent behind?"

"It was this woman," said Ashley.

"A woman?" asked Kevin. "Just one woman?"

"Hush," said Melissa quickly.

"Yes. She killed the two jackals who made me crash by throwing knives at them. She fought the third one with her bare hands. It tried to run away and then she got it with knives too."

"Can you describe this woman?"

"A little taller than me, long blonde hair, wore all black. She wasn't wearing any heavy clothing even though it's freezing out. The cold didn't seem to bother her."

"What was her skin color?" asked Morgan.

"White, why?" Morgan shook his head.

"Was she pale?" Ashley thought about it and realized the woman was rather pale.

"Yes." Melissa looked at Morgan concerned.

"Vampire?" she asked. Morgan nodded.

"It's what I've been thinking since I saw that mess. It's the only thing which would be strong enough and not leave a scent behind."

"Why would a vampire save Ashley though?" asked Kevin. "No offense Ashley, but vampires aren't generally generous with their help. Plus it's daylight out. What vampire goes out in the day?"

"If she stays to the forest and stays covered up," said Morgan, "there's plenty of places she could stay out of the sun. Did she tell you her name Ashley?"

"No," said Ashley, "but she knew mine." All of the family looked at her concerned. "She told me she wasn't my enemy yet. In exchange for saving my life, she said I had to give you this." She pulled the envelope from her coat and held it out to Morgan.

"She wanted me to have this?" asked Morgan.

"She knew your name too," said Ashley quietly. "She knew that I was coming here."

"How could she know that?" asked Nathaniel. Morgan said nothing as he turned over the letter. He frowned at the lipstick stamp and opened it up. Inside was a single piece of paper. From what Ashley could see through the back of it, it wasn't a letter but a picture. Morgan held the picture up and his frown deepened.

"Gods damn it," he whispered.

"What is it dad?" asked Nathaniel. Morgan slammed the picture down on the table for everyone to see.

It was a drawing of a longsword coming up the paper. Halfway up the blade began to change into a rose. The sword point was visible through the rose and the rose was bleeding down the blade. It was done expertly and the detail was exquisite. Melissa snarled at the picture, but nobody else knew what it meant.

"Dad?" asked Nathaniel.

"It's Karin," he said as he stood up. "She's back."

"Who's Karin?"

"Not a very nice person. Melissa, can you get on the phone and call Katie." Melissa nodded. Morgan rose from the table and pointed to Ashley and Nathaniel. "You two are coming with me. The rest of you are staying here."

"Where are we going?" asked Nathaniel.

"We need to get Ashley's car towed into the shop. Be prepared for trouble Nathaniel." Nathaniel nodded. Kevin stood up looking upset.

"Why don't I get to go?"

"Because I know Nathaniel and I can take care of ourselves out there." Kevin looked wounded by his dad's words at first, but Morgan wasn't finished. "I want you to stay here and protect the family. We can fight, but Lidia and Samuel can't yet. I don't want to leave your mother and sister up to the task in case anything bad happens. Can you watch the house for me Kevin?" Kevin's disappointment changed to a moment of pride.

"Of course dad."

"Good. We'll be back soon."

Morgan led them out of the house and they went back to the barn. He opened the doors and went in search of something. Ashley peered in realizing she'd never really been in the barn before. She knew it was something of a small auto body shop in itself. Nathaniel pulled her back out as her dad dragged out a heavy trailer. Nathaniel grabbed the other end and they started to attach it to the back of the truck. Ashley realized they meant to put her jeep on it so they could tow it into town.

"Who's Karin?" asked Nathaniel. Morgan sighed.

"Get in the car."

Ashley had never seen Morgan look so down and sad about something before. They all got in the car and began their descent down the mountain. Nathaniel didn't say a word, but looked at his dad intently. Ashley knew he wouldn't give up until he got an answer. She would've told him to stop, but she wanted to know too.

"Karin is a woman I used to know a long time ago." Morgan finally said. "We grew up together and we used to date. We were a lot like you and Ashley are now." Nathaniel and Ashley shared a look before they looked back. "I decided we had to go our separate ways after high school. She was obsessed with me and said I couldn't go. I knew then it really had to end and I left."

"Did she know you were a werewolf?" asked Nathaniel. Morgan shook his head.

"No, thankfully she never did. Thirty years after high school I ran into her again." Ashley frowned. Morgan talked about this like it was so long ago, but he didn't even look fifty. She wondered how old he really was. "I was shocked to see her again, it was by complete chance. To my surprise, she didn't look any older than I did. I found out she'd become a vampire in college and had been moving around ever since. She didn't attack humans and she seemed so much calmer. One thing led to another and we started dating again for a bit."

"I take it that didn't go well," said Nathaniel. Morgan shook his head.

"It was a dumb idea from the start. I knew what she was so our relationship would've never really worked anyway. I thought it was just some old fling and enjoying time with an old friend. Then I found out the truth."

"She was still obsessed. Our chance meeting hadn't been chance at all. She'd been stalking me for years looking for the right opportunity to jump back into my life. I told her to leave. She refused and again I just left her where she was. She was almost mad back then and almost hurt a friend. I thought she died, but somehow she must've survived.

That picture Ashley brought us was Karin's favorite personal symbol. It's tattooed on her back."

"So she's back for you?" asked Ashley.

"Yes. Only this time I don't think she wants to go out with me. I think she's back to settle some kind of grudge. A grudge that could extend to all of us." They pulled up next to Ashley's jeep and stopped. Ashley sighed. It was completely dead in her eyes.

"Don't worry Ashley, we'll get it fixed," said Morgan. "I just need you to do something for me."

"What?"

"I need you to lie to your dad. I need you to say you skidded off the road and got in an accident. I know your dad is good at telling when people lie, but you have to do this." Ashley nodded and started to think up a good story. "Nathaniel, take the other end and let's get it up on the trailer." Nathaniel nodded and braced himself on the other side of the jeep. Ashley watched in amazement as the pair of them shoved her jeep away from the tree and back into the street. It was in neutral and the wheels slid decently, but there was a lot of brute force going into play here. When they finally had it up on the back, Morgan pulled out his cell phone.

"Nathaniel, hook up the jeep. I'm going to call Ashley's dad right now. You ready for when I hand you the phone Ashley?" Ashley nodded and worked up some fake tears and coughing. Morgan started up the call and started pacing.

"Alex? Hey this is Morgan. I'm doing alright. I'm calling because Ashley got into an accident on the way to my house. Yeah she's alright, just slid off the road into a tree. I think she was going a little too fast, hit a little bit of black ice, and lost control. Yeah I've got her here." Morgan held the phone out to her. She choked her voice up a bit before taking the phone.

"Hi dad."

"Hey, are you alright?"

"Yeah. I'm just a little shaken up."

"Good. What happened?"

"I…I don't know. I was just going up to see Nathaniel and suddenly I was off the road. I tried to slow down, but I hit the tree first."

"Okay. You called Nathaniel before me?" Ashley shrugged even though her dad couldn't see her.

"His family fixed the jeep once before. I wanted to see if they could do anything."

"Good thinking, but you should call me first. Even if you did wreck your car and want to hide the fact." Ashley smirked. That wasn't the fact she wanted to hide, but if her dad believed it, that was fine with her. "You sure you're okay?"

"Yeah."

"Okay. Put Morgan back on the phone please." Ashley nodded and handed the phone back to Morgan.

"Hello. Yeah I'm giving her and her jeep a lift back into town. We'll get started on it right away, we have her insurance in the glove box, but feel free to drop by. We'll be back in the shop in about an hour. Oh and Alex, good choice on getting her the jeep. Ashley may only have a few bumps and I say the reason for that is because the jeep took the brunt of it." Morgan listened for a bit more and Nathaniel gave a thumbs up to his dad. Morgan nodded.

"Alright, we'll see you in town. Here's Ashley. No problem." Ashley took the phone.

"Hey dad."

"I'll see you when you get back into town, alright?"

"Okay. I'm sorry I didn't call you first."

"It's alright. I'm just glad you're not hurt." Ashley laughed.

"Yeah me too."

"I'll see you soon. I love you."

"Love you too dad." She hung up the phone and handed it back to Morgan.

"Good job," he said. "Now let's get out of here."

"Leaving so soon?" asked a sweet voice. Ashley knew that voice and turned to look into the forest. Morgan turned faster and took a step in front of both of them.

Karin was back. She was where Ashley's jeep had crashed and was leaning against the tree. A long hood was drawn across her head to keep the meager sunlight away from her.

"Karin," said Morgan angrily.

"Hello to you too, you big puppy," laughed Karin. "What? No big hug for an old friend?"

"You're not my friend anymore. I told you to leave me alone."

"And soon I will. Soon I will never bother you again," she said nastily. Morgan snarled and took a step forward. Karin giggled maliciously. "Not in front of the kids Morgan. Ashley isn't a part of this."

"Neither is my son!" Morgan barked loudly. Karin frowned.

"Your son? Your kids?" she spat. "They were supposed to be my kids too."

"You can't have kids," said Morgan. "You knew that when you changed and nothing will ever change that."

"Ha! I have many kids. My children are here, you'll meet them soon enough. Until then, enjoy. I'll be seeing you again real soon."

Karin cackled and flew backwards into the forest. She was as quick as Ashley remembered. Nathaniel started after her, but Morgan caught him and held him fast.

"No. She wants us to follow her," said Morgan. "We can't pursue her alone and we can't leave Ashley alone."

"She doesn't want Ashley," said Nathaniel.

"Yes she does," said Morgan quietly. "Get in the truck. We need to be going." Nathaniel growled, but Ashley tugged on his hand and he relaxed. They all climbed back in and Morgan started to call someone. He plugged his phone into his truck and hit speaker phone so they could all hear.

"Hello?" asked Katie.

"Katie, it's Morgan. Has Melissa called you yet?"

"Yes. She told me psycho bitch is in town. I thought she was dead."

"So did I, but we just saw her."

"Damn vampires. They're harder to kill than weeds."

"Agreed. Karin told me she has children here in town."

"Children? Vampires can't have children so that must mean…"

"She's infected other people and they're in town," finished Morgan. "I think we've got a full nest on our hands."

"Damn. We have to root this out quickly Morgan."

"I know. She's made it clear she wants my family and Ashley as the targets."

"Poor Ashley, is she there?" Ashley leaned forward.

"I'm here Katie."

"I don't want you to worry Ashley. We've got a real problem on our hands, but we'll keep you safe." Ashley smiled.

"I know. I'm starting to get used to being in danger."

"Good girl. So what's the plan Morgan?"

"I'm taking Ashley's jeep back into town. After we get that resolved, we'll work out a system to watch her house."

"Sounds good. Keep me posted. Katie out." Katie hung up the phone and Morgan smiled.

"Katie out," he joked. "She still thinks like a Hunter."

Ashley knew bad things were about to happen, but there wasn't a lot she could do about it. She just had to take everything in stride and not panic like before. She could trust Nathaniel and his family. They would watch out for her.

CHAPTER 4

A DANGEROUS ALLY

"You really did get lucky," said Alex as he eyed her jeep in the shop. He ran his hand over the crushed door and sighed. "I'm so glad I got you a jeep now instead of something cheap."

"Agreed," said Morgan. "She's safe and that's all that matters."

"It is. What did the insurance company say?" Morgan held up his hands.

"I haven't called them yet, you came here a little faster than I expected. I seriously doubt it will be a problem. Accidents from black ice are too common here. The company seems to expect it."

"I'm sure. I'm just surprised how banged up the jeep is."

Ashley stood in the back near Nathaniel and watched her father. He was suspicious of the accident. Nathaniel held her hand tightly and gave her a reassuring look. She felt better until her dad looked back at her again.

"I'm not," said Morgan. "She slid around a lot up there and scraped more than one tree over the ice. If the snow hadn't been deep enough where she crashed, I think her jeep might've become a pinball in the forest." Alex gave a small smile.

"I guess. I forget how much heavier the ice and snow are near your house."

"And the plows don't usually come up our way," continued Morgan. "We get a lot more build up." Alex nodded and looked back to Ashley.

"Well have you learned a lesson about how dangerous the road can be?"

Ashley nodded. Before she'd come here, she'd never heard the term black ice before. Anyone who lived with snow and ice however, knew the term intimately.

"Don't worry, we'll have it fixed up before you can blink," said Morgan. "I'll get on the phone and get everything settled with the insurance and we'll make her brand new." Alex shook his hand with a smile.

"Thanks Morgan. You're the best mechanic in town."

"I'm the only mechanic in town." Alex laughed and smacked him playfully on the shoulder.

"There's that too. Ready to go Ashley?"

"Yeah dad."

"Are you coming Nathaniel?" he asked. Nathaniel nodded.

"If you'll have me Mr. Jameson."

"Sure, why not. Ashley could use some cheering up after all this. Do you mind if I borrow your boy Morgan?" Morgan waved him off.

"Take him. He's more trouble than he's worth."

"Thanks dad," said Nathaniel cheerfully as they walked out the door. They all climbed in Alex's truck and started back home.

"You should be more careful up there Ashley," said Alex.

"I know dad. I'm sorry."

"I know you are. I also saw inside the jeep that you weren't in four-wheel drive." Ashley thought about it and realized she hadn't been. "How many times have I told you if you're driving through the mountains you should always be in four-wheel drive? That alone probably could've saved you."

"Thanks for reminding me."

"I'm not trying to belittle you Ashley. I'm trying to get you to think. Those roads are dangerous. Just because your boyfriend is in the car doesn't mean I'm not going to tell you what's right and what's wrong." Ashley nodded and kept her mouth shut. Her dad could tell her anything he wanted. As long as he didn't know the truth they were okay.

When they arrived home Ashley took Nathaniel up to her room and closed the door quietly. Nathaniel looked out her window at the town and frowned. Ashley stood next to him and held his arm.

"Do you think they're in town?" she whispered.

"I do."

"What are you going to do?" Nathaniel kissed the top of her head and smiled.

"The same thing I always do. I'm going to protect you and everyone else." Ashley smiled and kissed him. Despite this frightening new enemy, Nathaniel was standing tall and confident. She liked how fearless he was. His strength was infectious and she felt they had nothing to worry about.

"Do you think it will be easy?" she asked quietly.

"No." Nathaniel's face became serious. "I think this could get very bad very quickly. Times are only going to get worse before they get better."

"Ashley?" called her dad from downstairs. Ashley stepped away from Nathaniel and opened her door again.

"Yes?"

"Can you come downstairs?" Ashley sighed and prepared for another talk.

"Yeah." She looked at Nathaniel and waved for him to relax. "I'll be right back." Nathaniel shook his head and followed her to the door.

"I'll come with." Ashley didn't want Nathaniel to have to suffer a boring lecture, but she couldn't say no to that smile. She couldn't tell him she didn't want him near.

They headed downstairs and Ashley felt something was wrong. The mood in the house seemed to have darkened. Maybe it was the actual darkness that threw her off. All the blinds had been pulled shut and none of the daylight could come in. She thought it a bit strange considering how much her dad had always liked the sun. Near the front door, she looked into the living room and kitchen, but her dad was absent from both.

"Dad?" she called out.

"I think he's in his room," said Nathaniel.

"And you would know that, wouldn't you?"

Before they could turn they heard a loud racking noise. Ashley's eyes widened and her heart skipped a beat. She knew that sound. She'd heard it once before when she'd talked to Katie. It was the sound of a shotgun being leveled right at them.

Ashley turned to see her father holding his shotgun and pointing it directly at Nathaniel's heart. She'd never seen him look so serious before in her life. There was a coldness in his eyes and a steadiness in his hands she'd never seen before. Nathaniel pushed Ashley back.

"Move away from him Ashley," Alex said calmly.

"Dad! What are you doing?"

"It's okay Ashley," said Nathaniel. "Get away from me."

"No! Dad, what are you doing?"

"I'm tired of being lied to and I want some answers."

"We haven't lied to you about anything Mr. Jameson," said Nathaniel quickly. Alex scoffed and took a hand off his shotgun. He reached inside his coat pocket and pulled out a long silver chain. Ashley didn't know what it meant, but Nathaniel twitched at the sight of it. At the end of the chain was a strange emblem. A pair of white wings were folded onto a knife. A golden white band wrapped them all together like a halo.

Alex spun the chain around his left arm and let the emblem hang off his hand before he took hold of his shotgun again. "Care to rethink your answer now Nathaniel?" Nathaniel gulped.

"What is that?" asked Ashley.

"It's the seal of the Hunter Order," said Nathaniel. "Whoever holds one is a trained hunter of creatures that don't exist." Ashley looked at the necklace again and then at her dad. He nodded and frowned.

"You're a Hunter dad?" she asked fearfully. He shook his head.

"I haven't been in years, but I never forgot the trade. I've never forgotten the traits of a werewolf either. So you want to start talking Nathaniel?"

"I'm a werewolf," said Nathaniel proudly. "Are you going to kill me?" Alex shifted his eyes from Nathaniel to his scared daughter behind him.

"It depends on what you tell me. No more lies from either of you though."

"No more lies from us?" asked Ashley. "What about you? When were you going to tell me you were a Hunter?"

"I'm retired Ashley. You should've never known what a Hunter was so I should've never had to explain it to you! First, and most important question," Alex nodded to his daughter, "are you bitten?"

"What?" she asked.

"No," said Nathaniel forcefully. "She's not a werewolf." Alex blew a sigh of relief.

"What happened to her today?" he asked. "Did you lose control and attack her jeep?"

"Dad!" Ashley yelled.

"It's a fair question Ashley," said her dad. "Your jeep had claw marks on them and I need to know if he can control himself."

"I can control myself," said Nathaniel, sounding insulted. "Jackals attacked Ashley's jeep." Alex lowered his shotgun an inch.

"Jackals? I knew there was a werewolf in the mountains, but we have jackals too?"

"We did. They've left for now," said Nathaniel. "We've got bigger problems and they don't want to get involved."

"Bigger problems?"

"Vampires." Alex scowled.

"We've got damned vampires too?"

"Yes. They're the dangerous ones, not me." Alex nodded and held his shotgun casually. Ashley was relieved, but Nathaniel wasn't as calm. Alex was still tense and his eyes screamed danger. It wouldn't take him more than a moment to raise that shotgun again and blow him apart.

"One last question," said Alex. "Have you been protecting my daughter?"

"Yes and I've paid the price for it."

Nathaniel raised his shirt and Ashley winced. She hated seeing his scars from fighting with the jackals. Even with his incredible regenerative abilities, nothing would take away the scars. A chunk of his side and arm were lighter and rougher due to jackal bites. Smooth lines were still visible from where claws had taken him. Alex looked over his body and grimaced. He held out his hand to Nathaniel.

"Then I suppose I owe you my thanks." Nathaniel lowered his shirt and shook Alex's hand. "Thank you for keeping my daughter safe."

"I was glad to."

"Now we still need to talk, but for now I don't think we have to do it at gunpoint," said Alex with a smile.

"Dad!" complained Ashley.

"It's alright Ashley," said Nathaniel. "He's not going to hurt me."

"Not yet," said Alex with a wink. "Let's have a seat." Alex led them into the living room and took a seat in his chair. He set his shotgun against his chair and Ashley and Nathaniel took the couch.

"How long have you been bitten Nathaniel?"

"Never. I was born this way." Alex looked at him in surprise.

"You're a purebred?" Nathaniel frowned.

"Not exactly how I'd put it." Alex waved his hand in apology.

"Sorry, I just wasn't expecting it. So your whole family is…"

"All seven of us." Alex whistled.

"I knew there was one or two on the mountain, but I never figured a whole family. You stay hidden very well."

"Not well enough apparently."

"I've been trained and you've been coming around my house."

"When did you figure it out?" asked Ashley. Alex smiled.

"Since the first day you two met in the hospital. I knew after he was the one who saved you." It was Nathaniel's turn to be surprised.

"That long?" Alex grinned.

"I found your tracks in the woods. They were too big to be a dog's or even a regular wolf's. When I saw you in the hospital was the biggest giveaway. Nobody just runs out into a snowstorm for someone they hardly know without dressing for the cold. You were so sick and shaky in there. The sheriff figured it was running down the mountain. It wasn't though, was it? You were suffering withdrawals from the moon." Nathaniel nodded. Ashley was astounded at her dad's awareness. He'd learned so much from observing so little and had put all the pieces together in one night.

"So why not the shotgun treatment then?" asked Nathaniel. Alex shrugged.

"Just because you're a werewolf doesn't mean you're a bad person. I learned that from years of being a Hunter. Plenty of people are born this way just like you are, nothing they can do about it. Sure some of them give into their wolf instincts and become more crazed animal than human, but some are just normal people. And no offense, but I figured this was just a quick high school relationship and I didn't think it would last anyway." Ashley crossed her arms offended.

"Thanks for the vote of confidence." Alex smiled.

"I was in high school once too. You date someone and think you'll be with them for the rest of your life, only to break up with them two weeks later." Nathaniel grinned, but Ashley was still annoyed.

"So Nathaniel, tell me all about this vampire problem." Nathaniel shrugged.

"I don't know much about it. We just found out only a couple of hours ago." They sat and talked for a while about everything the two of them had seen and learned that day. Nathaniel told Alex all of the basics from what his dad had told him. Ashley told him all about her terrifying scene with the jackals and about Karin's sudden arrival. Alex asked questions about all the minor details they'd forgotten or otherwise didn't know.

"So we don't know much yet," said Alex. "We have to find out where these vampires are and stamp them out."

"That was the plan," said Nathaniel.

"I'll keep an eye out and look around myself. I'm not worried about your family Nathaniel. It'll take more than a few vampires to take out a den of fully grown werewolves. I'm more worried about them coming into the town. I'll bet they're already here considering they know you're here. The town will be safer for them than the woods will be." They sat in silence for a minute as Alex contemplated all that he'd learned. His thoughts were disturbed as Nathaniel began to laugh.

"So this may seem kind of strange, but I'm glad it turns out you're an old Hunter," said Nathaniel.

"Why is that?"

"Because now we won't have to watch your house as much. Ashley has a defender living here." Alex nodded.

"I'll take a few days off work and get the house set up. If they plan to target my daughter they'll discover real quick they chose the wrong house to mess with."

"Hey dad," started Ashley, "do you know about Katie?" Alex paused.

"Katie? She's involved with your family too Nathaniel?" Nathaniel looked amused.

"Not quite. She's like you, an ex-Hunter." Alex looked shocked.

"You're kidding me. I've known her for years and she's never shown any sign."

"She is," said Nathaniel. "She's a friend of my family and she has the same necklace you do."

"Well I'll be." Alex rubbed his face. "And here I thought I knew everything about this town."

"Yeah, how do you think I feel?" asked Ashley.

"I would've preferred you never knew about any of this," said Alex. "But I guess it can't be helped now. Grab your things. I think Morgan and I need to talk."

"Already?" asked Nathaniel.

"If there are vampires in the town, we don't have time to just wait around. We need to pool our resources if we're going to take them on. I'm hoping I can leave the shotgun here?" he asked as he looked at Nathaniel. Nathaniel nodded.

"Probably a good idea." Alex disappeared into his room but kept talking.

"I'm hoping your dad won't attack me just by learning what I am."

"We're friends with Katie so I somehow doubt it." Alex reappeared as they were putting on their shoes.

"Good. I hate it when they bite first and ask later. It really is a pain in the ass."

"I know how that feels," said Nathaniel as they left the house. When they were in the car and pulling out of the driveway, Ashley tapped her dad's shoulder.

"We're going to have to talk about your past later. I feel like suddenly I don't know anything about you."

"We will, I promise."

The drive to the body shop was quick enough. Alex didn't talk much. His eyes were focused and Ashley assumed he was probably thinking about what to say to Morgan. Going to talk to Morgan was still a dangerous thing for him. Nathaniel had asked if he should call ahead, but Alex had told him no. He didn't want Morgan to worry about him like he was worried about Morgan.

They arrived and went inside. Ashley sniffed when she saw her jeep was already being dismantled by one of Morgan's employees. Her poor baby would be out of commission for a while if she had any guess. She'd gotten so used to her car that now that it was gone, she wasn't sure how she'd manage without it.

"Where's your dad?" asked Alex. Nathaniel pointed to the office. Alex nodded and they headed in. Morgan was on the phone as they entered and he had Ashley's insurance paperwork in front of him.

"Just a minute everyone," he said quietly. They all took their seats and waited patiently as Morgan talked. Ashley expected to wait for a while, but Morgan hung up the phone rather quickly. She wondered if his quick looks at Nathaniel had anything to do with it.

"Insurance companies," said Morgan angrily. "I despise every single one of their agents."

"They are a pain," agreed Alex.

"Did you forget something?" asked Morgan. "I expected all of you to be gone longer."

"We all need to talk," said Alex as he pulled out his Order pendant. He laid it on the table and Morgan eyed it darkly. He sat in silence for a while, but Alex didn't show any hostility. He was smiling and didn't have any weapon on him. He even kept his hands on Morgan's desk so Morgan could see he wasn't about to pull anything.

"Nathaniel, close the blinds please," said Morgan. Nathaniel quickly closed the blinds to the office so the employees couldn't see them anymore. "You're a Hunter Alex?" Morgan sounded hurt.

"Retired," said Alex plainly. "And you're a werewolf." Morgan grinned.

"Still active, my job is harder to retire from." Alex smirked.

"Indeed it is. I hear we have a vampire problem in town, want any help?" Morgan sighed happily.

"I thought this conversation was going to go in a much darker direction. Yes, we'll gladly take any help we can get."

"Like I said, I'm retired," said Alex. "I only hunt down things that are hurting or killing innocents. I haven't heard any horror stories in town about people being killed by giant wolves, so I'm guessing your family is good."

"Only trouble we've caused have been some scuffles with jackals in the past year. Some of them have caused some real problems, I nearly lost a son to them." They all looked at Nathaniel.

"I saw the scars," said Alex. "Must've been one hell of a fight."

"It was," said Nathaniel.

"It certainly was. Nathaniel, will you and Ashley step outside for a minute?" asked Morgan. "Alex and I need to discuss some things in private."

"Good idea. I'll see you in a minute Ashley." Nathaniel took Ashley by the hand and led her out of the office. When the door was closed, Morgan leaned forward and put his hands together.

"This is a very awkward position you've put me in Alex."

"I know how you feel. This is why I came to your office so we can get this out of the way right now. The less time we worry about this, the more we can work together."

"The thought of working together sounds grand, but it's your past I'm worried about. Are you truly retired?" Alex sighed and took his old pendant back. He eyed it miserably before he put it back in his pocket.

"Trust me Morgan, twenty years ago we wouldn't be having this conversation. I would've walked in with a gun and never thought twice about it. But that all changed in my last couple of years as a Hunter."

"Why? Why did you leave the Order? I know they don't have a history of letting people leave kindly."

"Two reasons. First was I found out Ashley was born. I couldn't be much of a father to her if I was putting myself in danger and hunting monsters all over the world."

"But you didn't raise her," said Morgan. "As far as I know, you hadn't even seen her until last year."

"I wanted to be there for my daughter Morgan, but her mother didn't. Ashley's mother knew what I was and what I did. You don't make many friends as a Hunter, Morgan. She didn't want some vampire creeping into our house in the middle of the night looking for revenge. I didn't want that either." Alex balled his hands into fists.

"You have no idea what it's like not being able to see your kid because you put them in danger just by existing. What's worse is Olivia was right too. People did come after me and I had to fight and move away constantly through the years. So to keep my daughter safe, I stayed away."

"It must've been very hard," said Morgan, "but you're wrong. If you'd come in here just a day before I would've agreed I had no idea what that feels like, but today brings new dangers. This vampire in our town is named Karin, and she's here for me. Because of my past, my family is now in danger."

"Then all things aside, I think we have a common ground to fight on," said Alex. "In this fight, I'm not a Hunter, and you're not a werewolf. We're two dads with kids we need to protect." Morgan held his hand across the desk.

"I believe you." Alex took his hand and shook it.

"I hope so." They let go and Morgan leaned back.

"If you don't mind, I'd still like to hear the second reason." Alex smirked.

"I thought you just said you believed me."

"I do, but it's strange how calm you are with talking to me. You're not tense or nervous. Did you have werewolf friends before?" Alex shook his head.

"In the Order, I was your stereotypical hard ass. I didn't have many friends and I certainly didn't befriend anything that wasn't human. I hunted because of the terrible things I'd seen creatures do to good people. I thought I was restoring order to the world."

"Sounds like what most Hunters seem to believe."

"Yeah well that all changed on my last mission," said Alex. "We were going to root out a few werewolves who'd been seen in the countryside. It was supposed to be an easy mission."

"And something went wrong?" asked Morgan.

"No, something went right. I cornered the whole family and had them at my mercy. Then I saw children." Alex turned to look away. "I won't lie to you Morgan, it's easy to go out and hunt something that looks like a monster. It's a different matter when your orders are to kill children. Since werewolves don't change until puberty, they couldn't change and they couldn't fight. They could only sit behind their parents and cry." Alex spoke with a heavy tone, but Morgan could see the sadness in his eyes when he looked back at him.

"That's when I began to doubt what I was doing. The creatures before me weren't monsters, they were people. We were hunting them just because they were different. According to the orders, not even the children were allowed to survive because they were infected. On that day I realized I couldn't do it. They were at my mercy and I couldn't take the shot."

"So you let them go?" asked Morgan.

"I did. I even shot my own partner when he caught up and tried to kill them. I told the family to run and never come back. I went back to the base and retired the same day. I was done."

"You've been through a rough life," said Morgan.

"And now I have a peaceful one and a family. I will do anything to make sure it stays that way."

"Me too," said Morgan. "I was once young too and have fought my own wars. Now I'm old and have a family and don't want to fight any more than I have to."

"Then let's find this bitch and finish it quickly," said Alex. Morgan chuckled.

"I've already killed Karin before. If anything, she's very resilient."

"We'll have to make sure she stays down for good this time." Alex stood up and held out his hand again. Morgan stood up and shook it. "If you'll excuse me, I have some preparing of my own to do now."

"I'm glad we had this talk."

"Me too." Alex opened the door and saw Ashley and Nathaniel holding each other near the door. He smiled and waved her over.

"Come on Ashley, we're going home."

"Everything okay?" she asked nervously. He nodded and she smiled. Nathaniel kissed her on the cheek and let go of her.

"I'll stay here," whispered Nathaniel. "You and your dad probably need to talk." Ashley nodded and rubbed her head against Nathaniel's chest. Nathaniel kissed her head one last time before she followed her dad.

"You're not supposed to grow up so quick on me," said her dad.

"I never thought my dad would actually give a boy the shotgun treatment either." Alex chuckled and got in his truck.

"Touché."

CHAPTER 5

TOOLS OF THE TRADE

They made a large shopping trip and Alex picked up a large number of strange things. It was a bigger grocery list than she'd ever seen him have before, but he came out pleased. When they arrived home he locked the door and opened all the windows.

"How much do you know about vampires?" he asked.

"Only what I've seen in movies? Nathaniel hasn't really told me anything about them," she said as she pet Roland. She started to refill his food bowl as her dad came into the kitchen.

"Alright. Most obvious and best defense against vampires is the sun." Alex pointed out the window to the sun. "In the day, always keep all the windows open. Vampires aren't hurt by just any light, but direct sunlight will fry them before you can say chicken tenders." Roland barked and began wagging his tail furiously. "I'm making a point pooch, not giving you a treat." Roland whined and Ashley pet him furiously.

"I knew the sunlight one."

"I figured, but just in case." He poured one of the giant grocery bags out and the table was covered in garlic. "Vampires are allergic to garlic. They won't go near the stuff. Get some garlic in their system and they'll go into shock. Get a lot of garlic in them and they'll die."

"That's a lot of garlic," said Ashley.

"That's the point. We'll put them around every door and window in the house. Plus some in the chicken I have for dinner." Ashley laughed and helped pull it all back into the bag.

"Vampires are also allergic to silver," said Alex.

"Like werewolves are," said Ashley. Alex held up a finger and smiled.

"Not quite. Silver to a werewolf is more like garlic to a vampire. They're highly allergic to it, but it won't kill them automatically. Silver is a holy metal and will tear a vampire apart, whereas it will just hurt a werewolf badly. Put a few silver rounds or a silver blade into a vampire and they'll turn to ash." Ashley looked up confused.

"Vampires turn to ash when they die?"

"Vampires are cursed things Ashley. They're the walking dead which require the constant consumption of blood to survive. Science can't explain them and neither can I. The moment a person is turned into a vampire, they're dead. Once something kills them, their body ages dramatically, returning them to the form they should be. Time catches up to them, turning them to ash."

"So you know a vampire is dead when it turns to ash?" Alex waved his hand and frowned.

"Yes. When a vampire turns to ash, it's dead for sure. Some weapons, like silver or sunlight, will turn them to ash instantly. But say a werewolf gets a hold of them and mauls them. They don't have any vampire killing weapon, but werewolves are big enough they can outright crush vampires. The vampires might lay there bleeding out for a long time before they finally turn to ash. They could have a chance to recuperate, but it's unlikely." Ashley had a thought.

"Who would win in a fight, a werewolf or a vampire?"

"One on one, I'd put my money on the werewolf. Werewolves are larger and stronger, plus they have natural weapons. Give the vampire some type of weapon, then it could be either or."

"When I saw Karin, she beat up a jackal pretty easily."

"Exactly, a jackal. Jackals are powerful, but they're no werewolves. Karin is also probably a very experienced vampire and knew what she was doing. I'd say it's a tossup between a jackal and a vampire. But then again, jackals usually are never alone. Karin also had a knife to finish them off." Ashley nodded and squeezed Roland for comfort. This was all scary talk to her, but her dad was just starting dinner as if they were talking about one of her classes at school.

"Why don't werewolves need anything special to kill a vampire?"

"You don't need anything special to kill anything, just some things work better than others. You can kill a vampire with anything if you know what you're doing. They're tough, but they aren't invincible. You know how they always pierce a vampire's heart with a stake in the movies?" Ashley nodded. "That works, but anything through the heart works. Take away a vampire's blood and they're as good as dead."

"What about crosses? Don't those work?" Alex shrugged.

"Hard to say. I've seen some people use them to great effect, but they never did a thing for me. People say it's all about the faith behind it, but I don't know about that. I've seen the greatest believers go down with crosses in their hands and others I would've never thought hold back mobs of vampires. I never bothered with them. I'll take a gun any day."

"Holy water?" asked Ashley.

"Same thing. Holy water all depends on who blesses it. If you watch the news, I'm sure you've heard lots of stories about holy men who didn't turn out to be quite so holy. Some cases it works, others it doesn't. I'd rather put my faith in things I know work. Speaking of which, I have something for you to take with you now." Alex went into his room and came back with a small canister. Ashley smirked and held it up to the light.

"Pepper spray?"

"Garlic spray," said her dad smugly. "Spray an unsuspecting vampire with that and watch them flip out. It probably won't kill them, but it will get them to leave you alone." Ashley nodded and pocketed the item. "I want you to promise you'll take that everywhere with you."

"I promise."

"Good. I've got a few other things I want to teach you. I'll show you how to spot a vampire, how to use a gun, and all kinds of tricks."

Ashley just nodded and felt the garlic spray in her pocket. She couldn't believe she was learning all this from her dad. For the first time in a long time, he felt like a stranger to her again.

"So what's your real past dad?" Alex frowned and put down the chicken he was preparing.

"Everything I've told you so far was true. I really was an orphan. Like many children out there, I was never adopted. As soon as I was old enough, I left the orphanage and joined the military. When you grow up feeling unwanted and alone, the last thing you want to be is that. I was a dedicated soldier for years. Then when I was twenty-two, my unit crossed paths with some feral werewolves." Alex frowned and he stabbed his carving knife through the chicken.

"We fought them off, but most of my squad was lost. We didn't know what we were dealing with and we paid the price. Nobody believed our story and most of us who survived were dismissed for medical reasons. I found myself wandering from town to town wondering if I was insane. Then a group of Hunters caught up to me and told me the truth. They brought me focus and asked if I was interested in avenging my fallen brothers. It wasn't a hard choice."

"You joined the Hunters," said Ashley.

"I did. It's not hard to lose yourself to revenge when you've got nothing else to lose. I learned later on that was how most Hunters are recruited. They play on people's fears and insecurities, turning good people into dangerous weapons. I got my revenge on those werewolves, them, and many more. How many of them actually deserved it I still wonder to this day. I learned all the dark secrets of the world and came to regret it." Alex sighed and pulled the knife out of the chicken.

"One mission brought me stateside and in my spare time, I met a beautiful woman." He smiled. "It was your mother."

"You knew mom while you were still a Hunter?"

"I did. We were the classic couple of love at first sight. We spent as much time together as we could. I would take constant vacations out to see her. Unfortunately one day a vampire came looking for me and your mother had to witness what I really did. She was less scared than I could've believed, but she said she couldn't see me again. She moved away and said she didn't want to risk anything coming after her. I never saw her again." Ashley wanted to hug her dad, but couldn't find the strength to get out of her chair. She just looked down sadly.

"I left the Order a while later. I received the letter about your birth and wanted to see you. I really did Ashley. I wanted to be there as you grew up." Ashley felt a few tears coming down her cheeks and Alex came over and hugged her.

"Why didn't you then?" she asked.

"Because your mother didn't want me to endanger you. I couldn't risk some old feud coming after your mom or you just to get to me. I had to stay away, far away, and never acknowledge you. It was the only way to keep you safe." Alex squeezed her tightly.

"When I wrote your mother, I had to put fake names and speak to her in code. You were never mentioned directly, and neither was our time together. We didn't want to risk anything getting into the mail and discovering our connection. For years I moved around and for years I was hunted. The hunting stopped after about five years and it seemed my past was forgotten." Alex pulled away from her and rubbed her hair.

"I enjoyed two years of peace and asked your mother if I could come see you. She told me she was happy I was enjoying freedom, but she wouldn't see me. She said if I truly loved you both that I would stay away. So I did." Ashley hugged her dad and started crying harder.

Her mother's deception suddenly made sense. Her mom didn't tell her her father was dead because she didn't like him, but because she wanted to protect her. She never wanted her to seek out her dad because she never wanted something to come after her. She sniffed and started laughing at the irony.

"Mom kept me away for all those years." She leaned away from her dad and started laughing. "And my first serious boyfriend turns out to be a werewolf." Alex started laughing and sat back.

"Your mother would be furious at me right now."

"I think she's happy for us." Alex sighed and stood up.

"I hope so," he said as he went back to the chicken. "Your turn to spill the beans."

"What?" she asked.

"Tell me everything about you and Nathaniel's family. Did you learn the truth the night the jackals attacked him? My guess is that's why you broke up for a bit." Ashley gave a bit of a nervous laugh and bit her lip.

"No, we got attacked once before about a month into dating. He had to change to protect me."

"And you stayed with him?"

"I was actually kind of excited. I also thought no one would've believed me if I told them my boyfriend was a werewolf." Ashley paused. "I can't believe you turned out to be a Hunter. If I had panicked about Nathaniel then you probably would've gone after him."

"Probably," said Alex. "If I thought he was trying to hurt you, then I would've gone after him in a heartbeat." Ashley sighed and leaned back in her chair.

"I really made the right choice not to freak out."

"Probably," he said again as he plopped a chip into his mouth. "So can I ask you now why you broke up? I assume it has something to do with him being a werewolf since you went to Katie." Ashley felt chills go through her body as she remembered that horrible night.

"We were ambushed by five jackals that night. Nathaniel defended me down to the bitter end, but…" Ashley shivered and found she couldn't continue. Alex looked at her sadly.

"He had to kill, didn't he?" Ashley nodded and put her head down. Alex washed his hands quickly and came over and hugged her.

"I'm sorry." She nodded and kept her head down. She didn't want to think about it. "I'm just happy you both came out okay."

"No, we didn't," said Ashley quietly. "Nathaniel got really hurt and I just ran away. I was so scared. I thought he was a monster." Her dad brought her chin up to look him in the eye.

"There was nothing you could've done. You're only human and it's to be expected that you'd be scared. What matters is that you went back to him later and showed you were there for him. It might've taken you some time, but you faced your fears, didn't you?" Ashley nodded. "Then that's what matters now." He let go of her and went back to preparing dinner.

"The family seems to like you enough."

"Except for Melissa," snorted Ashley. "I don't think there's anything I can do to impress her."

"Melissa is very defensive of her children," said her dad. "She's a scary woman. I wouldn't want to be on the wrong side of her."

"How do you think I feel?" asked Ashley.

"With her cold stares, probably the same as this chicken." Ashley watched him slice the chicken apart.

"Yeah that's about right."

"You should have a break for a bit now. Vampires are a much bigger problem than you and Nathaniel dating."

"So what's going to happen with the vampires?" asked Ashley.

"First thing we have to do is find them. Then we have to run them out of town. Vampires are like ants. If you see one, you can bet there's a lot more wandering around. If you don't get them all out of your house at once, they'll just keep coming back." Ashley gulped and admitted her fears.

"I'm scared dad. I don't know what to do."

"I know," he said quietly. "Fortunately, the rest of us do. What you can't learn from us, we can handle." He stabbed his knife into another chicken.

CHAPTER 6

BRILLIANT SNOW

Two weeks passed since Karin had appeared and there had been no more word from her. Nathaniel's family hadn't found anything and neither had her dad or Katie. It was as if Karin had just come back just to taunt them. She voiced her opinion to everyone, but Morgan quickly shot her down.

"She's out there," he promised.

The families left it at that and simply went on prepared. Just because a threat was out there didn't mean they got to avoid their jobs or school. Ashley had expected more instant action like with the jackals, but the vampires were a different breed. For the time being, they were remaining quiet.

"I can't believe winter is almost over," said Kara at lunch, breaking Ashley's concentration.

"I can't wait," said Liz. "I'm so sick of all this ice and snow."

"I love it," said Nathaniel. Nathaniel didn't usually join them for lunch, preferring to go out or hang with some of his friends, but on occasion he joined them. Today was one of those lucky days.

"We should do something before spring," said Caitlin. "All go on some crazy trip." Her face brightened suddenly. "We should go skiing!"

"Where can you go skiing around here?" asked Ashley.

"Nowhere," said Kara. "There's a resort about an hour or so away though."

"That's somewhere," teased Nathaniel.

"What a coincidence!" said Kara delightfully. "So is my fist." she finished with a scowl. Nathaniel gave her a toothy grin.

"Any day small one."

"How many of us actually know how to ski?" asked Liz. Caitlin, Nathaniel, and Liz held up their hands. "Half of us would be sitting on the sidelines. I say no."

"You can ski?" asked Ashley to Nathaniel.

"Snowboard, but it's all the same to me."

"I'm surprised you never learned to ski Kara," said Caitlin. Kara gave her a surprised look back.

"You want me to put on small pieces of wood and throw myself down a mountain?" She laughed. "How stupid do you think I am?" Nathaniel was already opening his mouth when Ashley stuck the last bit of her sandwich in his mouth to shut him up.

"I can't believe you do that," said Liz.

"Why not? Works on the dog." The girls laughed as Nathaniel chewed. He swallowed it down and smiled back at them.

"I don't know what you're all laughing at," he said. "Who got the sandwich in the end?"

"He's got a point," said Jeremy as he sat down next to Liz. Liz hugged him immediately and snuggled up close.

"Hi!" she said happily.

"Hi."

They rubbed each other's faces before kissing. Kara gagged and Ashley silently agreed. Liz had been dating Jeremy for a few months now, but their mushiness was getting out of hand. They'd let it go as dating bliss the first month, but this was ridiculous. When they finally managed to untangle each other, Jeremy leaned over to see everyone.

"What'd I miss?" he asked.

"Caitlin wants to do something with the snow before it all vanishes," said Kara. "We already ruled out skiing."

"What about sledding then?" he asked quickly. Kara and Nathaniel perked up a little bit and Liz smiled.

"Sledding?" asked Ashley. "As in getting on little plastic things and going down tiny hills?"

"Yeah, only replace tiny hills with giant ones."

"That could be fun," said Caitlin, looking around for support.

"I love sledding," said Nathaniel.

"It could work," said Liz. "What do you think Ashley?" She shrugged.

"I don't know. I've never been sledding either." They all looked at her in shock. "What? I didn't grow up in the snow."

"Sledding is both fun and hilarious," said Kara. Liz looked at her confused.

"Why is skiing stupid, but sledding is fun?"

"Because it's easier to jump from a sled than skis. Plus the hills aren't as big nor crowded with hundreds of people."

"Excellent, sledding it is," said Nathaniel. Liz and Caitlin cheered moments before Liz was pulled into another kiss fest by Jeremy. Kara shuddered and looked at Ashley.

"Remind me never to get one of those…" she waved at Nathaniel and Jeremy. "I'm sorry, what do you call those parasites again you have clinging to your backs?"

"You'll want one someday." Kara scoffed.

"I think I'm more likely to suffer the plague and the town burning down first."

"What horrible odds," laughed Nathaniel. "So sledding? This Saturday?" They all agreed just as the bell rang for them to go to their classes.

Saturday morning came and Ashley found Nathaniel at her door a little before noon. He was dressed for the snow and he had the face of a child on. "Ready?" he asked eagerly. She laughed at his giddiness and started to put on her coat.

"Bye dad." Alex waved to them from the living room.

"Have fun you two. Be safe."

Nathaniel had driven one of his family's trucks down for the day. It wasn't big, but it had a camper over the back. Normally they would've taken Ashley's jeep, but it was still in the shop. Morgan had said they would fix it like brand new, but she hadn't expected it to take so long.

"When am I going to get my jeep back?" asked Ashley.

"You're lucky your jeep isn't in the junk pile. Do you realize how much of it we have to replace? It's taking hours upon hours to dismantle the thing, who knows how long it'll take to put it all back together. Plus we have to order dozens of parts, new doors…" Ashley sighed and hit her head against the seat.

"Stupid jackals," she swore.

"Yeah they did a number," said Nathaniel. "We can fix it, just give us some time okay." Ashley mouthed an okay to him and looked back out the window.

"Are we still picking up Kara?" she asked.

"Yes we are."

Ashley realized she would've known that if she'd been paying attention to where they were going. They were only a few blocks away by the time she'd asked. They pulled up to the Fortune house and the top window was thrown open.

"A siege! A siege at the main gate!" shouted Mr. Fortune. Ashley smiled, but Nathaniel charged forward with his hand up.

"We've come for your loot! Hand over the fortune!" Ashley didn't know if he meant Kara or money, but Mr. Fortune growled and pointed at them.

"Never! Fire the cannon!" Nathaniel's smile vanished and the main door flew open. Mrs. Fortune was holding the door and Kara came barreling out of it with a sled. Nathaniel saw too late that the walkway had been sprayed down so it'd turn into a slick, icy slope.

"RAAAAAAAAAAAAAGH!" shouted Kara as she dropped onto her sled. Nathaniel tried to move out of the way, but his feet couldn't find a good enough purchase to leap. Kara mowed him down and nearly flew into the truck. She rolled out a few feet away and slid across the snow. A string in her hand connected her to the sled and she brought it to a stop.

"Touchdown!" she screamed triumphantly. Her father cheered from the window. Ashley was laughing as she helped Kara up. Nathaniel rose unsteadily and waved goodbye to Mr. and Mrs. Fortune.

"We'll bring her back soon," said Nathaniel almost bitterly.

"Have fun!" said Mrs. Fortune.

"Bring her back safely or I fire the real cannon at you! Har har!"
The top window slammed shut and Kara's dad vanished from view.
Kara opened the camper on the truck and put in her sled.

"Can you imagine that that was my dad's idea?"

"I really can," snorted Ashley.

They headed up to the hills and pulled off on a pathway Jeremy had
claimed was great for sledding. Jeremy's car was already there when
they arrived, but they saw no Jeremy, Liz, or Caitlin.

"Where'd they go?" asked Ashley.

"I don't think they went anywhere," said Kara as she pointed to the
car. The windows were steamed over. Ashley wretched.

"Doesn't explain Caitlin," said Nathaniel. He raised an eyebrow.
"Or does it?"

"That's gross," said Ashley. Nathaniel grinned and snuck over to
the back of the car.

"Come here," he whispered to both of them. Ashley stood her
ground and shook her head stubbornly. Kara tiptoed after him. He put
his hands over the back of the car and motioned up and down. Kara
nodded and tried not to giggle.

"EARTHQUAKE!" they shouted before pounding up and down on
the car. The car wobbled up and down uncontrollably and they heard
shrieks from within. A door opened and Jeremy stuck his head out.

"Why?" he demanded. A snowball hit him and sprayed inside the
car, bringing a shriek from Liz.

"Because you're gross," said Ashley.

"At least he's dressed," conceded Kara.

Jeremy came out of the car and Liz followed him. Ashley didn't
think she could be redder than if she'd been left out in the snow all day.

"You were late," said Jeremy defensively.

"No, you just came early," stated Nathaniel. Kara guffawed and walked away. Nathaniel started laughing suddenly and followed Kara. Ashley shared confused looks with Liz and Jeremy as only Kara and Nathaniel caught some hidden joke.

"Where's Caitlin?" asked Ashley, hoping to change the subject. Liz shrugged.

"I couldn't get a hold of her. I tried all this morning, no response."

"So we sled without her," said Jeremy. He opened his trunk and pulled out two sleds. "I'm hoping someone else has sleds."

"Yeah we do," said Nathaniel as he opened the truck. "I also brought snacks and drinks so we don't have to end early."

"I don't see anywhere to sled here," said Kara. Jeremy pointed down a path.

"It's not too far of a walk and there's a decent hill."

Kara held her sled above her head and charged down the path. Jeremy held the two thin sleds he had in one hand and held Liz's with the other as they walked. As much as she wanted their cuteness to end, she felt cold without Nathaniel's hand in hers. She reached for it but realized he was long gone.

"Wait for me!" he shouted as he raced after Kara, sled over his head. Ashley sighed and trudged through the snow with Jeremy and Liz.

"They're excited," said Jeremy.

"That's Nathaniel and Kara for you," said Ashley with an edge of bitterness. Liz gave her a surprised look.

"Somebody's in a mood," she said.

"I'm cold," said Ashley as she put her face into her scarf. Up ahead they saw Kara break off the path with Nathaniel right behind her. They all walked faster to catch up and Ashley saw the hill Jeremy must be speaking of.

It was a good clearing of trees and bushes which enveloped part of the path. The hill was pretty steep and when it finally cleared out, there wasn't much room to stop before one hit the bushes. Nathaniel and Kara were at the top and waving their disc-like sleds above their heads.

"LETS…" started Kara.

"DO THIS!" finished Nathaniel before he leapt into the air.

Kara dropped into her sled and shot down the hill. It took Nathaniel a second more as he waited to hit the snow, but when he did, he blasted down the hill. They all watched as Nathaniel and Kara came down the hill in a blaze of snow. Their trip probably lasted only ten seconds, but what a ten seconds it was.

Ashley watched as they pulled on the sleds and shifted their weight about to move around. They shifted back and forth, yelling at each other. They tried to swing at each other like children as they picked up more and more speed. They came across the trail and Ashley was sure Nathaniel waved as he went by.

Nearing the end of their course, Ashley wondered how they'd stop. Kara was leaning and it looked like she was heading for a controlled roll out. Not if Nathaniel had to say anything about it she wouldn't. He came close enough that he took hold of the side of her disc. Kara gave a last furious shout before Nathaniel raised it and tipped her into the snow. Liz covered her mouth and Jeremy laughed. Nathaniel had plucked the disc straight out from underneath her and had it in hand as he turned back.

He should've thought about abandoning ship same as Kara had. Instead he'd looked away and now there was nothing but bushes in front of him. Kara's disc came up like a shield and he screamed hilariously as he crashed through the frozen foliage. Ashley ran after him and arrived just as Kara stood up. She was laughing and pointing where Nathaniel had gone in.

"Serves you right," she giggled.

Ashley looked through the clear path Nathaniel had cut through. He rose about ten feet away, covered in branches and snow. He gave Ashley a feral grin and tromped back over to her.

"And that is sledding," he said cheerfully. He held out Kara's disc to her. "I think you dropped this."

"I was wondering where that went."

"You two are crazy," said Ashley with a smile.

"Your turn," said Nathaniel, holding his sled out to her.

"No, I'm good." she tried to say, but Kara grabbed her by the arm and was dragging her up the hill. There was an excited shout as Jeremy flew past them with Liz only a few feet behind. At the top, Ashley looked down the steep hill and gulped.

"Get your feet in to hold you," said Kara as she wiggled into the snow with her sled. "Then when you're ready, let go." Ashley followed her example and sat down slowly. She saw Nathaniel waving and pointing at Kara.

"What's he doing?" she asked. Kara looked down at Nathaniel.

"I think…" she started and finished with a shriek. Ashley took hold of Kara's sled and spun her around, sending Kara down the hill. "I was supposed to do that to you!!!" Ashley grinned and let go of the snow.

The rush was amazing. She loved the sudden speed that came with the first boost down the hill. The part she didn't like was her stomach rolling into her and not being able to control her descent. She put her feet in to slow herself down, but the snow snapped her leg right back to her. She shrieked in pure terror as her sled began to spin and she had no idea where she was going.

"Bail!" she heard someone shout.

How did she bail? Which way? Her sled came to a sudden stop and her mind was made up for her. She tumbled out into the snow and came to an abrupt stop face first in the snow. She spat powder and rolled over to see Nathaniel laying nearby holding onto her sled.

"Thanks," she laughed.

"No problem." He stood and patted the snow off himself. "Keep your eyes forward and don't kick the snow. You started spinning yourself." He came over and gave her an icy kiss. She shivered, but smiled all the same.

"Thanks, I hadn't noticed," she said sarcastically. "Your turn."

"Nope. Our turn."

Ashley looked at him and the sled curiously. There was no way they were both fitting on that thing. He led her back up the hill and said nothing else. He wedged the sled in and told her to get on. She climbed on and Nathaniel draped himself around her. His enormous frame meant most of him was hanging off the sled.

"There is no way," said Ashley.

"We can do this," he said as he nudged them out of the snow a bit.

At first they didn't go anywhere and Ashley thought they were too heavy, but inch by inch they crept forward. The sled pulled itself out of the snow and used their weight against the hill. Ashley screamed as they began to pick up incredible speed. Their combined weight practically threw them down the hill. Nathaniel laughed in delight, always keeping his face next to hers.

"Speed bump!" shouted Kara and out came her disc upside down. Ashley squealed as they careened towards the small hill. Nathaniel yanked them to the side.

"Break left!" he shouted.

They turned, but it wasn't enough. They skimmed across Kara's sled and suddenly found themselves airborne. They both screamed as their sled left them and they were hovering inches above the snow. Nathaniel curled up around Ashley and they hit the ground hard. A small puff of snow burst up all around them and they rolled for a few feet.

Ashley was about to be angry with Kara and then Nathaniel sat up. Snow covered his entire face and he gave her a crooked grin. She laughed and fell back into the snow. She screamed seconds later as Nathaniel tried to give her a frozen kiss.

They went up and down the hill countless times. Ashley began to see the appeal of this kind of snow sport but it was exhausting. She was the first to tire out and Jeremy and Liz soon joined her on the sidelines. Only Nathaniel and Kara seemed to possess the endless strength to climb back up.

"I'm going to get something to drink. Do you two want anything?" said Ashley.

"I'll take a soda," said Jeremy and then he looked at Liz, "and for you?"

"I'm good."

"I'll be right back."

Ashley looked up the hill and laughed at Nathaniel and Kara as she left. They were running uphill at full speed, eager as children to be the first to the top. She wondered how long they would continue to race each other. Ashley smirked as she walked down the trail. If it were up to those two, they would probably do it all day.

Ashley opened up the back of Nathaniel's truck and rummaged for drinks. She found a soda for Jeremy and she took a water for herself. She wondered if Nathaniel or Kara would want anything. Kara was a soda addict so it was a safe bet she wouldn't turn down one. Nathaniel was a bit trickier to predict what he wanted. After a moment she simply shrugged and grabbed another water and soda. He could have his choice if he ever stopped sledding.

"Ashley Lebell, I presume?" Ashley let go of the drinks. The dark voice belonged to a tall, thin man she didn't know.

"She is," said another man next to him.

They both stood about twenty feet away from Ashley and she had no idea when they'd arrived. They wore long winter coats and large brimmed hats. Ashley was instantly uneasy by their presence. They looked normal to her, but something seemed wrong about them.

"Who are you?" she demanded quickly.

"Our names are unimportant," said the first one. "You must come with us."

"No."

"That would be an unwise decision," said the second slyly. His mouth opened slowly and he showed off a pair of shiny fangs. It felt like Ashley's heart skipped a beat as she understood the two men's appearance. They were vampires like Karin. They were out in the open, but sadly there was little sun to speak of. The sky was filled with lifeless, gray clouds which only existed to make the day bleary. The vampires were safe from their greatest enemy and Ashley knew she wasn't much of a threat to them. Only Nathaniel could fight them and he was off sledding.

"You will come with us," said the first strongly. "If you refuse, we will kill all your friends here and make you come with us anyway."

"My boyfriend will kill you if you try," she said angrily. The two laughed at her anger.

"Perhaps, but will he be able to stop us before we get to your friends? They are only human you know."

"And humans are so very fragile," whispered the second.

Ashley didn't know what to do. She had to get Nathaniel's help, but what these two were saying made her scared. Would they willingly die to kill her friends if she didn't cooperate? She didn't know the answer to that. She would guess no, but was this really something she could afford to guess on?

"Come," beckoned the first.

Ashley shook. She couldn't go with them and she couldn't refuse them. An idea came to her as she remembered the garlic spray her dad had given her, but she shook it away just as quickly as it'd come. The spray was in the front of the truck, not in her pocket. She remembered how fast Karin was and she didn't think she could jump for it before they grabbed her.

"Quit stalling," demanded the second. "You're coming with us."

Her face felt suddenly warm as the vampires approached her. The sun had come out just for a moment. The vampires didn't slow as their clothing and hats blocked the sun's light from reaching them. She was on her own!

Then the vampires shuttered and backed away. They squirmed and shrieked as their skin began to burn. Ashley didn't know what was happening, but she threw back her head and let loose a panicked howl. She threw herself in the back of the truck and slammed the door shut behind her.

The two vampires didn't pursue her, but began to run away screaming. Smoke was rising from them and Ashley saw they were burning. Somehow the sun was touching their skin despite their outfits.

They bolted into the woods and Ashley was grateful for their disaster. Whatever the reason, they were gone now and she blew a sigh of relief.

She screamed in panic as the truck rocked as Nathaniel landed on it. He took a flying leap off and launched himself into the woods after the vampires. Ashley crawled to the front of the truck, grabbed the garlic spray, and started after Nathaniel. She saw the other three coming down the trail at a jog.

"What's happening?" asked Kara.

"We heard screams," said Jeremy.

"I don't know," Ashley lied. "I heard a howl and then some screams coming from that way. Nathaniel just ran past to check it out."

"Let's go find him," said Kara. "That boyfriend of yours flies like the wind."

"Agreed," said Ashley and they all started to jog after him. She didn't want to go fast, but the rest of the group wasn't slowing down. She was worried he'd changed into a werewolf and would be seen.

"Where are you Nathaniel?" shouted Liz. Ashley had a feeling he couldn't respond, but was surprised when he did.

"Over here!" He was off the path a bit, but they found him standing next to piles of clothing on the ground.

"What's going on?" asked Kara.

"No idea, but someone is missing some clothes." He pointed to the ground and they saw two full outfits on the ground. Ashley gulped as she recognized the clothing and saw ash around them. The two vampires had met an untimely end in the snow. She looked at Nathaniel to see if he'd been the cause, but the look he shot her said he wasn't the one.

"Weird," said Liz. Kara bent down and examined the clothing. She ran her finger through the ash and looked ahead.

"We have to leave," she said quickly.

"Why?" asked Liz.

"There's something terrible around here." Nathaniel and Ashley shared worried glances. Did Kara understand what had happened?

"Like what?" asked Jeremy. Kara stood up and gave them all a terrified look.

"Streakers," she said with a gasp. Jeremy started laughing.

"You think we have naked people running through the woods?"

"What else could it be?"

"I don't know, but it's freezing out."

"It would explain the screaming," laughed Liz.

"It must be something," said Kara. She looked at Nathaniel suddenly and asked inquisitively. "What are you so worried about?" Nathaniel shook.

"Ugly naked people." The group laughed and Kara started gagging. They were tired, so instead of relaxing the group decided to split up and head out. Kara came with Nathaniel and Ashley and Liz went with Jeremy.

"Those two are cozy," said Kara as they were driving away.

"First serious boyfriend Liz has had in a long time," said Nathaniel.

"Yeah, but damn. You two weren't this lovey-dovey when you first got together. It's almost gross."

"You're just jealous," said Ashley.

"Yeah, only single girl around now," laughed Nathaniel. "Whatever shall you do?"

"Be a lot happier than if I was dating you guys," said Kara and it was Ashley's turn to laugh.

"And a quick comeback shuts down Nathaniel."

"You're dating me," said Nathaniel confidently. "What does that say about you?"

"Avoiding my challenge, are you?" asked Kara.

"Of course. You're the only girl who will hit back." Kara grinned and Ashley leaned over to smack Nathaniel on the chest.

"I'm not afraid to hit back," said Ashley.

"Fine." Nathaniel turned to Kara. "You're the only girl who will hit back and make it hurt." Ashley scowled, but Kara just smiled.

"That's what I'm talking about." They headed down the mountain and stopped at Kara's house. She saluted them both as she took her sled and headed inside.

"We'll have to race again sometime," she said.

"You bet," said Nathaniel. They waited for Kara to get inside before they headed for Ashley's house. "Well that was exciting," he said as they were on the road.

"What? Vampires showing up and turning to ash somehow?"

"I was talking about the sledding. Kara's really fun to race against." Ashley gave Nathaniel a look to be serious. "Yes, the vampires were kind of surprising too."

"I mean, what were they doing out there?"

"You tell me. What did they say?" Ashley frowned.

"They said I had to come with them. They said if I didn't come with them they'd attack everyone else." Nathaniel finally became serious.

"They wanted you?" His hands balled into fists. "Then they got what they deserved."

"How did it happen?" Ashley asked. "They just started smoking and ran off in front of me."

"I didn't get them," said Nathaniel. "Must've been the sun."

"How? They were all covered up. The sun didn't get Karin when she was out."

"I don't know, there was a lot more cover in the mountains than where we just were. It was earlier in the day too when Karin showed up so the sun wasn't entirely up then."

"Maybe my dad knows," said Ashley as they pulled up to her house. "Dad?" Ashley shouted as they came in.

"In the basement!" he called back. Ashley led Nathaniel down. Her dad was going over some new project he was working on when they arrived. "How was sledding?"

"It was fun," said Nathaniel. "Until two angry vampires showed up." Alex dropped the papers he was holding and looked up.

"Is everyone okay?"

"Yeah," said Ashley. "They came after me when I was alone. They told me I had to go with them or they would hurt everyone else."

"Did they say why?" questioned her dad.

"No. They just told me I had to go with them."

"What happened?"

"I was trying to think of a way out when they just started screaming," said Ashley. "The sun came out and even though they were covered up, they started burning. I jumped into the truck and they ran off. I howled and waited."

"I heard the howl and ran for her," continued Nathaniel. "I could see the two vampires running off and I chased after them. They were trying to get back under the main cover of the forest, but they collapsed before they got there. They were ash when I was able to reach them." Alex snorted and stood up.

"They weren't very smart," he said. "From what you've told me, I'm guessing they were low ranking vampires trying to gain favor from their master so they tried to get Ashley. Nobody expects vampires to attack in the middle of the day, even if it is overcast. The sun was burning them, just not from above."

"How?"

"Winter is a vampire's best friend and worst enemy depending on the area," said Alex. "There's less sun and it's usually cloudy, giving them free rein. However, winter also brings something out which is very dangerous on a sunny day."

"Snow." Nathaniel perked up and smiled. "Winter brings snow." Alex nodded.

"Snow."

"How does snow kill vampires?" Ashley asked.

"It doesn't, but sunlight is sunlight. It doesn't matter whether it comes straight down from the sky, only that it touches them. Ever wonder why people can get so tan in the snow? It's because the snow reflects the sunlight back onto us. We don't usually realize it, but vampires are a thousand times more sensitive to the sun than we are. Those vampires might've covered their heads, but they got a healthy dose all the same."

"I don't like that they were after Ashley," said Nathaniel. "Why her?"

"Simple, because she's the easiest target," said Alex. "Your family are all werewolves. The only ones in your family who can't change are your two youngest siblings' right?" Nathaniel shook his head.

"Samuel has been able to change for about half a year now. Not that it matters, Samuel and Lidia are both home schooled."

"Which puts them next to your mother all day," Alex said more than asked. "Where was your garlic spray Ashley?" Ashley smiled sheepishly.

"In the truck…"

"Keep it on you at all times," her dad said angrily. "I'm serious."

"I know, but it was the middle of the day."

"You always have to be prepared." Ashley just nodded to avoid saying anything else which might get her in trouble. "Any idea where they came from?" Nathaniel shook his head.

"They didn't leave any tracks and their clothes didn't smell like anything." Alex cursed.

"This is why I hate vampires. You should go tell your dad Nathaniel. This could be just the beginning."

"Okay." he turned to leave and Ashley looked at her dad sadly.

"Can I go with him?" Alex smirked and waved her off.

"Just be home for dinner okay?" Ashley hugged her dad and ran after Nathaniel.

"Thanks dad! I will be." She took Nathaniel's hand and they headed back to his truck. "Lidia and Samuel are homeschooled?" she asked.

"Yeah, we all were until we were old enough for high school." Ashley thought hard.

"No you weren't," she said. "Liz said you were her crush in grade school."

"What, you think just because I was homeschooled I didn't have any friends? I met a bunch of people through my dad's work and other events. This is a small town Ashley, we know everybody."

"Oh. Why were you homeschooled?"

"Because we're werewolves," he said as they drove off. "When it's near our time to start changing, we can get really weird. Some kids freak out, some become recluses, some super aggressive. It's just better if we can stay at home until we're used to the changes."

"So?" she laughed. "That's not a werewolf thing, that's called puberty."

"Oh really? When you hit puberty did you grow claws and eat a squirrel?" Ashley stopped laughing and looked horrified.

"Tell me you didn't." Nathaniel laughed.

"No I didn't." He shrugged. "That was Kevin."

CHAPTER 7

GHOULS

The coach blew his whistle and Ashley slowed to a walk, putting her hands behind her head. She was red in the cheeks and sweat was dripping down her face. The track meets were going well, but damn if they didn't make her tired. It was cold out, but she wished she was wearing shorts instead of her running pants.

"Good job everyone. Let's call it a day."

Ashley took in a deep breath of the cold air and followed everyone else. She saw the track captain Mark walking just a bit ahead of her. When their eyes met, he turned away almost instantly. He was kind, but ever since she'd started dating Nathaniel, he'd never really spoken to her.

"Hey Ashley," said Mary as she caught up to her. "Let's walk a lap before we go back."

Ashley nodded and turned to follow the track with Mary. They didn't say anything until they were halfway around the track and everyone was long gone from sight. "What's up?"

"Not much. I just wanted to ask you about the vampire attack. I've never really gotten a chance to yet."

"They just came after me and told me I had to go with them. The sun reflected off the snow and turned them to ash."

"Wow. What were they like? I've never seen a vampire before."

"Really pale and they made me feel uneasy. They were all covered up, but not enough apparently."

"I still have a hard time believing they're here," said Mary. "It's scary to hear about all this stuff and not see any of it."

"I think it's scarier to see it and not be able to do anything," joked Ashley. "At least you can fight back."

"Yeah, but I'm not much of a fighter. My bark is worse than my bite."

"Your bite still does something," said Ashley.

"Is something bothering you?" asked Mary. Ashley shook her head.

"No. It's just I feel useless. These vampires are everyone's problem and there's nothing I can do to help." Mary stiffened suddenly and stopped. Ashley stopped next to her. "What?"

"I think you better try at least," said Mary quietly. Ashley looked up and jumped.

There were two men walking towards them. They didn't work for the school and they were dressed normally. They walked without hats and the sun shined brightly on their faces, yet Ashley felt Mary was right. Their faces were pale and she felt the same uneasiness again.

"What do you want?" asked Mary, already backpedaling towards the school.

"We want you to come with us," said one of the men.

"We can do this the easy way or the hard way," said the second, cracking his knuckles. They were both fairly large men and Ashley didn't know what to do. If they were vampires, why weren't they burning?

"Why?" she asked.

"You'll make a nice gift for Karin," said the first with a sneer. Ashley wasn't sure why they weren't running. The two men stopped in front of them. "What's it going to be?"

"You know we aren't coming with you," snapped Mary.

"One way or another, you are."

The first man's hand snapped forward faster than humanly possible and took Ashley's arm. Ashley tried to break free from the man, but his grip was unnaturally powerful. He grinned as he pulled her closer. Ashley hated his creepy smile and stopped resisting. He yanked her forward and she let his momentum carry her fist into his nose. There was a nice crunch and he cried out in pain. His hand didn't release her however, it only became tighter.

Suddenly his grip fell away and he screamed in a greater pain. Mary moved to Ashley's side and kicked the man as hard as she could straight into his crotch. He bent over in agony and Ashley kicked him to the floor. The second man grabbed Mary from behind and lifted her into the air. Ashley scrambled to hit the man, but he kept Mary in front of him.

"Get up you fool!" yelled the man at his friend. The other man was trying to get back to his feet. Ashley kicked him in the face and he rolled over hissing. An unnatural growl left Mary's lips at that moment. The man holding her loosened his grip on instinct as he realized what he was holding. He knew one of the girls might be a werewolf. If she transformed in his hands his chances of survival would drop to zero.

Mary wasn't planning on changing, but she knew how to use her heritage to great effect. She pulled the man's arm up and bit down ferociously. Sharp teeth ripped straight through his jacket and skin. The man cried furiously and threw her off of him as quickly as he could. Mary hit the ground and came up in a roll. Blood dripped from her mouth and she spat out a piece of the man's jacket.

"Let's go!" shouted Ashley. Mary turned with her and they bolted for the parking lot. The man pulled his friend to his feet and they started a futile chase. On top of being terrified, both girls were track runners. They easily made it across the school and into the parking lot before the men gave up halfway. Ashley's jeep was in the shop, but her dad had a small rental car for her to use now. She opened the door and let Mary in the other side.

"What was that?" cried Ashley. "Why did they attack us?"

"They mentioned Karin. That tells us everything we need to know," said Mary angrily. "Head to my dad's shop." Ashley nodded and tried to calm her pounding heart.

"Okay." After a minute she looked at Mary and saw her blood stained cheeks and shirt. "Are you okay?"

"Yeah, none of this is mine." Mary was dabbing her mouth with her shirt. "I don't know what he was, but he tasted nasty."

"I never thought you had a thing for vampires." Ashley tried to joke.

"Those weren't vampires though," said Mary. "It was the middle of the day and they were in the sun."

"They weren't human."

"I know. I'm hoping my dad knows." Ashley pulled out her phone and handed it to Mary.

"Can you message my dad? He'll want to know." Mary took the phone without a word and sent him a brief message. Her dad had always taught her not to reveal too much over the phone so she kept it simple.

Emergency. Morgan's shop. Karin.

She handed the phone back to Ashley just as they pulled into the parking lot. Her phone was already ringing.

"I'm safe dad, can you come to Morgan's shop?"

"I'm on my way. You can explain when I get there, I just wanted to make sure you're safe."

"I am. I'll see you when you get here." They headed in through the open door and Mary announced their presence loudly.

"DAD!" There was panic and fear in her voice and they responded instantly. Morgan, Nathaniel, and Kevin came away from their work and rushed over.

"Mary! What happened?" Morgan looked her over quickly as Nathaniel checked Ashley. "Where are you hurt?"

"I'm not," she said quickly.

"We were attacked at school. Two guys came after us while we were at the track," said Ashley.

"They told us they were sent by Karin," finished Mary. Morgan's eyes darkened and he stood up as tall as he could.

"Let's go Kevin," snapped Nathaniel. "We're going to hurt some people." Kevin looked as if he'd been told Christmas had just come early. He threw the wrench he had over his shoulder and strolled after his brother.

"No," said Morgan darkly. Nathaniel turned to argue but his dad shot him such a fierce look even Nathaniel's rage was quelled. "They won't be there anymore."

"We can't just let them get away with this," shouted Kevin. Morgan eyed his other son with a terrible look.

"They won't. Mary, is that their blood?" Mary nodded. "Go put on your work clothes and bring your shirt back to us. We need their scent."

"I also have this." Mary pulled the piece of jacket she'd torn off. Morgan took it eagerly.

"Good girl. Go get changed. Ashley, is your dad on his way?" Ashley nodded. "Good. I want him in on this."

Ashley realized she was shivering. It wasn't that cold out, but something about what had just happened made her shake. It reminded her of when the jackals had come after her and Nathaniel. Nathaniel saw her shaking and hugged her.

"You okay?" She nodded slowly. Just feeling his touch calmed her down. She knew he would always keep her safe.

"Ashley!" called her dad from outside. She let go of Nathaniel and stepped into the doorway.

"I'm here dad."

"What's going on?" he demanded as he stepped inside. Morgan looked at his sons.

"Close the doors and shutters. We're closed." They nodded and split up to close all access to the shop. They were fortunate it was the afternoon and only the family was working.

"Your daughter and mine were attacked at school just now," said Morgan. Ashley didn't like how calm he sounded when he spoke. A man like Morgan wouldn't be calm in a time like this. His words seemed to carry an underlying tone of hatred and rage. His face was tense and his eyes were burning. "Two men who claimed to be sent by Karin."

Alex became just as tense as Morgan. His fingers clutched themselves into fists and his teeth became locked. He barely opened his mouth when he spoke. "They came after our daughters."

"Yes," said Morgan. "Ashley, tell us everything that happened." Ashley told them quickly everything she knew. The story wasn't long, but everyone listened intently. Mary came back wearing a white tank top and had her shirt in her hand.

"You say they were stronger than normal and stood in the sunlight?" asked Morgan.

"Yes," said Ashley and Mary.

"Sounds like a couple of ghouls to me," said Alex.

"What's a ghoul?" asked Kevin.

"A ghoul is a human who's been given vampire blood," said Morgan. "It doesn't change them, but it does make them very powerful."

"It also acts like a drug," said Alex. "Ghouls become reliant and addicted to their new masters. They become slaves. Vampires love to use ghouls to do what they can't in the daytime."

"And they sent them after our girls," said Morgan.

"Now it's our turn to go after them," said Alex. "I won't let this infestation get any worse."

"Neither will I. If we're lucky, these ghouls will lead us right back to their masters."

"Do we have a trail?" asked Alex.

"In a way." Morgan held his hand out to Mary. She tossed him her bloody shirt and held it up for Alex to see.

"Mary here happened to get a nice bite out of one." Alex's smile made him look like the devil himself.

"Ghouls bleed just like normal humans do."

"Ghouls have scents just like humans do."

Morgan held the shirt up to his nose and inhaled deeply. He immediately picked up his daughter's scent and picked a trail through it. He could smell the fear she had known from being attacked. It made his blood run wild. Then the scent of the blood touched his nose and he knew something else.

He could practically see the man in his mind's eye. He could almost taste the man's rancid smell. His blood was contaminated by something terrible. Morgan could taste his pain and his eagerness to get the girls. After failure, retreat would be his only option. He would flee like the rodent he was, back to his house of masters.

He passed the shirt to his sons and held the man's torn jacket to his nose. There was little trace of his daughter on this one, only the man. His stink was even worse on his clothing. It was a unique scent; one he hadn't smelled in town. This man had not been walking through town recently. He'd been in the hills somewhere, somewhere secluded but with easy access to town. He wouldn't be hard to find.

"We'll find him," said Morgan confidently as he passed the cloth off to his sons. "We'll start tonight."

"We have to wait?" asked Kevin angrily.

"We want the element of surprise Kevin," said Alex. "They might expect us to chase them immediately. Besides, we won't cause as much of a scene once the sun goes down. It'll be too cold for most people to go out."

"Ghouls aren't immune to cold like their masters," said Morgan. "They need to be indoors just like people do for this kind of cold."

"You always did work best at night anyway," said Nathaniel to his brother. Kevin grinned.

"You always did work best in the snow."

The brothers pounded their fists against each other and snarled. Alex held Ashley as Nathaniel's family looked about evilly. Morgan held his boys strongly and gave them both determined looks. They met their father's powerful gaze and held their heads high. Mary watched them happily, baring her teeth just the same. Ashley held her dad's arm nervously.

The wolves were at war now.

CHAPTER 8

SHADOWS HUNTING SHADOWS

**"A**shley? Can I come in?" asked her dad as he knocked on her door. Ashley sat up and closed her laptop.

"Yes." Her dad came in smiling suspiciously. "What is it?"

"You need to pack a bag for tonight. You're spending the night at Kara's." Ashley looked at him in surprise and looked at the clock. It was already past eight, much later than she'd usually go to a friend's house. Plus with everything that had happened today with the ghouls, she would've thought her dad would never let her leave the house again.

"Why?"

"Because I have to go out tonight and I don't want to leave you here alone with everything that's happening." Ashley looked at her dad suspiciously.

"Where do you have to go?" Her dad sighed.

"I have to go hunting."

"This late?" asked Ashley, not quite understanding why he was feeling down. He took a deep breath and his face became serious.

"I'm going hunting for vampires tonight." Ashley stood up.

"What?"

"They're getting to be too dangerous Ashley. The ones that attacked you and Mary today pushed it too far. Morgan, Katie, and I are going to go take care of them tonight."

"What about Nathaniel and the rest of his family?" Alex chuckled.

"I thought you'd know by now almost nothing attacks a pack of wolves in their territory." Ashley nodded and bit her lip. "He might be there tonight too."

"This is going to be dangerous, isn't it?"

"I don't think so. There's always an element of danger in this, but not with the group I'm going with. We should be fine. I just want to make sure nothing comes after you while I'm gone." Ashley realized just then that her father was dressed like the night sky. He had a dark blue long coat over his clothing and black leather gloves on. She trembled slightly as her father reminded her more of an assassin than a contractor at the moment.

"What are you going to do to them?" asked Ashley. Alex frowned and left the room.

"Pack a bag quickly. We need to be going." Ashley gulped. Her dad was going to do exactly what she thought.

A few minutes later she had a quickly assembled bag and headed out the door with her dad. His eyes kept darting back and forth as if he expected to be attacked on the lawn. He carried a large roll up bag with him that made Ashley uneasy. She didn't want to think about what was in it.

The drive over to Kara's was quiet. Ashley didn't say anything and her dad looked too concentrated to speak. His eyes had become hard and fearless. His face had become tense and in a strange way, Ashley thought he looked younger. He looked more alive than she'd ever seen him, all of his senses at their peaks. He was retired from both his work as a soldier and Hunter, but the trade had never left him.

They arrived at the house of Fortune and the door was flung open when they were mere feet away. In the doorway were Mr. and Mrs. Fortune with Kara in the background. Mr. Fortune came out loudly.

"Mr. Jameson, good to see you again."

"Hello Mr. Fortune." They shook hands and Mrs. Fortune hugged Ashley.

"Hello again Ashley," she said before patting her off in Kara's direction.

"Hi," muttered Ashley as she went by.

"How's the house holding up?" asked Alex.

"Not a problem with her yet, but you should know that. You helped build it."

"I take pride in my work," laughed Alex. "I like to make sure everything stays to the standard I made it."

"A man should take pride in his work," said Mr. Fortune. They both laughed again and Alex looked at Ashley sadly.

"Thanks for taking her for the night."

"No problem at all. She's such a good friend to Kara, she's welcome anytime." Alex moved in and rubbed Ashley's shoulder.

"Alright kiddo, time for me to be off." Ashley gave a small smile and hugged him.

"Okay dad. I'll see you tomorrow."

"Yup, I'll come get you in the morning." He let go of Ashley and felt incredible. If only he'd had a daughter waiting for him to come home after every mission years ago. He felt a need to survive and succeed. "Have a good night everyone."

"Goodbye," they all said. Only Mr. Fortune held his hand out and followed Alex.

"I'll walk you to your car. Best make sure you get there in one piece."

"Oh dear," laughed Mrs. Fortune. "I'm sure the walk to the curb is safe."

"You can never be too sure." He closed the door for his wife and the street drifted back into silence.

"You have a great kid Alex."

"Thank you."

"Which is why I want you to make sure to be safe tonight." Mr. Fortune eyed Alex seriously as they walked.

"I don't know what you mean," said Alex quietly. "I just have to do some work out of town."

"Your line of work doesn't set a man on edge or terrify his daughter. Anything you want to tell me?"

Alex took a deep breath as they reached the truck. Mr. Fortune had a keen sense for danger and he was no fool. Alex wouldn't lie to him and expect to get away with it.

"Earlier this afternoon a couple of men tried to attack Ashley and her friend Mary at school."

"Mary..." started Mr. Fortune. "You mean Mr. Lexington's first daughter, sister to Nathaniel, Ashley's boyfriend?" Alex raised an eye to Mr. Fortune. Mr. Fortune hardly ever dealt with the townspeople, yet he seemed to know everyone. Alex smirked. The man probably had a list of everyone in town.

"Yeah. The girls got away alright, but those men are out there."

"I take it the sheriff doesn't know?" Alex shook his head grimly.

"No. Mr. Lexington and I are going to teach those boys a lesson the old fashion way." A knuckle popped as a tight fist was formed. To Alex's surprise, it wasn't his.

"Best kind of lesson," growled Mr. Fortune. "Need any help?"

"No, we can handle it. In case they avoid us and come looking for Ashley again, I just want to make sure she's somewhere safe for the night."

Mr. Fortune straightened and his chest puffed out. Mr. Fortune had never felt more honored in his life than right now. Alex was worried for his daughter's safety and was entrusting him and his family to watch her. As someone who had lost a child, he knew how hard it could be to trust another. He held his hand out to Alex and looked him in the eye.

"Alex, I can promise you come Hell or high water, Ashley will be safe in my house." Alex shook his hand and smiled.

"I know. Thank you." Mr. Fortune turned away and stormed towards his house. The entire way he began to mutter almost insanely.

"Time to mount the defenses. Full alert!"

Alex couldn't tell him the full truth, but he trusted Mr. Fortune to be fine. He was as paranoid as they came and his house was built like a fortress. Even if he didn't have the expected weapons to fight off vampires, Alex was pretty sure he could still bring them down in waves.

Alex drove into downtown and parked in front of Katie's diner. It was shut down for the night, but he could still see a light on inside. He saw Morgan's truck was already there when he stepped outside. He pulled his large bag out of the back and slung it over his shoulder.

He checked the weather again before he stepped into Katie's place. The wind was practically dead and it was colder than sin out. The sky was littered with clouds, obscuring the moon and the stars. It was a dark night indeed. It reminded him of the old days when he went out hunting. Bad things had a way of happening on nights like these.

Everyone in the diner looked up as he entered. He saw Morgan leaning against the counter and to his surprise, Nathaniel sitting at it. Nathaniel was drinking some water and eating the last meal Katie had made that night. Katie was sitting at one of her tables with a roll out bag laid out in front of her and it was filled with guns. She was checking a rifle as he entered.

"All set Alex?" she asked without even looking up.

Alex grinned and laid out the same bag as Katie on the table. They were both bags from their days as Hunters and they were armed just the same. He pulled out a couple of pistols and holstered them inside his coat. Nathaniel looked over and whistled.

"You are bad people."

"Yes we are," said Katie as she rolled her bag back up. Alex pulled out his shotgun and grinned at Nathaniel. It was the same one he'd pointed at him just a few weeks ago.

"But tonight, we're on your side," said Alex.

"Two dads with the same purpose," said Morgan approvingly.

"Then why is Katie coming?" asked Nathaniel.

"Vampires are bad for business kid." Katie pulled her long blonde hair into a thick ponytail. She tucked it into the back of her coat and wrapped a scarf around her neck. "Or if you want the more sadistic reason," she said with her usual southern drawl, "because I think this is good fun."

"Creepy," laughed Nathaniel. As ready as he was to assault the ghouls which had come after Ashley and his sister, he was still young. He was not yet hardened to this inevitably dangerous and bloody quest. He was the young pup standing with three old veterans. Alex and Katie had stormed more vampire hideouts than they would ever care to admit. His father had been in plenty of territorial battles in his day and he'd already had such battles against Karin. This was something new to Nathaniel, but merely just another exercise of discretion to the others.

"You sure you can handle tonight Nathaniel?" asked Alex as if he were thinking the same thing.

"I've seen worse," said Nathaniel. "Besides, this is our mountain and we don't like to share."

"Just checking," said Alex. "I suppose it'd be foolish to ask if either of you need a weapon?"

"It would," laughed Morgan.

"Again, just checking. What's the plan?"

"We'll all take my truck," said Morgan. "You two will meet Kevin in the field while Nathaniel and I stay back. If anybody's watching, we don't want to tip them off that my family is looking for them."

"And they won't see Kevin?" asked Alex. Morgan grinned.

"Not by a long shot. From there he'll lead the way with his nose. If need be Nathaniel will follow him up if the trail gets weak. It's cold out there and we know the ghouls at the very least have to be indoors. Odds are their masters will be with them. Whatever safe house they're in, we find it and take it."

"Straight to the point. Just the way I like it," said Katie. "Let's do this."

Alex wasn't sure they would find them so easily, but he kept his doubts to himself. He wasn't a werewolf. He probably didn't know this mountain half as well as they did and he couldn't track like they could.

The drive over to the school was quiet and to Alex, very awkward. He'd never felt comfortable driving towards danger. The heavy weight of the pistols pulled on his body. How many times had he waited in the cold car heading towards some secret hideout? It was a good thing this area wasn't often patrolled by police. It was very hard to persuade a policeman a truck full of people and guns were just out for a nighttime drive.

At the school, he and Katie got out of the truck. Morgan handed a radio to Katie as they exited. "We're going to drive away and look around. Contact us when you have a direction."

"You've got it."

Katie and Alex headed through the school and towards the track field. Katie wore the same type of clothing as Alex. As they'd stepped outside, they'd both wrapped dark scarves around the lower half of their faces. They were taught to blend in with the night and that's exactly what they did. Even though Alex had never worked with Katie before, he felt absolute confidence walking next to her. She stood, walked, and talked like every Hunter he'd ever known. No matter where they'd been trained, they were trained the same so any Hunter could work with another.

"This has to be the strangest mission I've ever been on," he said to break the tension. Katie giggled.

"That's right. You've never worked with wolves before."

"No I haven't. I'm not sure about their methods. The trail could easily be gone by now. Kevin could be as easily spotted as us." They headed out into the field. There were few streetlamps in the area, leaving the field in almost total darkness.

"Since you've never seen them transformed, I'll give you a break," whispered Katie. "But let me tell you, nobody is going to spot Kevin."

Alex was about to ask why but his hand suddenly went for his pistol. His eyes saw it far before he registered the wolf in the field and years of training came into effect. His pistol was half drawn before Katie held out her hand.

"Relax," she said. "That's him and that's why I said nobody will see him."

Alex nodded and wondered how long Kevin had been there. He was lying in the grass watching them cross the field. His fur was as dark as the sky and he was nearly impossible to see. Alex was sure he'd only seen him because Kevin's head had moved to watch them better. It was a nervous crossing for Alex. Katie may have been right at home with them, but Alex had had too many bad experiences walking towards such a creature.

"Ready to get to work?" she asked. Her voice was quiet but Alex was sure Kevin could hear her better than he could. The wolf rose stealthily and started to move towards them. Alex felt every hair on his body rise and every muscle tense. Kevin wasn't fully grown yet and he was already quite the werewolf. He should've guessed it by Morgan's size, but it was still an intimidating sight.

Kevin sniffed at both of them and nodded. Alex knew he just wanted their scents to keep track of them. He tried to slow his beating heart, but it was impossible with something that big looking him in the eye. Katie pulled a small bag out of her pocket and pulled out Mary's shirt from earlier and the piece of jacket.

"Here you go."

Kevin rubbed his nose all over the samples and inhaled deeply. He'd smelled the man before, but his senses were even greater as a wolf. In a few moments, he felt he knew more about this man than the man did. His nose pulled him away from the shirt and along the grass. There was blood in this grass and it was a smell he now knew. There were only the smallest of drops in most places, but to him, they shined like beacons of scent. They went around much of the field before the trail led out of the school.

"He's on the move. Back side of the campus," said Katie into the radio. Kevin was out of the school and started skirting around the town. Morgan pulled up in his truck.

"Get in." Alex took the front seat and Katie took the back.

"Where's Nathaniel?" asked Katie.

"He's in the bed," said Morgan. "I want him to be ready to get out as soon as we need."

"Let's go before Kevin leaves us behind," said Alex. Kevin was already around the corner and Morgan drove after him.

Kevin thought about what this man must've done after the school. He'd expected much of the trail to disappear, but it kept going. These men did not arrive at the school by car. They had walked. The man had made some effort to cover his wound, but there was still the occasional drip to keep the scent up. He didn't smell like the rest of the town either. Kevin wasn't sure if the man had showered in a week. His foul stench upset his nose, but if his nose hurt, that meant he was going the right way.

Near the edge of town, the smell suddenly vanished. No more trails became apparent and Kevin guessed they must've finally met someone with a car. There were multiple scents so they all must've split up when they came to town. They were out on the mountain somewhere. He hid and waited for his dad to come over.

Morgan stopped his truck and walked into the trees. Alex had to admire the man's tact as Morgan looked like he was stopping to use the bathroom. He couldn't hear anything, but he knew Kevin must be barking about what he'd found to him. Morgan came back after a bit and started them out of town.

"Kevin says the trail ends here as they got into a car. We can still follow some of the smell, but it will be much harder now."

"Out of town?" said Katie. "Unless they're driving hours to get to us, there are only so many places they could be."

"No, they're close enough. Karin wouldn't want to be so far out," said Morgan confidently. He stopped the truck just outside of the town. No light but the truck's for miles. Morgan patted his hand on the outside of his door twice.

"You're up."

Alex turned around as the truck sagged and bounced as the heavy werewolf hopped out. He expected Nathaniel to be lighter than his brother, but his white coat took him completely by surprise. He understood why Kevin had said Nathaniel worked best in the snow, he looked just like it. Nathaniel crossed into the forest and stopped next to his brother.

"You have a midnight wolf and a winter wolf?" asked Alex amazed. "Such a rare trait of coats."

"I know," said Morgan. "Kevin took after my side and Melissa's dad was a winter wolf too."

Alex was truly surprised by their coats. They were stunning wolves and they brought excitement and fear to him. Alex had seen a pair of wolves like this work together only once and they had filled his nights with dread. Most experienced hunters wouldn't even hunt a pair like this at night in winter. As soon as the boys ran off into the woods they became invisible amongst the scenery.

They wouldn't be seen unless they wanted to be seen.

Nathaniel and Kevin took opposite sides of the street and ran along sniffing. The strange stink of the ghouls was faint, but they could find it if they tried. They didn't expect to get anything unless the men turned off the road or stopped for some reason. Morgan drove slowly and kept his eyes peeled. He doubted he'd get anything by sight though. He'd have to leave this to his boys.

A few miles down he heard barking from Nathaniel and slowed the truck to a stop. Nathaniel and Kevin crept into the road with their noses down. Something in the road stunk like one of the men. Kevin found the stub of a cigarette near the road and barked for his brother to look at it. This was it. They were still on the right trail and ran back into the forest.

"This is why I tell people smoking is bad," said Alex with a chuckle.

"Those things can kill you," said Morgan.

"Yeah, especially if they lead angry werewolves to your door," said Katie.

They all shared a quiet laugh and kept going. It left a trail and an unmistakable scent with every cigarette. Ten minutes later the road split, one heading down the mountain and one further up. The boys split up and returned only moments later. The trail disappeared down the mountain, but up the scent continued. Alex didn't know these roads very well, but he knew there were only a couple of houses over the next few miles. They would be at their target soon.

It was getting late and Kara had turned off the movie they were watching. Ashley rolled out the sleeping bag on the floor and Kara collapsed on her bed. Every light in the house was off and the sky provided almost none. Clouds covered the stars and the moon was absent this night.

She laid on her side and looked outside. Somewhere out there her dad and adopted family were running around in the darkness. They were using every shadow to their advantage and searching for vampires. She trusted her dad and the others to hide, but how can someone hide against a creature of the night?

Something soft pattered gently against the window. Ashley sat up and tried to see what it was. Drops of water were hitting the window. The rain started light and then it disappeared. The dark sky suddenly turned into a white mist. An unexpected snowstorm was descending over the town.

"It's snowing," said Kara, not even moving from her sleeping position.

"This late in the year?"

"We can have snow through April if we have a bad winter. Coming from California though, I guess you're still not used to this."

"I haven't even lived here a year," reminded Ashley.

"This winter has been kind of rough. Started early and odds are, it's going to end late."

"I like storms," said Ashley. "I don't like how cold they are, but they're kind of fun to watch if you're inside. It makes me feel very peaceful." Kara snickered from her bed. "What's so funny?"

"My dad used to tell me storms came when something evil was at work. Whenever something really bad was about to happen, the world would cover the area in water and snow in an attempt to bury it. That way nobody knew it ever happened." Ashley smirked.

"It seems to storm here year round." Kara finally rolled over and gave Ashley an evil smile.

"Tells you what kind of town this is, doesn't it?"

"We'll go from here on foot," said Morgan as he pulled his truck off the road and turned off the engine. "We don't want to alert them that we're coming."

"They could still be a long way off," said Alex as he grabbed a few weapons from his pack.

"Not for us," said Morgan. "We can carry you if you like." Nathaniel and Kevin opened their mouths in silent laughter.

"No thanks," said Katie. "I'm not so old I can't hike a bit." She hung a shotgun across her back and had a pair of pistols at her side. She checked her hunting rifle and kept it in her hands.

"Do all of you Hunters use the same things?" asked Morgan as he pulled off his jacket.

"No, but we use the same principle," said Alex as he checked a pistol. "RPM."

"RPM?" asked Morgan.

"Range, power, mobility," said Katie. "If you don't know what you're up against, you always keep at least one of each. A weapon good for range." She hefted her rifle. "A weapon strong enough to take down anything." She nodded to her back where the shotgun was hanging. "And something small and mobile, usually a pistol."

"And you never leave home without something that doesn't take ammo," said Alex as he strapped a long hunting knife to his leg. He had two pistols and a rifle like Katie, but he didn't bring his shotgun tonight. He kept a .45 pistol slung under his arm. It was no shotgun, but he was more accurate with it and it still would bring down anything he pointed it at.

"You two go find them," said Morgan to his kids. "When you do, one of you come back and lead us. I'll be staying near these two." Both boys nodded and disappeared once more into the night.

"Let's just hope they don't have sentries," said Katie.

"That could make the whole night go to hell," agreed Alex.

"If anyone spots those two before they spot them, I'll be ashamed of them," laughed Morgan as he went around the side of the truck.

Alex had to hold himself back as he heard the cracking of a man changing into a wolf so nearby. It was hard not to pull out his .45 and shoot through the truck. He looked at Katie and saw even she felt like doing it.

Even though he knew it was coming, Alex almost turned his rifle on Morgan as he came around the corner. Morgan was a giant of a man and as a werewolf looked more like a werebear. He was so thick that if Alex had started shooting, he wasn't sure the few rounds would stop Morgan.

They kept a good pace through the forest after the werewolf. He was going at a gentle walk, but his size and powerful legs made it a jog for Alex and Katie. They kept off the street and every once in a while, Alex and Katie would scan the horizon with their rifles. They were both equipped for night vision but never saw anything. Morgan just shook his head and kept going as they checked, forcing them to run after him once they were done.

"Some of us can't see in the dark," hissed Katie.

Morgan just shrugged, or at least Alex thought he did. It was extremely dark out and they could barely see where they were going. They didn't risk flashlights so they just had to trust their feet and follow the dark outline of Morgan.

Alex felt the night getting colder as they ran. His body stayed warm with every step, but any moment they paused the chill set in. The sky groaned and light began to sprinkle down onto them. The clouds hadn't parted for them, only gifted them with one of the last snows of the year. The snowflakes came down tentatively, barely holding themselves together for their trip to the Earth. If visibility was bad before, now it would be impossible.

A small grumble came from up ahead and the former Hunters trained their rifles for trouble. They saw Kevin coming towards them, barking something quietly to his father. Morgan nodded and greeted his son.

"You found them?" breathed Katie. Kevin nodded and looked back the way he came.

"How many miles?" asked Alex. Kevin paused and held up two claws. "Two miles isn't bad." Kevin raised and dropped a third claw after a moment's thought. "Two to three miles."

Morgan barked something and Kevin responded. They spoke for a minute before Kevin turned and sat down next to Katie. Katie looked at him uneasily.

"You know I don't like doing this."

"Really?" demanded Alex, realizing what they were doing as Morgan sat next to him. He didn't know if he could ride a werewolf. He didn't even like riding horses. "I don't think so."

"It's better than wasting our strength running three miles, uphill, in the snow," sighed Katie.

"I…I just can't," said Alex. "I'm already uncomfortable."

"We're not out here tonight because we like it," said Katie. "We're out here because they went after your little girl." She slung her rifle over her shoulder and stood over Kevin. He stood up slowly and took Katie off her feet. She found the comfiest seat she could and leaned forward.

"You coming?" asked Katie.

Alex looked at Morgan and gulped. He stood over him and waited just like Katie did. The moment Morgan rose, Alex's stomach lurched badly. He felt hundreds of pounds of solid muscle beneath him connected to sharp fangs and claws. Images of every werewolf who'd ever charged him danced before his eyes. He'd never let a werewolf get this close before. Morgan's soft fur felt thick in his hands and with every step he took, Alex felt he was about to be turned upon.

"It's okay Alex," said Katie reassuringly.

"I am not okay," he said tensely.

"Some people love riding these big guys."

"They've never been on the wrong end of one."

"I heard Ashley is quite good at it." Alex looked at Katie mortified. "She rides Nathaniel all the time." Alex gulped and felt his insides groan.

"Please never say that again. I will thank you for it."

Alex had no idea how long it took to get to this house, too long in his opinion. He saw the lights up ahead shining blearily through the snowfall. Kevin slowed down first and dropped down for Katie to get off. Alex didn't wait for Morgan to slow and leapt off him as quickly as he could. Katie came over and put a hand on his shoulder.

"Not so bad," she said with a small smile.

"I don't care how this ends, I'm walking back to the truck. I'll walk back to town if I need to." Morgan looked hurt, but advanced without a word. Alex took down his rifle and held it for strength.

The house before them was a large cabin hidden from the world. The road wasn't even visible out here. There must've been a trail hidden somewhere now by the snow. All the blinds were closed, but lights were on all over the house. Smoke drifted out of the chimney in a feeble attempt to push back the storm.

"Where's Nathaniel?" asked Katie. They followed Kevin's head as he pointed him out.

Even with Kevin pointing, they almost missed him. Nathaniel was lying just at the edge of the forest, not too far from the house, but just enough to be out of the light. When he laid down the snow seemed to just grow on him and add to his beautiful coat. It was slowly building up around him, erasing his presence from the world. His eyes were nearly closed to hide all traces of him, but he opened them as they approached. Icy eyes peered out and Alex felt like the weather was angry at him.

"You're sure this is the place?" Kevin nodded. Nathaniel didn't move from his hiding place. Morgan held up a claw and sniffed at Katie's coat pocket. She pulled out the samples and Morgan went over them compulsively. Then he crawled around the cabin quietly, smelling the car, door, ground, and walls. He came back and nodded gravely.

"How do we want to do this?" asked Katie.

"I say we just walk in the front door," said Alex. Everyone looked at him in surprise. "Katie and I walk up to the front door and pose as lost travelers. We can get a look inside before trying to storm the place."

"We're either going to get pounced or shot," said Katie.

"Exactly. If they try and jump us, we can take them. If they have guns, we want to know who has them. You three come in wherever you think you can, preferably behind them." Kevin held up his paws and shook his head. "I don't command the pack, don't ask me. You figure it out." Morgan barked something at his boys and they moved with him. Nathaniel trailed a wave of snow behind him as he walked.

"You were one of those ballsy hunters, weren't you?" asked Katie as they walked to the door.

"It works in my experience," said Alex. He took his rifle and laid it just to the side of the door. Katie laid her rifle and shotgun and rifle on the other side. "How good is your quick draw?"

"I prefer the shotgun for a reason." Alex laughed before pounding his hand against the door.

"Hello?" he called out. He pounded on the door harder. "Hello is anyone home?" Katie looked impressed by the level of distress he projected. "Please," he called out as he banged on the door. "We're just lost travelers."

Warm air spread across them as the door opened. The home was brightly lit and they could hear the fire cackling somewhere. A pale faced woman was standing in the doorway smiling.

"What's wrong?" she asked sweetly.

"Please miss," said Alex with a chill in his voice. "My wife and I here were traveling down the road and we ran out of gas. We're freezing out here."

"Please come in." People started to come into the living room. They were all pale and shaky looking. Alex noticed one had a bandage wrapped around his arm. Katie leaned down feigning cold and reached slowly towards her weapons. The woman smiled and showed off a pair of shiny fangs. "You came to the right place."

"We certainly did," said Katie cheerfully. Her shotgun came up to the vampire's midsection. She hissed and Katie pulled the trigger, blasting her back into the house with a hail of silver.

At the same time, Alex's hand flew into his coat and came back out with his pistol aimed past the woman. He fired into the packed crowd, aiming for the bandaged man. They scattered, but he and Katie managed to drop three in the first volley. He smiled as the man with the bandage fell and he took cover.

"Prepare to die monsters!" shouted Katie. "You came to the wrong town!" She blasted the cabin with her shotgun, shooting through walls and tearing apart the house. A scream came from one room as a stupid ghoul didn't have the brains to duck. She pulled away and ducked as a few pistols came around the corners and began firing wildly.

"Reminds me of the old days," said Alex. He fired his pistol slowly into the house, trying to make his shots count as Katie reloaded her shotgun. Bullets hissed by them and made them pull further away from the door.

"I counted three vampires," said Katie, "the rest ghouls."

"Agreed, there could be more."

The gunfire stopped. Inside a vampire had willed a few of her minions to break the glass and go out the windows to surround them during the gunfire. A few ghouls reloaded their meager weapons as their brethren started out into the night.

Screams filled the air as ghouls didn't go out the windows, but were yanked out. All the vampires inside saw were giant claws reaching in, and then their servants were gone. Windows burst all over the house as the giant monsters made their rounds. The vampires cursed angrily.

Outside Katie reached inside her coat and pulled out a long bottle. She popped the top off and the scent of powerful alcohol reached Alex's nose. She held the bottle out towards him. "Drink?" she laughed.

"No thanks, I'm trying to quit." Katie laughed and took a swig of the bottle. She coughed and smiled.

"This stuff can kill you," she hacked before she stuffed a rag in it and lit the other end. Alex grinned and began to fire his pistol into the house. First rule of the Order, no evidence must ever be left behind.

Katie tossed in the flaming bottle and it shattered against the hardwood floor. Dark liquor spread across the floor and the thirsty fire chased after it desperately. The couch caught on fire and the rug began to burn.

Ghouls came out shooting, spraying the entryway with bullets. They were poor shots though. They were scared and too inexperienced with their weapons to be much threat. Alex and Katie leaned in and blasted them backwards into the roaring flames. Shrieks came from the side of the house and they realized the ghouls were just bait. The vampires were trying to escape to fight another day.

One vampire leapt free only to have something large pounce her straight back through the wall. She tried to fight back, but the werewolf on top of her was huge. She'd not been expecting it either and it tore into her before she could utter a shout of denial.

The other leapt into the night hoping for freedom and instead hit the snow. She couldn't understand how the snow had risen up to meet her and felt stronger than steel as they rolled. It took her a moment to realize the snow was furry and a large head was turning for her with large jaws. She was not on the snow at all, but on the back of an angry werewolf.

She screamed and held on for dear life. The werewolf thrashed about dangerously as it tried to catch her in its mighty jaws. She had no chance to attack back or even make a run for it. Its head could almost reach all the way around and it would only take one bite to bring her down.

The werewolf ducked low and the vampire saw the night sky descend upon her. Powerful jaws ripped her off the werewolf's back and she found herself tumbling in the snow once more. Only this time the werewolf was on top of her. All of her mighty strength came to a quick end and she knew no more.

Nathaniel met his brother's fearful gaze. Dark ichor dripped from Kevin's jaws as he contemplated what he'd just done. She was a vampire, but she looked just like a human. Kevin walked away from her and put his head on his brother's shoulder. Nathaniel told him it was okay. It was never easy the first time.

The vampire stood suddenly and Nathaniel roared angrily. She hissed and tried to leap at them. A rifle cracked to their left and the vampire burst into ash in front of their eyes. They looked back and saw Alex holding his rifle up. They nodded thanks to him and looked back to the vampire. She didn't look like a person anymore. She was just a pile of ash. In a way, she was dead before they'd ever found her.

Alex dropped his rifle against the door again and headed inside after Katie. Morgan was prowling around inside and Alex took it as a sign that the house was clean. Katie was already pulling out wallets and checking ids. He headed into the other rooms in search of anything that would lead them to the real masters.

"All out of state people," shouted Katie. "Looks like they all came in from Minnesota." Alex tossed the room apart in search of any secret folders, computers, or the like. He found nothing and went to the next room.

"I doubt anything is here," said Katie.

"So do I, but it never hurts. Morgan will you check the car outside for anything." Morgan climbed back out the window and Alex instantly felt better. There was nothing here. He moved to join Katie in the kitchen.

"Nice liquor cabinet. Whoever lived here knew how to spend the winter," said Katie.

"Unfortunately they drank a little too much with the fire going," said Alex with a smile. They emptied the cabinet and anything flammable and spread it all over the cabin. The fire swam around like a mighty serpent, growing mightier with each passing second. When they felt they'd fanned the flames enough, Alex and Katie stepped outside to admire their handiwork.

The house was roaring in agony as the flames danced in the windows and through the cracks. It screamed black smoke into the sky and begged for the end. The world failed to hear its cries though as it continued to snow softly. The storm would conceal its smoke and the forest would hide its fire. The snow would never allow the fire to grow past its base, so the fire clung to the cabin greedily.

Morgan and his sons stood together and howled to the moon above. The victory was theirs tonight. The woods shook in fear of the great wolves and their songs. Alex and Katie didn't even raise their weapons in salute. They just stood side by side and let the heat wash over them.

The first victory was theirs.

CHAPTER 9

WE RUN ALONE

Ashley's eyes opened the minute the first rays of dawn touched them. The storm had already passed and now a new day was coming to life. But the sun didn't hold the same warmth as it used to. It wasn't a symbol of comfort, just a sign of safety. The vampires would stay away another day.

Laying in bed, hopelessly tired but unable to sleep, she wondered how her dad and Nathaniel had faired. There were no messages on her phone and they didn't reply to her. Ashley didn't know when they'd be back. Her dad had only said he was going for the night, but what if it was longer? Part of her secretly hoped they'd never found the vampire's lair last night. It was easier to imagine them scouring the mountain through the snow than fighting. If they hadn't found them, there was no chance they could be hurt. Maybe they were so intimidating the vampires would just leave like the jackals had. Then they'd come back, just like the jackals had…

Ashley texted them again, staring bitterly at her phone that didn't respond. Patience flared to anger and she lay there spitting venom quietly. It was better than letting the fear creep in. If they were hurt or needed her help, there was nothing she could do. She couldn't track them and even if she could magically appear at their sides, it wasn't like she could help. What did Ashley know about fighting? Teenage ideas of becoming a doctor or veterinarian to aid her werewolf family teased through her mind.

Time passed by in leaps and bounds. One moment the sun had barely risen and the next it was an hour later. Every time she glanced at the clock time moved forward at least ten minutes. When the clock struck eight, Kara stirred in her sheets. Ashley welcomed the distraction.

"It's too early to get up," said Kara as she rubbed her eyes.

"I could hardly sleep," said Ashley.

"Allow me to make it up for you." Kara slumped back into her pillows and snored loudly. Ashley shook her back and forth, but Kara just remained there stubbornly. It wasn't until Ashley plopped a pillow over her head and tried to lay on her did Kara sit up.

"You're terrible at this sleepover thing, aren't you?"

"Come on, I'm hungry," said Ashley.

"Why do you need me for food?"

"Because your family will interrogate me if I'm alone. Now come on." Kara rolled out of bed and popped to her feet. She rolled her whole body, cracking it in several places before relaxing.

"That was gross," said Ashley. Kara smirked.

"You're just jealous."

Downstairs they found Kara's mom standing ready in the kitchen with a batch of pancakes just waiting to be made. Mr. Fortune was reading the paper and constantly peeping out the blinds. Ashley noticed every time he looked outside, he used a different window at random. It was as if he expected snipers to shoot him dead any moment. He had dark circles under his eyes.

"Did you sleep dad?" asked Kara.

"I believe I lost about three minutes before 4AM." He growled. "I'm losing my touch." Ashley looked at him in alarm. Kara just gave him a thumbs up and took a plate of pancakes. They had a large breakfast and were upstairs washing up when they heard Mr. Fortune shout proudly.

"Success!"

"Yay," mumbled Kara as she brushed her teeth. Ashley went over to the window and saw her dad outside.

"My ride is here," she said happily.

Her dad looked tired, but okay. Mr. Fortune met him halfway and shook his hand. They were talking quietly as Ashley picked up her things. She didn't know what they were talking about, but she could guess. Mr. Fortune was giving her dad the rundown of his security measures and apologizing for having slept three minutes.

"Next time you should hang out longer. Come earlier or something," said Kara.

"I will.." Kara gave her a two fingered salute. Ashley met her dad in the doorway and smiled.

"Hi dad."

"Hi there." He hugged her and she smiled. He wasn't hurt. "Did you behave?"

"Not a peep out of her," said Mr. Fortune proudly. "House was quiet all night, no issues."

"That's good," said Alex with a yawn. "You ready to go?"

"Yup."

"Good. Thank you again." He shook hands with Mr. Fortune who shook back vigorously.

"It was my pleasure. Bring her by anytime." He winked at Alex before closing the door. Ashley gave her dad a curious look as they walked away.

"What was that?" she asked.

"Mr. Fortune is a good man," chuckled her dad once they got in the truck. Once the doors were shut, he continued. "He figured I was up to no good last night. He supported me and asked me to bring him along sometime." Ashley looked at him bewildered.

"You told him about the vampires?" Alex waved his hand.

"No. He just thought we were teaching some inappropriate boys a lesson."

"Oh. So did you find them last night?"

"Some," he answered, the amusement leaving his voice. "A few vampires, a lot of ghouls. They weren't all there, it was just a hideout. We took it out no problem."

"Nobody hurt?" she asked.

"No. We took them by surprise and it was over in just a couple of minutes. I got home around two, which means Morgan probably got home about three. Sorry I didn't respond to your message earlier, but I was out cold. Last night kind of wore me out."

"I'll let you sleep when we get back," said Ashley. "Maybe I'll see Nathaniel and see how he's doing."

"Not today," said her dad sternly. "Today could be dangerous to be out. We don't know how they'll react when they discover we took out their nest. Besides, I think Nathaniel wants to get some sleep too."

"You're up," she said defiantly.

"And I'm still tired. No means no Ashley. You can see him tomorrow. Today I want you to stay home. I'm sure you have homework to do anyway."

"Yeah, because with everything that is going on, I'm totally focused on homework," said Ashley sarcastically.

"You can see him tomorrow," repeated Alex before he changed the subject. "I got to see them changed," he said quietly. "Morgan, Kevin, and Nathaniel I mean." He smirked at Ashley. "I see why you fell for him."

"He looks good even as a wolf," said Ashley smugly.

"Winter wolves, rare breed. Katie told me you've ridden on his back before. Is that true?" Ashley heard the tone of his voice change and wondered if she was in trouble. There wasn't much point lying so she didn't.

"Yeah. It was weird at first, but I've gotten really good at it. Have you ever ridden a werewolf?"

"Only briefly," said Alex. "If I can help it, I'll never do it again. I'd buy you a horse if you said you'd never do it again either." He sighed and gave her a soft smile. "But I don't suppose that's going to happen."

"I don't think the horse would be very happy," laughed Ashley. Alex grinned.

"No, probably not."

They made it home and Alex made sure the house was secure. When he was content that everything was safe, he brought Ashley in and locked up the house. He didn't spare any time in heading for his bedroom and collapsing.

Ashley felt bad for her dad. He was a fit man, but he wasn't young. He wasn't up to hiking through storms in the dead of night anymore.

She didn't know how cold it was last night, but it was bad enough for snow.

She waited about an hour before she decided to sneak out. It took her only two seconds to realize her plans to see Nathaniel had been thwarted. The key rack was empty. Nathaniel lived far into the mountain and there was no way she could get there without a car.

She tried to call him, but received no response. Nathaniel was still down for the count as well it appeared. Ashley paced her bedroom, watched a movie, and did practically anything to keep herself distracted. All of it was useless though.

There was only one thing she could do to comfort herself. She opened her window and looked out to the mountain. Somewhere out there her boyfriend and his family were sleeping soundly. If she couldn't call him or go see him, there was only one other way to communicate with him.

She raised her flute to her lips and began to play one of her softer melodies. She wished she could stand on top of the roof and play, but the window would have to do. The music was soft and she was sure it couldn't reach into the mountains. With each song, she gradually raised the tempo. Soon she had a few of the dogs in town howling with her. It was hard not to smile so she could keep playing. A few notes were dropped, but she kept the overall song together.

She jumped as the door flew open. Her dad was glaring at her with dark and weary eyes. She froze in place and let the song fall away. If she was playing loud enough that she hoped wolves might hear her in the mountains, it was pretty obvious her dad could hear her too. He walked over to the window and closed it. He locked it, pulled the blinds, and held a warning finger to Ashley.

"What part of sleep and it could be dangerous don't you understand?"

"I'm sorry," she mumbled. It'd been a long time since she'd seen him mad. Exhaustion and fear practically glowed in his eyes when he spoke to her.

"They may try and get revenge on us today," he said again. "The last thing we need is you standing in the window and making enough racket for the entire town to know about. All of us are sleeping and you're up here painting a big sign that says please kidnap me. Do you understand what I'm saying?"

"Yes dad." Alex let out a deep sigh.

"I don't mean to be angry with you, I'm just worried. You're my daughter and I don't like the thought of you being defenseless. I don't know what I'd do if you got hurt because someone came after you because of me. It's the whole reason I couldn't see you your entire childhood." He held her shoulders and smiled. "Now can you please promise you'll be quiet and stay out of sight today?"

"Yes dad," she said sincerely.

"Thank you honey." He kissed her on the head and headed back downstairs. "I'm going to try and get some more sleep."

Ashley closed the door and laid down on her bed. Her dad was right. Out of everyone involved in this, she was the only one defenseless. The only one who was in the same boat as her was Lidia, and she wasn't even ten.

No revenge came that day. Her dad slept for only a couple more hours and they had a quiet dinner. She heard back from Nathaniel and agreed to meet him the next day. She didn't tell her dad that they were going walking in the hills, but that they were going to Nathaniel's house. Her dad was rightfully paranoid, but she couldn't just hide all the time.

The next day she drove up into the hills and stopped near one of the many trails she and Nathaniel liked to walk. As usual, he was there first, standing cheerfully in the fresh snow. While it still felt cold outside to Ashley, Nathaniel was beginning to downsize in clothing. He'd traded in his coat for a simple long sleeved shirt. Ashley noticed his boots and pant legs were a bit wet as she left her car. He must've run the entire way there.

"Hi there," he said as he skipped towards her. Ashley just smiled and let him kiss her on the lips. "How are you?" Ashley just shrugged and started their walk.

"How was going after the vampires?" she asked quietly. Nathaniel grinned and strengthened his stride.

"It was exciting. Kevin and I were tracking them for what felt like forever until we finally found the house. It was like hunting, only the prey was so much more aware than usual. A deer can only run away, but vampires and ghouls can fight back. It took a lot of patience to find them and then I had to wait for your dad and Katie to catch up."

"I'm just glad nobody got hurt," she said as she clung to his arm.

"Me too. Kevin almost got a good surprise, but fortunately your dad was there. He showed us vampires don't always like to die." Ashley nodded and laid her head against him as they walked. They said nothing for a long time and simply enjoyed the path.

Winter and spring were battling each other to see who would reign over the land. Winter had struck a mighty blow with the storm, but spring would win in the end. The snow was weak and crunched beneath their feet. The plants rose out of the snow's frozen embrace and reached for the sky. The sun grew stronger with every passing day and the plants took the melted snow into their roots.

"What's on your mind?" asked Nathaniel. She snuggled her head against him.

"Not much, you?"

"Trying to figure out what you won't tell me," said Nathaniel. He slowed his step and looked at her worriedly. "What's wrong?" Ashley sighed and let go of his arm.

"I don't like this. I don't like that you're hunting vampires with my dad and your family."

"Neither do I," said Nathaniel, sounding insulted. "It's not exactly what I'd call a fun time. Tracking them was exciting sure, but not fighting them."

"No, I don't mean it like that," said Ashley. "I mean that all of you are out there hunting them, fighting for the town and all of our lives. My dad, Katie, your dad, you, and even Kevin are involved now. And what am I doing?" She looked at him hurt. "I'm at a friend's house trying to pretend nothing is wrong."

"There isn't a lot you can do." He took her hand, but she pulled it back quickly.

"I know! That's just it! I hate that I can't do anything. My dad is a skilled Hunter, you're some mythical beast, and me..." She waved her arms pathetically. "I'm just me. I can't do anything special."

"And you don't want to," said Nathaniel.

"Yes I do. I want to help you." Nathaniel sighed and held up her hand. He pulled her light glove off and admired her hand.

"You have beautiful hands," he said. "Delicate skin. No scars. No roughness from lots of hard work."

"What?" she asked confused.

"And no blood on them," said Nathaniel seriously. He put his hand next to Ashley's. "My hands look tougher and while you can't see it, they're stained red. It's not something you want. I can see in your eyes you don't want to hurt people."

"No I don't," said Ashley as she put her hand in his. She closed her fingers around his and felt his warmth against her cold hands. "I don't want to hurt people. I want to protect the people I care about." Nathaniel smiled and pulled her over for a hug. He kissed the side of her head.

"You're wonderful," he said. "I hope you never change."

"I want to change."

"What?" Ashley took a deep breath and plunged herself off the ledge. There would be no coming back from this question.

"Will you bite me?" she asked quietly. Nathaniel pulled away from her.

"What did you say?" he asked shocked.

"Will you bite me?" she asked louder. "Will you let me be a wolf with you?" He took another step away and looked away from her.

"I…ah…no. No I won't."

"Why not?"

"Because you don't want to deal with it. If I bite you it would change your life forever."

"I know."

"No you don't. Why do you want to become a wolf anyway?"

"I want to be able to fight back. I want to be able to protect you and everyone else." Ashley sniffed. "I want to be a part of the pack, not just following it."

"You're always with me," said Nathaniel. "I've even taken you out on the full moon to run with my family."

"No, you take me out to ride. I can't run with your family because I'm not a wolf. I can't talk to your family. I can't join them because I'm not one of them. When you run, you run alone without me. I want to join you."

"I'm pretty sure your dad would shoot me," laughed Nathaniel.

"No he wouldn't."

"No, I know for a fact he told my dad one day if I ever changed you he would shoot me. Your dad tolerates us Ashley, but he doesn't like us. We were working together the other night and he almost shot us then."

"He'll learn to deal with it," said Ashley. "I want to be a werewolf."

"And the answer is no!" snapped Nathaniel. "I'm not biting you, so leave it alone." He walked away from her and looked back angrily. Ashley met his fierce look with tears.

"Why?" she whispered. "Why don't you want me to be with you?"

"Don't turn it into that, because that isn't what this is about!" shouted Nathaniel. Ashley took a step back as she felt she'd touched a nerve. Nathaniel's eyes became hard and his body grew slightly. He flexed clawed fingers at her and brandished sharp teeth.

"You want to become a monster?" he barked. "You want people to be afraid of you? Do you want to be judged just for what you are?" His body reverted to normal, but his face was just as fearsome. "Do you really want to have the power to kill?" The words came out in a hiss and Ashley felt as if Nathaniel had just physically struck her. She staggered back as he turned away from her. She didn't know what to say.

Ashley watched him walk down the path and didn't follow him. She desperately wanted to, but she had to compose herself first. She had to calm her jumpy nerves and stop the tears trying to reach her eyes. She'd expected Nathaniel to reject her idea, but she'd never expected him to react like that. Is that what he really thought of her idea? That she wanted to kill? It's amazing how different it sounds when you say you want to protect someone and when you say you want to kill. To some the two are different subjects, to others they're the same. Nathaniel obviously thought that way. Ashley started after him. If he'd wanted to be left alone, he would've left so quickly she'd never be able to follow.

Still she practically had to run to catch up to him. Even if when he was just walking his longer and more powerful legs made him faster than her. She slowed to a walk when she was next to him and looked him in the eye. His face looked more pained than angry. "I'm sorry," she said. Nathaniel sighed and let his hand slip into hers.

"I know."

"I didn't mean it like that." Nathaniel nodded.

"I know again." She stopped and pulled Nathaniel around to look at her. She rubbed his face and frowned.

"Is that how you feel? Do you think you're a killer?" Nathaniel gave her a weak smile and rubbed his head into her hand.

"I don't think I'm a killer." He paused and took both her hands into his. "I do think I've had to do some very bad things before."

"No one blames you," she said quickly. "You do what you have to do."

"I know. It doesn't make it any easier." He let go of her and walked off the path to a downed tree. He wiped away a small layer of snow and sat down. Ashley followed him but she didn't sit down. Nathaniel rubbed his face and leaned back. "I try and be cheerful about everything. I try and be strong for everyone else, but I can't do it all the time Ashley." Nathaniel looked at her with tired eyes. "I don't want to do all this. I do it because I have to."

"I know," said Ashley. She knelt down in front of him and smiled. "I wouldn't be dating you if you liked this." Ashley saw darkness in

Nathaniel's eyes. It had grown so much it'd almost completely quenched the light of innocence. He had the same look as every war veteran who'd been in the trenches. His fights weren't sadly from hundreds of feet away with a gun, his had been close. They'd been vicious and they'd scarred him in more than one way.

"It's easy to do it when it's happening," he said quietly. "When I thought those jackals were going to hurt you, I took them apart without even thinking about it. I let instinct take the wheel and we both know what happened. When we were tracking the vampires last night, it felt like a game at first. Then we arrived and I felt the game was over. We were there to do bad things. When the first ghoul stepped outside, I knew what I had to do." Nathaniel shuddered and held his head. "It's easy to do it. The hard part comes afterwards when you have to think about it." Ashley rubbed her hands on his legs.

"Have you told your dad this?"

"Yeah. We've talked about it a lot and we still do. I know it was for a good reason every time, but still..." He put down his hands in hers and frowned. "Somewhere out there, someone cared for those people. Now they're never coming home."

"But they came out here," said Ashley. "It was their choice. I've never seen you start a fight like that. The other night was because they came after us. They started this, not you."

"Whatever they started, we still killed them," said Nathaniel. "Whether it was right or not, I will never know." He sighed and brought her close. Ashley moved to sit on his knees and hug him. Nathaniel kissed her and looked up thoughtfully. "I'm sorry I won't turn you."

"It was a bit dumb for me to ask," said Ashley.

"Maybe one day," said Nathaniel, "but not for this. If you ever become one of us, I want it to be because you want to be with us, not because you're afraid." Ashley kissed his forehead.

"You know I want to be with you." Nathaniel put his head against her chest and took a deep breath.

"I know you do. I just don't want to do it anytime soon. Besides, from everything I've heard, turning from a human into a werewolf is weird. I don't know if you'd be able to help us anyway."

Nathaniel laughed and looked back to Ashley with a grin on his face. His mirth was back and it made her happy, but she could still see the change in his eyes. These kinds of experiences weren't right for someone Nathaniel's age. He was aging more and more by the day, maturity and responsibility forced upon him. This was what he didn't want Ashley to suffer.

She held his hand and rested herself up against him. One day they would run side by side as wolves and be happy, but not today. She wanted Nathaniel to change her because he wanted to, not because he felt he was forced. He needed to believe that being a werewolf was a good thing again. Ashley kissed his head and smiled. She would wait however long she had to. It would be worth it.

CHAPTER 10

SCOUTING THE FUTURE

"I'm busy," shouted their history teacher as the phone rang in their class. The students whispered excitedly as he walked over to the phone and picked it up. Their teacher was notorious for despising interruptions in his classroom and would yell at anything which caused them, including other members of the staff. He was on the phone for less than ten seconds when he slammed it back down.

"I thought you disconnected the phone?" asked one bold student.

"I did. They keep reconnecting it." The students laughed and their teacher stuck his thumb towards the door. "They want you in the counselor's office Ashley." Ashley looked up surprised.

"Why?"

"How the hell should I know? Get outta here so I can finish my lesson." The class laughed again and Ashley stood up to go. "Take your bag. I guess you're sneaking out of the last few minutes." Ashley gathered up her things and headed for the door. Nathaniel brushed her leg with his hand as she headed out.

"Hands on your pencil Nathaniel," said their teacher, not even looking back to see if he'd moved. Nathaniel held up his hand to prove he'd never put down his pencil.

Ashley wondered why she'd been called into the office. She didn't remember doing anything wrong of late. She hadn't missed any classes and certainly wasn't failing. She assumed it must be something else and just went in expecting some boring talk.

"Hello there," said Margaret, the office secretary. "Mr. Evans will see you." Ashley looked at Mr. Evan's door confused.

"My counselor is Tom," she said, pointing to a different door.

"We know, but Mr. Evans wants to see you. Just knock on the door." Ashley went over and knocked twice.

"Come in," he said immediately. "Ah Ashley, you can close the door."

Ashley closed the door and took a seat. Mr. Evans was a pudgier man in his late forties. His skin was a bit pale, despite the open window next to him bringing in the sun. He was beginning to bald and he didn't seem to be aging well.

"Is there a problem?" she asked concerned.

"No no," he said quickly. "I'm just calling you in to review your school records and talk to you about what your plans are for the future." Ashley nodded slowly and Mr. Evans smiled. "I am a counselor you know. It's what we do."

"Then why am I speaking to you?" Mr. Evans raised a bushy eyebrow and leaned forward.

"Just because I'm not your designated counselor doesn't mean I can't give you some advice. You've only been here a year but it appears you've become a bit snappy." Ashley sighed and leaned back in her chair. It was best to just let the man talk so she could go. He shuffled a few papers together and laid them in front of her.

"You've been a rather stalwart student. Judging from your records here, you're quite gifted in English and History. It's hard to say you've been bad at anything. You haven't gotten below a B since you came here. You've been involved on the track team and I understand the coach will be very sad once you're gone. A very good record for a new student." Ashley just smiled and accepted the compliment. "With this you can go to a lot of places. Have you considered what you're going to do after high school?"

"For now I'm just going to the community college down the mountain?" Mr. Evans frowned and looked at her papers again.

"Are you sure you just want to go to community college?"

Ashley frowned. He said she could go a lot of places, but that wasn't true. Applying to colleges meant meeting deadlines. Ashley had been a little preoccupied with everything that had happened last year to think about sending out applications to colleges. She didn't even know any of the colleges out here.

"I'll probably transfer later, but for now community college will do."

"Any college in my experience is good," agreed Mr. Evans. "Anything you want to study in particular? Any careers in mind?" Ashley shrugged again.

"Not yet sir. I don't really know what I want to do yet."

"Most kids your age don't know what they want yet. I suppose community college is good for that very reason. You can go and get all the basic classes out of the way and discover what you truly like. Once you find a subject, you can transfer out in a few years."

"That was the plan," said Ashley as she eyed the clock. A few more minutes and the bell would ring. Hopefully she could get away to her next class.

"It seems to be a much better plan than your boyfriend's. You've done much better than he has, that's for sure." Ashley narrowed her eyes. Where was this coming from? He opened another folder and whistled. "He's definitely not the scholar. He'll be graduating, but nowhere near as spectacularly as you. I'm not even sure if he's applied to any colleges."

"What does this have to do with me?" Mr. Evans sat back and shrugged.

"He's your choice, but I just thought I should be counseling you from all aspects."

"I don't think you're allowed to tell me Nathaniel's personal information."

"No, I suppose I'm not, but it's not like it matters anyway. The boy doesn't have much of a future. Not anymore." Ashley scooted back away from the counselor.

"What did you just say?"

"We both know his family is mixed up in more trouble than they can handle. As one of our finer students and as a counselor, I'd hate to see you mixed up in all this." Ashley stood up.

"How do you know all this?"

"Because I work for them," he whispered. "Now sit down, I'm not going to hurt you. If I had wanted to, I would've done it when you first came into the office." Ashley eyed him warily, but lowered herself back to her seat.

"You're a ghoul." She said more than asked. He nodded.

"Not a polite term, but I suppose fitting. The real reason I brought you in here was to apologize about the whole event on the track field." Ashley was ready to run and scream for help, but she calmed herself. What could she tell everyone? That this man worked for vampires, but he wasn't one. She cursed quietly at how ignorant everyone was. "The incident should've never happened. Those men were acting on their own and not of our lady's wishes."

"They still attacked me," spat Ashley.

"They did and they would've been properly punished once we found out. Unfortunately for them and many others, there appears to have been an accident and the house they were in burned down." Mr. Evans put his hands together and shot her a bemused smile. "Terrible timing too. The last snowstorm hid all the smoke and fire, so nobody knew about it for days."

"Should I feel bad?" asked Ashley.

"No, I suppose not. Either way, the event shouldn't have happened and Karin has personally told me to apologize to you."

"I'd accept the apology if she never came back."

"You can partially accept it then. She wants you to pass on the word that she is pulling her children out of town. The forest seems to be cruel to them and they're moving. You will not get harassed again by any fools out trying to prove their worth." Ashley was intrigued now.

"So she's leaving for good?"

"I wouldn't say that," said Mr. Evans. "All I've been told is she's leaving town. Whether she's coming back or not is entirely up to her. You think she'd let a man like me know her plans?" He chuckled. "Now you may think I'm a monster…"

"You're right."

"...and in some ways you are right, but I'm still a counselor. I've worked this job for over ten years and I know a good student when I see one. You may not know what you want to do in life, but you have a good future ahead of you. You could do great things and I want to see you fulfill your potential. There's just one thing you need to do."

"And what's that?" Mr. Evans sighed.

"You need to leave Nathaniel. The further you get away from that family the better. There's no stopping the kind of trouble coming. I'm begging you to stay away from him." Ashley frowned.

"You actually mean that, don't you? You're trying to protect me."

"With every fiber of my being." Ashley stood up and grabbed her bag.

"That doesn't mean much," she said bitterly.

"Look I know how you feel. I was once young and in love too."

"No, it's not that. You said *with every fiber of my being*. You belong to Karin now. None of you belongs to you anymore." Mr. Evans grumbled and stood up. Ashley wasn't afraid of this old man, ghoul or not. "I will tell Nathaniel everything you told me. They'll know about you."

"This is your last chance."

"And yours," said Ashley confidently. "You better not be here later."

"This will be the last time we meet. Now get out of my office." He pointed a finger towards the door. Ashley walked out with a smirk as the bell rang. She wasn't afraid of him. She'd tell Nathaniel and her dad everything Mr. Evans had told her. They didn't appear to know about her dad or Katie either.

At lunch, Ashley found Nathaniel and told him to meet her after school on the track. They could walk and talk there. She whispered to him about Mr. Evans being a ghoul and to be careful. He just nodded and said it was a good idea to talk later. He had something to tell her too. She asked if it was about the situation with Mr. Evans, but he said no. It was about them.

The last two class periods of the day went by agonizingly slow. Ashley had never before experienced the horrid wait everybody feels when their significant other tells them they need to have a talk, and then doesn't talk to them. What did he have to say that couldn't be said in front of their friends? Was there a reason he didn't have lunch with her today? Why couldn't she tell if he was happy or sad? Worse, she had no one to tell by the time she would see him. The only good friend she had in class was Liz, and Liz was the master of disaster. She'd probably tell her Nathaniel was breaking up with her. She put her head down on her desk. She didn't need to talk to Liz, Liz was already in her head spelling out her doom.

The final bell rang and she almost sprinted to the track. Nathaniel was waiting for her with a smile on his face. Ashley used it to calm her fears, but she didn't know if his smile was genuine.

"Hey," she said.

"Hey," he whispered back. He kissed her cheek and they walked down the track. "So Mr. Evans is a ghoul?"

"Yeah. He told me to stay away from you. He also told me to pass on that Karin and everyone else were pulling out of town. Your little assault scared them."

"Good. Let's hope they stay out."

"Do you really think they'll just leave?"

"Mr. Evans did leave early today, but I don't think he's the only one. I think there are ghouls in the school and town that will act as Karin's eyes and ears. She'll be back."

"We'll get her then," she said. She took his hand and slowed their walk. "I want to say I'm sorry again." Nathaniel looked at her confused.

"Sorry? Sorry for what?"

"For asking you to bite me. I was just really scared and I don't like feeling weak. I just wanted to be like the rest of you." He kissed the top of her head.

"Maybe someday. For now, I like you just how you are." Ashley leaned up against him.

"You're not mad?"

"I was for a little bit, but I understand. I'm sure it's not easy to stand around and not be able to do anything."

"Then what did you want to talk about?"

"Oh that." Nathaniel took his hand away from her and dug inside his backpack. He brought out an envelope and handed it to her. Ashley opened it to see two tickets inside.

"What are they?" she asked.

"I wanted to ask you if you wanted to go to prom with me." A large smile crept across Ashley's face.

"You jerk," she laughed. "I thought you were mad at me."

"Excuse me for not asking in front of everyone."

"Of course I'll go with you," said Ashley. She jumped up and kissed Nathaniel, only to pull away with a frown. "Is it safe to go?" Nathaniel shrugged.

"We can't just sit inside all day because we might get attacked. Besides, I know you didn't go to your junior prom and we didn't go to the winter dance. I figure we might as well get in one dance before we graduate." Ashley grinned and took his hand again. Today was looking a lot better than she'd thought.

CHAPTER 11

SWIRLING DRESSES

"Why did you bring me here?" whined Kara as the girls went through the mall. Liz and Ashley had to practically drag Kara out of her house and through the mall. "I don't even like dances or dress up. I'm not a pretty girl."

"You're here in case we need a second opinion," said Liz.

"The dress looks slutty and dear god how can you walk in those shoes," said Kara plainly. They hadn't even tried on a dress yet and Liz scowled. "I will bet you five bucks I'm right."

"Depends. Which one of us are you betting on?" laughed Ashley. "If it's me I'll take the bet."

"What about me?" complained Liz.

"I don't want to lose five bucks." Liz smacked Ashley with her purse and Ashley and Kara just laughed. There weren't too many stores around here which had formal dresses, so their trip wouldn't take too long. Ashley personally wanted Kara there to level out Liz. Liz was one step away from going into super girl mode and Ashley wasn't sure she'd survive.

"Why aren't you going to the dance?" begged Liz. "It would be so much fun with the three of us."

"Yeah, because I totally want to dry hump with some stranger," moaned Kara.

"Some of us know how to dance," said Ashley as they went into a store. "You just don't want to ask out a guy." Kara frowned and looked away.

"If a guy wants to date me, he should have the balls to ask out me."

"Yes, but you scare them all away," said Liz. Kara didn't respond, she just put her hands out like claws and made a scary face.

"So you do have some interest," laughed Ashley. "I never thought I'd see the day when you didn't deny you wanted a guy."

"One wouldn't hurt," admitted Kara. "The problem is finding a good one. I've looked this whole town over and haven't found a single one worthwhile."

"I think Jeremy is pretty good," said Liz, sounding hurt.

"He's nice Liz, but do you really think he could put up with me?" Ashley openly laughed and Liz looked offended. Jeremy was a nice guy, but very timid and reserved. If there was an open challenge, Jeremy would not be the first guy to step up to the plate. He'd probably be near the back if Ashley had to guess.

"What do you want in a guy then?" asked Liz.

"I don't know. Someone strong and smart? Maybe a guy who can think on his feet and isn't afraid to jump at life. He should be taller than me, but then again," Kara held her hand over her short body, "that part isn't hard to find."

"Please stop describing my boyfriend," said Ashley. "You're making me nervous."

"I'm not describing Nathaniel," said Kara angrily. "I said strong *AND* smart. Your boy is an idiot." Kara stopped and looked around.

"Little paranoid?" asked Liz.

"He always pops up with a smart comment right about now. I was trying to find out where he is."

"He's not here," reassured Ashley. "He hates shopping, lots of people, and I'm pretty sure civilized areas. He's probably running around the woods acting like an idiot." Kara held out her hand to Ashley and smiled.

"Case in point, even Ashley agrees."

"Enough boy talk," said Liz powerfully as she held her hands out in awe of a store. "It's time to be girly." She ran into the store like an excited five year old. Ashley followed her with a smile on her face. She couldn't help but giggle as Kara took a deep breath and pushed past the doors.

Mannequins stood everywhere as faceless models. Each one showed off a beautiful dress and some were more elegant than others. It was a nice touch that some of them looked like they were dancing while others were just standing there bashfully. Between them were rows of racks all filled with dresses. Different sizes, colors, and styles, they were all there. The store didn't cater solely to prom, but the owner wasn't stupid. He knew the best way to make money at this time of the year. He stood behind the counter with a large smile on his face. With every excited girl that came in, his smile only became bigger.

Ashley went past Liz and looked casually for what she wanted. Liz's head was moving and yet no words escaped her mouth. She might've gone into shock or a seizure, nobody would've noticed. Kara stayed near Ashley and did her best to not let the other girls touch her. They were an infectious breed and she feared being touched by them. Ashley pulled out a tight yellow dress and before Kara could see what she was doing, Ashley held it up against her.

"Oh yes. Definitely your color." Kara looked at the dress in utter disgust. Even Ashley had to admit it was a very ugly color, but she just wanted to see what Kara would do. Liz magically appeared at her side.

"Is Kara actually trying on a dress?" she begged. Kara hissed and Ashley put the dress back.

"No I'm just teasing."

Liz sighed and went back to looking for dresses for herself. Ashley pulled a few dresses aside and looked at each of them in the mirror. It was hard to find a dress with some kind of straps. Everybody was going strapless now and Ashley despised the fashion. Strapless bras were a pain and you spent the whole night fearing your dress might come loose. They worked decently for some girls, but Ashley didn't have the chest to hold it up.

Liz found dress after dress that she wanted. Ashley secretly promised herself to be as far away from Liz as possible the day she might get married. Fortunately Liz spent most of her time trying to get into a dressing room and then coming out displeased with the dress. Ashley tried on a few, but couldn't find anything she really liked. She and Liz were talking about a new dress when Kara spoke up behind them.

"What do you think? Too Jessica Rabbit?"

They turned around slowly to see Kara in a dress. They and the rest of the store gawked openly at her. She was wearing a long sparkly red dress and she looked amazing. Her bare arms were in front of her, holding a strong pose instead of the innocent girl's look. The dress could barely hold her chest and made her breasts perk up wonderfully. The dress was form fitting right down to the slit at its base where Kara was holding her bare leg out. The dress looked like it was made for her.

"Oh. My. God," said Ashley slowly. Liz almost broke down into tears next to her.

"You look so hot!" she proclaimed. "How did you pull this off?" Kara spun around and showed off the dress. It made Kara look quite beautiful and almost sexy, but something was wrong with it. Kara was too stiff and proud to move how the dress wanted. With how she held herself she looked more like a girly man in a dress than a sexy woman.

"It's not bad," said Kara. "Bit too tight for me."

"Not at all!" said Liz. "I demand you buy this dress. You look too amazing to not have this." Kara shivered and stuck her hands out.

"Yeah that's about as long as I can be girly. I need to take this off."

"No!" cried Liz.

Ashley giggled as she saw Liz try and fight Kara all the way to the dressing room. Kara nearly struck Liz when she pulled out a camera and tried to take a picture. Ashley wasn't sure if Kara got away or not, but she was laughing. She was having a much better time than she'd expected. She went back to the dresses and wasn't sure what would look good on her. Liz had many ideas, but Ashley felt most of those ideas were a bit much.

She was walking towards the back when she saw a mannequin off to the side modeling a dress she hadn't seen. She stared at it awestruck for a moment. She walked around it to check the back and sides. When she was satisfied, she stepped back and admired it. Liz came by saying something about Kara but Ashley just pointed at the dress. Liz's words died on her lips as she looked at the dress and back to Ashley.

"Oh yes."

Ashley was in the bathroom cleaning herself up when she heard the doorbell ring. She smiled and slipped on her shoes. She checked herself in the mirror one last time to make sure everything was in order. She wasn't one for makeup and despite Liz's begging, Ashley had put on very little. Nathaniel always said she had a beautiful face, why ruin it with expensive face paint?

Downstairs Alex opened the door and greeted her date. Nathaniel stepped in holding a small box which contained a flower. "Good evening Mr. Jameson."

"Good evening Nathaniel. You ready for the night?" Nathaniel looked around eagerly.

"All I'm missing so far is my date. Is Ashley ready?"

"Yes," said Ashley as she came out of her room.

Nathaniel gawked as Ashley came down the stairs. She came down slowly so she could show herself off. She was in a long sapphire dress which almost reached her feet. The two straps came up front and wrapped around her neck. The dress was tight for the most part and covered everything she wanted it to. She liked how it left her shoulders and arms bare though. She couldn't wait to see Nathaniel's gorgeous blue eyes next to this dress.

Her long black hair had been straightened and a pair of long bangs came down her front as the rest flowed down her back. Nathaniel was impressed that she wasn't wearing tall heels like the rest of the girls, but instead small shiny black flats. He wasn't sure if she disliked heels because of how they felt or if because she was already tall. He'd have to remember to ask at some point.

Ashley's beautiful moment was instantly ruined as her dad slid to the bottom of the stairs with a camera. A few bright flashes later and Ashley's smiling face went to a strong disoriented. She held up her hand and complained loudly, but Alex was relentless. He moved from position to position, snapping more shots than he should've had film for. Nathaniel just grinned until Alex stopped.

"You missed your calling dad," whined Ashley.

"Hey, I haven't had any pictures for eighteen years," said her dad. "I'm just making up for it." Nathaniel greeted Ashley at the bottom of the stairs and took her hand.

"You look beautiful," he said as he kissed it. He held onto her hand and put a corsage of beautiful flowers around her wrist.

"Thank you. You look pretty good yourself."

Pretty good was an understatement. As much as Ashley liked her boyfriend, he was the dirty type. She'd never seen him not covered in dirt, grease, or some kind of slime. He loved his dirty work and he stayed in the wild probably more than he stayed at home.

Tonight he was cleaned up and she'd never seen him so handsome. His long bleach blonde hair was combed and cut just above the shoulder. He'd scrubbed his entire body and for once didn't smell like a dog. He wore a fine suit of dark black. The shoes had been wiped clean, his pants and coat pressed, and the shirt was ironed. The only color on his outfit was the sapphire blue tie he'd gotten to match her. Ashley felt his light skin and hair was more than enough to offset the darkness of the outfit.

Once again, the moment was ruined by a hail of flashes. Alex circled both of them, taking picture after picture. Ashley tried to complain, but Nathaniel put his hand around her and leaned in for each picture. Ashley realized they probably wouldn't get free until her father's photo lust was quenched. They posed and posed until at long last he was finished.

"I like your necklace," said Nathaniel with a grin. Ashley played with the thick cord and grinned back. It was the only non-formal thing about her. It was the necklace Nathaniel had given her last year. It meant more to her than any diamond necklace.

"You kids look good," said Alex. "Aren't you forgetting something Ashley?" Ashley realized she was and rushed into the kitchen. She came back with the small flower for Nathaniel and pinned it to his coat. Alex took a few more pictures and Ashley giggled girlishly. She'd never had a night like this before.

"So what's the plan?" asked Alex. "Dinner and then the dance?"

"Yup," said Nathaniel. "I've got a special place in mind."

"He won't tell me where," said Ashley.

"Surprises can sometimes be more fun," winked her dad. "Now go have some fun while you're still young." Nathaniel held the door open for Ashley both for the house and the truck. He'd borrowed his dad's truck and Ashley was surprised once more by the cleanliness. The truck had been cleaned from the inside out and it had even been expertly waxed. He closed the door behind her and got in the other side.

"Aren't we feeling formal tonight?" she laughed as they drove away.

"I feel weird." He fidgeted with his coat and shook his body like a chill had crossed through him. Ashley smirked and played with his coat a little.

"You really do look nice."

"Thanks, but don't get used to it. I prefer going all natural if you get my meaning." He winked and looked longingly out the window.

"I thought that was supposed to be after prom, not before." Nathaniel started laughing and hit his hand against the steering wheel. Ashley couldn't stop herself from giggling.

"Well said.."

"So where are we getting dinner?"

"The few nice places we have around here are booked solid tonight. It's not just us kids either. You wouldn't believe how many adults see this as their date night and an excuse to get fancy. I'd almost think it was cute if they weren't taking our spots."

"So…" said Ashley slowly. "Where are we going?"

"It's a secret," said Nathaniel with a smirk. Ashley scowled and looked out the window.

"There's only so long you can keep it a secret."

"And I plan to until the very end."

They drove around for a bit and Ashley noticed the roads were filled with cars. Almost every vehicle contained a well-dressed couple. The backwards mountain town had suddenly become fancy overnight. Nathaniel told Ashley to close her eyes after a few minutes. Ashley indulged his fun and sat back with her eyes shut. She had no idea what he was planning, but she was excited. She'd never been out on a date like this and she couldn't help but feel girly.

The truck came to a slow halt and Nathaniel opened his door. Ashley almost opened her eyes but he said to keep them shut. She grinned and stayed where she was. He opened her door and helped her out. She kept her purse over her shoulder and Nathaniel led her up the curb and down the street a little. Ashley heard people talking and she wondered why she couldn't look yet. Finally Nathaniel stopped and whispered for her to open her eyes.

"And I bet you thought I was romantic."

Ashley sighed as she saw the sign for The Myst, Katie's diner, above their heads. The Myst was a good place to go, but nowhere near what she'd hoped. She'd expected something fancier and shinier. Bright lights and fine tables, not dark and like a bar. She gave Nathaniel a small, but disappointed smile.

"Yeah. For a moment there I did." He opened the door without a word and waited for her to walk in. Ashley headed in with her head down and waited for their booth.

"Don't you look pretty," said Katie as she came over. "And with this fancy man in tow, how nice of you two to drop by."

"This is our spot," said Ashley, trying to find the good in it. Katie grinned and Nathaniel took Ashley's hand.

"Let me show you to your seat," said Katie as she headed back. Ashley saw a few patrons looking at them surprised. She felt incredibly overdressed and out of place. She was so focused on everyone else that she failed to notice the black curtain hanging up ahead of them. Katie pulled it aside and Nathaniel stepped Ashley through.

"I guess I am a bit romantic after all," he whispered deviously.

Ashley gasped as she realized the curtain cut the diner in half. On the other side was a single table in the middle of the floor. A white cloth covered it and it held three long red roses and a lit candle. Nathaniel walked Ashley over and held out a chair for her. Ashley sat down and looked about amazed. Katie had closed off this section for them and them alone.

"It was all your boy's idea," said Katie as she approached the table. "He asked if we could separate the area and make it all pretty. I thought it was a strange idea, but I've got to admit. The boy has good taste." Ashley looked at Nathaniel and couldn't help but smile. He'd tricked her so beautifully. "I'll bring you some drinks and leave you two alone for a bit." Katie disappeared behind the curtain.

"You really came up with this?" asked Ashley.

"I thought it'd be fun. I'm not too fancy, but this is nice. Besides, this place is special to me." He ran a hand across the table and took her fingers into his. "This was the first real date we had. That makes this place more special than anywhere else in town." Ashley was at a loss for what to say. She'd never expected Nathaniel to be such a wonderful sap.

"I don't know what to say." Nathaniel kissed her hand.

"Just enjoy the night."

Enjoy it she did. Nathaniel hadn't just cornered off their own little area, he'd brought special food in. They had warm bread, a small batch of potatoes, and a boiling hot steak cooked just right. Ashley enjoyed every bite and just when she thought she could eat no more, dessert came out. A thick slice of a fudge filled cake with a scoop of vanilla ice cream on top. The cake was warm and Ashley could see the ice cream melting along its side. Small rivers of fudge and vanilla intermingled. Everything in Ashley's stomach vanished immediately and her body told her there was room for more.

Nathaniel spooned off a small bite and held it out for Ashley to eat. Her mouth closed around the spoon and her mouth was filled with ecstasy. The dessert practically melted in her mouth. Sweetness like she'd never tasted moved across her tongue and dripped down her throat. Her mouth was both warm and cold as the warm cake mixed with the ice cream. She savored each moment as she gulped it down. Nathaniel took a bite and a look of happiness came that must've rivaled her own.

They left the diner about an hour later and Ashley thanked Katie. She'd never expected such a wonderful meal from there. Katie told them to have a good time and shooed them off to the dance. They arrived at the dance a little late and they were met with nothing but noise.

The music was pounding and the lights were almost nonexistent. There was a tiny crowd of seniors dancing in the middle of the floor with a DJ a little bit ahead of them. There were tables out for punch and small snacks near the side. Ashley wasn't sure she could eat another bite. They found a small table to put their things down on and headed to the dance floor.

They found Liz and Jeremy shaking it up in a corner. Liz squealed and hugged both of them before returning to Jeremy. She was in a white and silver strapless dress she'd found after a few stores of searching. Kara had been right about the dress being a bit revealing and the shoes. Ashley noticed with some amusement that Liz's high heels were absent and she was dancing barefoot.

Nathaniel put his hands around her and they let the music take them. Neither of them knew how to properly dance. They just moved with the beat and stamped their feet. They clapped their hands and shouted with the songs they knew. They kept the corner to themselves and danced as long as they could. Ashley found herself sweating and getting much more tired than Nathaniel. She kissed him and left him on the floor with Liz and Jeremy while she went for a drink.

"Don't we look nice?" asked a sarcastic voice near the punch bowl. Ashley turned around to see Monica, the popular girl she'd punched last year, standing next to her. She wore a tight black dress which in Ashley's opinion did not go down long enough on her legs.

"You look good too," said Ashley spitefully. "Would you like some punch or is that too many calories?" Monica smirked and leaned against the table next to her.

"No thanks. I drink better stuff now." Monica gave Ashley a toothy smile. Ashley frowned and looked at Monica carefully. It was hard to see good detail in the dim lights. "How's that big puppy of yours? Still running around under moon filled nights?" Ashley stepped back and threw her cup away. Monica's hints weren't exactly subtle and she was getting tired of dramatic introductions.

"You're with them?"

"Yes. Looks like you and I will get to settle that fight after all. Only now Marten will be on even ground with your dog." Ashley leaned forward and looked at Monica closely. She was paler than she remembered, but her teeth didn't look sharp. She grabbed Monica's arm. Before she could snap it away, Ashley felt her warm skin.

"You're not one of them," laughed Ashley quietly. "You're just a little ghoul."

"For now," said Monica angrily. "I'm still better than you and your toy."

"No you're not. You know why you came to talk to me instead of Nathaniel?" Ashley said quietly. "It's because you're afraid of him. You only came to talk to me because you think you're stronger." Monica looked ready to snap back at her, but Ashley cut her off. "I know Karin doesn't want you telling me this either. When she finds out you're going to be in trouble for ruining the surprise." Monica looked at her with dangerous eyes, but Ashley saw she was right. Monica had never thought very far ahead and now she was going to pay for it. Marten loomed out of the darkness to appear at her side. Ashley thought something was going to happen when her counselor stepped between them.

"Everyone having a goodnight?" he asked menacingly. He poured himself a glass of punch and looked at the three of them.

"Yes," said Monica bitterly.

"Good. You kids should be back on the dance floor."

Ashley took the hint and headed back to Nathaniel. She could feel the white hot hatred of Monica's stare on her back. She hoped the looks stayed on her instead of her new dress. She'd be livid if Monica found a way to ruin it tonight.

The quick songs changed suddenly to a slow tune and all the couples came together. Nathaniel was waiting for her with his hand out and a smile on his face. "May I have this dance?" he asked. Ashley smiled and gave up her hand. She allowed Nathaniel to drag her close and start their slow dance. He put his head down on her shoulder and Ashley could almost feel how happy he was. His elation almost made her forget Monica.

"I have some bad news," she whispered.

"What?" he asked quietly.

"Monica is a ghoul, Marten too." Nathaniel kissed the side of her head.

"I know. They're not alone either. A few of the kids here are ghouls."

"What should we do?" Nathaniel brought his head around and kissed Ashley slowly. When he was done playing with her lips, he kissed her forehead.

"Nothing. Forget about them. Tonight is all about us."

"But what if…" He held a finger to her lips and smiled.

"We'll deal with it later." The soft song ended and the speakers began to thump loudly once more. Nathaniel brought her hands up and began to move quickly. "Tonight is all about us," he repeated. Ashley couldn't help but move her body with Nathaniel's. It was hard to think about vampires or ghouls when she had Nathaniel's infectious smile right in front of her.

They danced almost until midnight. Liz and Jeremy said they were leaving for the night and Ashley agreed it was a good idea. She was getting tired and Nathaniel was still filled with boundless energy. She walked on shaky legs back to their table and they collected their things. When they were almost to the door, Nathaniel surprised Ashley by suddenly picking her up. She gave a small squeak in surprise, but Nathaniel held her confidently. When Nathaniel reached the door he simply kicked it open and walked out, leaving Ashley laughing in his arms.

Back in the truck, Nathaniel drove off through the town. Ashley sat in the seat next to him and leaned up against him proudly. She was sweaty and gross, but she'd never felt as beautiful as she had tonight. Nathaniel kept his right arm around her front and she almost fell asleep against it. She pulled her head up after a while and smiled at Nathaniel.

"Do you want to go for a drive in the hills?" Ashley asked suggestively. Nathaniel shook his head and glanced back to the side mirror.

"We have company," he said sternly. Ashley started to turn, but Nathaniel held her steady. "Don't look. They're just a bit behind us in the brown car." Ashley cocked her head to the side to see out the mirror. She could see the car behind them, but she couldn't see who was in it.

"Are you sure?" she asked.

"I've been just driving around so we could be together. I haven't taken any real direction and they've been behind us every step of the way."

"Who would follow us?" asked Ashley. Nathaniel gave her a sad look.

"Who do you think?" Ashley scowled and muttered a few curses.

"Vampires are ruining my prom night? Oh pull over the car and stay put. I'll deal with them on my own." Nathaniel snorted.

"Angry prom girl. I think they'd be safer facing me."

"What are you going to do? Think we can lose them?"

"This isn't a big city. The only way you lose people out here is some dark driving through the mountains. They can see better in the dark than even I can so it's kind of pointless trying to lose them."

"Don't fight them," said Ashley quickly. Nathaniel looked at her surprised and she shrugged. "You look really good in that suit. I'd be sad if you ripped it." Nathaniel chuckled and nodded to Ashley's purse.

"Message your dad. I'll drop you off and we'll see if we can't catch them in the open. Maybe we'll see who's following us up close." Ashley crossed her arms.

"But that involves going home. I don't want to go home yet."

"Don't worry about it." Nathaniel kissed her cheek quickly and went back to the road. "We have lots of nights we can sneak out on. It doesn't have to be just this one." Ashley growled and pulled out her phone.

"I swear when I find them," she grumbled. Her dad picked up the other end and she spat angrily. "Hi dad. Yes I'm coming home already. We have a car following us. Small brown car. What? Some vampire is ruining my prom night. Why else do you think I sound angry?"

"We'll come in from Hadren street," said Nathaniel.

"Did you hear that?" asked Ashley. "He got it. Okay. Yeah. We'll see you soon." She hung up the phone and smiled. "Dad is going to be sitting on the roof with a rifle."

"Does this mean he'll shoot me if I give you a kiss goodnight?"

"No. He likes you."

"I know he does. I'm just teasing." Ashley sighed and leaned up against Nathaniel.

"I'm really angry at that car."

"Me too, but I can't rip this suit."

"No, that would be saddening." She hugged his arm and nuzzled her head against it. "Stupid vampires."

"We'll clean them out for good," said Nathaniel.

"What about Monica and Marten?"

"I have no idea. I'll talk to my dad about it."

Ashley sat up as she recognized her street. Nathaniel pulled into the driveway and held the door open for her as usual. Ashley didn't want to get out, but she couldn't really get close with Nathaniel right there. Her dad could see them and he had a gun.

Nathaniel walked her to the door and they both looked back as the brown car pulled past. Ashley saw Marten and Monica staring at them with hate in their eyes. They were not alone in the car either. Another couple they didn't know was sitting in the back. One of them had eyes that glowed red in the dark.

"I really hate that girl," said Ashley.

"Me too. I'm surprised they didn't stop."

"Pity they didn't." Nathaniel gave her a big hug and kissed her hard on the lips. As they parted they gave each other smaller kisses. Ashley leaned against the door and frowned. "This is not how I wanted my prom night to end."

"I know." Nathaniel kissed her again and stepped away. "I guess this means we'll just have to go out on another date."

Ashley didn't know whether to frown or smile as he walked away. She liked the idea of going out again, but she was so angry her night had been ruined. She walked after him and got one last kiss before they said goodnight. She watched him drive away from just inside the house.

She was heading upstairs upset when her dad came down. He was coming out of the attic with his rifle in his right hand. "Have a good night?" Ashley groaned and just walked past him to her room.

"Right up until about ten minutes ago."

CHAPTER 12

A MIRACULOUS MAY

All the trouble in the world couldn't keep Ashley down in the middle of May. So many good things happened at once it felt like Christmas had come early. Finals were just about done and soon she would graduate high school. On May 12th she turned 18 and Nathaniel arrived with the best present of all. Her jeep was finally fixed and looked brand new. It'd been fixed a week earlier, but they'd decided to save it until her birthday.

Her dad surprised her with a small birthday party at the house. Nathaniel, Liz, Kara, and everyone else she knew were there. Ashley had screamed when Nathaniel had walked her in the door and everyone had jumped out yelling surprise. A wall of confetti covered her and the room was filled with laughter. They immediately began to sing Happy Birthday and her dad walked out with a cake in his hands. Eighteen lit candles danced in front of her eyes. She blew them all out and the crowd cheered.

"Did you know about this?" Ashley asked Nathaniel as she walked away with some cake.

"Of course. Who else would drive you around and waste your time while they got set up?" He went in to kiss her and she put her plate of cake in his face. Everyone laughed as she peeled back the plate to reveal a frosting covered Nathaniel. He was smiling cheerfully even as people took pictures.

"What an awful waste of cake," he said. He hugged her suddenly and came at her with frosted lips. Ashley shrieked happily as Nathaniel smeared cake across her face. There were plenty of clicks from cameras. When they separated Ashley was laughing and Liz met her with a paper towel.

"Oh I'm going to get you," she laughed. Her laughter was drowned out by a soft crooning from all the girls present. Nathaniel was kneeling down so her dog Roland could lick the cake off his face.

"Okay even I admit that's cute," said Kara from across the table. Ashley let the cuteness continue for only a bit longer before she wiped his face clean.

"The party is supposed to be about me," she said cheerfully as she pulled him back to his feet.

They didn't do much other than eat cake and hang out, but Ashley felt it was more than she could've asked for. She remembered her birthday last year and smiled. She'd been with her mom in the hospital watching her deteriorate, but her mother had still surprised her with help from the staff. Some of the nurses had come together to make a cake and decorations for Ashley. Her mother had always done whatever she could for her birthdays, even on her deathbed. Her mom promised it wouldn't be the last great birthday she had either. As her friends talked, Nathaniel held her, and her dad brought out more food for everyone, she had to agree. Somewhere out there her mom was happy for her.

The party lasted about two hours and when everyone had gone home, her dad said he had one last surprise for her tonight. He was going to take her out for a birthday dinner in addition to the surprise party. Ashley didn't know how much more she could eat, but she was happy to go.

Just before dark, they got in his truck and Ashley was surprised by their third passenger. Alex patted the backseat and Roland jumped in eagerly. She pet him furiously before looking at her dad intrigued. "Where are we going that allows dogs?"

"We're eating at the kennel tonight," laughed her dad. Ashley looked around town as they drove, but she didn't quite get it.

"So seriously, where are we going?"

"To have dinner with the rest of the family. It's not a birthday unless you get to spend it with the relatives." Ashley raised an eyebrow. Her mom had been an only child and her dad was an orphan.

"Who?" she asked bewildered.

"Since it's your birthday I can't call you dense," smiled Alex. "Where do you think we're going?" Ashley looked at the road and saw they were heading out of town.

"We're going to Nathaniel's?" she asked. Her dad nodded.

"Morgan promised us quite the barbeque tonight. I figured it was about time I met the whole family for real too." Ashley looked ahead more excited now. She was getting a second celebration with Nathaniel's family. Roland barked excitedly from the back seat.

They arrived to see most of the family out in the backyard. Morgan was standing over a large barbeque and waved them to the side gate. Nobody could talk over the barking dogs as Roland scurried to the fence. Morgan's four giant dogs fought over the space at the fence where little Roland sniffed. They barked at each other and chased each other up and down the fence.

Alex tried to get the dogs to sniff him before coming through the gate, but for once the dogs had no interest in a stranger. Nobody from their house cared about these strangers, so why should they? They almost pushed Alex and Ashley over to try and get at the small dog in their midst.

"They're friendly," shouted Morgan over the racket.

Roland barely made it inside the gate before four large noses came over him. He tried to sniff them all back, but he was only one dog. The other four must've surprised him because the moment he found a way to slip past them he was running across the yard. Mops, Bear, Dozer, and Chomper all chased after Roland barking. They were bigger but not faster.

"That should keep them entertained for a while," laughed Morgan as the dogs ran back and forth. Lidia shot out of the open backdoor. Without even bothering to say hello to Ashley or Alex, she immediately screamed and chased after the dogs.

Ashley left Alex as Nathaniel came out. Nathaniel showed her they were cooking quite a feast for her birthday. They had ribs, small steaks, and chicken all together. They owned one of the biggest barbeques Ashley had ever seen. Morgan had built it himself and designed it to have different compartments for different meats.

Melissa brought out extra side dishes for everyone to snack on. She met Alex with a bright smile and for once Ashley felt her dark gaze was missing. Either Melissa had lightened up on her or she knew how to be the perfect hostess. Ashley didn't hear a single snide remark. She wasn't sure what had changed, but she hoped it stayed this way.

The sky darkened and Ashley felt the night couldn't get any better. They all sang Happy Birthday to her and this time instead of being presented with a cake, she received a platter of ribs. She could never hope to finish it but both her dad and boyfriend promised her help. The family all sat down and ate quietly. The food was so good nobody spoke. The only background noise was the dogs playing.

The dogs stopped their barking and turned their heads to the driveway. The talking vanished with the barks and all of Nathaniel's family went quiet. They all slowly turned with the dogs and cocked their heads to the side. Ashley looked for what was wrong, but she couldn't sense anything. To her surprise though, her dad turned his head and looked towards the front of the house.

"Are you expecting more company tonight?" Alex asked. Morgan shook his head.

"I was about to ask you the same thing." Alex and Morgan shared a tense look. Morgan's eyes were filled with doubt and anger. Alex shook his head.

"I already told you I split my tie with the Hunters long ago. And if I'd wanted to call them, I wouldn't have done it while my daughter and I were here." Morgan nodded.

"Sorry. I had to check."

"I would've too if I were you. Who else would be coming here?" Ashley leaned over to Nathaniel.

"What's going on?" she asked confused.

"Cars are coming up the road," he whispered back.

"Ah." Ashley was getting tired of not being clued in all the time.

"Nobody good would be my guess," said Morgan. "Melissa take the kids inside." Melissa nodded and scooted Lidia, Samuel, and Mary inside. "Kevin," Morgan winked at his son and nodded to the trees, "the night is your friend." Kevin nodded and ran into the forest. "Nathaniel, you come with me. Alex, you and Ashley stay inside just in case."

"You think there's a fight coming?" asked Alex.

"I don't know, but at this hour and out this far, I doubt it's just people who are lost."

"How much time do we have?"

"Few minutes." Alex pointed to the door.

"Get inside Ashley. I'll be in in a minute."

Ashley kissed Nathaniel really quick and went inside. Morgan and Nathaniel went out front and Alex ran to his truck. He pulled a large case out from underneath his seat and started to jog back inside.

"What window can I cover you from?" he asked Morgan. Morgan looked at the case and back to Alex.

"Expecting trouble?" he asked with a smile.

"When there's a rogue vampire in town, always." Morgan grinned and pointed to a window on the top floor.

"You can see best from my room. Just don't turn on the lights and don't do anything stupid."

"I promise I won't do anything unless something attacks you." Morgan clapped him on the back as he ran inside. When he was inside Morgan put his hand on his son's shoulder.

"Interesting family your girlfriend has got there."

"I think so."

"Good. Now don't do anything stupid with Ashley. I think Alex would shoot you before asking questions." Nathaniel realized his dad's words were serious and he'd just received a father son talk of some kind.

"Thanks dad. I'll keep that in mind."

"Good. Now let's turn on the lights and greet our guests." Nathaniel opened a little compartment next to the front door and flipped all the switches inside.

Their front yard was naturally pitch black at night due to being so far outside of town. Now it was lit up like it was in the middle of the city. They'd put lights in all the trees near their house for twenty feet. Light was suddenly spread in great arcs all across their house and the surrounding area. Alex had to take a few steps back in the upstairs room to stay out of the light. He held up his hunting rifle and looked out the window. With his scope he could see all three cars coming up the road.

All three cars looked generic enough. They weren't uniform and their driving seemed casual. They were driving slowly and had their lights on so Alex knew they weren't hiding. He couldn't see who was in the car, but he kept his rifle trained on them. Whether it be human, werewolf, or vampire, his silver shells would still deal a killing blow.

The three cars stopped just in the Lexington driveway. Morgan counted ten in all and tensed as he saw them. They were all a bit shorter and had scraggly hair. Some had scars on their faces and he knew their smell. These men were jackals. Something wasn't right though. If the jackals had come to attack them they wouldn't have driven up so casually. The men looked unhappy to see them, but nobody was acting threateningly.

Then someone opened the passenger door on the middle car and an elderly man stepped out. He shared the same traits of the other men, but he was much older. His hair was a fine white and his face was clean shaven. He wore finer clothing than the rest of his family and had a more regal pose. A heavy wrinkled brow struggled to raise so he could look up. Morgan relaxed.

"Stay here Nathaniel."

"Is that their elder?" asked Nathaniel quietly.

"Yes. Stay." Morgan moved to meet the elder halfway and bowed.

"Welcome, my name is Morgan Lexington." The old man bowed his head a little.

"I thank you for your welcome, my name is Thomas Hainlot."

"Is there something I can help you with Mr. Hainlot?"

"No, I just came here to inform you of my arrival and departure. I heard about the vampire that's pursuing you. I also heard she used some of my family as practice."

"I'm truly sorry if I've brought any harm to your family."

"Those vampires took nine of my family from me Mr. Lexington. Do you have any idea what that phone call was like to receive?"

Morgan bowed again and truly felt bad. He'd only known about the three that went after Ashley. Karin must've been staking out her territory in the jackal's land. That would certainly explain why they couldn't find her.

"I'm sorry. I had no idea."

"Now you do. I want you to know I don't hold you responsible, even if some of my family does." Mr. Hainlot looked back and was met with many angry stares from his family. "But you did not endanger my family by living here, the vampire did."

"I will make her pay. I promise on my own family she will." The old man nodded and smiled.

"I respect the offer, but there will be no need."

CHAPTER 13

FROM PREDATOR TO PREY

Karin led the way through the forest with her small group behind her. They were out of the mountains, but not out of the forest quite yet. She'd chosen this place because neither Morgan nor any of his wolves would come out here. This was too far past their territory. And as long as they were bound to the town and the mountain, Karin would take advantage of the open land here.

The group behind her were her loyal servants. They were all recently turned vampires and slaves to her will. They could still think and act on their own, but her word was law. She was in their blood and mind now. All of them had thought to benefit and discover a new life from her powers. Now they knew the consequences of their actions. They didn't complain though. Karin smiled mercilessly. She didn't allow them to complain.

"Karin, are you going to tell us what we're doing out here?" asked one of the males. Karin wheeled on him and shot him a dark glare.

Most of them had gotten the idea, but this male still mocked her with her bare name.

"How dare you," she hissed before she struck him to the floor. He had the strength now to survive the vicious blow, but it still hurt him. The others watched nervously as Karin eyed them. The male held up his hands to defend himself.

"I'm sorry! What I meant to say was, may I ask what we're doing out here, Lady Karin?" Karin smiled again. She loved having "Lady" in front of her name. It made her feel so important. How she wished the world hadn't changed and that noble titles weren't almost gone. But alas, there was nothing she could do about it. Instead she just enforced the policy with all of her underlings.

"I suppose now is as good of a time to tell you all as any." She patted the knives in her coat. "Today I'm teaching you all to hunt. Not how to hunt humans, as I know you can all do that, but something much bigger."

"Werewolves?" asked one of the females, nervously. Karin shook her head.

"No, werewolves will come later. Werewolves are the level I need to train you all to, but you're not ready yet. Tonight, we hunt down jackals."

"What's a jackal?" asked another.

"Jackals are the underling cousins of werewolves. They're not as powerful, but they're still very dangerous. The remains of a defeated family are out here. We're going to kill them." Many looked nervous. It was a feeling Karin could appreciate. She remembered her first time trying to hunt something bigger than herself that had claws and large teeth. It wasn't a pleasant memory.

"How will we kill them?" asked the cocky male from before.

"You are a vampire now and you must understand your new abilities. You have strength with which few things can compete. Jackals and werewolves will most likely be stronger than you, but not by much. You need to realize despite their size, you can still hit and hurt them. Since your fists won't finish the job however, you need to learn to use these." Karin pulled out one of her long knives and held it for all to admire. "A werewolf is tough, but like all livings things they can bleed. Go for the head, the heart, or any artery you can find. Cut them in the right places and they will die just like anything else." Karin sheathed her knife in her coat.

"Are they made of silver?" asked one of the girls as she examined her own knife.

"No. Silver is just as deadly to you now as it is to werewolves. It's best not to carry a weapon you're allergic to, no matter how effective it may be on the enemy."

"Why not use a gun with silver bullets?" asked another.

"Because guns are loud and guns are noisy," said Karin. "You're hunting a pack animal here. If you fire a gun, every single one of them is going to know where you are for twenty miles. Guns also attract the attention of humans who want to investigate. Guns leave behind bullets which can be traced. When you're hunting a wolf, it's best not to bring something that stinks. Take a deep breath and tell me what you smell." They all took in deep breaths and were quiet for a moment. "Well?" Most shrugged their shoulders, but a few responded.

"Dirt?"

"Moss?"

"The forest?" Karin nodded.

"Exactly. The forest has a distinct, crisp smell. Wolves can smell far better than we ever will. If a wolf gets even a whiff of gunpowder in the forest, they'll know something is afoot. Now can any of you tell me why I had you scrub your clothes and yourself clean before we came here?"

"Because of our scent!" said one of the girls excitedly. She was the only one in the group who had kept enthusiasm after being turned. Karin had to admit she liked her and planned to make her a favorite.

"Yes and no. I did want you to get rid of your smells, but there's something important you all need to know about being a vampire. It's our greatest strength and weakness against the wolves. As vampires, you no longer have a scent. Your body will never sweat again, never have a pulse, or anything a werewolf can follow."

"How is that a weakness?" asked the male.

"Because since you have no smell, everything else around you becomes your smell. If you've been feeding, but never shower, you'll smell like blood. If you've been firing a gun, you'll smell like gunpowder. Since you have no scent, you begin to smell like everything else. So you must remember to change your clothes and shower if you have anything you need to hide from a wolf. Otherwise your smells will show them your past, what you've done, where you've been, or anything else you might fear them knowing. Understand?" They all nodded. "Good. Now we'll be entering the jackal's territory soon. Stay quiet and follow me."

Karin led them deeper into the forest. She was amazed the jackals were still living so close to Morgan's family. She'd learned that they'd already had a confrontation before with Morgan's son Nathaniel. Combined with the ones she'd killed, the jackal family had lost eight members in less than six months. Jackal families were generally bigger than werewolf families, but Karin knew their numbers must be low.

After about twenty minutes of walking, Karin placed her hands on her knives. The jackals could find them at any point and she needed to be ready. She wouldn't allow any of her minions to panic, but that didn't mean they would be effective fighters. For all she knew, they might all die tonight. She wasn't honestly worried. If these six didn't work out, she'd find another group soon enough. She needed to weed out the weak ones before she would attack Morgan directly.

Her followers were beginning to get nervous the further they walked. They didn't know how to find the jackals other than with their eyes. They could see through the darkness with ease, but that didn't mean anything. Jackals wouldn't just be waiting for them out in the open. They'd be hidden in bushes and in trees, disguised with the wild. They'd be low to the ground, blending in in a small pit of dirt. Her minions weren't old enough or powerful enough to see things like she did.

Karin's night vision went beyond normal sight. She could see in infrared now and detect their body heat. She could see the warm blood pumping in their veins as they walked. She could hear the beating of their hearts even if they were sitting completely still. When their hearts were pounding, it sounded like a loud drumbeat in her ears. If any of her underlings paid attention tonight, they would hear the same thing. Their ears weren't trained to hear heartbeats yet, but even they might notice the loud thumping in the heat of battle.

"Lady Karin," whispered one of the females.

Karin stopped and looked back. The female was pointing a few feet away from herself at something in the dirt. Karin stepped in for a closer look and realized it was a small patch of mud. There was a paw print embedded in it, but none around it.

"Good girl," she whispered back. "This is a jackal print. Most wolves can run through the forest and not leave a trail. We go this way." She moved ahead and kept low to the ground. Her eyes scanned the ground for any leftover tracks.

They went another half an hour without any more signs before Karin heard them. The jackals were quiet, but there were multiple heartbeats nearby. They were faint, but too loud to be human. The bigger the animal, the bigger the heart.

She waved for her group to get low. Karin drew her knives silently as she crept forward. The heartbeats were still faint and she wondered how far off they were. Then one became loud as it started to run. She paused as she realized it was heading straight towards her. She threw herself to the ground and waited. It was too easy for the jackals to just be coming to her.

Only one jackal came into view. He slowed his run and came to a halt not far from her. She grinned as it stood up for her to see. This jackal was old, very old. Like most immortal beings though, older didn't mean weakness, it was a sign of power. It meant they'd survived long enough to see generations. They were strong enough to survive the inevitable conflicts of life and smart enough to live on.

This jackal was an old male. His brown fur was mostly gone, replaced by a sleek silver. He was bigger than most jackals and could almost pass for a werewolf. Karin noticed with eagerness the scars across his nose, face, and body. This old jackal had seen his fair share of fights in his days. He shook his body and began to change. Karin cocked her head curiously as he began to change back into a human. When he was done, a fit naked man in perhaps his sixties stood before her.

"Stand up vampire. Let me see all of you." He knew where she was. Karin rose to her feet and held her arms out. She spun around for him and made no effort to conceal her knives.

"Like what you see old man?" she asked seductively.

"Old. Yes, I am old." The old man shook his head and rolled his shoulders. "I know I'm old because it's harder to get out of bed in the morning. My back creaks and my body aches. Do you know how else I know I'm old?" Karin frowned as the old man pointed at her. "I'm a grandfather. I've had many children and they've had many children. I've even got a few great grandkids. And do you know what drives me mad? A vampire like you taking away my babies." Karin planted her feet and eyed the old man.

"I've heard that some of my family was lost in a territorial fight with some werewolves. It's horrible, but that was their choice to fight. What I can't stand to hear is when a vampire like you kills them for fun. I hear you've been hunting the jackals here because they're young and not experienced yet." The old man cracked his knuckles. "How about you take on someone your own age?" Karin grinned and let her fangs sit on her lips.

"I would love to." She rolled her knives in her hands. "Care to play?" The old man shook his head.

"No. Young people play. I'm here on business."

The old man's voice deepened as he changed again. Karin laughed with delight and waved for her little ones to attack. They ran forward frightened, but eager to survive. They would fight this old beast until their last breath if they wanted to live. Sure she'd lose a few, but this kind of experience would be invaluable to the ones who lived.

The jackal roared and suddenly the entire forest was filled with noise. Barking and howling came from every direction. Karin looked about in surprise and suddenly picked up a lot more movement than she had before. To her, the forest was alive. She could hear the heartbeats of dozens of jackals. Only the smallest blurs of heat were coming to her, but she could see through the darkness without infrared. The jackals had been in holes all around the forest covered in thick mud. The cold mud had hidden them from her sight and had dampened the sound of their hearts. They must've been fully buried with only a hole for air to breathe and hear out of.

The old jackal hadn't been lying. He wasn't there to play; he was there for business. And his business was killing Karin and every vampire in the area. He hadn't come by himself, but had brought along his entire family and then some. Karin had brought her minions out to fight a few young jackals for experience. Karin knew she couldn't beat this kind of ambush if she had ten experienced vampires instead of the half dozen newborns she had. If they didn't run, they were dead.

Her underlings paused as they felt her confusion. They expected only the greatest of bravery from their mistress and they found fear. Their momentary hesitation was the worst mistake they could've made. The elder jackal plowed into them and whipped his arms around. They all left the ground behind and flew scattered into the forest. Some rolled head over heel across the ground as others crashed into trees.

None of them were lucky. Jackals surrounded and tore at the downed vampires before they even had a chance to recover. Most of the vampires didn't even have time to scream they were ripped apart so quickly. The jackals weren't fighting them for food or territory, but for revenge. Their attacks were angry and more dangerous than ever.

Karin wasn't waiting to see what fate the jackals had in mind for her. She took one leap and went straight up into the sky. She broke branches in her ascent and came out above the forest. The darkness was left to the forest floor below as she stood atop the tree. An ocean of stars shined down upon her. On any other night, she would've stood there and gawked at their beauty. Not tonight though. Tonight they seemed to shine only to set the scene for her demise.

She leapt as fast as she could from treetop to treetop. She'd felt like she'd never moved faster before in her life as she darted about. The forest below was angry at her and it looked like the trees themselves were coming to claim her. They all shook as jackals clambered up them and leapt about unseen. She barely managed to dodge them as she continued her race to escape. She dived for an exceptionally tall tree and ran up its side.

On top of the tree, Karin paused. Now she could look down upon all of the forest and all of the forest was moving. Her infrared eyes picked up far more heat than she'd expected. There were not dozens of jackals down there. There must've been more than a hundred. The elder had come for her not with his family, but a small army. There would be no running for her tonight.

"If that is the will of fate then." Karin threw her long jacket off and tossed it into the night. She unbound her long hair and let it flow in the wind. She tore off her long sleeve shirt and let it fall behind her. Underneath her shirt was a tight shirt that covered her front but not her back. On her pale white back was a tattoo of a sword piercing a bleeding rose. Karin bared her teeth and held her knives up above her.

"You have called me into battle and I will not refuse. Face me, for I am WAR!" The jackals roared in answer. Karin leapt as high as she could into the sky and relished the rush of cold air. Her momentum faded and she saw the jackal force rising for her like an angry ant swarm. She flipped herself in the air and let gravity take her back down to them.

She screamed right back at the jackals as she dropped into the lead one. It leapt for her and they met in the open sky. Karin hissed as she slashed it across the nose and rolled over its back. She drove both of her knives into the next one and took them off the tree. Karin slashed back and forth as they tumbled through the air and back towards the earth below. They crashed through the treetops and came to the floor with a mighty crash.

Karin rolled off the dead jackal quickly and came up fighting. She slashed at the nearest jackal and leapt into the next. The jackals kept rushing her, but she moved through the fray as fast as she could. Her strikes weren't killing blows. They were just strong enough to injure the beasts and keep them at bay. She danced back and forth, barely managing to keep them away from her.

A heavy roar came from behind her and Karin turned just in time for the elder jackal. The others parted for his leap into her. Karin managed to bring up one of her knives in time to pierce its chest, but she couldn't stop the elder's weight and momentum. He crashed into her and rolled them. Karin tried to stab at him, but he kept his weight on her arms as they rolled. When they came to a stop he was on top and she was pinned.

"You cannot kill War!"

The elder snapped his jaws around her head in response. There was a lot of cracking and Karin went limp. The elder rose from her calmly and shook his body. He reverted to a human once more and spat on Karin's corpse.

"I disagree." One of the other jackals approached him and handed him a long coat. "Get rid of the bodies," commanded the elder. "We were never here." The jackals nodded and went about their work. Mr. Hainlot looked back at Karin.

"You were dangerous War. After seeing how mad you truly were, I'm glad I came here. Your death was for the best." He nodded to his bodyguard and walked away. Their work was done here.

Morgan was amazed at Mr. Hainlot's story. He was definitely the elder and true alpha of their family. He must've been someone of great importance to just come out here and do this. He'd brought who knew how many jackals with him and they'd demolished Karin and her minions.

"Then the vampire Karin is dead," he said to make sure. Mr. Hainlot nodded.

"As I said, I did the deed myself. She will never trouble either of our families again. We also traced her back to a house about twenty miles away in the hills. I can't say if the house was abandoned originally or not, but it was overrun with vampires. We took care of them."

"Thank you very much."

"You don't need to thank me. It needed to be done. Now about this issue between your family and mine."

Morgan's relief turned to tension. This was a topic he did not want to come up with this man. Mr. Hainlot stared at him with a deadpan look for a moment before speaking.

"It is ludicrous." Morgan was filled with relief again. "My family had their land and you had yours. Some of them tried to move in on your territory violently and they paid the price for it. It's hard to say, but it's the truth. They should've never been so foolish. I've taken the liberty to relocate my family away from these mountains." Morgan was shocked.

"What?"

"Yes, they're not safe here. I can talk all I want, but their grudges with your family will remain. I'd rather see them relocated to somewhere safe closer to me than try and settle a vendetta with you. As of tomorrow, we will all be gone."

"I'm sorry to make them leave." Mr. Hainlot smiled.

"No you're not." Morgan sighed.

"I am and I'm not. I don't like the idea of people being forced from their home, but I will not stand any threat to my family." Mr. Hainlot nodded.

"Nor I." Morgan turned to Nathaniel.

"Get everyone out here please, especially Alex." Nathaniel nodded and headed back inside the house. "Kevin! Come on back." A moment later the family came out front and Kevin hopped over the fence. Morgan held out his hand to them.

"Everyone, this is Mr. Hainlot. Mr. Hainlot, this is my family. My wife Melissa, my sons Nathaniel, Kevin, and Samuel." They all waved as their names were called out. "My two daughters Mary and Lidia." Lidia waved extra enthusiastically. "And that's my son Nathaniel's girlfriend Ashley and her father Alex. We were having sort of a late night barbeque before you arrived, would you like to join us?" Everyone stared at Morgan in surprise. The other jackals looked absolutely revolted by Morgan's offer, but Mr. Hainlot smiled.

"Thank you, but no. We must be going, I just had to come here and tell you all that has happened so there will be no confusion. Mr. Lexington." Mr. Hainlot and Morgan shook hands. "You've got a good looking family, don't lose any of them."

"I won't. Take care of yours Mr. Hainlot."

"I intend to. Goodnight."

"Goodnight, have a safe drive down."

Mr. Hainlot went back to his car and Morgan went back to his family. One of the younger jackals opened the door for Mr. Hainlot and he got in. They all got in afterwards and started to drive away. Morgan and the others waved happily as they left. After they were gone, Lidia tugged on her dad's shirt.

"Does this mean all the monsters are gone?" Morgan bent down and picked up Lidia.

"Yes, I think they are."

He gave her a big kiss and set her back down. They finished the barbeque that night filled with laughter and relief. The vampires were all gone. The jackals were all gone. The mountain was theirs for good and nothing could've made the night taste so sweet.

CHAPTER 14

AN INVITATION

"It is now with great pleasure, that I introduce to you the newest graduates from Robert's High school!" shouted the principal. There was a wave of cheers coming from the assembled parents and family in the crowd. Ashley stood proudly in the bleachers as everyone cheered. It was the end of the year. They were done with high school.

The rest of the year had been a breeze without worrying about vampires or jackals. In a way, their disappearance from the town couldn't have come at a better time. It allowed their stress to be focused only on studying. She came away with some pretty handsome grades for it and couldn't have been happier. One chapter of her life was over. Now a new one could begin.

Standing in the bleachers next to her was Nathaniel. She'd been worried he might not graduate, but he'd laughed at her. He said his grades weren't that bad, he just wasn't the stalwart student she was. When they'd practiced the lineup for graduation she'd been amazed to see him next to her. Then he reminded her that her last name was Lebell and his was Lexington. Down and across in the other row, Kara had asked if Ashley was really the one with better grades.

Graduation from Robert's High had gone by so much faster than she'd anticipated. At her old high school graduations, had taken forever. Her old school however had many more awards, presentations, and about four times as many students. Smaller schools may not have the grandest of ceremonies, which Ashley supposed was a downside for the parents, but they were much quicker, which she was sure every student appreciated more.

They filed down one at a time toward the end of the yard. This was their moment of reprieve before they were ambushed by eager parents. The schools didn't allow people to keep their graduation gowns anymore so they were forced to turn them in for their diplomas.

Ashley walked and waved to her dad and his work friends. They were all cheering at the top of their lungs like boys at a football game. Ashley enjoyed the strange reception as she walked past. A teacher silently glared at her for waving and not being more professional. Ashley just shrugged and kept walking. What was he going to do? Give her detention?

More hooting and cheering came down the way. Nathaniel's family was probably cheering for him since he was just a few steps behind, but Ashley waved to them too. She heard a few shouts of her name, most of them from Lidia. Morgan had a giant clammy fist in the air he was waving back and forth. He jostled Melissa to be more positive, but she seemed bitter even today. Ashley locked eyes with her and walked a little faster. Was this woman ever happy with her around? Away from the graduation lines, Nathaniel caught up to her and laughed.

"We did it!"

"It's finally over."

"I'm just amazed it happened," said Nathaniel. "I see the table for L's. Let's go and get out of here." He led her over and they waited in the very short line.

"There seems to be a lot of tension between your parents," whispered Ashley to Nathaniel. He nodded and kept walking.

"They've been arguing a lot lately. I'm not sure over what." He turned in his graduation gown and took his diploma with a smile. He stepped to the side and Ashley did the same. They thanked the teacher who was at the booth and walked away in each other's arms.

They lost sight of anyone else they knew as the crowds mixed. Fortunately Nathaniel was tall enough to be spotted amongst the students and Morgan was tall enough to be spotted amongst anyone. Ashley found her hands going numb as she shook hands with everyone over and over again. Her dad and his friends had caught up with them and she and Nathaniel were passed back and forth like pinballs. They were there for the amusement of the parents and were trophies to be shown off.

After being congratulated, hugged, and shaken a dozen times, they began to push their way out. It helped to be with Nathaniel's family and her dad's friends, most of which were large construction workers. They forced the crowd to part before the wave of giant men. Ashley and everyone smaller stayed quick on their heels before the crowd could re-assimilate them. Only Lidia was safe, perched on her father's shoulders above it all. Once they were out in the street heading towards their cars, Ashley relaxed.

"It's weird."

"What is?" asked Nathaniel.

"We go through all that stuff and now we're just walking away. It seems rather anticlimactic to me."

"Would you rather be celebrating all night?" joked Nathaniel.

"No, it's just…I don't know what to do now."

"Good because you don't get a choice," laughed her dad. "We're going out to dinner. All of us."

"Sweet! I'm hungry," said Nathaniel.

"What a surprise," said Ashley. "Where are we going? Wait, let me guess. Katie's?"

"Not today," said Morgan. "We're getting slightly fancier food. The Italian place Giovanni's."

"Noodles!" cheered Lidia from her dad's shoulders. Ashley had never been to Giovanni's before, but she'd heard good things. They piled into their cars and headed out before the main crowd of students could leave.

Giovanni's was a nicer place than most. It was certainly one of the better maintained places Ashley had been to in Reiner. The wooden exterior was fresh and recently scrubbed. The floor was made of cream shaded tiles and the staff were dressed professionally. Morgan had reservations for them and they went to a back room with a long dining table. Ashley wanted to sit closer to the edge, but she and Nathaniel were forced into the middle.

If there was one thing her dad and Nathaniel's family agreed on, it was food and how to eat it. Alex might've been the only human male there, but by the way he ate, he could've been a part of the pack. Ashley thought it was so funny they ate so quickly considering everyone had their own plate. Nobody was about to steal from them. Regardless of the matter, they ate like they were starving. Even if Ashley did think the noodles smearing Lidia's face were cute, it was still gross. Manners weren't so much of an issue here.

They received more congratulations throughout the dinner as they ate. Ashley wondered how many times she could get congratulated for doing something almost every other teenager did. They talked about the future and she discovered Nathaniel would go to the same college she did. He would be working more in his dad's shop than studying, but he'd still go to school. When the talking slowed Morgan took Melissa's hand and leaned towards Alex.

"Melissa and I were thinking of something since our recent problems have vanished."

Melissa took her hand back and crossed her arms. Ashley thought Melissa didn't think very highly of this and had been bullied into it. She tried not to smile at her discomfort and kept her eyes on Morgan.

"My cousin Samson is getting married in three weeks. Originally we couldn't go because we had to stay in town due to those issues. Since that has all been resolved though, we've decided to go again. And…we'd like to invite Ashley along for the trip."

Nathaniel nudged Ashley and smiled. Ashley grinned. Going to a wedding with Nathaniel's family. This could be all kinds of fun. She turned to her dad to see his initial reaction. He finished his bite of food and smiled.

"Sounds interesting. Where is this wedding?" he asked.

"In Colorado."

"That is a long way," laughed her dad. "Going to fly out or drive?"

"I like a good road trip as much as the next guy," said Morgan, "but from here to Colorado is a bit far. We'd be flying. Since we invited her we'd be paying for Ashley's ticket."

"No I can get that," waved Alex between bites. "How long would you be gone for?"

"Three days is what we're planning on. The first day will be travel. The second day would be the wedding. Third day would be recovery and come on home."

"And you said your cousin?" continued Alex in a more serious tone. "Is he a cousin by blood or marriage?" Morgan leaned back and smiled. Even Ashley knew what her father was insinuating here. Would this be a human or werewolf wedding was what he was really asking. Ashley wondered if there was honestly any difference.

"No he's a blood relation. Youngest son of my uncle Tom. Took him a while to find a girl, but he finally managed it," laughed Morgan. "We thought he'd never get married at this rate."

"Some people do take longer than others," said Alex. He looked at Ashley. "What do you think? Would you like to go?" Ashley nodded.

"I think it'd be really fun." Alex looked at her deeply for a while. She wondered what he was thinking. Was he still afraid of all of them being werewolves? Or was it just her being off with her boyfriend's family?

"I suppose there isn't any harm in it," he finally said and she hugged him. Melissa sighed and excused herself to use the restroom.

"Thank you dad."

"You better be on your best behavior. I trust you'll keep a good eye on her Morgan?" He gave Morgan a dark look.

"Of course. She'll be in good hands." Ashley took Nathaniel's hand just as Morgan spoke and Alex eyed them.

"It's those hands I'm worried about though." Everyone at the table laughed except for Ashley. She went bright red and had to turn her face away from her dad.

"Yay Ashley is coming! We can dance all night!" said Lidia as she shook about in her chair.

"So what are your weddings like?" asked Alex. Morgan grinned.

"Like nothing you've ever seen."

CHAPTER 15

DIFFERENT MOUNTAIN, SAME CROWD

Ashley had at first been excited about going with Nathaniel's family on vacation to a wedding, but over the past few weeks, she was beginning to regret it. As fun as it could be, it was also a large area for her to get judged in. She didn't know the people, the traditions, or anything. Then there was Melissa's sweet little surprise for her.

Melissa obviously didn't want Ashley there and seemed ready to make her life as difficult as possible. A few days after she'd been invited Melissa informed her that she'd been volunteered for the wedding band. Nathaniel had assured her it wasn't a professional band, just a bunch of musicians gathered to play. This didn't make Ashley feel any better when Melissa presented her with over a dozen songs she said might be played when they were there. Ashley knew a challenge when she saw one. Melissa was either going to make her look good in the band or she was going to make her look like a fool in front of a crowd.

Ashley wasn't willing to give Melissa the chance. She studied the music vigorously. She probably spent more time practicing music than she'd studied for her finals. She went over each song again and again until she was comfortable with each one. Luck was on her side as most of these were simple dance songs. Most of the notes were repetitive and there was nothing too complex. The slow songs would be incredibly simple.

It wouldn't be the last party she went to this summer either. Kara told her a week after she returned there would be a going away party for her. Ashley looked at her concerned. "Going away party? Where are you going?" Kara grinned and flexed her arms.

"I'm not going to college like you guys. I'm going into the army."

"The military?" asked Ashley.

"You bet. I already know how to shoot a gun and fight, but they're going to teach me how to do it better. I'm going to learn all kinds of skills you'll never touch in college."

"When are you going in?"

"In less than a month," said Kara. "I better see you at the party."

Ashley looked at Kara sadly and told her she would be. Kara was one of her best friends in this town and she'd be sad to see her go. She supposed she should've expected this kind of career out of her, but she didn't want it to happen. She wished they could all stay together just like always. High school was over though and they all had new lives to find.

The day of their flight came and Ashley was back to being excited for a break. She wasn't sure how to feel about Kara or anyone else leaving yet. The trip might be challenging, but at least she knew how to face those challenges. She packed an extra set of clothes, her nicest dress, her flute, music, and everything else she would need. When Nathaniel came to the door to get her, she was ready to go.

They drove into the very same airport Ashley had arrived in. Going through security took a lot longer this time with eight people, but they eventually got through. Their flight was a clean straight shot and Ashley was trembling with excitement as she got on the plane. She swore she wouldn't fall asleep this time.

"You ready?" asked Mary as they stepped on.

"I can't wait!" giggled Ashley.

"Yeah, maybe with you here Nathaniel won't freak out for once," said Kevin as he sat in the seat in front of them.

"You're not much better," said Mary bitterly as she sat next to him.

"Better than the crybaby back there." Nathaniel kicked Kevin's seat and rocked him forward. Kevin glared back at him, but Nathaniel just grinned. He was shakily putting on his seatbelt and opening the window. Kevin sat down and it sounded like he was doing the same thing.

"What was that about?" asked Ashley.

"Nothing," said Nathaniel a little too quickly. She'd never seen him this jittery before. He kept glancing out the window and ahead.

"Did you have caffeine before we left or something?" she asked. Mary turned around in her seat.

"Both Nathaniel and Kevin have a slight phobia of flying," she said annoyed. Kevin pushed her back to her seat and Ashley was sure she heard him tell her to be quiet. She looked at Nathaniel and took his hand.

"Is that true?"

"Let's just say I'm not used to having my feet off the ground," he said with a forced smile. "I'd much rather run to Colorado first."

"See you in a month," retorted Kevin.

"It'd take you two," snapped Nathaniel. Kevin surprisingly didn't get out of his seat. It might've had something to do with his belt buckle being so tightly fastened down.

"You two wonder why mom and dad sit in a different part of the plane," sighed Mary. "I asked them to swap with me. They said no deal."

"It'll be alright," said Ashley to Nathaniel. She could feel his heart racing just by holding his hand. He tried to keep a calm face, but his eyes said he was uncomfortable. "This'll be my first flight."

"How? I know you flew to Montana."

"I fell asleep through literally the entire thing." Nathaniel smirked and looked out the window.

"You're lucky. I wish I could do that."

"I'm excited to go. This time when I get on a plane, I'll actually be able to enjoy it. I won't be going somewhere scary and alone this time." Ashley meant the words, but that wasn't why she said them. Nathaniel calmed down and rubbed her hand. If she made him feel bad about the last time she'd flown, he'd forget all about his problems. She didn't have to be sad. He just had to believe it.

"I'm sorry," he said. "This time the journey should be a lot more exciting."

"Oh I don't know," laughed Ashley. "I can't exactly say my year in Reiner has been boring."

"True." Nathaniel rested his head against the seat and played his fingers in hers. He fidgeted momentarily and then stopped. He looked down at his cramped legs disappointed.

"That's the other reason I hate flying. I don't fit anywhere."

"How do you think I feel?" asked Mary.

"You fit easier than all of us," said Kevin. "What are you talking about?"

"Yeah but you don't!" she complained. "You keep falling into my seat. At least Ashley wants to be close to Nathaniel."

They all had a quick laugh and the plane began to pull away toward the runway. Ashley felt her body tingle with excitement as the engines grew louder next to them. She grinned at Nathaniel and placed her hand over his. He tried to smile at her, but his hand didn't hold hers. Both his hands tightened their death grips on the armrests and his hands turned white.

Ashley leaned against him and Nathaniel calmed down a little. Ashley didn't do it on purpose though, she just wanted to look out the window. She gawked openly as they pulled away from the ground at an alarming speed. She laughed silently as the city turned into a tiny speck and they were sailing into the clouds. Nathaniel put his head down on her and Ashley could hear his pounding heart.

"Here I thought you liked going fast."

"Not this fast," said Nathaniel through gritted teeth.

"You coward," whispered Kevin from the front.

"You're not any better," said Mary.

"I'll hit you," snarled her brother, but Mary just laughed.

"That would require letting go of the seat."

Ashley giggled with her and stayed close to Nathaniel the entire flight. He managed to calm down enough that his skin color came back, but he never left his seat. When the stewardess asked if he wanted anything, he declined quickly despite being hungry. The less he had to move the better. Ashley fed him some of her snacks, but the boy was hopeless.

She on the other hand was having the time of her life. She loved the strange feeling of flight and looking out the window. The land below looked like a painting more than the Earth she lived on. She hardly watched the inflight movie as she preferred the sky all around her. How had she managed to miss all this the first time?

The flight only took a couple of hours before they were descending in Colorado. Ashley held onto Nathaniel's hand tightly as the plane touched the ground. He was almost shaking by then. Ashley tried to support him, but she'd never felt a plane land before. It bounced angrily at first and she thought something had gone wrong. She held his hand in as much of an attempt to soothe him as well as herself. When the plane had come to a halt they both breathed steadily.

"That wasn't too bad," he said shakily. Ashley nodded and stretched a little in her seat.

"You two are such babies," said Mary as she stood up.

"Shut up," said Kevin as he stood up looking white as a ghost. It took them a little while to get off the plane and by then both boys were looking happy again. She thought they might kiss the airport floor. Ashley and Mary shook their heads when both boys had to run to the bathroom. Neither of them had been willing to risk walking around on the plane to even use the restroom.

"I hope you never have to go across the ocean," Ashley said to Nathaniel when he came back out.

"I'll take a boat."

"Nice cruises were invented for people like my sons," said Melissa as they went to get their luggage.

"I'd love to take a cruise," said Kevin. "Now that is a vacation."

They took their luggage and Ashley wondered how they were going to get wherever they needed to go. Nathaniel told her they'd be renting a car. When they were heading toward the rental station however, a loud voice called out to them.

"Little brother!" shouted a man near the entrance. Ashley and the family turned around to see another giant staring at them. He didn't have Morgan's facial hair, but the man could've been a cloned copy of him. He was bigger than almost everyone in the airport with the obvious exception of Morgan. People scattered to avoid the two giants as they went for each other.

"Ben!" shouted Morgan as they hugged. "What are you doing here?"

"I came for the wedding. You weren't the only one who was invited." They separated and the kids immediately flocked to the man. He laughed and gave them all a great big hug. Lidia squealed as uncle Ben picked her up and spun her around.

"You're all getting so big!" he exclaimed. "Gosh, what has it been, a year?"

"Two years uncle Ben," said Kevin.

"We missed you at Christmas," said Mary. Ben smiled and held them all again.

"This Christmas I'll make it for sure." He stepped aside from the kids and gave Melissa a light hug. "Melissa, good to see you again."

"Good to see you too Ben." Ben looked over Melissa's shoulder at Ashley surprised. He let go of Melissa and smiled. "And who's this little lady who isn't intimidated by me?"

"This is Ashley," said Morgan. "Ashley, this is my brother Ben." Ashley held out her hand.

"Nice to meet you," she said with a smile. Ben looked at her hand oddly and then looked back to the kids.

"Who picked up this little beauty?" Nathaniel stepped over and grinned. Ben laughed and moved in for a hug. Ashley squeaked as he picked up both her and Nathaniel at the same time. "So my little pup of a nephew grabbed a girly of his own." He set them both down. "It's nice to meet you Ashley. You can call me uncle Ben, or Ben for short."

"Okay," she said, feeling crushed. Ben and Morgan were definitely brothers judging by their hugs.

"You have all your things?" Ben asked Morgan.

"Yeah we're all set. We just need to rent a car." Ben dismissed the idea with a wave of his hand.

"I've got you covered. I rented a van. It'll be a small squeeze, but we should all fit. I didn't expect an extra body so we might all have to get cozy."

"It's no problem to rent a car," said Morgan.

"Nonsense!" said Ben. "We can all fit in and it'll save you a few bucks."

Ben led them outside and opened the large van he had. It would be a very tight squeeze Ashley decided. Every seat would be filled and all of their bags couldn't fit in the back. As the two largest members, Morgan and Ben had to take the front seats. Kevin, Mary, and Melissa had to sit in the middle. Nathaniel, Ashley, Lidia, and Samuel had to take the back with Lidia and Samuel sharing a seat. Many of them had bags on their laps as they drove away.

"Little cozy," reiterated Ben.

The drive to their hotel was an uncomfortable two hours with little said. They listened to music and had the windows rolled down out of necessity. With so many people cramped in such a small space, it was only a matter of time before the van got hot and began to smell. It was dark when they finally arrived and everyone was relieved to get out.

The hotel was extremely nice, but seemed to be in its down season. Ashley learned it was a main hotel for a nearby ski resort and most of their business was in the winter. Since all the snow was gone, so were most of their customers. The manager at the front of the hotel looked very happy to see them as they walked in.

"Hello," he said brilliantly. "How can I help you today?"

"I have four rooms under Morgan Lexington," said Morgan as he passed off his bags to Ben. The manager checked his computer quickly and came back smiling.

"Yes, we have all the rooms set up for you. I just need to check your ID and I'll give you all your room keys." The transaction only lasted a few minutes with the manager explaining everything available and passing out the keycards for their rooms. They stepped back so Ben could set up his room and Morgan began to pass out the keys.

"Alright everyone, here are the keys. We're all near each other. Before I hand these out, I want everyone to know we're going to meet back here for dinner in twenty minutes." he explained. "Your mother and I will be in room 107." Melissa took her key and headed down the hall with her bags. "Kevin and Samuel, you're in 111." He gave the boys a dark look as he handed them the two keys. "I expect there to be no fights and nothing broken."

"Us fight?" asked Kevin innocently as the brothers threw their arms around each other. "Never dad."

"Any problems and you two will be sleeping on the floor in our room you understand?" The boys nodded and grinned. They walked to the hall before bolting away to their room. Morgan turned his shifty eyes away from the boys and looked at Mary. "Here's a key for you. Lidia, you be sure to always hold onto yours. You're in 108. If you want to come to our room at any time Lidia, you just knock on our door okay."

"Okay!" said Lidia happily as she took her key.

"We'll be fine," said Mary. "Let's go you." Mary walked down the hall and Lidia skipped after her. Morgan turned back to Nathaniel and Ashley smiling. Ashley was in shock as he headed them a pair of keys.

"Your room is 113. I trust you two not to get into any trouble."

"Of course, dad," said Nathaniel. "Somebody has to be the good example around here."

"Yeah that's what worries me." Morgan laughed.

"I can't believe I'm not rooming with Mary," said Ashley quietly. Morgan looked at her with a smile.

"You're both adults Ashley. You've been with my son for almost a year and you've both been through more than most couples go through in a lifetime. You've been at my house more than your own this past year. Even if my wife is angry with you at times, we've always liked having you over. You're like family Ashley and you'll be treated like family."

"Thanks dad," said Nathaniel.

"Thank you," said Ashley bashfully. "I'm glad you let me come here."

"As far as I'm concerned you can come with us anytime you like." Morgan rose up to his full height and took a deep breath. "Now if you'll excuse me, I've got to go face my wife." He chuckled as he walked away. Ashley looked amazed at Nathaniel, but he just smiled and led them down the hall after his dad.

Their room was larger than Ashley had expected. There was a large queen size bed waiting for them, a closet with cupboards for all their clothing, and a small TV across the bed. Nathaniel dropped their bags and Ashley checked the bathroom gleefully. It was huge for a hotel room. It had a long shower, beautiful granite counters, and a large sink. She came out to find Nathaniel laying on the bed smiling.

"This place is wonderful."

"Agreed, but I'm starving." He sat up on his elbows and smiled. "Let's put away our stuff and go get dinner."

"I've got a better idea," said Ashley. Nathaniel started to ask what, but Ashley leapt at him. He caught her in midair and rolled her down next to him laughing. She kissed him and held him close. This was so wonderful.

They left a little while later for dinner. The hotel had a buffet area and they all had a large helping. There was almost no talk about the wedding, only the appearance of uncle Ben seemed to matter. The kids all wanted to hear where he'd been. Ben had no family of his own. He was very nomadic and was always exploring the world. From the sound of his stories, he must've had friends from here to Russia. They never got around to the part about how he made a living and Ashley never asked. She just enjoyed how much she was included.

It was late after dinner, but neither of them felt tired so Ashley and Nathaniel went for a walk around the hotel. The nights there were still cool by any normal standard, but it certainly wasn't Montana. Ashley felt more at home as the nights more resembled her time in California. It wasn't quite as hot as she'd like, but it was closer. They were almost back inside when they heard Ben.

"Just a moment you two." Nathaniel turned them about and smiled. His uncle was leaning on a tree nearby. Small smoke rings were coming out of a pipe perched between his lips.

"Hey Ben," said Nathaniel. "Still pulling off the Pop-eye look?" Ben held the pipe out and grinned.

"I do enjoy a good pipe once in a while." He tapped it against the tree and walked towards them. "How are you two enjoying the night?"

"It's nice," said Nathaniel. "I already miss the snow."

"You'll have to come back in the winter," said Ben. "You'd feel right at home here. How about you Ashley? Enjoying yourself?"

"Yes," she said as she held Nathaniel's hand proudly. "It's beautiful out here."

"I always thought so." Before they entered the hotel again, Ben stepped in front of them. He put out his pipe for good and smiled at both of them. "Interesting necklace you have Ashley." Ashley smiled and felt the smooth cord around her neck. She held it up for Ben to see.

"Haven't seen that in a long time. I'm surprised you kept it," he said to Nathaniel.

"You said it was a family gift." Nathaniel nudged Ashley. "Remember when I said my uncle gave it to me?" He nodded to Ben who just smiled.

"Made it myself," said Ben. "It's supposed to be worn by members of my family only." Ashley suddenly felt ashamed and wondered if she'd gotten Nathaniel into trouble. She felt like she should take it off, but she didn't know what to do. She played with the cord nervously. Ben just grinned.

"I guess this means Nathaniel brought you in. I'll have to bring another present at Christmas I guess." He laughed and held open the door for them. "You be sure to take good care of my nephew Ashley."

"I will."

"Good and as long as you do, I'll consider you my third niece." The words almost stopped Ashley, but Nathaniel kept her walking. Ben waved at them from the door. "Have a good night!" he said as he disappeared back outside.

"Did he mean that?" Ashley whispered to Nathaniel.

"Probably. You should know by now most of my family stays pretty close. I think since they brought you out here, they think you're family now too." Nathaniel shoved her playfully, but kept her fingers with his. Ashley didn't know what to say. Nathaniel's family was a part of hers now in some strange way. When did that happen, she wondered?

Back in their room, Nathaniel began to get ready for bed. Neither of them were that tired, but there wasn't much left to do now. Ashley watched him take off his shirt as he headed into the bathroom. She felt both want and sorrow as she watched his strong body go past. His scars reminded her of the beast underneath the man. They were one and the same. The same could be said about the rest of his family. They were unlike everyone else here, herself included, but they had brought her in. She was one of them.

"Find anything good?" asked Nathaniel a minute later, emerging from the bathroom. The TV was on, but Ashley wasn't on the bed. She was leaning against the wall behind him waiting for him. She wrapped her hands around and hugged him. Nathaniel smiled as he felt her cool arms and body against him. His eyes raised as he realized he could feel her body against his back. He looked down and saw her clothes laying on the floor.

Ashley pulled Nathaniel around and kissed him. She had no more words for him as she wrapped herself over him. She kissed him like she'd never kissed before, feeling his warm body against hers. She pushed them back to the bed and collapsed over him. His hands came across her as she pressed herself down. This was something they'd waited too long for. She didn't want to tell Nathaniel how much she loved being with him anymore. She wanted him to feel it.

Nathaniel rolled her onto her back and looked deep into her eyes. She laid back slightly embarrassed, but proud of herself. He grabbed the remote and flicked off the TV behind them. In perfect darkness, Ashley felt Nathaniel come closer.

CHAPTER 16

RESURRECTION

Three boys were sitting around a campfire in the middle of the woods. They all had long scraggly hair and their clothing was dirty. The remains of a deer laid nearby mostly pulled apart. Pieces of it were still hanging on sticks over the fire.

"I still can't believe Mr. Hainlot wanted us to abandon this place," said one.

"Will you drop it already Mikey?"

"No, it's so ridiculous. We had a war band here and we could've wiped out both the vampires and the werewolves. All of the forest and mountain would've been ours."

"Now all of this place is ours," said the third. "Don't forget, since the rest of them ditched town this place is ours."

"A lot of land for free," laughed Mikey. "Sounds almost too good to be true."

"Which means it probably is," said a dark voice. All three of them got to their feet quickly and turned towards the voice. They couldn't see anybody, but they could smell her.

"Who's there?" asked the third. He stepped in front of the other two and puffed out his chest. This was a great opportunity to show off his superiority to his friends and claim leadership of the pack. The others glared at him, but said nothing.

Suddenly the forest went quiet. A strange darkness spread across the trees and blocked out the starlight from above. The three boys moved into a defensive triangle around the fire.

"Stay where we are and nothing can take us by surprise."

The other two seemed to agree and kept their eyes on the forest. The smell of the woman disappeared along with everything else. Then it became harder to see and they realized the fire was going out. The wood stopped burning and the fire fell to only the smallest of embers. Almost all light vanished and the three boys became tense.

"Who are you?" demanded the lead boy again. All the hairs on the back of his neck stood up as he felt the woman behind him. Something slid into his back and suddenly he couldn't move anymore. He could feel the woman's cold breath as she whispered into his ear.

"I am Death." The boy fell to the ground without a word. He heard the sudden cries of his friends as Death fell upon them. Then all was silent. His eyes stayed open, but he would never see again. He would never do anything again.

The darkness disappeared and the woman stepped away from the three dead boys. Her hair was a long, glossy black and her eyes just as dark. Her skin was the palest white and her lips ruby red. She wore a long black dress which showed off only her arms and a small bit of her legs. There were no visible weapons on her.

"As beautiful of a performance as ever Death. Now come take your leash back before I infect your dog."

Death came over to where another vampire awaited her. She was a bit taller than Death, but nowhere near her beauty. Her hair was gray and thin and her skin blotched. It wasn't pale like a vampire's, but looked closer to a dying patient in the hospital. Her eyes were a faint yellow and Death paused at her putrid breath. The woman wore thick pants and multiple heavy coats.

In her hands were three long, heavy chains which led to the next vampire. The chains led to a large metal collar around the girl's throat. She was much smaller than the other two and didn't look older than eighteen. She had short blonde hair and vibrant blue eyes. She looked the most normal with her clothing, but something was off in her eyes. There was a maddened look to her as she tried to move towards the fresh corpses. She hissed and yelled, tugging on her collar and chains. The sickly woman yanked on the chains.

"Calm down you pathetic mess."

"Let me go!" screamed the girl. Death walked over to the girl and held her chin. All at once a certain calm came over her. She stopped her thrashing and looked at Death obediently.

"Famine. Control yourself." Famine nodded and tried to relax. Even when she was controlling herself her body shook uncontrollably. Death took the chains from the sickly woman.

"Pestilence, lead the way." Pestilence half laughed; half coughed.

"She's probably long gone."

"She's here. I know she is." Pestilence sighed and pointed.

"This way."

They walked for a few minutes and ignored Famine's cries as they did. She whined as they walked away from the boy's bodies. Death yanked on the chains to keep her in line but didn't say anything to calm her. Pestilence stopped at a mound of dirt.

"Here we are. Start digging."

"In my nice dress?" begged Death. "Famine dear. Find our friend." Famine looked at Death sadly. Death pet her head and smiled. "One of those boys is for you if you do." Famine's eyes went wide and she dove into the dirt mound. Dirt and mud flew everywhere as she swiped it away in great heaps. Death stayed back to avoid the mess. Pestilence didn't even bother moving and let the dirt cake her coat without any complaint.

"Found her!" declared Famine happily. Famine pulled at a leg and out came Karin's corpse. She was covered in dirt and had obviously been there for a while. Her head was smashed in considerably. Pestilence started laughing.

"I think she found what she was looking for."

"Bring her back to the bodies," said Death.

Famine nodded and ran back to the boys. Karin's body bounced along the ground as Famine dragged her. Famine let go of her leg next to the fire and looked at Death. Death studied Karin's body with Pestilence nearby.

"She got smashed up by something big," hacked Pestilence.

"Angry jackals. Stupid girl, you jumped in before looking," said Death.

"Still, she's not in bad shape. She got lucky." Death nodded in agreement. Famine started whining nearby like a sad dog.

"You did a good job. You can eat whichever one you like." Famine waited only until the word eat was uttered before she leapt onto one of the boys. She bit deeply into his neck and started sucking hard at the cooling blood within. Pestilence pulled out some rope from her coat and tied it to a boy's foot.

"Alright, let's get her going again." Pestilence leapt up into a tree and tied the other end to a thick branch. She hauled up the body until it was hanging upside down about six feet up. Death put Karin underneath the body.

"Here goes." Death stabbed two fingers into the boy's neck and pulled them out quickly. Blood began to flow freely out of the boy and dripped into Karin's open wounds.

"How long do you think it'll take?" she asked Pestilence. Pestilence shrugged from the treetop.

"For her to be awake, shouldn't be too long. For her head to be fixed? That could take a while."

"Blood fixes everything," said Death.

"I'm surprised they didn't leave her out in the sun. We can't bring her back from ash."

"Some creature was lazy with her death. She wasn't even buried properly. Whoever disposed of her probably just threw her in a nearby hole and threw some dirt on top of her. They must've thought since she was dead that she was dead." Pestilence laughed and clapped her hands.

"Some people are so stupid."

CHAPTER 17

THE PREMARITAL RUN

Ashley awoke to soft daylight playing across her body. She rose slowly, feeling the soft sheets cling to her. Her whole body was sore and she felt more tired than she'd ever been before. Each stretch brought a new pain, which in turn brought a new smile. Something inside made each painful move feel magical.

The clock said it was nearly noon. The wedding wasn't until four in the afternoon, so they still had plenty of time. The sunlight was seeping in through the cracks in the blinds. The room was silent and she found she didn't have the will to get up. She pulled herself onto Nathaniel and kissed his bare chest.

She couldn't see his eyes through his messy hair, but she could see a slow smile creeping to his lips. She could feel his thumping heart just beneath her face and she grinned. His hands came up and pulled her closer to him.

"Good morning." His head lifted and his face appeared through his hair.

"Good morning," he said as he planted a kiss on her lips. His touch was warm and she felt how rough his lips were. Never before had she felt so tender against his firm body. Her whole body tingled at his touch as if he would pounce her. She braced herself for another attack, but he did no such thing. He just held her and planted soft kisses against her head.

"When did we go to bed last night?" she asked.

"I have no idea," he said smugly. He put his head back down and sighed happily. "All I know is I feel like I do after a full moon. Exhausted to the core." His grin became so wide she saw his sharp teeth sticking out. She kissed his chest and laid still.

"How do you think I feel?" she said. He groaned and stretched proudly. Ashley enjoyed the ride as her whole body twitched over his.

"I don't think we have to get up yet," he said slowly.

Ashley smiled and held him tightly. She didn't want to get up yet, she wasn't sure if she could. Nathaniel laid as still as the grave and his breathing became softer. His breathing became light and she felt him drift back into his dreams. He was as tired as her. She nuzzled her head on him and thought about the night.

She'd been ashamed at first. She had been nervous to show her body to Nathaniel. She knew it was pointless with the lights out, he could see in the dark anyway. In a way, she'd felt his shyness too and had been surprised by it. Nathaniel had lost his clothes a lot turning into a werewolf. She'd never assumed he'd be shy to show himself to her.

She didn't feel embarrassed now. She felt right laying on top of Nathaniel with only the sheet to cover them. This was their moment and nobody else's. She'd chosen right in him and nothing could change that. She felt the strength to move away return to her, but she didn't want to. She liked this bed of muscle and skin below her. She liked feeling her head rise and sink with every breath he took. His warmth was hers now.

As soon as the clock struck noon the phone began to buzz incessantly next to them. Nathaniel stirred and looked at the phone angrily. Ashley just kissed him and smiled. "You don't have to pick it up." He raised his head and sighed.

"It's my dad."

Ashley stiffened suddenly. It was just a phone call, but for some reason she felt like she'd been caught. Nathaniel held her firmly with one hand before picking up the phone with the other.

"Hello? Yes. Lunch at one?" Nathaniel checked the clock. "Yeah that should be fine. We'll be there. K. Bye." He hung up the phone and put his arm back over Ashley.

"I could go for some food," said Ashley.

"So could I."

He kissed her and started to lean up. Ashley pulled back a little and allowed Nathaniel to stretch some. He sat up completely and threw his arms around her again. Her body ached as she sat on her knees to stay with him. He seemed content to sit there, but Ashley had to move to the side.

"I'm sore," she whined happily. Nathaniel smirked and held her chin.

"I think a shower would be good." Ashley nodded and allowed Nathaniel to lead her out of bed. She was surprised he just walked her to the shower and didn't even bother bringing the sheet with him.

This was the first time she'd really had a chance to admire his body. He might've been able to see in the dark, but she certainly couldn't. Looking at him as he turned on the shower and tried to get the water warm, she thought he looked exactly as he felt. His long arms and legs were strong, firm from constant work. His back was hard as steel and could've been polished rock for all she knew. She found it almost amusing that with how fit he was, he had a tiny bit of chub on his sides and stomach. She'd never really realized it before, but his body had to keep some fat on him. She knew there was muscle coiled underneath, but it wasn't as obvious as the rest of his body. He turned and held his hand out.

Ashley took it and felt her side flash with pain. Her own muscles were bunched up and tight still. The hot water promised her relief, but she couldn't get over how sore she was. She looked to her left and studied her form in the mirror.

Her skin was soft skin was bruised. She could see a few lines across her back where Nathaniel's hand had been. There were a few dark spots across her front which she felt gingerly. Nathaniel had nibbled at her expertly last night, but not left any wound.

"My dress better hide this," she said somewhat proudly.

"It will," said Nathaniel as he pulled her under the water. Ashley let the water soak her body and she relaxed happily.

"You've never seen my dress."

"I trust your tastes."

She started to argue when he drew her close for another kiss. Ashley held him close. They kissed, laughed, and held each other as they washed. Ashley felt she'd never been through such a thorough scrub in her life. Even when she was sure she was clean, she kept at it. She didn't want to even imagine Nathaniel's family smelling this one on her. They didn't end up leaving the shower until ten minutes before they had to leave.

They got dressed quickly and found their way to the lunch area. It was mostly empty by the time they arrived, but they spotted Morgan and Melissa seated at the far end. Everyone else was in the buffet line getting heaps of food before moving back to their parents. They joined Samuel in line before heading back to the table.

"There they are," said Morgan. "I thought you two would never wake."

"Sorry," said Nathaniel.

"I wasn't speaking to you two, I was speaking to them," said Morgan, pointing a finger at Kevin and Samuel. "Trying to sleep through the trip eh? What'd you do all night?"

"The pool stays open all night," said Kevin. "So does the spa."

"We know. Your father and I were out there for quite a while," said Melissa with a large grin. The boy's smiles dropped as their lie was seen through.

"We might've explored a little," said Samuel quietly between bites.

"Shush," snapped Kevin as he jabbed his brother.

"We'll talk about it later," said Morgan.

They all ate their food happily and Ashley was glad the attention wasn't on them. Nobody looked at her or Nathaniel weirdly so she took it as a good sign. They were almost finished when Morgan looked at Ashley.

"There's something you need to know about werewolf weddings Ashley. The wedding starts in the afternoon and it goes on well past night. The first part is what we call the premarital run. It's a gathering of all the werewolf families to see how the new couple runs and moves together. It's kind of a weird approval/disapproval stage where we see if the couple is truly compatible."

"Okay, and that's what we're going to later?"

"Yes. It consists of three parts. The first part is the introduction of the families and guests. You will be specially introduced since you're not one of us. A lot of people are going to come around you, sniff you, and come to know you. This is very important since uninvited guests at our weddings usually get a very rude greeting."

"Do I have to do anything or just have to stand there?"

"Just stand there. There's a small path you have to walk so all of the families can see you. Nothing hard, I just don't want you to be surprised." Ashley nodded.

"Then what?"

"Next comes the run. It's where the families run together as a giant pack. You'll be on Nathaniel's back as usual. You may actually see a few humans riding on werewolves so you won't be alone."

"She's never alone!" complained Lidia. "I'm there."

"That's true," laughed Morgan. "The last bit is the party. It's a small feast with lots of music and dancing. There we usually give our blessings to the new couple and wish them luck."

"Okay, should I bring a change of clothes?"

"I wouldn't. I think you'll be good in your dress and Nathaniel's cloak. It shouldn't get too cold out there tonight. If it does, you're probably sitting around and not near the fire."

"I was wondering about that. Is this like a camping thing?"

"It's all set up out in the forest, very little civilization out there. You got kind of lucky this time. We're set up near a rest stop so you can use the restroom instead of a bush." Ashley looked at him half pleased, half grossed out. She'd never even considered that fact.

"It never used to be around a bathroom," said Melissa. "Finally we girls got together and put a stop to that. Using the restroom outdoors at a formal occasion gets old really fast, let me tell you." Ashley smiled and laughed a little. Melissa was speaking to her and her voice wasn't filled with hate. What a nice change.

"You didn't bring heels, right?" asked Mary. Ashley shook her head.

"Do I look crazy to you?" Mary held up her hands showing she meant no offense.

"Just checking. You wouldn't believe how many girls try."

"Yes I would," said Ashley, immediately thinking of Liz.

"What time are we leaving here?" asked Nathaniel.

"I'd say about three," said Morgan. "We'll all meet in the lobby and go out from there."

"Not long then," said Kevin as he checked his watch.

"Nope, so we'll get started," said Melissa. "Come on you, dress up time." Lidia sat back in her chair and rolled her eyes. She finally took her mother's hand and left with her obediently.

"I thought Lidia liked getting dressed up," said Ashley confused.

"She does," said Mary.

"Then why did she look upset?"

"She enjoys being dressed up and feeling cool," said Kevin through a piece of bacon. "But this is also Lidia, and getting dressed up and pretty takes time. It means taking a long time doing nothing." Ashley imagined Lidia trying to sit still and understood what Kevin meant.

"Mom is pretty much the only one who can get her to sit still long enough," said Samuel.

"And even that is a challenge," said Morgan. "I think I'll avoid the room for a bit and shop for some last minute things."

"I'll go with you," said Mary quickly.

"Smart girl," said Kevin.

Ashley and Nathaniel finished up their breakfast a few minutes later and went back to their own room. They had at least an hour to kill before they had to get ready. Ashley hit the bed as soon as she got back and felt all her strength leave her. She was snoring contently a minute later.

"Wake up," said Nathaniel an hour later.

Ashley groaned, but sat upright. Amazingly she felt as if she'd slept better that last hour than she had the whole night. It might've had something to do with Nathaniel not being within arm's reach the whole time. Nathaniel was combing his long hair as she came to and he pointed her to a can on the nightstand.

"What?" she asked confused.

"Drink it." Ashley took the can and sipped it. A powerful taste of acid and syrup rushed down her throat and she almost gagged.

"What is that?" she asked.

"Liquid caffeine," said Nathaniel with a devilish smile. "Trust me, you're going to need it." Ashley grumbled and took the can with her to get ready. She took quick, hard sips as often as she could as she cleaned herself. Nathaniel didn't need to get prepared much. She on the other hand had so much more to do.

Nathaniel was watching some program on TV when Ashley came out of the bathroom fully dressed. He turned off the TV and eyed her eagerly. She wore a long black dress. The dress was open and free flowing at the bottom, but at the waist up it was tight and showed off her lean frame. It showed off little cleavage, yet Nathaniel thought it appealed more. The tightness of the dress showed something was there, but she wasn't freely flaunting it. The dress covered up to her shoulders but left her arms bare. In the open space around her neck sat the wolf pendant he'd given her. Her black hair washed down the back beautifully, not clashing with the dress, but enhancing it.

"Well." She spun in a small circle for him. "How do I look?"

"You look stunning," he said as he rose to his feet.

"Thanks." Ashley smiled and felt the dress. "This was my mother's dress." A small tear appeared in her eye, but it never sank to her cheek. "I think it fits me."

"I think so too," said Nathaniel.

"I was worried it'd be too much black," she said before pulling out Nathaniel's cloak, "but with this." She threw his cloak around her, covering her with white fur. "I think we'll make a good contrast."

"We know who the light and dark one is in this relationship," he said with a laugh.

"We all hide our true colors," said Ashley sweetly. She kissed him and looked him over. She'd expected him to be getting ready, but he'd done nothing other than tidy himself. He wore dark brown pants and a button up black shirt with his normal tennis shoes.

"I thought you'd be more dressed up."

"I will be, but my suit isn't worn the same way as yours. You have a fancy dress and I have a fancy fur coat." Ashley frowned but understood. She couldn't imagine Nathaniel trying to go about in a full suit and then having to change into a werewolf. She thought of him as a werewolf wearing a suit and that brought a smile to her face.

They met the rest of the family and uncle Ben in the lobby. They were all dressed very casually and Ashley felt out of place. Both Melissa and Mary were in flowing skirts with fine shirts, but they didn't even come close to the formalness of Ashley's dress.

"Ashley you look more beautiful than the rest of us," said Ben. Ashley blushed and unconsciously moved her dress about.

"Until you all change," said Ashley. "Then I'll be the one standing out."

"You look okay," said Lidia as she came out from behind her mother. "I guess you can stand by me."

Ashley smirked and knelt to hug Lidia. Lidia's hair had been combed thoroughly to give her nice wavy locks and there were bows in her hair. This was perhaps the first time Ashley had ever seen her completely clean top to bottom. She wore a cute blue and white dress. She clacked her little black shoes together and gave them all a toothy grin.

"My apologies," said Ben as he bowed to Lidia, "you are easily as fair as Ashley." Ashley curtsied back to Ben, but Lidia didn't. Instead she stuck out her finger and retorted powerfully.

"You bet I am." Everyone laughed except for Melissa who picked Lidia up by the back of her dress. Poor Melissa must have so much trouble keeping order and manners in this family.

"Let's go," said Morgan as he threw a large bag over his shoulder. All of the boys picked up a bag and followed him. Nathaniel carried his on his left shoulder and held Ashley's hand with his right.

"What's in there?"

"Supplies for the wedding," said Nathaniel.

"It's the duty of every family to bring something out to the party," continued Morgan. Ashley wondered how heavy the bulging bags were. She assumed there was probably a reason all the boys were carrying them.

Ashley expected to head for the car when they headed out, but she was surprised when they instead walked into the forest. They headed up a hill with their giant bags over their shoulders. Ashley walked next to Nathaniel, carrying only her small handbag but she was having the most trouble. Her little flats and nice dress weren't exactly made for hiking.

Once they'd left the hotel behind, the family moved off to a secluded area and left Lidia and Ashley waiting. They came out a few minutes later as wolves with their giant packs secured on their backs. Ashley wondered if it was safe to do this so close to the hotel. She didn't have their powerful senses though, so she just left it to them to know if they were being watched or not.

She patted Nathaniel as he came near and threw on his riding cloak. The bags he had on were near the back and she found she had somewhat of a seat amongst them. She was also comforted to know the baggage would help block any chance of her dress revealing anything on the ride. The cloak should do the job, but it was reassuring to know if it didn't, something else would.

"Are we going fast?" she asked Nathaniel. He shook his head and Ashley hugged him. "Good, I don't think I could handle it in this dress." He laughed and waited for her to get in position. Ashley also didn't think her body would appreciate a fast ride right now. Morgan barked for them to advance and away they went.

The wolves long strides still meant they were moving swiftly even without running. Ashley relaxed a little on Nathaniel's back and admired the forest. Its trees and plants were different than those she was used to, but the scenery wasn't. The forest air was still cool and calm. The silence she was so used to was in the air. It didn't matter which forest or mountain they were in; this was still a wolf's life. Even if she was only human, she felt right at home here. Escaping into the wilderness like this had become more of a home for her than the city she'd grown up in.

Ashley watched Ben move with the pack and realized he didn't quite fit in. He moved near the front with his brother, but he stayed a little to the side. He was a member of his family, but not of this pack. His movements weren't as subtle or in sync with the rest.

After walking for some time, Ashley heard barking ahead and looked up expectantly. She'd never seen any other werewolves besides Nathaniel's family before. Uncle Ben hadn't been much of a difference since he looked so much like his brother, but they were coming to a gathering of dozens of werewolves. Families from all over would be gathering for this event. It would be her chance to see what other werewolves looked like.

They rose over a hill and Ashley gasped in delight. There were wolves everywhere. They varied in size and color as much as the trees in autumn. Some families were mingling while others stood apart and waited for the festivities. Nathaniel's family seemed to be the average pack size at seven. From what she could see, there were a few smaller, probably newer families in the works. One group which sat apart though had to have at least a dozen members.

And there were people! Ashley saw there were many normal humans riding atop werewolves just like her. Males and females of all ages sat casually amongst the great wolves. Morgan had told her there would be other humans mixed in, but she'd never imagined so many. She couldn't believe this many people were being brought into werewolf families.

The best part was they all looked accepted. None of the wolves looked angrily at the humans with them. Ashley had expected someone to have some kind of aggression towards them, but nobody seemed hostile. Morgan led the way down the hill and barked loudly to announce their arrival. All of the other families turned their heads and barked back excitedly.

They were deep in the forest, but it was amazing such an event like this could be kept a secret. There were nearly thirty werewolves in attendance and it didn't appear they were the last family to arrive. She didn't know how nobody could notice and she voiced her opinion to Nathaniel. He growled something to Lidia who turned on her mother's back.

"Nathaniel says it's a big forest." Morgan barked something. "And dad says they have people watching the boundaries of this area. We see everything before they see us."

So they had sentries guarding the campsite. Now it made sense why no one would ever find them. They wouldn't even have to hurt wayward hikers either. Anyone with a sense of self-preservation who heard wolves wouldn't wander further into the area. She wondered what happened to the people without common sense.

They approached another steep hill which had a long white rug going down it. Most of the wolves were gathered around it and she figured it must be for the ceremony. Morgan kept his family a bit towards the back with the other wolves with humans.

"You got a real beauty there," said a woman. Ashley looked back confused at first. Then she realized the woman was speaking about Nathaniel. She leaned down and pet Nathaniel's head affectionately.

"I know. Thank you."

The woman nodded and went back to talking to a man nearby. There were four other humans there that she could see and to her great surprise, only one was her age. The woman who'd spoken to her was middle aged and so was the man. One man was old enough to be her grandpa and he was still riding a wolf. The remaining girl looked to be a year or two older than her.

"Ladies and gentlemen!" shouted a voice in front of her. Ashley turned to see a man in robes standing at the front of the white rug. He wasn't a priest Ashley decided. He was probably another werewolf just in human form. It was probably out of respect so their human guests could understand. "We are here today to celebrate the union of two families. Mr. Samson Rotic and Ms. Emma Comet. I can see many old friends here. I can also see many new friends many of us do not know. At this time will any unknown guests come before the bride and groom for presentation." Nathaniel nodded to Ashley and she understood. This was her turn to be shown off.

"First however," started the man, "we must introduce our two greatest guests this evening. Will you all please welcome Mr. Samson Rotic!" The announcer stepped aside and held his hands out to his right. There was a round of barking and applause. Ashley watched with some amusement as some of the wolves stood on two feet and actually clapped their paws together.

Samson was a lean werewolf with a bit of a big head thought Ashley. He had darker fur, a good mixture of brown and black going down his back. Under his head was a thin patch of grays and whites which went to his belly. He walked with pride and obvious happiness. He rose to his full height for all of the crowd to see before settling back down.

"And Ms. Emma Comet."

Ashley was surprised to see the bride come out of the forest as a normal woman. She had dark curly hair and was almost as tall as Ashley. She wore a long white wedding dress, complete with laced sleeves and gloves. She had no veil on her head and she walked down the path carefully. Ashley wondered why she'd come down as a human. Her first thought was maybe she just wanted to wear the dress, but then it occurred to her that she might be human. She'd always assumed someone would be turned into a werewolf before they got married. After seeing some of the older couples riding nearby, she thought maybe that wasn't always the case. The bride stopped next to the groom and placed her hand on his head. The groom barked something and then the bride spoke after him.

"Thank you all for coming. We're happy to see everyone here and for those we don't know, we can't wait to meet all of you."

The announcer moved off to the side to give the floor to the couple. He hopped onto a large rock to oversee the ceremony. The oldest man stepped off his wolf and moved to make his introduction. Ashley watched as all the wolves leaned close as he walked down the aisle. After a few introductions, Morgan growled something and Lidia looked at Ashley.

"Dad says you need to get off Nathaniel to walk down."

"Okay." Nathaniel laid down so Ashley could get off of him with some decency. She smoothed down her dress quickly to get out any wrinkles and noticed Nathaniel had shed on her. She plucked the white hairs from her dress as fast as she could.

"It's almost your turn," said Lidia excitedly.

"Hold this for me Nathaniel," said Ashley as she threw off his cloak. To Ashley's great misery, a large gust of wind moved past them just then. Ashley's hair billowed behind her madly. Her dress was fortunately long enough that when it shifted in the wind it didn't reveal anything.

"Who is that back there?" shouted the announcer.

Ashley froze as all eyes unexpectedly turned to her. She tried to stand composed and quiet, but the wind kept making her hair dance back and forth. Morgan barked to the crowd. Lidia stood on her mother's back and translated for those who were human.

"The Lexington family, here with our guest Ashley Lebell." Some of the people were looking at her as if something was wrong. A few wolves took a step forward and their lips went up slightly. Nathaniel stepped in front of Ashley and growled.

"You bring a dangerous guest to our midst Mr. Lexington," said the announcer. "What would cause you to bring one of *them*?" Ashley tried to understand what they or she had done wrong. Sure she wasn't a werewolf, but there were plenty of humans there. Morgan barked back.

"What do you mean?" asked Lidia. The announcer stayed quiet and tried not to look at Ashley. One of the other werewolves barked at her and made her jump. Nathaniel's family went quiet and looked at Ashley. She hated not knowing what was being said. The tension was killing her.

Then the tension vanished as Lidia started laughing. She laughed so hard she rolled off of her mother's back. By the loud cry of panic that followed, Ashley guessed Lidia hadn't meant to do that. The rest of the family followed suit and started chuckling. Ashley poked the back of Nathaniel's head.

"What?" she asked. Morgan barked something to the announcer and the other wolves. Most of the wolves instantly relaxed, but a few still shied away from her glance. "Lidia?" asked Ashley. Lidia reappeared giggling as she climbed back onto her mother.

"They thought you were a witch."

Ashley looked at the crowd stunned. They had thought she was a witch? How? What did witches even look like? She was just in her long black dress and black flats. Was it because she was wearing all black or something?

"Our apologies Ms. Lebell," said the announcer. "I'm afraid we had you confused with someone else."

"It's alright," she said still confused. She'd have to remember to ask Nathaniel about this later.

"If you would please," waved the announcer. "Come down the aisle so we may see you as one of us."

Ashley walked down the path as confidently as she could. It was weird how calm she was considering she had dozens of werewolves on either side of her. This would be a terrifying scene for any normal person, but she was used to it by now. She didn't see the gigantic wolves sniffing at her, she saw normal people just like Nathaniel.

While most of the wolves treated her just like any other guest, there were a few who still stayed away from her. They sniffed at her from a distance and seemed reluctant to do even that. They avoided her when she looked their way and honestly seemed afraid. Ashley couldn't help but smile at how odd it was. The giant werewolves were afraid of the normal human girl. She reached the couple up ahead and curtsied to them.

"Thank you for coming," said the bride. The groom merely barked and sniffed loudly.

"Thank you for having me," said Ashley. She rose and walked slowly back toward Nathaniel.

Nathaniel nodded to her when she got back. Ashley didn't immediately get back on him, but stood with her arm draped over him. She was already sore and tired of sitting. The next guest was walking down the path, but Ashley sensed many eyes were still on her. She'd made quite an impression on the crowd without having to do anything.

The introductions lasted only about five minutes and then all the guests were accounted for. Ashley thought they were going to go when the final guest strode down the aisle. It had never occurred to Ashley that the bride herself would have to do the same thing. This confirmed for her that she was not a werewolf and her scent had to be brought up just the same. Only when she walked past, the wolves barked their approval happily and bowed their heads in honor. The bride walked with elegance and strength amongst the mighty wolves. She was merely a human, but she walked as if she were the queen of them today. Ashley admired the strength she projected.

"Today we are here to see this great couple become one," said the announcer proudly. "These two will leave their families and make a new pack of their own." The wolves barked loudly. "But no pack can survive if they cannot move as one. Today we will follow them on the path they have chosen. We shall see how well suited they really are for each other." Ashley thought the words were dangerous to hear at your wedding, but neither bride nor groom flinched. The bride stood next to her fiancé and cracked her knuckles.

"Are we ready to ride?" she asked the packs of werewolves before her and was instantly met with approval. "Then unload your burdens and let us be on our way."

"We're going to drop everything over there," said Lidia, pointing to a clearing up ahead. It wasn't too far away and Ashley started to walk when Nathaniel barked at her. "You should get on. It gets crowded." Ashley climbed onto Nathaniel's back and instantly understood what Lidia meant. The clearing was large, but dozens of werewolves filled up any space easily. They jostled against each other, pushed and shoved just like any other crowd. The smallest wolf present was still twice a human's size, so staying up high was the wisest move.

Bags were dropped and deposited all over the place. Anywhere seemed to do, just as long as one's pack got everything in the same area. Most of the packs looked the same and none of them were named, but

Ashley felt that probably didn't matter. The wolves could simply sniff out whatever they needed.

"Are you helping?" asked the older man, pointing to Ashley.

"Helping?" asked Ashley, turning about as Nathaniel moved around. "Helping with what?"

"Those of us not riding set up everything while they run. You don't quite look like you're set for a hard ride." Ashley looked at Nathaniel who only shrugged. He barked something at Lidia who in turn looked at Ashley.

"It's up to you. People who don't ride and old wolves don't usually run, so they set up while we're gone." Ashley looked at the old man and back down to Nathaniel. Her body ached and she wasn't dressed much for riding, but she didn't know anyone in camp. She was trying to think when she saw something alarming approaching them.

It was another Nathaniel. A pure white wolf was making its way through the crowd. Ashley noted its fur wasn't quite as brilliant as Nathaniel's, but it was close. A few wolves were following this one as it met up with them. They barked and sniffed at each other in greeting.

"Hi!" said Lidia in greeting to all of them. Ashley just waved. She didn't appreciate how much the other white wolf was staring at her and Nathaniel. "Her name is Danica," said Lidia. Melissa barked quickly at Lidia and she sat back scared. Why didn't Melissa want to tell Ashley that?

She looked back at Danica and remembered something Melissa had once told her. Other wolves cherished the winter wolf look. Other girls their age would be coming after Nathaniel and his brilliant coat. Here was another winter wolf, a female, eyeing Nathaniel eagerly and Ashley dangerously. Nathaniel didn't change his posture, but Ashley found herself leaning forward. No words were spoken, but she knew instantly she had a rival.

"Miss? You staying?" asked the older gentleman. Melissa said something and Lidia looked at her.

"It would probably be better," said Lidia. If Melissa wanted to leave her behind, then that settled it. Ashley looked at the older man and shook her head.

"No. We ride as one." She patted Nathaniel affectionately.

"It's going to be a rough ride," said the older man. "Most people don't go on this for a reason."

It was true. Ashley saw most people had disembarked from their werewolf companions. Only one other remained on a wolf at this point. To her surprise, it was the other girl her age. The look on the girl's face said she was afraid of the same thing Ashley was.

"Wouldn't be the first time," laughed Ashley. "I'll be fine."

"Okay then. Good luck out there." The old man turned away to go help the others with the bags. Danica barked something and departed. The wolves behind her followed obediently. She hoped one of them snagged her before the night was done.

A war cry of some kind sounded at the far end of the camp. The soon to be married couple had ridden into sight. Emma was rearing back on her fiancé's back, crying out like a hunter. She had a spear in her hand which she planted into the ground. She threw back her head and let loose a long howl. Samson threw back his head and made the howl much more impressive.

"Here we go!" shouted Lidia as all the wolves began to howl.

Ashley looked for any semblance of rank or order, but there was none. All of the wolves were still mewling about, dropping bags or greeting friends when the howls went out. They all arched their heads and filled the sky with their piercing sound. Ashley howled right alongside Nathaniel.

The bride shrieked like a banshee and Samson bolted into the forest. Some of the wolves began to leap after them while others waited for the way to be cleared. Ashley saw Nathaniel's ears go down and braced herself. They were going fast today. They were going faster than she'd ever gone before.

Samson and Emma gained a great lead on the rest of the wolves as they'd started the race without telling anyone. Only the closest wolves were able to stay on their trail. The rest began the run slowly, allowing their packs to form up around them. Many of them crashed into each other for a chance to get ahead. Ashley held on to Nathaniel and trusted his nimbleness to get them through the crowd unharmed.

Then they were free in the forest. Ashley forgot about the run and marveled at the scene she was in. Dozens of gigantic wolves thundering across the ground all at once. A pack of bulls couldn't have made more noise. The sky darkened as every bird took the sky in a panic. Every small animal scurried to its den and shook furiously in fear. A storm of beasts had arisen and Ashley doubted there was anything which could halt them.

They ran through the hills at an alarming rate. The forest became a blur of fur as they moved with the other packs. Up ahead they could still hear Emma's shouts as she rode. Ashley and the other girl let loose their own cries as the beasts plowed their way through the foliage.

Ashley's whole body was aching and her fingers were white from holding on to Nathaniel so tightly. Her eyes couldn't keep track of the rapid movements and she felt sick, only she didn't have any time to be sick. Everything was happening so fast her instincts drove her to hold on and stay steady. There was no room for error. One wrong move and she'd be tumbling in the dirt behind Nathaniel. All of the stampeding wolves would probably not even notice she was there.

The run was not without foul play either. A race which was supposed to be all about the bride and groom was hardly just that. Other families were competing to see who could be the fastest and the strongest. More than one wolf was tripped or barreled into. One came into their group and tried to shove Kevin to the ground as they came around a bend. Kevin slid himself behind the wolf and barked angrily. Another came in the opening and tried to slide into Nathaniel's legs.

Ashley couldn't stop herself from screaming as Nathaniel leapt. He cleared the wolf in a single leap and planted his back foot on its face. He pushed off and forced the other wolf into the dirt before touching back down. Ashley bounced badly, but her limbs had a death grip on Nathaniel and she stayed. The other wolf snarled and started to come closer to Nathaniel as he landed, but he'd made a terrible mistake. He'd assumed since he'd pushed Kevin out of the way the boy would simply stay back. Kevin smashed his way under the wolf and threw him off the course with glee. Ashley looked around her, realizing what a madhouse she was in. The brothers barked congratulations to each other and kept going. Ben moved in behind the brothers and barked viciously. Nobody came back to bother them again.

Ashley kept an eye out to see if anyone else in the family had been bothered. She was worried about the bobbling Lidia now. Lidia knew how to keep herself in place for a rough ride alright, but it was a different matter if there was a fight. Whether it was out of respect or fear though, no issue started near Melissa. Ashley had a feeling everyone was honorable enough to not fight near a child. One probably innocent wolf came too close to the run and Morgan barreled him off the path. Even amongst so many other wolves, she could see Morgan was still one of the biggest present. He might've been the other reason nobody bothered them.

The ride only lasted ten to twenty minutes, but to Ashley it felt like it might've been an hour. The packs only slowed when they came back in sight of the camp. Ashley loosened her fingers on Nathaniel and laid down. She understood why the old man had said most people didn't take these trips. She sat up again and cheered to the other girl. They both looked frazzled, but they were proud of themselves. They'd survived the harsh ride with the wolves.

The bride stood next to her mount and cried like a war goddess one last time. Then she smiled and laughed, leaning up against her soon to be husband. Sweat glistened on her brow as she raised her arm. The wolves howled all around her and Ashley clapped her hands. She had a feeling the wolves approved of their ride. They would be married.

CHAPTER 18

BATTLES IN CELEBRATION

By the time they'd returned from the premarital run, the camp had been setup. There were tables and chairs set up along with food and drink. The wedding couple disappeared for a while as everyone else went to change. When they all left, Ashley found the only other girl who'd ridden through the premarital run. She extended her hand happily.

"Hi. I'm Ashley Lebell." The girl smiled and shook her hand back politely.

"Samantha Trevor." Samantha was a much smaller girl than Ashley. She must've barely been five feet tall. She was a small little thing with curly brown hair and big brown eyes. "I don't think we've met before. Did your pack come from around here?"

"No, we're from Montana. I think the groom is my boyfriend's dad's cousin," said Ashley.

"Oh nice. I'm from here. No relation, we're just friends with the bride."

"Okay," said Ashley. "I can't believe we did that run," she laughed. Samantha gave her an exhausted look and laughed back.

"It was scary." she giggled. "I've ridden my fiancé Henry before, but never like that."

"You're engaged?" asked Ashley more girlishly than she'd hoped. Samantha held up a shiny ring and grinned.

"Yup. I'm terrified to go through that run, but…" She looked down a bit and laughed. "He's definitely the one for me. What about you? You said yours was your boyfriend?"

"Yeah, Nathaniel and I are just dating. We just graduated high school together."

"Wow you're both young," said Samantha. "I thought you were older."

"Barely eighteen," smirked Ashley.

"Sam!" shouted a voice behind them. People were beginning to return to the camp. Samantha waved at someone and moved past Ashley.

"It was nice meeting you," said Samantha. "I'm sure we'll talk again later."

"Bye!" said Ashley cheerfully.

She looked at everyone coming back and was kind of surprised at their clothes. Almost nobody was dressed formally. Most of the men were dressed in large pants secured by a thick belt. Their tops were more like the top of a robe, very loose and kind of open. Some of the women wore tighter versions of the outfit, but most were in dresses like herself. She spotted Nathaniel's bright hair amongst the mix and went to him.

"Nice outfit," she said amused. He pulled on the loose clothing and smiled.

"You like it?"

"Not as formal as I would've guessed."

"Tradition," said Nathaniel. "Weddings weren't always a safe thing for werewolves, so they wore these outfits to allow for an easy transformation. Whether we need to fight or flee, we can do it without being constrained. We've never really changed in all the years I guess."

"Except for the girls," said Ashley as she looked at the multitude of dresses.

"Girls do tend to enjoy dressing up more than guys," agreed Nathaniel. "I honestly think we just hide behind tradition and wear these because we're lazy."

They found the rest of Nathaniel's family nearby and joined up. Everyone eventually corralled around the white path from before. Ashley was surprised to see there were no chairs for them to sit in. They all just kind of stood around and made sure they had a good view.

A few men stood on top of a few rocks and relaxed themselves with some violins and other simple instruments. Ashley watched amused as they played with their instruments for a while before they all came in together. A soft melody drifted down to the crowd and everyone became quiet. Nathaniel pointed to the end of the path as a few men took up their places.

Samson Rotic stood as a human with a few of his groomsmen. He was a little shorter than Ashley had expected. He had long black hair and darker skin. He shook hands with his groomsmen and best man. They whispered eagerly and just then the music changed. Classic wedding music began to drift down the aisle which filled their ears and excited their hearts. Ashley turned expectantly with Nathaniel.

Women in dresses were filing down towards the end of the carpet. As spectacular as they were trying to show themselves off, nobody cared about them. The only one they cared about was the bride, Ms. Emma. She strode down the aisle with her arm in her father's. The stout rider from before was gone and replaced by a blushing young woman. She was giggling happily as she came closer to her husband to be. Ashley held Nathaniel's hand tightly as they watched Emma's father pass her off to Samson.

The ceremony was very short and their vows beautiful. Ashley found herself scooting into Nathaniel and letting him hold her with both arms. She listened to the beauty of their words and felt as if she could sink into Nathaniel. Nathaniel must've felt the same as he dropped his head onto her shoulder and nuzzled close to her. When the priest announced their marriage was complete and the groom and bride to kiss, Ashley started to clap with everyone else. She missed the kiss though. Nathaniel had pulled her head back and kissed her instead.

Everyone applauded as the married couple walked down the white carpet and back out into the clearing. They headed off the path and a few people followed them. "They're going for the usual photography and such," said Nathaniel as everyone else went to the tables. "For now we all just need to sit and relax for a bit. A good time to meet everyone." Ashley didn't know anybody in the crowd except for Nathaniel's family and two others. She spotted Samantha sitting nearby and waved to her.

There was another she'd never been introduced to, but there wasn't a doubt in her mind who she was. Only Danica could have such natural bleach blonde hair. She and Nathaniel were the only ones who stuck out so dramatically and everyone constantly looked at them. Danica had to be near their age or possibly a little younger. She wore a tight green dress which made her eyes look like emeralds. There were a number of boys fawning over her, but she remained uninterested. It was obvious she was so used to being loved for her beauty that the interest of others did not bother her.

It was the way she looked at Nathaniel which bothered Ashley. Here was a man just like her. He was tall, handsome, and shared her illustrious coat of snow white fur. The only time her beautiful lips curved unpleasantly was when she locked eyes with Ashley. This girl in all black which held onto Nathaniel and claimed him as her own.

Ashley had more than one fight with Danica just by looking at her. Danica wanted Nathaniel from the first look and Ashley was determined to show her how much Nathaniel belonged to her. She put an arm around Nathaniel and kissed his cheek to reassure herself. Nathaniel smiled and returned the gesture. He seemed completely unaware of the invisible duel going on around him.

Ashley turned away from Danica and enjoyed some food with everyone else. There was no real meal here, just hundreds of appetizers. Ashley piled herself a small plate of treats and munched on them cheerfully. Everyone was in high spirits and showed it. Old friends talked and family reunited from all over the country. Ashley found herself laughing with people she didn't know and listening to stories of others she'd never met.

A quick whiny of a violin silenced the crowd suddenly. Everyone looked at the man with the violin as many other musicians assembled themselves around him. The man began a slower melody as he looked at the returning bride and groom. Samson took his wife's hand and led her in a dance. The crowd watched enthusiastically as he twirled her around. As the song became faster, so did their footsteps. The crowd began to clap as the couple moved as one. The song ended and everyone clapped louder. Samson kissed his bride and then addressed the crowd.

"Today we form a new pack, but today is a day of celebration. A day for all packs to come together and enjoy. So come on out! Let's get this wedding started!" The crowd cheered as Samson pointed to the band. The lead member nodded and began to play furiously. The beat became much faster and in Ashley's opinion, crazier.

Men began to rise left and right and held their hands out to ladies. Nathaniel rose and extended a hand towards Ashley. "May I have this dance?" he asked smoothly. Ashley smiled and took it. Nathaniel barely waited for her to be up before he pulled her out onto the dance floor. Everyone was joining in, forming a circle of dancers around the newlyweds.

Ashley hardly knew how to dance and neither did Nathaniel. She'd certainly never danced to music like this before. It was primitive, a weird mix of folk song and tribal music. She had no idea how she was expected to move to it.

Fast was the answer. As she was about to discover, werewolves didn't dance like most people did. Their dancing was fast paced and always on the move. Ashley found herself bobbing after Nathaniel as the crowd surged. The dancers jumped and clapped seemingly without pattern. Many of them danced with their eyes closed and just let the music take them. So attuned were they to the other dancers they didn't need to see.

Nathaniel may not have known how to dance normally, but he seemed right at home here. He spun with the crowd easily and never missed a beat. He stomped his feet with the others and clapped his hands above his head. Whereas Ashley spent most of her time fearing she'd trip over somebody, Nathaniel swayed back and forth easily. He laughed at Ashley's apparent awkwardness and took her hands in his. Ashley just let her body go loose and followed Nathaniel.

She wasn't sure how long she'd been dancing when her belly began to ache. She wasn't so sure about jumping around on a full stomach. She'd also needed to use the restroom for a while now and this wasn't helping. She kissed Nathaniel at the end of a song and told him she'd be right back. He nodded and continued to leap about with the others.

Just outside of the dancers, Ashley spotted Samantha. She was sitting on a bench and clapping with the dancers. She paused to wave at Ashley. "Any idea where the bathroom is?" Ashley asked. Samantha nodded and pointed down a path.

"It's down this way. I could use the restroom myself so I'll show you." Ashley followed Samantha away from the party and welcomed the silence of the forest. "You're quite the dancer," said Samantha suddenly.

"I try," said Ashley. "I can't keep up with Nathaniel though. He just never runs out of energy."

"Welcome to doing anything with werewolves. I'm just lucky Henry doesn't like to do too much dancing. His idea of a little dancing is almost all I can do."

"Nathaniel never gets bored dancing," said Ashley. "He'll probably do it all night." A woman passed them and said hello. Ashley could see a small shack up ahead. "Where did they find a bathroom out here?"

"They didn't," said Samantha solemnly. "They built it quickly for the wedding. It probably won't survive one good storm." Ashley silently agreed as they approached the building. It didn't look well-built and there was obviously no real facility. There were only three doors to the small shack. "It's no worse than a port-a-potty," said Samantha somewhat depressed. "I'll just warn you to hold your breath."

Ashley opened a door and felt the smell might push her back out. It was a tiny dirt room with an old toilet propped up in the corner. The only light was from the cracks along the ceiling which let in the sun. A box of paper covers and toilet paper was next to the toilet. She pulled down the simple wooden lock on the door and grimaced.

"It's better than going in the middle of the woods," said Samantha as they were walking away. Ashley had to give it at least that. With so many people around, she doubted she'd find a private space anywhere in these woods. The walls of the shack had made it more preferable. When they got back they saw the dancers were still going. Ashley could see Nathaniel jumping amongst them.

"You're right," laughed Samantha. "He never does get tired."

"Never ever," agreed Ashley. She was having a great time. She had a feeling nothing could go wrong today.

"Ashley?" Ashley flinched at the sound of Melissa behind her. Even Samantha shot a hesitant look past her to the tall mother. Ashley turned around slowly.

"Yes Melissa?" Melissa had a dangerous smile on her face.

"The band could use another player right now and I felt since you were just standing around..."

Ashley narrowed her eyes, but said nothing. She felt it was no coincidence that just as she was getting comfortable and making a friend, Melissa decided now would be a good time to interrupt. Melissa's bright eyes said she was right. Ashley had a bad surprise for her.

"I'm sorry. I completely forgot about it and left my flute in the hotel." It was the truth and Ashley was glad to have forgotten. She would much rather talk and dance than play with the band. Melissa's smile didn't lose any of its glamour as she suddenly produced Ashley's flute case.

"It was in the supply bag. I found it when I was unpacking." Ashley took the case from her and opened it. She could see her flute inside along with her sheets of music. She didn't know how Melissa got it in the bag, but she was trapped now. "I'll inform the band for you," she said with delight and passed by them. Ashley sent daggers into Melissa's back with her eyes, but it was all she could do. She sighed and looked at Samantha defeated.

"Wow she's intimidating," whispered Samantha.

"Tell me about it," said Ashley.

"Was she with the family you came in with?" Ashley nodded sadly.

"Mother of my boyfriend." Samantha cringed.

"I've been on the wrong side of that look before. I take it you did something to make her mad?" Ashley looked past Samantha to Melissa and a man she was speaking with. Melissa waved her over and Ashley felt a boulder sink in her stomach.

"You have no idea," she whispered to Samantha as she headed over. The band had paused for a moment and Ashley felt all their eyes moving towards her. Melissa brought her over with a warming smile.

"Everyone, this is Ashley. Ashley, this is Thomas, the lead player right now." Thomas eyed her nervously.

"Melissa says you're a pretty fierce player." Ashley was completely blown away by the man's thick accent. "You think you can keep up?"

"I'm sure she can," said Melissa. "I'll leave her in your hands Thomas." Melissa practically skipped away. Thomas watched her go and smiled at Ashley.

"Dangerous woman there. You seen the music we've been playing?" Ashley pulled out the sheets of music Melissa had given her. She suddenly prayed Melissa had actually given her the right music and not just random notes. Thomas flipped from song to song and smiled.

"Yup those are them. See the numbers on the edge there? Different for each song, I'll just call out a number and you can switch to them." Ashley nodded.

"I can do that."

"Right. It'll be nice to have a good flute in this mix."

Ashley placed her case with the others and quickly began to assemble her flute. She was sure she knew most of the basic songs by heart. She'd just need the notes for the more complex ones. Thomas and the others started up another song as she prepared herself. She blew a few practice notes and waited patiently for the song to end. She waved to Nathaniel as he skipped amongst the dancers.

The song came to an end and everyone clapped. Thomas held out four fingers and Ashley quickly found the sheet. She pressed her flute up against her lips and nodded to Thomas. The music started up again and Ashley let her notes flow with it. It was a quick song, but the beat only changed a few times. The hardest part for Ashley was just getting enough air to play until the next break.

After the first song, Ashley fell into rhythm with the rest of the players and began to enjoy herself. She'd never played with a full band before. She'd enjoyed listening to how her notes mixed in with those of the other players. The music was so powerful all around her. She shifted back and forth as she wanted to dance and play at the same time.

Something bright caught her eye amongst the dancers. She saw the flow of Nathaniel's hair and smiled at his rapid movements. Then she realized more shining hair was moving through the crowd. Danica! The girl was amongst the dancers and swirling rapidly. She kicked off the ground and leapt just as fiercely as the rest. She moved her body like a true dancer. She knew when to be suggestive and when to be powerful. Many eyes fell on the beauty of her movements, but she matched none of their looks. She had eyes for one of her own.

Ashley almost forgot how to play as she saw Danica move next to Nathaniel. She matched his moves and they flowed around each other. Nathaniel grinned eagerly at the challenge. To him this was all just a fun game. He was laughing as he danced and she came with him. Danica gradually brought her moves closer to him with each passing minute.

Ashley looked at Melissa and saw she was watching the dancing with great interest. She passed her gaze over to Samantha and she looked concerned. The look she gave Ashley said there was foul play afoot here. Melissa had planned this little adventure well. By putting her with the band she had a chance to shame her. Now that Ashley was doing a good job, she was trapped into staying while Nathaniel danced alone.

Danica danced next to Nathaniel quickly and beautifully. Even Ashley had to admit the girl was a natural. She'd never have moves as graceful or seductive as the white haired girl. When Danica laid her arms on him Ashley felt her temperature rising. Danica shot her a look which she said she was taking Nathaniel and there was nothing she could do about it. Ashley was so angry she missed the next couple of notes. As the song ended, she could see Melissa giggling a bit.

Then Danica put down the last weight on the scale and sent Ashley overboard. Nathaniel thanked her for the dance and Danica planted a quick kiss on his cheek. Ashley felt she might crumple her flute with her bare hands. She turned away so she didn't throw her flute through the crowd like a spear. Thomas and the others paused as they saw the fumes coming off of Ashley. She was a bomb waiting to blow and they were all the closest targets.

"You okay?"

Ashley shot him a threatening look and then smiled cruelly. She had a way to stop all this. All of the tools she needed were in her hands and standing right in front of her. She scattered her music notes and pulled up the song she was thinking of. She held it in front of Thomas and commanded.

"Wait for me to start then play this." She took in a deep breath and stepped away from the band. Thomas passed the number back so everyone knew what song.

"Are we going to do it?" asked one of the players. Thomas nodded only slightly and shot a sideways glance to the player.

"One thing me ma taught me, never provoke an angry witch." The other players all nodded and waited.

Ashley stepped down from the small hill and blew a colorful line of notes. All eyes came to her as she approached. The song started slow and quiet. Ashley used its quiet melody to step into the crowd while nobody was dancing. She played softly and began to move her feet to the music. When she was sure all eyes were upon her, she let loose.

Thomas took the cue and the rest of the band backed her song. The beat was growing stronger and faster. Ashley danced forward and back, waving her long black hair around her. Ashley couldn't move more than her feet while playing, but move them she did. She slid forward and clapped her feet against the cool earth below. The crowd started to dance, but it was much slower than the music called for. They were too interested in this dark haired girl whirling through the crowd.

Ashley felt the tempo begin to rise and made her move. She stopped her dancing and advanced quickly through the crowd. She found Nathaniel waiting for her in the middle and Danica not far. Ashley slowed her steps in front of him, blowing sweet notes all around him. She walked slowly around him, never missing a beat. He turned as she went, watching her amused. When she stood between him and Danica, she leaned back against him and began to backpedal. Danica shot her a foul look as the crowd laughed at her obvious slight. Ashley almost couldn't continue to play she was smiling so hard.

After she'd scooted Nathaniel away a bit, she turned on him and began to rock back and forth. Nathaniel began to shift with her. Ashley tried not to smile as she danced around him the best she could while playing. Some in the crowd began to clap as they moved around each other. Any other day Ashley would've been embarrassed, but not now. This was her dance as much as Nathaniel was her boyfriend. She wanted Danica, Melissa, and every other girl to see this.

The more she danced, the more she played. Soon the speed and the notes didn't belong to the original song anymore. It became her song, a unique play of music just for them. She moved faster and intertwined Nathaniel in her music. She lost sight of the crowd and the forest. All that existed in her world right now was Nathaniel and the music. She spun around faster and faster until she suddenly came to a stop. Somehow she knew the music was done. Just as the band hit their final notes she stopped playing and held her flute into the sky like a sword.

The crowd cheered and clapped. Ashley was aware of them once more and she felt the sweat coming down her face. She wasn't sure how she'd pulled all that off, but now she felt tired. She gasped happily and looked about the crowd for Danica's bright blonde hair. Despite being so unique, she was not to be found. Nathaniel took her and leaned her over before she could say a word. His lips met hers and the cheering only became louder. When they parted she rubbed his face and smiled.

"You never cease to amaze me," he said as he pulled her back upright.

Ashley just smiled. She wasn't sure she had the strength to speak right now. The sound of heavy cups beating against each other drew everyone's attention to one of the tables. The crowd parted and Ashley saw the bride and groom were looking at them intently.

"I just wanted to say that was beautiful," said the bride as she clapped her hands. Ashley did a small bow. The groom spoke up to Nathaniel.

"What's your name son?"

"Nathaniel." The groom held up his mug and smiled.

"Nathaniel, your witch can play a mean song."

The crowd laughed and Ashley joined in. Cheers came out for more songs, but Nathaniel fortunately waved them down. She'd gladly play again in a bit, but she needed a drink after that. Thomas was more than happy to entertain them while they waited for Ashley to join back in.

CHAPTER 19

ACCEPTANCE

Ashley was relaxing at the table with Mary and Samantha when she saw people were starting to clean up. A large number of guests were packing up food and drinks, collecting trash, and clearing the tables.

"I thought the party lasted all night?" she asked Mary.

"It does," said Nathaniel as he came to clear their table. "We're changing location for the night party."

"Why?" asked Ashley.

"Wolves, we're kind of a nomadic group," said Mary. "We're always on the move." Ashley felt she should've expected this. She stood up and started to help them clean up things.

"Nathaniel." Ashley felt the hair rise on the back of her neck as Melissa appeared behind them.

"Yes mom?"

"Can I borrow Ashley for a moment?" Nathaniel looked at Ashley and smiled supportively.

"Of course. We can finish up without her."

Ashley really wished he would've said no. She didn't want to be left alone with Melissa any more than she had to. It was bad enough that she intimidated Ashley. Now she knew she was actively trying to sabotage her relationship. Melissa turned and headed out of the camp a little. Ashley was growing less and less tolerant of Melissa's little antics too. She wasn't sure how much longer she could pretend to be nice to her. She stopped when they were next to the bags of supplies they'd brought for the wedding.

"It's been a long time since you and I have gotten along Ashley," said Melissa suddenly. "I'll admit, it's not easy for me to see you around my son." Ashley sighed and decided to bite the bullet.

"I'm sorry. I know I can't ever reassure you." Melissa smiled and started to unzip one of the bags.

"I've been mean to you. I've ignored you. I've made life for you in my household as unpleasant as possible. Yet you keep coming back." Ashley held herself as tall as she could.

"And I always will."

"Oh to be young." Melissa sighed and rose with a large paper package.

"Honey?" asked Morgan as he came down the path. "You ready to go?"

"Yes dear. I just figured Ashley might need this if we're going to the next party." Melissa handed her the package as Morgan came down the hill. Morgan kissed his wife and grabbed most of the bags. Melissa took the last few and together they left Ashley standing there.

Ashley looked down at the package curiously. It was heavy and yet the package folded easily. She pulled the paper apart and was surprised to see a white cloth on the other side. She pulled what she thought was a coat out, but it was much too large. The package fell away and the cloth unfurled before her.

It was a cloak. It was a riding cloak just like Nathaniel's. It was just as white as his fur and was lined with silver. The edges had fur as did the hood. It was so soft and warm. Ashley felt like she was holding a little piece of Nathaniel when she threw on the cloak. It fit her perfectly, unlike Nathaniel's which hung like an oversized comforter. This was a cloak for her.

"Wow," said Mary as she came down the hill. Ashley turned to her and blushed.

"Your mom gave it to me." Mary smiled.

"I guess this means mom likes you again. You know she makes those herself." Ashley ran her finger through the cloak.

"I can't believe she made this for me. What did I do to change her mind?"

"You fought for Nathaniel today," said Ben as he came down the hill. "You didn't let the she-wolf take him away. You not only stood your ground, you brought the fight. I was standing with Morgan and Melissa when you pulled your little stunt. They were very impressed." Ashley blushed.

"Thank you."

"You best run along Mary," said Ben. "I'll bring Ashley to Nathaniel."

"Okay, see you in a minute," said Mary as she ran off. Ben put a large arm over Ashley's shoulders and brought her up the hill.

"I know you're still getting used to this Ashley, but you're doing pretty good. You see, Melissa never disliked you, she just didn't know if she could trust you. She was afraid if trouble came again, you'd just run away like you did before. She sent Danica after Nathaniel not because they make a cute pair, but because it would test you. She was expecting you'd just sit back and watch it all happen." Ben laughed and thrust his fist forward. "But you showed that girl! Made her look like a fool in front of the whole party." Ashley knew she shouldn't be laughing, but she couldn't help it. She'd defeated Danica and won Melissa's approval in the same moment.

"Just do me a favor tonight, okay?" said Ben.

"What?" Ben looked around and bent down to whisper to her.

"Stay with the family all of tonight. I really doubt anything would happen, but…" Ben shrugged. "You know how jealous and petty some girls can get." Ashley nodded and kept that in mind. "And here's your ride!"

Nathaniel was approaching as a wolf. His tail was wagging and she could see the surprise in his eyes. She pulled her hood over her head and stood next to him proudly. They looked one and the same now. Nathaniel barked his approval.

"You kids have fun," said Ben. "I'm going to go get changed so we can go." Nathaniel laid down so Ashley could climb on. When she laid down on his back she felt like she'd become invisible. She blended perfectly with his soft coat as they walked. She only lifted her head when they were in formation with the family. Everyone was looking at her with a smile.

"Ashley is all pretty now!" shouted Lidia. Ashley threw back her hood and let her black hair mesh with the white fur of the cloak.

"I'm always pretty." Lidia giggled and Ashley looked down at Melissa. "Thank you for the cloak, it's beautiful." Melissa barked a welcome back to her. A minute later Ben appeared behind them and Morgan barked for his family to advance.

As they walked, Ashley saw Danica's beautiful coat amongst the wolves. Her eyes were focused on her and Ashley shot her the smile of a victor. This was her family to ride with and nobody else's.

"It's supposed to be quiet out here!" shouted Alex angrily at the forest. "Either come inside or quit making such a racket!" He slammed the door and headed back to the living room. The basement door was filled with scratches and barking. "Be quiet already!" shouted Alex at the dogs.

All of Morgan's dogs were barking and had been all night. No matter what he did he couldn't get them to shut up. He'd finally had to shut them in the basement to at least block out most of the noise. All he'd wanted was a nice relaxing night and watching some movies on Morgan's giant TV. Was that so much to ask for?

The only trouble with the Lexington's going on vacation was their dogs. Alex had volunteered to housesit for them while they were away. He took a few days off work and was more than ready to relax. He brought Roland up to the house and left him with the other dogs. They might all be dancing at a wedding and sitting with people they'd never met, but Alex was alone. As he relaxed in Morgan's giant chair, Alex sighed happily. This was his idea of a vacation.

He'd also found an unexpected treat in the form of Morgan's liquor cabinet. He knew Morgan enjoyed a good drink once in a while and Alex had to admit the man had good taste. Morgan was such a big guy that it would certainly take a lot to get him drunk. Combine that with him being a werewolf and Alex suddenly understood why he'd never been able to out drink him. Either way, he was sure Morgan wouldn't mind if he helped himself to a shot of this and a shot of that.

He lounged happily. There were empty glasses strewn all over the table and the TV was blaring. He envied Morgan's house out here up in the mountain. Half the reason Alex had moved to this town was to get away from the noise and the lights, but they still existed somewhat in town. Out here though, there was nothing. The darkness was pure and the silence was to die for. He could be a very happy man living out here.

Out in the wilderness that he loved, dark figures began to move towards the house. They were just as dark as the sky and as silent as the night. They came from all directions with one thing on their mind. To find the man in the house and silence him.

Ashley gasped with delight as the trip came to an end. They'd gone further up into the mountains and left civilization behind. They were on top of a large clearing with nothing around for miles. The area was lit only by torches, campfires, the stars, and the moon above. There were tables set up, filled with food and drinks. They were one of the last families to arrive and the camp was being assembled rapidly.

They dropped off their supplies and Ashley went about helping anyone who was human while Nathaniel's family changed. Many people complimented her cloak and musical talent. She just blushed and tried to help lay out anything she could. The supernatural strength of the werewolves made the creation of the camp very quick. Giant containers of ice, kegs of beer, piles of wood, and anything else large could be carried by a single person. Ashley soon found herself standing around more than helping.

"Ashley, help us get this party started!" shouted Thomas as he pulled out his violin. A smile grew on her face and she rushed after him with her flute. He was gathering band members at a table. There was a rush of music sheets and instruments being handed out. He handed a sheet to Ashley and asked her if she could keep along. She put her flute together and grinned.

"Whenever you're ready!" she said.

"Ladies and gentlemen!" shouted Thomas. "If we may have your attention please!" All eyes fell upon him as he stood on top of the table. "We are here tonight to celebrate Mr. and Mrs. Rotic!" A cheer came up from the people. "And I say we celebrate!" He drew a long note along his violin before he began to play loudly.

Ashley chimed in almost instantly as did a few others. When the others had their instruments out and ready, they simply jumped into the song halfway through. It was a beautiful jumble of music with no real pace or rhythm, but it was certainly uplifting. People cheered and the drinks were poured by the dozen. Laughter began and Ashley looked into the sky as she played a long note.

Now this was how to spend a night.

"What is wrong with all of you!" demanded Alex angrily.

The dogs continued to bark and scratch at the door, but Alex wasn't about to get up for them. He waved his hand at the other side of the house and took another drink. The ice clinked in his glass and he sighed as the drink was no more.

He laid his head back and easily blocked out the sound of the dogs. He wasn't sure what glass this was but he knew it felt damn good. It has been too long since he was this relaxed.

The dogs continued to pound at the basement door as people moved through the house. The leading vampire had planned a bigger assault, but the front door had no lock on it. He'd simply pulled it open and slipped inside with the others behind him. They walked tenderly across the floor, careful not to make the slightest squeak on the wooden floors. He had been ready to pounce at the sound of the man, but his voice portrayed him to be drunk and sleepy. He would be an easy kill.

The vampire peered around the corner and saw Alex sitting in a chair next to the couch. It looked like a large lounge chair and its back was to the vampire. The man could not hear him coming nor was he in a position to see him. The vampire's fangs came out.

Nathaniel pulled Ashley away from the band after a few songs and brought her over to their table. Lidia and Samuel were dancing with a few kids nearby and the parents were all clapping with them. Mary was even trying her luck dancing between the tables with a few other girls. Ashley was amazed no boy had asked her to dance yet. Then she noticed the dangerous eyes of Morgan following his little girl and she thought she might know why she was alone.

Nathaniel gave her a kiss and sat on the table and put his foot on the bench. Ashley stood next to him and tasted something bitter on her lips. She looked at Nathaniel who had a bizarre smile on his face.

"Have you been drinking?" she asked. Nathaniel pulled up a tankard from behind him and took a quick swig before putting it back down. Uncle Ben cheered behind him as he brought more glasses to the table.

"Maybe," said Nathaniel and Ashley laughed. "Care to try it? It's really good!"

"No thanks. I'll watch you instead."

"Nonsense!" said Ben loudly. "It's a celebration of the highest order. You're adults and you may have a drink with the rest of us." Melissa stepped over and moved the mug away that Ben had offered.

"If you're going to give the girl something, at least give her something good." Melissa pulled a different cup aside and handed it to Ashley. "Trust me on this one Ashley."

Ashley took the cup and basked in Melissa's good mood. She hadn't seen her look so happily on Ashley in a long time. She took a sip of the beer carefully and was instantly surprised by its taste. It wasn't bitter or strong like she'd expected. It was actually very sweet and light. Melissa looked at her and waited for approval. Ashley tilted the cup back and took a big gulp. Ben and Morgan cheered and emptied their glasses at once. Nathaniel hugged Ashley with one arm before going back to his drink. Melissa held up her glass and clinked it against Ashley's. They knocked back the glasses and Ashley felt warm.

"So this is what happens at the night party?" she asked. Nathaniel shook his head.

"Naw, just part of it." He hopped off the table and took her hand. "May I have this dance?"

"One more drink first," said Ben. Melissa elbowed him off the bench and he fell back laughing. Morgan clapped the table and almost fell backwards himself he was laughing so hard. Melissa just smiled at Nathaniel and Ashley.

"You two go have fun." Nathaniel pulled Ashley away from the tables and held her hands as they danced. Ashley laughed as Nathaniel leaned in to kiss her.

"Are we starting to have a good time?"

"I don't think I could be any happier than I am tonight," laughed Ashley as she kissed Nathaniel. "Nothing could ruin tonight."

The vampire snapped around the side of the chair and before Alex could even utter a word, the vampire's teeth sunk in.

CHAPTER 20

TRUE DANCE OF THE NIGHT

And all at once the vampire knew he'd been tricked. His teeth sank not into a man, but the cold plastic of a dummy. A mannequin sat in the empty chair fully dressed and looking like it was watching TV.

The jarring sound of a shotgun took the room and the vampire was blown off the chair. The other vampires looked around panicked before more shells scattered through the room and took them apart. They sizzled and burnt into ash as the torturous silver shells embedded themselves into their flesh. None of them could find their attacker before he dropped them. Those who survived the initial volley retreated back into the hallway or the dining room.

Alex reloaded his shotgun quickly and knocked the closet door open with his shoulder. There was a closet behind the chair with not a full door, but a bi-fold door so he could sort of see through it. He'd seen the signs of the vampires coming and he'd been ready. It was easy to set up the dummy and make the vampires believe he was drunk and helpless. The dogs were both the hardest and easiest thing to plan. They could've scared away the vampires if they thought he was onto them. On the other hand, they also announced when the vampires had arrived and Alex was waiting for them. He grinned as he stepped into the living room.

It was time for the prey to become the predator.

He stepped into the dividing room between the kitchen, the hallway, and the living room. He blasted a vampire in the dining room before he turned his attention to the hallway. Vampires and ghouls alike tried to find places to hide from the deadly man. They leapt into rooms and even back outside as the shotgun blazed down the hall. Alex walked with a calm demeanor as he hunted the vampires.

The door to Mary's room came open and a vampire forced Alex against the wall. A quick butt from his shotgun sent it stumbling back. He spun the shotgun around to face the vampire and it turned to dust a moment later. He felt the last shell exit the shotgun and he let the weapon fall to the floor.

The side door to the upstairs came open, but Alex shouldered it in the vampire's face. Alex put his foot against the door to hold it shut before he drew his pistol. He fired a few rounds through the door before back at the front door where they were trying to regroup. Crashes of glass came from both the dining room and living room and Alex felt his surprise advantage was about to wear out.

Fortunately the vampires seemed confused by the chaos which made their ghoul subordinates even more confused. One was wounded by the door and couldn't escape without coming into Alex's line of fire.

Eager to escape, he tried the basement door to see if there was another way out.

What he found were four enormous dogs on the other side just as eager to get at the invaders in their home. The ghoul tried to close the door, but their large noses and heads wedged the door open. The ghoul was hurt and the four dogs easily overpowered him.

The ghoul went down screaming and the dogs burst into the hallway just as the vampires did. They hesitated in surprise as the single dangerous man suddenly had allies. Neither the dogs nor Alex hesitated and their attack was renewed with even greater vigor. The dogs were dangerous to the ghouls, but to the vampires they realistically posed no threat. The dog's bites hurt, but they didn't have the strength to bring them down.

No, the real threat came from Alex. The danger from the dogs was not their teeth, but their size and the fact that once they clamped onto an intruder, they didn't let go. They hindered their movements and made them easy targets for the Hunter in their midst. Alex had two pistols and every shot found a target.

In the crowded hallway, there was no victory to be had for the vampires. They fled to the windows they'd entered from and disappeared back into the night. The dogs pursued them to the windows but didn't leap after them. They didn't trust the forest right now and all they wanted to protect was their home. Alex wasn't stupid enough to follow after the vampires and stayed behind the dogs.

"Good dogs," he said as he pet them. The dogs barked suddenly and Alex turned just in time to see one last vampire. It caught his wrist before he could fire and bit into his neck.

Ashley was among the crowd of partiers who were hooting and hollering as they left the forest. The dancing had gone on well after midnight. The fires had died down and soon they were left with only embers and the diamonds in the sky.

Ashley was pretty sure she was a bit drunk. Every time they'd gone back to the table, Ben had another drink waiting for both of them. He and Morgan were in constant competition to see who could drink more. They slammed mugs against each other and threw them back. Ashley giggled every time she saw the two squabble. She was instantly reminded of Nathaniel and Kevin at the dinner table.

She wasn't sure when the bride and groom had left, but it was much earlier than everyone else. Melissa explained it usually happened this way. While the guests partied, the newlyweds would sneak off into the forest and get a start on their honeymoon. Ashley had been curious what werewolves did for their honeymoon and decided to ask.

"Same thing everybody else does," said Melissa with a raised eyebrow. Ashley went red and Melissa started laughing. She handed Ashley another drink and left her to her embarrassment.

Lidia surprisingly stayed up for the entire night. When they'd all transformed back into wolves though, Lidia collapsed on her mother's back. It wasn't long until Ashley could hear Lidia snoring contently.

For Lidia's sake, they went back down slowly. Ashley was kind of glad too because she wasn't too sure she could handle a fast ride right now. Nathaniel seemed full of energy, but he also didn't seem quite there. Ashley held on tightly as Nathaniel seemed to miss a step once in a while. She wished she could have a picture of the camp dispersing right now. Dozens of giant wolves all managing their way down the mountain, some so drunk they could hardly walk. Ashley laughed at the thought and received many funny looks for it. She had trouble trying to stop laughing and she held a hand to her mouth. Maybe she'd had more than she thought.

Ashley wasn't sure when they arrived back down at the hotel. It barely felt like any time had passed at all, yet she knew at least an hour must've passed. Her body was sore and tired from the ride and night. Her head hurt and her neck was stiff. She wondered if she'd fallen asleep a few times herself.

Nathaniel set her down and went off to change with the rest of his family. Ashley wasn't sure how much longer she could stay awake. Melissa came by and held Lidia's unconscious form to Ashley. Ashley just nodded and held Lidia while Melissa went to change. Ashley grimaced as she took Lidia. Either Lidia was getting heavier or she was really that tired.

While the trip back had felt brief, holding Lidia until Melissa came back felt like an eternity. Ashley was finally relieved and they headed down the hill to the hotel. Nathaniel kept his arm around her waist to make sure she didn't stumble. She blinked furiously as the bright lights of the hotel met her eyes. They entered slowly and started to head to their rooms when the man at the front desk called to them.

"Excuse me sir?" started the man at the front desk. "You're Mr. Lexington, aren't you?"

"Yes I am!" shouted Morgan happily. "Did you need something?"

"While you were out there was an emergency phone call for you from a Mr. Jameson." The family went quiet and Ashley suddenly felt awake again.

"When?" asked Morgan, his voice suddenly calm and focused.

"About two hours ago. He said to call him as soon as possible."

Morgan nodded and led the family past the front desk and towards their rooms. Ashley wondered why Morgan wasn't saying anything or calling her dad back. When they got to their rooms, he waved everyone into his. Once inside he picked up the phone and dialed Ashley's dad. He clicked a button and put the phone back down. He'd put it on speaker phone and they could all hear it ringing.

"Hello?" asked Alex. Ashley felt the room grow tenser as they heard her dad's voice. He sounded in pain.

"Alex, it's Morgan."

"About time you got back," said Alex. "Is the room secure?"

"Yes Alex, you're on speaker phone with my family and Ashley. What's the emergency?"

"Karin is the emergency." The room went silent. Ashley could feel the tension in the room spike and Morgan looked at the phone darkly. "She's back Morgan."

"How?"

"I don't know, but vampires don't always die easily. She sent her lackeys to attack your house tonight."

"Are you alright?" asked Ashley quickly.

"I'm alright honey. They weren't that quiet and I was waiting for them. Either way, we've got vampires in town still. I took one alive and he's told me some very bad things. You need to get home and quick." Morgan looked at Melissa.

"Call the airport and see when we can get out of here." Melissa nodded and stepped onto the balcony to call. "What have you learned Alex?"

"Karin isn't acting alone. She's working with other powerful vampires and has formed a group we Hunters knew as 'The Four Horsemen.' Karin has dubbed herself War and I think we all know where she's going with it."

"The Four Horsemen?" asked Kevin.

"An old biblical term," said Alex. "Four riders who ride at the apocalypse. They're called Famine, Pestilence, War, and Death. I haven't heard of one of these groups in a long time Morgan, but they can't be up to good."

"I believe you," said Morgan. "Are you safe?"

"None of us are safe right now, but I'm about as safe as I can be. I do know one thing for sure. Karin plans to ride tomorrow night after the sun sets."

"Then we better get back before she starts," said Morgan.

"You should. I'll try and get any more information out of the one that I captured."

"Stay safe Alex. We're coming back as soon as we can."

"I will. And Ashley?" Ashley leaned forward to speak into the phone.

"Yes dad?"

"I promise you I'm okay. Just stay with all of them and stay safe yourself." Ashley nodded and found herself almost crying.

"I will dad."

"I'll see you all soon." The phone buzzed as Alex hung up.

"What's the plan dad?" asked Nathaniel.

"All of you go to your rooms and pack. As soon as you're done, get some sleep. We're on the soonest plane out back to Reiner."

"I don't know if I can sleep now," said Kevin.

"You better. We may not get a lot of sleep before this is all over."

"Sounds like you've got a real problem there brother," said Ben. "I think you better count me in on this." Morgan smiled and patted his brother's back.

"I can't ask you to come, but I'd be glad to have you." Nathaniel pulled Ashley out the door and opened their room.

"We need to pack."

Ashley nodded. Her mind was absent as she put her things away. All she could think of was vampires attacking her dad. She changed her clothes and packed her dress away sullenly. It had been such a good night, just like her prom. Every time she dressed up and did something fun the vampires had to come back.

When they were all packed up, she and Nathaniel just laid in their bed and waited. She drifted in and out of sleep, holding onto Nathaniel dearly. She hoped this wasn't the last night they shared a bed. One time she woke up as the phone rang. It was Morgan telling them they'd be leaving in two hours. Nathaniel said they were ready and they went back to lying next to each other silently.

Nathaniel stroked Ashley's cheek as they stared into each other's eyes. His eyes said he was worried. Ashley saw a dangerous future in them and she held him tighter. Things would never be as happy as they'd been only a few hours ago. He kissed her and kept her just as close.

"This will end badly won't it?"

"Yes, but I promise you no matter what we'll be together in the end."

CHAPTER 21

INTERROGATION

They crammed themselves back into Ben's van and headed for the airport. There wasn't much talking and most of it was done between Morgan and his brother as he filled him in on the attacks and Karin. Ashley listened carefully and learned more of Karin's past.

They'd had a battle like this once before. It was before they'd even had kids when they'd last fought Karin and it had been in Louisiana. She'd brought a small mob of vampires with her and had attacked the town Morgan was in. Karin was so crazy she didn't even bother to hide her presence. Many people were hurt before Morgan, Melissa, and another group of werewolves had finished them off.

Ashley was surprised to hear that was where Katie was from. She was a Hunter at the time and had gotten involved in the conflict. She and Morgan met when Katie helped him fight off the vampires. After a night of saving each other's lives repeatedly, they'd become close friends and still were to this day.

They arrived at the airport and got on the plane. The situation was so serious that neither Nathaniel nor Kevin worried about flying. They had to get back to town as soon as possible. Ashley called her dad periodically to make sure he was okay. He sounded tired, but okay. She'd have to trust him to stay that way until they made it home. Ashley smiled every time she saw the sun out the window. At least her dad had one ally on his side for now.

They were barely in the airport before they all ran to where they'd left their cars. They hopped inside and raced back to town. The family only stopped once for bathroom breaks and to pick up as many snacks as they needed. They ate on the road and enjoyed more caffeine than was healthy. Nobody had slept well last night except for Lidia. She was too young to truly understand what was going on. It took them a few more hours to get back to the Lexington house. Ashley watched the clock and the sun anxiously. Soon they would be out of time and light.

Morgan pulled his car into the driveway and they all immediately jumped out. Just outside of the house, Ashley could see the windows were broken where the vampires must've come in through. Barking could be heard from inside the house as the dogs heard them coming.

Morgan pulled open the door and the dogs immediately bounded out to greet them. He pushed his way past the dogs and saw his defiled home up close. There was blood on the walls, bullet holes, and most of their decorations had been scattered or destroyed.

"Alex!" he called.

"I'm in the basement."

Morgan shoved Mops aside to get downstairs. The basement was brightly lit and in the middle of the floor was a vampire tied to a chair. He was gagged, blinded, and bound more times than necessary.

Morgan smelled Alex before he saw him. Alex appeared out of a cluttered corner where he'd been neatly disguised amongst the mess. He had a shotgun in his hands and his eyes looked tired. "It's about time you got here," he said with a smile.

"Sorry we missed the party," said Morgan sadly.

"The house is a bit of a mess, but it's secure for now." The rest of the family came into the basement and Ashley threw herself at him.

"DAD!" He caught her and kissed the side of her head.

"Hi honey. I'm fine."

"I was so scared for you." They separated and Alex smiled.

"It'll take more than a few vampires and their lackeys to bring down your dad."

"I'm sorry about all this Alex," said Morgan. Alex waved his hand.

"Don't worry about it. They weren't that good, except for this one." Alex nudged the vampire with his shotgun. "This one was real clever and waited quite patiently. Almost got me good." Alex showed them his neck where a bite mark was still present.

"Oh no," whispered Ashley.

"Is that why you're in the basement?" asked Morgan sadly. "Afraid of the sun?" Alex just laughed.

"No. I stayed down here because they've been trying to sneak down here all night and day. They've tried to set your house on fire, but they're easy pickings in the open. They've been trying to get down here at your gas reserves to blow your home to kingdom come. As for this," Alex rubbed his neck, "it wasn't a real good bite. This guy here thought he could bring me down from behind, but I had a little surprise waiting for him." Alex pulled out a jar and held it up for the family to see.

"What is it?" asked Samuel.

"Garlic," said Morgan.

"It's an old trick we use against vampires. Rub a thick layer of garlic across your neck and anywhere else they might bite you. You might stink to high heaven, but a vampire can't bite you. If they do, like this guy did here, they find themselves going into shock."

"That explains how you captured him," said Kevin.

"Yup. Dragged him down here and tied him up. I got rid of the others who attacked and I've been down here ever since." Alex saw Ben and held out his hand. "We haven't met, I'm Alex, Ashley's father."

"Uncle Ben, Morgan's brother. You can just call me Ben."

"Nice to have you Ben. I have a feeling we're going to need you before the night is up." Morgan prodded the vampire. The vampire tried to shake in response, but he was too tightly bound.

"What'd you get out of him?"

"Not much," said Alex. "Mostly the obvious stuff. They were coming here to ambush your family. When they found me here instead, they were just going to kill me and move on. Once they figured out you were gone it told me they were waiting for you. Karin was talking through him for a bit and I was tired of her chatter. All of this was to make sure he couldn't show Karin anything through his eyes."

"See through his eyes?" asked Nathaniel. "How is that possible?"

"Vampires can make links through blood with their underlings," said Alex. "Most of the time it's just so they can talk telepathically, but it can do greater things. Depending on how strong the bond is, they can see through their eyes and hear through their ears. If the blood bond is strong enough the master can even make them move around against their will."

"Spooky," said Samuel.

"Very spooky," agreed Alex. Morgan walked over and pulled at the binding around the vampire's face.

"Let's see if she wants to talk." He ripped away the gags and blindfolds so the vampire could see and hear them. The vampire hissed and tried to bite him, but couldn't reach. "Karin," said Morgan angrily. The vampire's head shook suddenly and his gaze became more focused. Morgan must've been waiting for it because as soon as it smiled, he slugged the vampire in the face. It brought its face back around and smiled with a few less teeth.

"Welcome home lover. What took you so long?" Morgan punched the vampire again so hard he knocked the chair over. The man just laughed on the floor.

"How many times do we have to kill you?" spat Morgan. "How many times until you get the point?"

"Until I get what I want from you, I shall never leave," sang the vampire.

"We rushed home just for you," said Morgan. "I hope you feel proud."

"Oh I am, but there was no rush." The vampire licked his lips. "I just threatened to attack today, but I never would've done it if you weren't here." It shot them all an insane look. "You can't have a party without the guests of honor!"

"When I find you…" started Morgan, but Karin cut him off.

"When you find us!" she hissed. "I brought some of my friends along for the ride. War cannot ride without her siblings after all. There are three others your friends must look for tonight. I ride with my sisters Famine, Pestilence, and Death." The vampire half laughed, half choked on its own blood.

"Your family versus mine! They will leave you alone though Morgan." The vampire spit on the floor and began laughing. "You are mine and mine alone! Come outside and look across the mountain.

We're waiting for you!" The vampire slowly lost its laughter as it regained control. The whole family began to talk when Morgan snarled.

"Quiet!" He gave them all a quick look to silence them. "To the roof," he commanded. Morgan led them outside and Alex took up the rear. Ashley winced as she heard his shotgun fire.

CHAPTER 22

GOING TO WAR

They all started to move and Ashley wondered where the roof access was. They all headed outside and she thought maybe there was a ladder she hadn't thought of. She paused to think how stupid she was when the Lexingtons began to climb up the house or just leap straight up. Morgan took her dad over his back and gave a huge leap up. Lidia clambered onto her mom's back as usual and Melissa scaled the house a moment later. Ashley held on tightly as Nathaniel picked her up and started running. He leapt up a nearby tree before kicking off of it onto the rooftop.

Ashley closed her eyes and took a deep breath as they soared through the air. She still wasn't used to fast flight movements like this and her stomach rolled into her throat each time. Nathaniel set her down gently on the roof.

"That was new," said her dad joyfully.

"They're out there," said Morgan darkly, stealing all the mirth from their group. The family stared into the distance and Ashley felt a little left out. She and her dad didn't have their superior vision and they especially couldn't see as well at night. Her dad took a step next to her and pulled out a pair of binoculars.

"These might help." He held up a larger pair to his eyes and they scanned the region.

"There," said Samuel suddenly. He pointed out ahead of him and the family turned their eyes. Ashley wanted him to give a more exact location than "there", but the rest of the family was tuned into his senses. Their link as a pack succeeded yet again as Ben patted him on the back.

"Good eyes Samuel."

"Good eyes indeed," said Morgan. "We see you…"

Ashley held her binoculars down and frowned. She couldn't see a damn thing. Just then four small lights appeared in the distance. She focused her binoculars on them and saw the four vampires. She recognized Karin, but not the others. They were all sitting on horses with torches in their hands. She gasped as she realized three of them were looking right back at them.

"What are they doing?"

"They're declaring their presence," said her dad. "They're showing themselves because they're not afraid of us."

"They will be when I get my hands on them," said Morgan.

On the other side of town in the hills sat the four horsewomen. They were all staring at their werewolf foes with glee. Only one was looking away, barely even able to hold her torch as she twitched on her horse.

"Oh calm down Famine," said Karin. "The fun will begin soon."

"Please let me go!" she whined as she thrashed at her chains. The vampire next to her yanked her chains painfully.

"She said to be calm." Death said sweetly. Famine calmed down almost instantly, eyeing her fearfully.

"You certainly have a way with her," slurred Pestilence.

"Don't talk Pestilence. You're getting mucous everywhere."

"Ha!" snorted the sickly woman. "They see us War, can't we get this started?" Karin grinned evilly.

"You all know who I want, you may take down anyone else who gets in your way. Have you decided who you want Death?" Death gave a sly smile.

"If he's worthy of my attention, he'll come straight to me."

"Then let the dogs of war be unleashed." Karin threw her torch into the forest behind her. The others all did the same and a patch of oiled ground started to burn. The four sat illuminated by the fire for a moment.

"You can almost feel the warmth," said Death quietly. She turned to Famine and reached to the back of her neck. "Go find your warmth sister. Go feed."

The heavy collar broke around Famine's neck and the calm girl's eyes went mad. The night air was ruined as the devil used her throat to scream. So powerful was her launch towards the town she threw her horse into the ground. She practically flew through the forest. She had a horse but it would never move fast enough for her. It didn't feel her insane desires and didn't have the same motivation she had. It had been so long since she'd last fed.

It would take her ten minutes to reach town, but there were houses closer to her in the wilderness. She would find every person she could and feed. Tonight she would gorge herself and drown the world in blood.

"They've started," said Alex. Morgan took Alex again and leapt for the ground. They all took to the air and hit the ground a second later. Alex was already racing back inside to gather his things.

"We've got multiple targets to hunt tonight," said Morgan loudly. "There's the four of them and we can be sure there will be other vampires and ghouls. Kids, tonight I'm going to ask you to forget everything I taught you. Do not stick to the shadows and do not be quiet. The entire town is in danger and I'd rather them see werewolves than be eaten by angry vampires."

"If you see a vampire, you go for the kill. You all know what they look like. Go for the kill and if possible, dump them in a fire. The jackals already showed us that if we don't fully kill them, the stronger ones can come back. Watch each other's backs and only start a fight you can win." Alex came back out with his large bag and threw it in his truck. He pulled out some pistols and laid them on the seats and then began to check his shotgun.

"You should stay here," said Morgan.

"Like hell I will. I'm a trained Hunter and just as useful in this fight. You'll need all the help you can get."

"Katie!" said Mary quickly. "She doesn't know."

"Yes she does," said Alex. "I called her while I was in the house. I'm picking her up and then we're going to the Fortune's house."

"The Fortunes?" asked Melissa confused.

"Their house is like a fortress," said Ashley.

"It is." agreed her dad. "We'll hold down there."

"Okay. Go there and hold down the fort. If any of us has a problem we'll come to you." Alex nodded and racked his shotgun.

"No problem." Morgan looked at his family.

"The vampires are most likely going to be all over town. We'll have to split up to take them all out. Your mother and Nathaniel are with me. Kevin and Samuel, you're going with your uncle Ben. Follow him and you'll be okay."

"What about me?" asked Mary.

"You are taking your sister to the den." Mary crossed her arms.

"That's unfair. I'm a part of the pack and I deserve to defend the town too."

"Don't be so eager to spill blood," said Morgan fiercely. Mary looked away shamefully. "I'm asking you to defend our cousins and your little sister. I'm not asking this because you're a girl, I'm asking because I trust you to take care of this. Samuel is too little to fight on his own, so it must be you. Can you do that for me?" Mary looked back and nodded.

"Yes dad."

"Good. Get your things Lidia, you're leaving now." Lidia nodded and bounced into the house and out of sight. Morgan held his brother's hand.

"Ben, I'm trusting you with my kids."

"I'll take good care of them."

"I know you will. Alex?"

"We'll be fine," said Alex. "Go on and get into town." Morgan nodded and held out his hand.

"I'm glad our families can fight as one." Alex took his hand and shook it.

"I'm glad too. Let's not leave one of these bastards alive."

"Agreed," said Morgan. "Let's go!" Morgan started running towards the town, changing as he went. The rest of the family started to follow him. Nathaniel paused and took Ashley's hands in his own.

"I love you," he said quickly before he kissed her. Ashley didn't gasp at the words or even feel surprised. She knew he'd felt those words for a long time now. She kissed him back and pushed him to follow his family.

"I love you too. Come back alive."

"I will." Nathaniel let go of her hands and bolted after his father. Soon Ashley couldn't see them anymore and could only hear their howls as they ran down the mountain.

"Ashley, let's go," said her dad from his truck.

"Do you want her to come with me?" asked Mary. "She could hide in the den with me and the other wolves."

"Thank you Mary, but no. I'd rather keep Ashley by my side. Take care."

Mary nodded and ran in to get her sister. Alex had thought about sending Ashley with Mary, but he had a bad feeling about leaving Ashley unattended. She cared too much about Nathaniel and his family. He hated to admit it, but his foolish daughter would probably leave safety and go looking for her boyfriend in the middle of a war zone. No, it would be better if she stayed in his sight.

Alex waited until he saw Mary leave through the sideyard with Lidia on her back before he drove away from the house. They were lucky it wasn't winter right now or it would've taken them twice as long to get down. He knew he could drive the mountain quickly, but they'd never beat Morgan and his family down the mountain. The wolves didn't have to abide by roads or worry about anything getting in their way.

"What do you think is going to happen?" asked his daughter fearfully. He looked at Ashley with a worried smile.

"I don't know, but tonight isn't going to be pretty." Ashley held her sides nervously and nodded. "Don't worry, I promise I won't let anything get you."

"What about Nathaniel and the others?" Alex smirked.

"They should be the last people you should be worried about. One werewolf is nasty enough, a full pack is twenty times more dangerous. Combine that with the fact that they have a purpose and are angry." Alex didn't even want to think about it. He'd only seen the results of an angry, dedicated pack once a few times before and they'd never turned out pretty. Their town would be in for one hell of a night, but so would those vampires.

The Lexington family pounded down the mountain as fast as they could. They ran as a pack and they howled as loudly as they could. Making so much noise would remind the vampires that they had a challenge coming to town. With any luck, it would keep them worried and give the people of Reiner a greater chance of escaping. Morgan let loose another loud howl and his family joined him. Howling like this would also bring courage to his children who were about to experience a battle of the likes they'd never seen before.

"We'll head straight for the other side of town," barked Morgan to Melissa and Nathaniel. "Ben, Kevin, and Samuel, you follow up behind us. Anything that gets by us, make sure it doesn't get anywhere else." The family barked in unison that they understood. Morgan prayed all would go well.

The town was already under siege long before they arrived. Screaming people filled the streets as the town burned. Karin knew they would arrive in town about the same time, but she'd sent her ghouls and underling vampires to the town earlier. Flaming bottles could be seen flying through the air. Ghouls ran around spreading chaos and vampires attacked at will.

It took every ounce of Morgan's will not to turn on the first group of ghouls he encountered. He forced himself to run past them and towards the more dangerous threat. Karin and her riders had to be dealt with first. He had no idea how long it would take to find them, but the sooner the better. And if Morgan knew anything about Karin, finding her wouldn't be a problem. She would be coming to find him.

Ben and the others leapt upon the ghouls and brought them down. The screaming in the area intensified as people saw the giant wolves enter town. Ben tore through another ghoul and chased after the next group. Samuel stayed on his heels and Kevin brought up the rear. Samuel seemed hesitant to attack the people. Ben felt bad for his nephew, but scolded him all the same. The boy wasn't ready for this, but if he didn't fight back, he could get himself killed. Ben would rather have the boy's innocence lost rather than his life.

The ghouls and vampires it seemed were being met with more resistance than they'd thought. There were many hunters and woodsmen in the town and most of them were well armed. Some of the streets were turning into shooting galleries as people gathered together for survival. Others were fleeing the town as fast as they could by either car or foot. The vampires had certainly caught the town unaware, but after a spell of madness, some of the townspeople were putting their feet down and fighting back.

Ben leapt upon an unsuspecting vampire and bit deeply into its neck. The vampire screamed and clawed desperately at Ben's mouth, but it was a futile attempt. Ben spat the dying vampire to the ground when out of the corner of his eye he saw another one leaping for him with knives. He turned with his mouth open and winced prematurely for the oncoming knives.

The vampire shrieked as Samuel met it in midair and rolled them onto the ground. Samuel's bite was weak and the vampire easily pulled away, but that was more than enough time for Ben. He wouldn't let the vampire get his nephew in a one on one fight. Wolves didn't work that way and Ben finished what Samuel started. He saw the nervous look in Samuel's eye and nodded to him in approval. The boy had to know what he'd done was a good thing.

A few ghouls came charging at them wildly. Samuel took his place next to Ben and stood his ground. Ben beamed at his nephew and felt he was getting the right idea. They both waited for the mob and grinned at their foolishness. They failed to see Kevin moving up behind them in their rage. Their attack was doomed.

Kevin was almost on them when the ghouls were torn to pieces. Another street was between Ben and Kevin and the ghouls had walked into someone's line of fire. There was a heavy rattle of a large gun and they were no more. Kevin peered around the corner and immediately had to retreat as the gun turned on him.

He'd expected an angry mob of humans moving as one, but to his surprise, there'd only been one man. He'd braced a large machine gun of sorts on a car and had sprayed it down the street. Kevin had no idea what kind of gun it was, but it certainly wasn't made for civilians.

"You alright?" barked Ben.

"Yes. Stay away from that street. Head around and I'll meet up with you."

"We stay together!" Samuel peered into the street and whined in fear as the bullets whizzed past him. The man knew they were down there and he wasn't moving until they were gone or dead.

"Go!" shouted Kevin and ran around the other way. He didn't know when he'd be able to meet up with them again, but he wasn't too worried about it. Uncle Ben could take good care of Samuel and Kevin worked better alone. Remaining unseen in the darkness was his specialty.

CHAPTER 23

THE SINNER AND THE SAINT

Liz grinned as she skipped down the street. She'd told her mom that she was going over to Kara's to hang out, but that was her little white lie. She was heading over to Jeremy's house. His family was out for the night and he said they wouldn't be back until around 2AM. It was the perfect opportunity for a little bit of alone time. Liz giggled to herself as she went along. If her mom had ever known she was going to spend time alone with a boy she'd have a total meltdown. Liz held a finger up to her lips as she skipped.

What her mom didn't know couldn't hurt her.

She was almost there when she heard screaming. She turned and tried to see where it was coming from, but the noise was a few neighborhoods down and she couldn't see anything. A few other people came out of their houses to see what all the commotion was about. Liz pulled up her hood and kept moving down the street. She really wanted to know what was going on, but didn't want anyone to recognize her. Sadly being the town gossip meant almost everyone knew her.

And then gossip became the least of her worries. She saw a burning object fly through the air from the adjacent neighborhood. It looked like a bottle of some kind. It came down on a house just in front of her and suddenly fire exploded across the house. She gasped and took a step back. People started shouting and more people flooded the streets in concern.

Unfortunately the streets were the last place anyone should've been as more projectiles came flying in. The bottles hit the street, trees, houses, and even people. Fires sprang up everywhere and soon nowhere was safe. Liz panicked and began running towards Jeremy's house as quickly as she could. People started screaming louder and she heard new noises added to the mix. Emergency vehicles began to blare all over town. Then a final noise entered which sent shivers down Liz's spine.

Gunshots.

She was almost to her boyfriend's house when she saw a mob coming down the street towards her. Men and women were screaming and shouting, not out of fear, but enjoyment. They were throwing the bottled fire and attacking anyone they happened across the street. She ducked into some nearby bushes and stayed out of sight. They charged down the street and passed her location. She tried to breathe easy, but she couldn't. She wanted to run to Jeremy's but her legs weren't responding.

She heard whistling coming down the street. The tune was cheerful and belonged to a pale man following slowly after the mob. He wore dark clothing and skipped every couple of steps gleefully. Something told Liz to stay away from this man. Her fears were confirmed when he stepped on a wounded man. He hissed with glee when he heard the man yelp in pain. He reached down and pulled the man upright like he was a child.

"They do all the work and I get the food. I couldn't ask for better circumstances."

His mouth opened wide and Liz saw a pair of shiny fangs. He clamped onto the man's throat and began to suck him dry. Liz had to clamp her hands over her mouth to not scream. He wasn't a man at all. He was a vampire! He tossed the man aside like a doll and wiped the blood from his mouth. His eyes suddenly passed over Liz and he licked the blood from his lips.

"Did that excite you?" he asked loudly. Liz tried to hide herself even though she knew he knew her location. "Or perhaps it frightened you?" The vampire gave a long laugh and advanced on her. He stopped just outside the garden and waved his fingers towards her.

"Why don't you come out of there?" he crooned. "Come to me. I can show you something greater."

Liz shook her head, but found herself standing up. She gasped as her legs moved jerkily on their own. She tried to hold onto the bush, but her hands weren't paying attention to her either. After a few steps, she found she couldn't take her eyes off his. He was drawing her in.

Her hands came up and her small coat started to pull away. The vampire smirked and continued to will her forward. Liz tried to look away, but it was useless. Her hands passed her neck and she felt the rough chain of her necklace. Her hand returned to her and she found the will to stand. The vampire looked at her surprised and Liz fumbled with the end of her necklace. Just as he moved towards her she found what she was looking for.

Liz held up her cross to the advancing vampire. He paused only for a second and then he came at her again. He reached out and took Liz's wrist and pulled her forward. Liz cried out as the vampire grabbed her throat with his free hand.

"A word of advice," he said cheerfully. "Crosses only work if you have enough faith. Your faith isn't strong enough." Liz whimpered, but that was all she could do. The vampire's hand was closing tighter on her throat and she didn't have the air to scream. The world started to go dark.

"I don't need faith for this to work!" shouted a familiar voice.

Both the vampire and Liz looked over to see Kara next to them. She had her cleaver sword in both hands above her head and brought it down as she spoke. The blade sliced neatly through both of the vampire's arms. Liz dropped free and the vampire screamed in agony as his limbs fell away. Kara brought her sword up again and dropped it onto the vampire's head this time. Liz squirmed and threw away the vampire's arms. Kara drew her sword back out and hacked him again. And again.

Liz sat horrified as Kara hacked the vampire until he was unrecognizable. She'd reduced the horrible creature into a pile of red chunks on the street side. When Kara turned to Liz she was covered in speckles of blood. The most bizarre smile covered her face.

"Let's go Liz. We need to get going." Liz wasn't sure how to move yet. Kara wasn't ready to waste time and she pulled Liz to her feet. "Liz?" Liz didn't respond. Kara drew back her hand and slapped her hard across the face.

"OW!" cried Liz.

"Snap out of it and let's go!"

Kara took her by the hand and they started to jog down the street. The town's screaming started to become more constant as they ran. The night sky was more lit up than usual which probably meant more buildings had been set ablaze. Liz heard a shrill cry behind her and turned just in time to see a vampire leaping off a nearby house towards them. Time seemed to slow down for her as the vampire came closer. She could see its fangs as it opened its mouth for her.

Time sped up as Liz felt Kara's boot kick against her back. Liz went tumbling towards the ground and Kara took her place as the oncoming vampire's target. Only Kara took a stance like a baseball player and she was prepared to make the vampire her unwilling ball. The vampire tried to stop its descent, but it couldn't defy gravity any more than Kara could. Kara planted her feet and swung her sword two handed through the oncoming vampire. The razor sharp blade sliced clean through the vampire and sent two pieces to the ground. Again Kara went to dismembering the already dead vampire. A moment went by and Kara turned to Liz again.

"Ready?"

Liz nodded but secretly began to fear Kara. That was twice Kara had saved her by mutilating both of their attackers. Her face showed no remorse for her actions and she was still smiling. Her eyes told Liz that Kara was teetering towards a dangerous abyss. Some inner madness was being released by the carnage of their town.

They ran further through the neighborhood and found only more screaming people. Some even fled from Kara as she looked like one of their attackers. Some people were running with torches and burning bottles. Liz stopped as one of the groups with fire started towards them.

"We need to go the other way," Liz said hastily. Kara didn't move at her suggestion. Her fingers tightened around her bloody sword. Liz grabbed her shoulder and pulled hard.

"Kara!"

Kara shook her off and began walking towards the crowd. The group seemed to consist of teenagers like them. They were hooting and hollering as they set stores on fire. Twenty feet away one of them noticed Kara walking towards them.

"Who's that?" asked a boy.

"Get out of here!" shouted another.

Kara didn't respond. Her stride started to become longer as she neared them. The five teenagers started to take steps backwards as Kara moved in for them. Kara leapt into the air just as a girl in the group recognized her.

"Kara?"

Kara hissed as she dropped into the first boy and split him down the front. The others cried as one and charged for their fallen friend. Kara spun around and sliced through another two. A fourth came at her with a burning bottle of liquor in her hand. The girl screamed as Kara drew her sword across her. The liquor bottle broke and splattered Kara's blade before the fire touched it. Sections of Kara's blade began to burn and Kara's eyes shined in the firelight. The burning alcohol seeped around her to give her a burning aura. Kara cackled in the fire as she turned to the last member of the group.

"Please don't." Liz gasped as she realized the girl was Monica. She looked paler than usual and was on her knees. "I never wanted any of this."

"Then you shouldn't have done it," warned Kara.

"I didn't want to! My mistress made me do it. She said she'd kill me otherwise."

"Stupid choice." Monica gave one last panicked scream as Kara drove her flaming sword into her. "If she didn't kill you, I would have."

"Kara!" screamed Liz. "What are you doing?"

"They're all monsters now."

"That was Monica! She wasn't a monster." Liz looked down and gulped as she recognized Marten was among Kara's victims. Kara walked towards her calmly.

"Our town is being raided by vampires. These people were infected and destroying our town. What was I supposed to do?"

"I don't know! But you can't just start killing people."

Kara frowned, but didn't say anything. Liz saw a shadow appear behind Kara and tried to warn her, but it was too late. A woman she didn't recognize grabbed Kara by the throat and sword hand and lifted her off the ground. Her skin was pale and when she spoke Liz could see sharp fangs.

"These were my children. You will pay for taking them from me."

"I'll kill you," gasped Kara.

"No. I'll make you suffer for years for what you've done. And you girl," the vampire stared at Liz, "you just stay right there unless you want me to break your friend's neck."

"She's already going to kill me," said Kara angrily. "Attack her."

"She can't and she won't," laughed the vampire. "Even if she charged me, what would she do? You were the only one with a weapon. This girl doesn't have the spirit to kill anyway. Do you?" Liz trembled. The vampire was right on both accounts and they all knew it. She wanted to help Kara, but she didn't know how.

The vampire was so distracted by its fun it failed to notice another shadow appear. Liz only caught the faintest sight of something darker than night and suddenly the vampire was screaming. Kara was dropped to the ground as something dragged the vampire away and smashed her along the ground. Kara brought her sword up again and by its fiery light, they were shown their savior.

The vampire was being dragged around by a giant black wolf. They couldn't tell exactly how big it was, but it was enormous. It had the vampire by clamping its mouth sideways so as to grab both of her shoulders at once and press them in. The vampire was screaming and flailing about, but there was nothing she could do. The wolf held her to the ground and tightened its jaws further. The vampire's body collapsed and she stopped moving. The werewolf spun around and tossed the woman into one of the burning buildings.

Liz was terrified. Her whole body shook and she didn't know what to do. Her town had gone mad. Her life had become a nightmare and she wasn't even sure if she wasn't dreaming right now. Vampires were real and invading their town. Kara seemed to have snapped and given into some form of primordial rage. Now giant wolves were here. What was going on?

The giant wolf moved close to the fire so they could see it better. Its entire body was covered in long black fur. Firelight shined in its eyes and blood dripped from its teeth. Liz held onto her cross and began to pray for their souls. This wolf looked like a creature from the depths of Hell itself. It had saved them from the vampire, but Liz wasn't grateful. She was sure it had wanted them only for itself.

"Come on!" screamed Kara. She held her flaming sword out in front of her. Some of the fire had gone out, but the fire that remained only made the weapon look more frightening. Liz looked at Kara in a new light. The girl may have lost it, but she might be their only chance at survival now. The wolf still didn't back down.

Its legs braced and Kara saw a charge coming. She let loose a battle cry and charged. It pounced and Kara tried to swing for it, but it cleared her head in a single bound. She turned in fear for Liz but the wolf didn't want her either. It landed on a nearby roof and snapped at a shadowy figure. Another vampire hissed and leapt clear for another building, but the wolf was right behind it. Its sharp teeth managed to catch one of the vampire's legs and the vampire screamed. They both crashed into a house before they tumbled into the street. The collision looked like it'd rattled both of them, but the wolf hadn't relinquished its hold on the vampire's leg.

The vampire hissed and rolled up to strike the wolf repeatedly in the face. The wolf shook its head and the vampire with it, but the vampire didn't seem to care. It was strong enough to hurt the wolf, possibly enough to even get away, but it knew if the werewolf righted itself, he would be done for. War had warned them of this. Werewolves were bigger and they had four legs. If they could stand evenly on the ground, they wouldn't be moved by even a vampire.

"HEY!"

The vampire looked back momentarily as he felt the voice was directed at him. The girl he'd seen in the street was behind him now. She had her large sword in both hands above her head. He knew that smile on her face. It was the joyful look he'd shared in many times. It was the look he had right before he was about to bring death to someone. He brought his arms away from the werewolf and swept for the girl. He had to knock out her legs or at least get her to jump. If she dropped that sword down he'd never survive.

Unfortunately the werewolf had other ideas. It sensed the sudden lack of resistance and pulled back on the vampire as it stood up again. The vampire screeched as he was rolled over and just out of reach of the girl. Kara drove her sword into its backside and the vampire spasmed. She jerked it out and he stopped moving. The black wolf dragged its body before it tossed this one into the fire. It turned around and looked at Kara differently. She didn't even hold her sword up to it as it approached.

"Friend?" she asked. It nodded its head. "Are you trying to get rid of the vampires and their wannabe friends?" It nodded again and she laughed. She held her sword over her head and pointed to the wolf. "Show me the way, my hellhound friend!"

The wolf cocked its head at her. After a moment of consideration, it knelt next to her and pointed to its back with its nose. Liz looked at Kara like she was crazy, but Kara's smile grew. She immediately jumped on the wolf's back and held her sword just above its side. She took a handful of fur into one hand and howled.

"Let's go!" The wolf bolted away down the street and Kara laughed the entire way.

"Kara where are you going!" screamed Liz.

"Hunting!" Her laughter disappeared as she leaned low on the wolf and her face became serious. She was hunting now and silence was their ally. Her ride didn't make any noise and neither would she.

Liz stood shaking as Kara rode off into the night. Kara had somehow transformed from weird mountain girl to crazy barbarian. The night was beginning to show their true forms in the face of disaster. Liz was ashamed of herself, but admitted she'd broken down. She was terrified and wanted nothing more than a corner to hide in. Kara however had leapt into the face of danger with steel in hand.

"Oh scared little girl. What will you do now?"

Liz looked down the street as a man came around the corner. He was dressed in all black which only made his pale skin even more apparent. She knew he was a vampire and she knew she was all alone. The vampire proceeded to walk down the street. "I can hear your heart pounding. It's a lovely melody." The vampire began to clap his hands at a rapid beat. "What do you say we quicken the tune?" It stopped a little bit away from her and frowned. Liz just stood there quivering in front of him.

"This is where you run," he said coldly. Liz wasn't sure what was going on. She wanted to run, but when she told her feet to move nothing happened. The vampire snarled and walked past her. It grabbed the body of one of the teenagers Kara had slain and held it up for Liz to see. The vampire bit deep into the boy's neck before pulling away violently. Blood poured freely and the vampire tossed the body right in front of her.

"I said RUN!"

Liz bolted down the street. She ran screaming and shouting for help. She tried to pray for help, but she was too scared to form a coherent thought. The vampire stayed behind her, jogging lightly and clapping his hands.

The street ahead of her was burning and the other direction was filled with screams and howling. She paused to figure out where to go, but the vampire didn't stop. She cried and ran the other way through the neighborhoods. The vampire started to speed up and she dashed to somebody's fence. Someone had to have dogs around here. She'd take anything which might save her.

The first yard had nothing and she clambered over the fence as fast as she could. The second yard had nothing and she kept going.

The vampire casually hopped over each fence and closed the distance a little more. By the time she cleared the fourth fence, the vampire was almost on her. She started to sprint for the next one when she was forced to stop only a few feet in. This house had a pool. Her sudden stop cost her as the vampire appeared behind her.

"Boo."

She screamed and he gave her a light push. Liz splashed into the pool and came up as fast as she could. The pool was surprisingly warm. The vampire kneeled at the pool's edge and dipped his hand in. He whistled loudly.

"Nice pool! These people must be pretty wealthy to afford this heating bill. You can stop running now by the way, there's nowhere you can go." Liz looked around for any type of help, but there wasn't any. The vampire was already faster than her and she was slowed down by the water. He was right. The vampire walked calmly into the pool.

"I feel very fortunate. I think killing someone in a pool is absolutely delightful. There's just something amazing about watching the whole pool go red as the blood seeps in."

Liz was terrified but her shaking had stopped. She didn't know whether it was the warm water or that she was facing her inevitable death, but her heart was calming. She had to make her stand now or she would die here. She held up her cross one more time.

"Stay back," she said firmly. The vampire laughed.

"You think that really works. You're dumber than you look." It took another step forward and Liz matched it. She put every ounce of her will into the cross and believed. It would work.

"You will not harm me," she said strongly. The vampire just chuckled and took another step forward. Liz held her ground and the vampire took another step.

Then something happened to the vampire. Its foot stopped before it touched the pool floor as if it'd struck a barrier. It hissed and tried to step forward again. Again it bounced off an invisible wall. It was working.

"You will go back!" The vampire frowned and then smiled.

"So you got me. But what are you going to do about him?"

The vampire's eyes strayed away from her to someone behind her. She turned with her cross held upright. There was nobody there. A wave of water covered her and she hunched over instinctively. The vampire's strong hands took her hair and then her arm to keep the cross away from him. It squeezed painfully on her wrist and she cried out as her hand opened. Her cross fell free and began to slowly make its way to the bottom of the pool.

"Humans. So easy to manipulate," said the vampire sweetly. "Now you're mine." It pulled her back slowly by her hair and held her neck open to him. Tears ran down Liz's cheeks but she didn't sob.

"I believe," she said quietly.

"So did I once," said the vampire. "I guess you'll find out the truth." Liz felt for her falling cross with her free hand. It was gone somewhere in the dark water.

"I believe."

"And you're beginning to bore me."

"I believe," she repeated as the vampire bit into her neck. She cringed as she felt his needle sharp teeth pierce her skin. Her blood thundered in her body as it tried to stay away from the undead abomination. It was of no use though. Her blood was its claim and she was going to die.

The vampire pulled away suddenly as light filled the area. Liz tried to look for help, but the vampire held her fast. The pool was lit up and the vampire started laughing.

"False alarm I'm afraid. Your savior was just the pool light. So tell me," it licked its already bloody lips, "do you still believe?" Liz nodded her head. "Then perhaps you can believe in me. What if I made you into my servant instead of killing you?"

"No," she said with all the spite she could muster. The vampire smirked.

"Fortunately I don't need your approval." She started to squirm as it went down to her neck again. She didn't want to be turned into a vampire. She didn't want to live as some servant of his. She'd rather die than be one of them.

The vampire pulled back again and this time he released her. Liz swam away and held her neck. She was barely bleeding, but the vampire was screaming. He thrashed about in real agony. His soft looking skin was beginning to wrinkle and he was beginning to smoke.

"The vampire tried to leap out of the pool, but it didn't have the strength to get out. His skin began to fall apart and he finally stopped moving. His skin turned from white to ash. The water pulled his body apart and he disappeared into a small dark puddle in the pool. Even his clothes melted away.

Liz sat on a pool step and started crying again. She didn't understand what was going on or how she was saved. The vampire's bite marks from her neck were gone. The vampire was gone. She just sat there unsure if any of it had ever happened.

As the ash puddle formerly known as the vampire dissolved, Liz saw something shining in the pool. She moved off her seat to go and see what it was. She ducked under the water and found the object.

Resting in the center of the pool light, shining brightly for her, was her cross.

CHAPTER 24

CHAOS IS UPON US

Death stood upon a tree and admired the carnage in the city. The ghouls were moving through the city herding the people around with fire. The attacks may have seemed random, but War had been more precise than that. War wanted the people to go where she wanted to achieve maximum carnage. When they were done with this town, there would be nothing left of it.

Pestilence was moving somewhere inside the town spreading her little charms to everyone she could meet. She would be a walking disaster to the people. She was so noxious that Death herself found it hard to stand around her, and she was dead. Pestilence had such foul things living inside her body it was beyond unnatural. Since she was a vampire, the diseases didn't like staying in her dead body. Disease likes fresh victims with open wounds. After tonight, she would infect most of the town with some type of plague.

Death turned her eyes to the far part of town that was filled with the most screaming. The ghouls would certainly destroy the town and

Pestilence would eventually kill its people, but nobody would make more of an impact than Famine.

Famine was the worst type of vampire imaginable. She didn't have any unique abilities like she or Pestilence had. She didn't even have the vendetta and planning skills of War. No, Famine had a mental disease when she was alive and it had carried over to her vampiric life. She always thought she was starving for some reason. In her human life, if she wasn't restrained, she might kill herself by eating too much. Now that she was a vampire…Death shuddered.

Famine was horrible. She fed like there would be no more blood in the world. When she had a victim, she would drain them down to the last drop. Worse, if there was a full crowd of victims, Famine wouldn't just take one. She would bite one and enjoy the first taste of their blood and quickly move on. In five minutes, she could convert more people into vampires than most vampires would in their entire lifetime.

Death hated releasing Famine. She caused carnage and confusion on such a massive scale it was unreal. Unfortunately she could never think much beyond her next meal which meant all of her newly turned vampires weren't controlled. If they fed off of their new master's influence, which most of them did, they would start to feed until the end of the world. It was an endless cycle that really could lead to the end of the world if they were smart.

Famine's terrifying strength was also her weakness. She wasn't smart. If Death didn't restrain her, Famine would always go looking for food. Her desires were so strong she would risk stepping into the open sun for more blood. Her followers would do the same thing. Death considered this a fortunate flaw considering she could never kill all of Famine's spawn. There were simply too many to count.

Death turned her head as she heard the howls of the approaching werewolves. She trembled with excitement as the group came down the hill and rushed into the city. They were the ones she was waiting for. One in their group would truly be worthy of a beautiful death. She had killed many people in her day, but she knew the most beautiful kills were done on those who resisted. The ones who could stare death in the eye and spit at its feet. Those were the people who Death wanted and perhaps one of them would be such a character. She leapt off the tree and into town. She would have to follow them and find her worthy foe.

Alex drove his truck down the mountain as fast as he dared. They were in a way lucky that winter had passed. Vampires and werewolves didn't care if it was snowy or dry, they'd run all the same. If the town had been snowed in right now they'd all be torn to pieces. Since it was summer the roads were clear and there was nothing hindering the people from leaving the city.

Ashley sat next to him clutching the door and gritting her teeth. She'd never taken these paths so quickly before and with every turn, she was sure they'd hit a tree. "I've driven in worse than this before Ashley. Don't worry."

"It's not that I don't trust you." They hit a large bump and they rocked in their seats. Ashley opened her eyes again and said in a long breath. "It's just hard to convince my body to trust you."

"You've ridden werewolves before and you're afraid of being in the car with me?" laughed Alex as he slid his truck around a bend. They were almost on the straight path back into town.

"I never said there weren't moments I wasn't scared on Nathaniel," said Ashley. Alex hit the long stretch of road and gunned the engine. They came over a hill and they got a good look at the town.

"Good god," whispered Alex. Ashley cringed next to him.

Reiner was burning. The far end of the town was in flames and they could hear the screaming from the opposite side of town. They couldn't see the fighting in the city, but they could hear the noise. Wolves howled, guns fired, and people screamed. Hell had come to Reiner for a visit.

"We're too late," said Ashley.

Alex looked at his daughter sadly. They'd only been driving for twenty minutes. This battle was long from over. It wouldn't end until either every vampire or everyone in town was dead. He pointed to the glove box.

"Open that," he commanded. Ashley opened it and found a dark handle waiting for her. "Take it." She gingerly pulled out a long pistol. It was dark with a silver top and compact. Her dad had shown her how to use a gun before, but today it felt so much heavier in her hands. Its grip was tough and she felt a dark aura coming off the weapon. She swore the devil himself swam around her heart when she held it.

"I don't think I can."

"I never wanted you to have a gun," said her father. "You should've never been exposed to one and you should have never had a chance to use one. Tonight there will be things out there that want to hurt us. Tonight it will be dog eat dog out there, kill or be killed." She started to put the gun back but her dad caught her hand and forced her to keep it. He kept one eye on the road and one on her.

"Ashley, if something comes out at you tonight, I want you to shoot and ask no questions. I hope you never have to squeeze the trigger, but if you have to, I want you to do it. Tonight this never leaves your side for any reason." He slammed the glove box shut and didn't say another word. Ashley held up the gun and cringed.

She remembered when she'd asked Nathaniel to turn her and he'd refused. She'd been so angry with him back then, but she understood him now. He was right. She didn't want to hurt people. She didn't want to shoot and possibly kill someone. She held the gun in her lap and tried to find the strength to keep it together. Nathaniel and his family were fighting out there. Her dad and Katie would be fighting. The entire town was in danger. She couldn't hide any longer.

The way into town was slow as people were crowding the streets. The fighting hadn't reached them yet and they had no idea what was going on. Alex honked at them to get out of the way, all the while shouting to each mob they passed. "We're under attack! Everyone with a gun get ready for the worst!" People screamed and panicked. Ashley wasn't sure if they heard her dad or would do what he said.

They arrived at Katie's diner and it was empty. People were scattering everywhere, but the shops had been abandoned. Ashley flinched every time she heard a gunshot as they approached. Her dad raised his voice and shouted up. "Katie! Let's go!" Ashley saw a shadow move on the roof and saw Katie. Katie had a long rifle in her hands and she was sniping into town. She took her time, lined up her shot, and fired into the distance.

"Like shooting fish in a barrel!" she shouted back. "Meet me inside." Alex led the way inside with a pistol in each hand. He turned on the lights and checked every door. There was a rattling in the kitchen and he swept his guns to the door. It opened a moment later and Katie stepped out.

"Grab the bags and lets go," she said. There were two large bags on the counter next to them. Alex grabbed one and Ashley took the other. She grunted at how heavy it was. "The town has gone mad."

"So we can see. How bad is it?" asked Alex.

"A good number of vampires and tons of ghouls. The ghouls are spreading the fires while the vampires are just attacking people. Fortunately there are enough people with good sense in this town to fight back."

"Did you see Nathaniel?" asked Ashley.

"I didn't see Nathaniel, but I did see a few of the others running around town."

"Are the vampires armed?" asked Alex as they headed for his truck.

"For the most part no. Looks like they're going in for the close fight tonight."

"Aren't we lucky?" growled Alex. "Let's get to the Fortunes and hope they're home."

"They're not," said Katie. Alex looked at her bewildered.

"What!"

"They aren't. I saw them mowing ghouls down left and right a few blocks down. He's got some kind of military grade machine gun too. I don't think they're in any danger."

"Why would they leave their house?" asked Alex. "They have the best position in town?" Ashley leaned forward scared.

"Kara," she breathed. "What if Kara wasn't home?"

"Oh god," said Alex. "If their kid is missing they're going to storm the town themselves."

"Should we help them?" asked Katie. Alex thought hard as they drove, but eventually shook his head.

"No. Everything going on right now is too chaotic to just jump in. We need to set up a strong point before we do anything rash. Besides, their house is close to all the action. I don't imagine we'll be bored."

"Probably not," said Katie. She rolled down the window and leaned out as they drove. Ashley suddenly understood why the front seat was called riding shotgun.

They took a left and Alex slammed on the breaks. Ashley leaned forward to see what all the commotion was. Katie wasn't shooting, but she had her shotgun trained. Alex was fingering one of his pistols nervously.

The street was filled with vampires. They were pulling at a few people they'd caught like wild animals. They were slobbering fiends, fighting each other for every bite. There had to be at least a dozen of them, probably more.

"What's wrong with them?" asked Katie.

"I don't know, but I think we should find a different street," said Alex. Some of the vampires rose from their finished meals and regarded the truck more than curiously.

"I don't think we have any more time," said Katie. "I say we plow right through them." Alex started to put his foot on the gas when all the vampires charged. Only they weren't charging at the truck.

A figure stepped out of the shadows and walked calmly towards the vampires. He was drinking something and didn't appear to notice the chaos around them. They might have mistaken him for a beggar if not for the dark blue cloak which seemed to shine under the firelight. He shifted his drink to his left hand before drawing a longsword with his right.

"Drive," commanded Katie. Alex stomped on the gas and rushed towards the mob. He doubted they'd save the man's life, but they could try. They were fifty feet away when the vampires collided with the man.

The man tossed his drink into the sky and cut the first vampire in half with one deft blow. The sword seemed to take the light of the flames, glowing as it struck them all to ash. He walked and killed methodically. Every time a vampire looked like it might get close enough, he moved so suddenly he was a blur.

Alex swerved his truck into the last few vampires and ran them down. He leaned out his window and shot them to make sure they were gone for good. In his experience, it was best to make sure they were dead. The price of a few bullets was worth it to make sure the undead went back to dead. When he looked back to the cloaked figure though, he was gone. The street was empty.

"Where'd he go?" asked Ashley.

"We did all see him then?" confirmed Katie.

"Yes, he was just here," said Alex.

"Get us out of here," said Katie. There was a loud thump and Alex and Katie almost blew out the windshield out of reflex. It wasn't a vampire or the stranger. A coffee mug rolled across the hood. "Alex?"

"Katie?"

"That's one of the mugs."

"There's something in it," said Ashley. Not willing to stick her hand outside during the vampire apocalypse, Katie flicked on her flashlight and pointed it to the mug.

"Three dollars. Enough for a coffee or hot chocolate. Please drive Alex." Alex floored it and the coffee cup fell into the street.

"Was that another vampire?" asked Ashley.

"No," said Katie. "I don't know what that was."

"Whatever it was let's hope it stays away," said Alex.

"But it killed all those vampires," argued Ashley.

"Yes, with extreme ease," said Katie. "Someone who can do that and just disappear is never a good sign. Let's hope it hunts a few more vampires and leaves before it gets bored."

"Do you really think there's something else besides vampires and werewolves here too?" asked Ashley.

"It wasn't a vampire and it wasn't a wolf," said her dad. "I don't know what it was, but it wasn't human. Nobody is that fast."

"It could've been a vampire," said Ashley. "We didn't see its face or body so we don't know."

"Vampires don't feed on other vampires," said Katie calmly. "Even blood crazed ones don't. Vampire blood does nothing to nourish them. Whatever it was, it was no vampire." Ashley wanted to ask what it could be then, but decided against it. She was already having trouble keeping track of everything unnatural in the world. How many different things were there?

The house of Fortune was brightly lit when they arrived and the front door thrown wide open. Katie led the way in and Alex took up the rear. Alex saw more of the crazed vampires coming down the street and swore. He slammed the front door shut and bolted the door. The door was reinforced, but they would find a way in sooner or later.

"What if they come back?" demanded Ashley.

"Then I'll open the door," said her dad as he pushed her upstairs after Katie.

"What if we can't get to the door?"

"Then odds are neither can they."

The door shuddered as the vampires threw themselves against it. The front window cracked as another pounded against it. Alex pushed his daughter up the stairs and pointed his pistols at both locations. Whichever location broke first would get the much deserved attention of his guns.

Katie checked the upstairs rooms quickly and nodded with approval. She'd never been to the Fortune household before, but it was a fortress. The master bedroom didn't even have a window and the only entrance was the hallway. They could make them pay for every step they took. Alex began firing from the stairs and Katie waved Ashley back.

"Stay here and cover us!" she shouted and went into what she could only assume was Kara's room. A vampire leapt up and hit the window with its fist. Katie almost fired when she realized the glass didn't shatter. The windows were reinforced. The vampire clung to the wall and pounded desperately against the glass. Katie watched small pieces of glass fall away. The vampire made a tiny hole and placed its lips against it to scream inside.

Katie walked over to the window and placed her shotgun barrel through the hole. With one squeeze of the trigger, the lawn was sprayed with ash. She saw a dozen vampires trying to climb through the downstairs window. Some were so desperate to get through they leapt at her window. She managed to shoot another through the hole, but she could only wait for the others to make new firing holes for her.

Ashley stepped into the room to look at the insane vampires. She'd thought all vampires were like Karin, so calm and cool. These things were monsters. When more came to the window Katie pushed her back again and moved to deal with them. Ashley noticed Kara's wall was strangely bare as she left the room.

Katie shot another vampire off the window and loaded new shells into her shotgun. Their eyes were disturbing. They were bloodshot and unfocused. These vampires looked like they were possessed. They paid no heed to their own survival or wellbeing. One was beating his head against the glass in the hopes of making the hole his fist could not make. Katie leveled her shotgun as more glass came out.

What could do this?

CHAPTER 25

ENDLESS HUNGER

Famine leapt into the town in a mad frenzy. The run had only taken her eight minutes, but those eight minutes had felt like an eternity. Her body ached and cried out in pain from starvation. She hadn't fed in so long and she thought she might actually die from it.

Now that she was in town, she almost felt like she didn't know where to start. Death had told her to go and eat and hadn't given her any restrictions. She was allowed to eat and eat and she wouldn't get in trouble until Death came back for her. She didn't know how long Death would give her so she had to use the most of her time. She didn't even slow down as she came up to the first house on the edge of town. She hurled herself at the door.

It collapsed without a fight and she rolled badly in the entryway. A door opened nearby and a middle aged man came out. Famine half flopped, half rolled into the man and dragged him down by his legs. He screamed and she rolled herself on top and bit hard into his throat.

Warmth filled poor Famine's body as the man's blood flowed through her. Her muscles grew stronger, her aching body eased, and her eyes glowed with power. Blood, sweet precious blood. This was all she ever needed. This was all she ever wanted. She could stay in this spot all night if the blood lasted.

A loud bang filled the house and Famine felt her body shoved off the man. A screaming woman had come into the room and seen her husband's peril. Famine hadn't even noticed her until the wife fired the gun. The wife dropped the pistol and began to shake her husband, all the while screaming for help.

Famine felt the hole in her side and the blood leaking from her. It hurt. She almost wanted to cry, but her mind brushed aside the thought. Pain was nothing compared to her hunger. As long as she fed, her pain would disappear. She could feel the bullet hole already closing. She looked at the crying wife and smiled. The old man had begun to lose his taste, but her...she was new.

Phones began to ring in town as gunshots and screams were reported. Neighbors left their houses to see what was going on. As Famine was feeding on the woman she saw the approaching neighbors. She absently dropped the woman to the floor and licked her lips. These people were new, and some of them were younger.

Men and women screamed as the wall suddenly exploded as Famine shot out of it. She didn't even touch the ground before she was on her next victim. Some people fled, but others charged towards her. She looked up eagerly with bloody lips. As long as they kept coming, she could do this all night.

Morgan, Melissa, and Nathaniel all ran as fast as they could through the streets. The vampires were still primarily on the other side of town, but the ghouls were everywhere. Morgan cursed himself at how stupid he'd been to just trust that Karin had been killed. While they'd been gone celebrating, she'd infiltrated the town and planned its destruction.

It filled him with anger and pity as they raced past the groups of ghouls attacking the town. As dangerous as they were, they were harmless compared to the vampires coming in. He could already hear the screams of people on the far side of town where Karin's group must've entered. They had to find the vampires and kill them before they could spread. He would have to trust his brother to clean up the ghouls behind them.

The only advantage they had tonight was their speed. The vampires were certainly fast, but they could never compete with a werewolf in an open run. While they were further out of town, they reached the edges of town only minutes after the vampires had. Soon they'd be across town and into the vampire's ranks before they knew what hit them.

They came around a corner and spotted their first prey of the night. A trio of vampires were sitting over a body, feeding upon it madly. Morgan watched them with concern as they ate. They didn't act like normal vampires when they fed. There was no elegance with these vampires. They ate more like wild dogs one meal away from starvation. They fought and hit each other between bites on the corpse.

The vampires were so intent on their meal that they didn't even notice the danger coming towards them. Only one lifted his head and thought he'd heard something, only for Morgan to take his head off moments later. His wife and son dragged down the other two quickly and the fight was over in seconds.

Morgan threw his vampire aside and looked at the man they'd dragged down. He couldn't even recognize the man with how badly he'd been mauled. The thing that concerned him was the man was still breathing. He was gasping for air and cringing in pain. Morgan looked at him pitifully and knew it wasn't the pain of his wounds that bothered this man, but the change occurring inside of him. The vampires had infected him and soon he would be just like them.

Morgan wished he could apologize to the man, but the man wouldn't understand his words. The man started to convulse on the street. Morgan didn't know what foul work made the people change so fast, but there was little he could do about it.

One quick bite ended the man's life and horrible fate. Anger boiled in Morgan's belly as he felt this was all his fault. These vampires were here because of him. His ears perked up and he listened to all the screams. He snarled and raced towards them with his wife and son in tow. They would have such a reckoning tonight that the vampires would wish they'd never come to town!

Famine felt bloated and swollen from all the blood she'd ingested throughout the night, but still the hunger drove her. It didn't matter how much she consumed, the horrid hunger never left her. Why was she always starving? Why was her stomach always in pain? Why!

It didn't help that the herd was thinning already. Much of the town was fleeing already from the apparent riot. Fires were lighting up the town and Famine suddenly found competition to feast. Most of the people she'd bitten before had turned into wild monsters. They attacked without hesitation and fought for blood as if it were all about to disappear. Her newly raised minions were fighting more than just people for food. More than once Famine watched as vampires tore at each other for the chance to get the first bite on a human. Loyalty was not an issue when it came to feeding.

War and Death's ghouls learned this perhaps the hardest. They assumed for some reason since they worked for the vampires that they were safe from retribution. They paid for their stupidity in droves. Famine herself had dragged down her fair share of ghouls for the blood beating under their skin. She certainly cared that they belonged to War and Death, but her pains didn't. Her compulsion to feed defeated her will every time and more fell to her need by the minute.

A nearby human started to run towards Famine. Famine ran towards them eagerly. The man was so scared about what was behind him that he didn't bother to look in front of him. She pounced for him, but discovered she was a moment too late. He fell into the street as one of her underlings landed on his back. The vampire immediately went for the man's throat and the man screamed in fear.

Then the weight came off the man. He looked up in surprise to see another vampire had pulled his attacker off of him. The attacking vampire thrashed and hissed, but the other didn't even bother.

Famine throttled the vampire in anger and yanked him close. The vampire tried to punch her, but she ducked under his swing and lunged for his neck. Famine wasn't much of a fighter, but when it was win or lose for her next meal, she didn't lose. Her strength was in her jaw and she used it to great effectiveness. The vampire whined in fright as Famine ripped out his throat. His blood tasted putrid and it made her feel sick to her stomach. She tossed the vampire aside and left him to bleed on the sidewalk.

"Thank you," said the downed man gratefully.

Famine spat out the vampire's blood and looked at the man eagerly. His smile vanished as he realized he was in just as much danger as before. His killer had changed to a different person, but a killer is a killer. Famine held the shouting man down and soothed her disgusted stomach. Fresh blood had a way of fixing everything.

The bliss which accompanied Famine's meal almost caused her to miss the commotion nearby. The screams of vampires were unusually high just then and it sounded like bigger competition had entered the area. Her ears perked up as she heard thunderous heartbeats and she rose off the ground to wonder what it could be.

Three large werewolves came around the corner, bringing down vampires and ghouls alike. Famine rose and wondered what to do. They were certainly dangerous and would undoubtedly hurt her.

Did she really want to run though? Their beating hearts called to her and there was an allure to them. Most of the people she'd fed on were not strong and their laziness was reflected in their blood. But these werewolves were different. They were strong, powerful, and in their prime. What would they taste like?

Drool dripped out of her open mouth as she started towards them.

Morgan flattened another vampire and quickly looked about. They'd wiped out over ten vampires who'd all been crazy to feed. They were beginning to multiply like crazy and he feared the town couldn't take much more of this. They had to stop the vampires from spreading any further.

When he looked down the next street, he saw a familiar face. The blonde haired rider from Karin's group was in the street. She had just finished ripping apart a poor soul and was eyeing him. Her once neat outfit was splattered in gore and her face was a mess. She had no wound on her despite looking like she'd been through the worst of it.

"There!" he snarled. His wife and son both looked down the street at Famine. "The blonde girl is the one." A faint noise in the air and their ears went up. It had sounded like a howl.

"Can you take her?" barked Melissa.

"We'll be fine. Go." Morgan barked back. Melissa bounded away from them and Nathaniel came up next to his father's side. Famine was looking at them curiously and seemed to be thinking. "Go around and get behind her son. We can't let this one get away." Nathaniel nodded and started to head around the houses.

Famine's gaping mouth only grew wider as she started towards Morgan. Morgan had Famine all wrong. A smart vampire certainly would've run away from the huge werewolves before her, but Famine was not normal. Her condition drove her to feed and she could not back down from such a large meal. She would no sooner back down from Morgan than Morgan would run from her.

Just before they met, Famine slid underneath the huge beast. As much as she wanted to feed, she wasn't so stupid as to take Morgan straight on. She barely avoided his large jaws and she kicked him hard in the belly. She was strong from all the feeding she'd done and she struck him like a hammer.

All she appeared to do was hurt her own hands and legs. Her limbs may have been like a hammer, but this wolf was the anvil. She kept sliding about to make sure its mouth never found her. Being underneath it protected her in some ways, but it endangered her in more.

Morgan was heavy as a man and even heavier as a wolf. Each time one of his feet dropped onto Famine it drove the wind out of her. She would've panicked if she needed to breathe. She felt bones crack and blood leak free, but she didn't care. Morgan rose onto his hind legs and Famine clamped onto his arm and went for a ride.

Morgan's skin was tough and his fur was nasty, but Famine bit hard into his arm anyway. Morgan snarled in pain and Famine's eyes shined in delight. How right she had been! His blood was ferociously strong and it made her feel just as strong. Her wounds healed and her aching disappeared. She sucked hard at the wound, desperate to get every last drop.

Famine's pain reappeared as Morgan drove her straight into the pavement below. Many bones in her body cracked and she almost lost him. Instinct and desire however continued her death grip on Morgan's arm. His blood was delightful and she didn't want to let go. Stars flashed around her as Morgan dashed her against the floor again.

Morgan took Famine in both hands and threw her off of him. The damned vampire was determined and his arm was really beginning to hurt. Her bite was so secure that Morgan lost a bit of flesh in order to tear Famine free. Famine bounced along the street and came to her feet looking disappointed. She'd lost her food and she wanted it back.

It was time to repay the favor and Morgan leapt at her with his mouth open. Famine dove backwards expertly and prepared herself to leap onto the wolf's back. As long as she could get at his blood, she would never be defeated!

And then suddenly, for the first time in her life, Famine lost her will to feed. She lost her desire to eat and kill. The only thought she had now was how badly she'd erred in her fight. Blood had always been her greatest weakness and distraction. She should've thought past it tonight.

Wolves didn't hunt alone. It had been barely a minute since she'd seen him, but she'd already forgotten about the white wolf. He'd come up from the opposite side of the street and grabbed her while she wasn't looking.

Nathaniel's jaws clamped around Famine's side as she came to her feet. He bit down as hard as he could and he felt her small body come apart. She didn't resist and didn't cry out in pain. She just looked down at her body as if wondering how this could've happened.

Famine looked back up to see the werewolf she'd bitten coming right for her. His mouth was open and he was coming straight for her head. She couldn't move if she wanted to. She didn't feel anything anymore. She made the effort to smile one last time before Morgan took her.

For the first time in her life, she wasn't hungry. It was a nice feeling.

CHAPTER 26

WALKING PLAGUE

Ben tossed aside another ghoul and saw with satisfaction Samuel was doing the same thing. Samuel was young, but he was learning fast. Training in the woods was fine, but nothing trained a boy more than real combat. Samuel was already learning to pick his battles and attack his opponents when they were unaware. He was already using his larger uncle as bait so when they all came after Ben, Samuel would strike from behind. The boy was clever.

In many areas, the vampires were already pulling back. They'd strode into town confident at first, but they were young and inexperienced from the look of things. It was one thing to face unarmed humans in the middle of the night, it was a different thing to face them once they were scared and armed. None of them were ready to face werewolves. More than once Ben had seen vampires abandon their ghouls to the wolves. They were scared.

Still, there were some older ones present. Ben had faced a few and they were far nastier. Samuel had helped him drag down the last one and had taken a nasty hit for it. Ben had been hoping to find one of the four women who'd started this whole thing. He imagined his brother was fighting them more at the back end of town. He'd almost gone to join him, but Kevin was still missing.

He was positive Kevin could take care of himself, but he wanted to be sure his nephew was safe. All these ghouls and vampires though were making it near impossible to find him. It didn't help he blended into the night better than anything alive. He barked for Samuel to keep up as they ran down the street. Kevin had to be around here somewhere.

Around the corner, his nose detected something foul. Something gross was lingering in the air. He paused to see a dirty woman walking down the street. Ben could hardly see her face, but he could tell she was the source. The vampire only laughed as she approached the two werewolves.

Kevin paused and sniffed the air. He and Kara had killed many vampires and ghouls, but there always seemed to be more. Even though they were in the heat of battle, he was beginning to like this Kara. She was fierce and warrior like. She had no fear even in the face of relentless death and met it head on. She might be a little crazy, but she was definitely to Kevin's liking.

The thick stench of blood was in the air tonight and it was beginning to get harder to tell where the next group of vampires were and what was just the town. So many people had been lost. It made him angrier just thinking about it and he raced off to another location. He tensed as he prepared to leap over a few fences to get to the next street over. Kara seemed to be a natural rider and sensed his movements perfectly. She tucked her legs in tighter and lowered herself to him just as he jumped. They landed in the next street and Kara didn't even bounce.

In the street was a small group of vampires who were viciously ripping at a nearby corpse. They'd encountered these vampires before and they made the least sense to Kevin. They were so hungry they felt the need to stop and consume all of their victims on the spot. In an odd way, it was a good thing as it spared much of the town as three vampires would sit down for a meal. Kara raised her blade and Kevin bared his teeth. It was time to put an end to this plague.

He charged into the group and snapped a vampire almost in half. Kara swung her sword deftly from his back and cut down another. The third tried to wrestle Kara off her mount, but Kevin reached around and pulled the vampire to the floor. Kara neatly planted her sword in him and he stopped his hissing.

Kevin began his customary ritual of throwing the bodies into a fire when he heard a noise. A faint howl came from nearby. He barked out in fear. "Samuel?"

"Lead the way demon dog!" shouted Kara. Kevin looked back to Kara and shook his head. This was family business. He pointed for her to get off and step aside. Kara looked hurt, but did as she was told. As soon as she was off, Kevin launched himself into the night.

Kevin pounded through the neighborhoods and came to the street where Samuel was. His brother was lying in the street mewing. He could see long cuts along his body and his breathing was heavy. Kevin rubbed his head against his quickly and looked him over.

The wounds were bad, but not too deep. Samuel's regeneration would take care of these in no time. He would just have to take care of his brother until he was able to stand on his own again.

He looked around him warily. Where was uncle Ben? He should've been with Samuel and kept him safe. Nobody was more capable than uncle Ben, so where was he? Why was Samuel hurt in the middle of the street?

The openness of Samuel's position alerted him to the trap just before it was sprung. Why else would Samuel be lying in the middle of the street with no attacker in sight? There wasn't even a corpse near him to show he'd killed his attacker. He was the bait and Kevin had taken it.

The quiet street suddenly erupted with mad shouts as people swarmed them. Ghouls came out of the houses and swarmed the brothers like ants. Kevin knew his brother was in no condition to run. Which meant there was only one thing he could do. Kevin leapt at the crowd and tore his way through them as quickly as he could. These were merely people with simple weapons. He didn't need to use any technique against these opponents, just his size and superior strength. He leapt about repeatedly so they couldn't surround him. His heavy body flattened anyone he landed on. He grabbed and threw them about like rag dolls and bit into anyone who came too close.

Something was off about these ghouls. They attacked with no regard to their own life and they had no fear of Kevin. They smelled strange and when Kevin bit into them, he swore they tasted different too. Something about their blood was rotten.

He crushed the last of his foes and realized he was correct. The last one approaching him was foaming at the mouth. These people weren't just ghouls, they were sick. He picked up his last foe and hurled him into a burning building. He spat repeatedly to get their blood out of his mouth.

"A pity, but it went about as expected," said a woman. Kevin turned his eyes towards a rooftop where a vampire stood. He recognized her as one of the four women responsible for the attack on the town. "It is so hard to make ghouls for me and it's nearly impossible for me to make another vampire. You do realize how many servants you just made me waste, don't you?" Kevin's body began to feel warm and it felt like needles were poking at his side. He shook his head and focused on the vampire.

"Hmm, just beginning to feel it? It is so hard to find a good disease capable of taking on werewolves. Your bodies are something else when it comes to fighting off disease. Most normal humans would be dying by now." The vampire leapt off the house and landed in the front yard.

"Forgive my manners, I forgot to introduce myself. You can call me Pestilence." Kevin snarled at the woman. Pestilence held her hands out to him.

"Not even foaming yet. Let's see if I can change that." Kevin barked viciously at her, but he didn't charge. He didn't want to leave Samuel alone and he didn't know if going near this woman was wise. There was a horrible stench to her. She was beyond decay. She was infested.

"You must be that one's brother. The young ones do go down so quickly." Kevin looked at her with a new hatred he'd never felt before. "You must also be related to that other one with him. He certainly put up a good fight, but he was worth it." Kevin's eyes widened as he understood why uncle Ben wasn't here. Ben would've never left Samuel here alone. Ben would've never gone down without a fight. He could see claw wounds on this woman and smell his uncle's scent.

Something inside of Kevin snapped and he lunged forward. Pestilence gave a bubbly laugh as Kevin charged into her. Kevin knew not to bite her, but his teeth weren't the only weapons he had.

He slashed at her with his claws. She was surprisingly swift, allowing Kevin to get only glancing strikes.

"You're fast, but you're slowing with every step." She breathed heavily at him and Kevin could smell how toxic her breath was. He tried to leap back, but she caught both of his hands and held him. She was amazingly powerful.

"Take it in you foul beast. There's nothing you can do to stop it."

Kevin threw his head forward and headbutted her so hard she shrieked in pain. Black blood squirted out of her eyes and nose and she fell backwards. Kevin took the moment to pounce her and ride her into the street. She hacked up something terrible and Kevin found himself leaping away from her. She rushed him and struck him so hard she lifted him off his feet. Before he could set down again, she smashed him into a burning building. Pestilence cracked her neck and spat on the floor.

"You're a fierce one for sure." A roar came from inside the house and Pestilence held out her hands. "Not done yet?" The wall came apart as Kevin came crashing back through it, fire tracing his every step. For a moment he truly did look like a hellhound.

"Fight back as much as you want," laughed Pestilence. "Sooner or later, your strength will fall. Every moment you spend near me puts you closer to your last breath." Kevin brought up his arm and Pestilence just smiled. The more he touched her, the more he'd infect himself.

Then she panicked as she saw a large burning board from the house come up in his hand. Kevin swatted Pestilence to the floor with one easy stroke. She tried to rise again and he swept her into the air. His final blow broke the board across her and sent her skidding down the street. He dropped what was left in his hand and started after her.

Then his feet no longer held him. He dropped to the ground and found himself coughing. His vision became blurry and it felt like his muscles were shrinking. His stomach heaved and his lungs labored furiously. Something was inside him. He felt sicker than he'd ever been before in his life. He tried to force himself to stand and almost lost consciousness. Fire seeped through his veins and he didn't try and rise again.

Pestilence rolled to her feet down the street. She was cut in dozens of places and she had to crack her arm back into place. She sighed and patted down her filthy coat. She walked back to Kevin leisurely, her smiling growing with each step.

"I told you your strength would fail. Everyone does in time. I'll give you credit for lasting this long. You wolves really are something else. I bet if I left you here to heal, you'd eventually recover. But the disease you're tasting is just what I give off by walking around." Pestilence rubbed her hands in the thick blood coming out of her wounds. She stood over him with her hands pointed like daggers.

"Well then, I'm afraid this is the end." Kevin winced and started to close his eyes.

"DEMON DOG!"

Kevin's eyes flashed open and he rose as he heard Kara's voice. Pestilence turned in surprise as Kara appeared screaming. She swung her sword full into Pestilence's side and wedged the blade in deep. Pestilence screamed in agony and tried to hit Kara. Kara let go of her sword and dodged the blow before she grabbed her sword once more. She yanked the blade out with a sickening slurp and brought it spinning back around for Pestilence. Pestilence's scream became a horrible gargle as Kara split her jaw and throat.

Pestilence flailed and spewed her foul ichor everywhere. Kevin moved to the side, but Kara was not so fast. The foul blood splattered against her clothes and bare skin. Kara's skin swelled all at once and she started coughing. Pestilence continued to shriek as she collapsed to the floor. Kevin found the strength to move forward and kick Pestilence as hard as he could away from Kara. Pestilence went through the open wall Kevin had created and disappeared into the burning building.

Kara smiled and started to stumble. Her eyes were beginning to fade and her words were slurred. Pestilence's foul diseases were already on her and they were acting fast. Kara started to talk to Kevin, but she was moving the wrong way.

"Don't worry hellhound, I'll save you." She dropped to her knees and began to cough some more. Kevin made his way slowly over to her. Now that Pestilence was dead, he could feel his adrenaline rush leaving him. His body felt heavy and weary.

"Bad person," mumbled Kara. She stabbed her sword into an already dead ghoul. "Burn the bodies..." She let go of her sword for the first time and fumbled with the ghoul's possessions. She pulled out a bottle of liquor and smashed it against her sword. Her blade only had the tiniest bit of flame to it left, but even that was enough to turn her weapon and the body ablaze. Kara stared at the fire for a moment before she collapsed next to it.

"No..." cried Kevin as he ran towards her. He collapsed next to her and put his arm around her. He yawned as his body reverted to being a human again as he tried to stay awake. His body needed all the energy it could to fight off the infections. He hugged Kara and her head rolled over to look at him.

"I know you..." she whispered. Kevin held her side tightly.

"And I you."

"I guess I wasn't strong enough to make it," she said before a coughing fit took her. Kevin shook her.

"No. No you'll make it."

"No I won't. I'm only human. You're something else, I think you'll make it."

"We will make it," said Kevin as strongly as he could. "I won't lose you too."

"Just promise me one thing," shivered Kara. Her hand came up and squeezed Kevin's tightly. Tears came to her eyes and Kevin saw she was afraid. "Promise me."

"What?"

"Don't let me rot or become like them. When you're strong enough, put me in there." Kara let go of his hand and pointed weakly to the side. Kevin followed her eyes and saw a large burning building.

"No I won't. You won't die." Kara sniffed and held Kevin's hand again.

"Promise me..." she whispered as the light left her eyes. Kevin shook his head and hugged Kara tightly.

He'd lost two people he'd loved tonight and he'd only just met one of them.

CHAPTER 27

LADY DEATH

Ashley sat nervously in Mr. Fortune's bedroom. She was sitting next to his safe full of guns and desperately wishing she knew the code to help her dad and Katie. The both of them were watching the staircase and Kara's bedroom window for attackers. Only a few vampires and ghouls had been foolish enough to attack them and most of them had been killed. Her dad and Katie were ruthless and for once, she didn't mind.

Her head began to hurt from the stress. They were in the perfect choke point in Kara's house, but she couldn't help but fear. Her town was being overrun by vampires. Somewhere out there Nathaniel and his family were fighting for the town. They were probably getting hurt. She tried to shut out the visions of one of them dying, but she couldn't help it. She imagined coming out in the morning to see Nathaniel lying in the street with so many others.

She fell over hard as if something had just struck her on the back of the head. She looked behind her, but there was nothing but Mr.

Fortune's clothes. Alex rushed into the room quickly with his shotgun aimed high.

"Are you okay?"

"Yeah, I just fell over. I'm fine."

"Okay, stay here."

He rushed back out of the room and Ashley felt something prod her head again. She sat up and rubbed the back of her head, but nothing was there. It felt like her brain itched and her thoughts became sporadic. She remembered everything about the defenses of Kara's house from what she knew. As far as Ashley knew, the place was impenetrable and the only way through was the stairs or window.

Something clicked in her mind. No, that wasn't right. There was something else she'd forgotten. There was a hatch right in front of her that went down to the basement. Her dad must've known about it, but he hadn't mentioned it. He must've assumed almost no one knew about it. It was practically impossible to find unless you knew it was there.

Ashley rolled up the rug and looked at the escape hatch. She knew she had to stay in place, but she was afraid for everyone else. She couldn't help Nathaniel or the others by just sitting around. The concerned voices in her head told her to open the hatch quietly. She could sneak out this way and make sure everyone was okay. Her dad and Katie were so busy they probably wouldn't even notice she was gone. She could see the basement floor below her. The ladder up was disguised into a series of shelves for storage. She slipped down quietly when a new voice entered her mind.

"Ashley don't."

Ashley paused on the ladder and thought about the voice. She'd heard him somewhere before. It was a while ago, but she knew she'd heard him before here in Reiner.

"Remember who you are." Remember who she was? Of course she knew who she was. She chuckled at the silly question as she headed down.

"Remember where you are." The voice became more urgent, but Ashley shrugged it away easily. She knew where she was. That was exactly why she had to sneak out. Her dad would never let her go willingly and she had to know everyone was safe.

"Ashley?" asked her father from the other room. Ashley flinched and wondered if she could go back up. Something told her Nathaniel needed her more and she should go. Her dad and Katie could take care of themselves.

"Ashley?" asked her dad again. Ashley shook her head and started to climb back up the ladder. What was she thinking? She couldn't go outside right now. She wondered where such crazy thoughts had come from.

Then she felt something heavy wash over her and she let out a gasp as all the air left her lungs. It felt like someone had punched her hard in the stomach. She coughed for air and tried to keep climbing. The wave came again and Ashley saw her worst nightmares become reality.

Her eyes went dark and she lost hold of ladder. Visions streaked through her mind depicting the most horrifying scenarios. She saw her town, her friends, Nathaniel and his family, and her father burning. She saw them crying out in pain and agony. They were all around her and reaching for her, begging for help. She saw horror, pain, and madness all rolled into one. Ashley took in a deep breath and used it all for one last scream.

Katie was still shooting down the stairway as Alex reloaded his shotgun when he felt it. Something unnatural moved through the house. It couldn't be heard or seen, only felt. His breath became cold and his heart quickened. He'd felt something like this before from his hunting days. Something much older and far more powerful had come for them.

Alex heard his daughter scream and practically flew into the bedroom. He saw the open hatch and looked down to see Ashley at the bottom. There was a flash of darkness as a vampire came over her and pulled her away. Alex screamed as Ashley vanished and he ran for the basement. Katie flattened herself against the wall as Alex launched himself down the stairs. In the basement, he saw a window barely large enough for a small person to fit through had been neatly removed. Ashley was laying just outside it when pale hands plucked her up and they disappeared from sight. Unable to even scream, Alex reversed course to the front door. The mad vampires were almost stunned to see a rage equal their own. A wall of lead and silver cut through the confusion.

A lithe figure stood at the end of the block, Ashley over her shoulders, and blew Alex a kiss. Then they were gone.

Katie caught Alex by the shoulder before he could run out into the night.

"Get off me! They have Ashley!" he screamed.

"I know! We'll get her back, but we're no good to her dead!" Alex took a deep breath and took a step back inside.

"Get your things, we're going now."

Katie's eyes moved away from Alex and looked back outside. He followed her gaze to see someone walking towards them. Alex aimed his pistol at the approaching man. He didn't look like a vampire, but he was obviously being controlled. He was shaking in fear and his walking was off. He was trying to fight some outer influence from making him walk towards the deadly pair.

"Ghoul," said Katie. "What do you want?" She aimed her pistol at the man. The man started crying but his legs kept him coming towards them.

"M...My master...bids me." The man shook and twisted suddenly. His head rolled around and when it came back, he looked completely different. His eyes were blank and a grin crossed his face. The master had come forth to speak with them.

"Beautiful Hunters, how I love the sight of you," said the man in a hiss.

"What do you want?" asked Alex.

"I have her." Alex pointed his pistol at the ghoul's head.

"Tell me where she is."

"I will. In exchange for her, I want you." The man pointed at Alex. Alex grimaced and Katie put her hand on his shoulder.

"We don't do trades for life or death." Alex shot her a damning look. It was his daughter and he would make these decisions.

"Oh I don't want his life so easily," laughed the man. "It would be so boring to just kill you. I want to fight you and then kill you. A duel."

"A duel for my daughter?"

"Yes..." The man held out his hands. "No guns, only blades and skill will tell our fate tonight."

"We're not walking out in the street unarmed," snapped Katie. "We'd be dead in two seconds."

"Not a problem."

The man snapped his fingers and dark figures appeared on the nearby house. Alex and Katie each tracked an oncoming vampire and began to wonder what was going on. "These are my most trusted underlings. They will escort you to me for our fight." The man turned and looked at the pair. "You will not harm either of these two and you will protect them against all harm. Any one of you who defies me will suffer for eternity. Do you understand?"

Both vampires nodded. Alex noticed something about these vampires. Even though their master commanded them through a mere ghoul, each of the vampires was genuinely afraid. This spoke leagues of their master. Alex lowered his pistol.

"What are you doing?" begged Katie.

"I accept your terms," he said. The man laughed and curtsied.

"I shall wear my finest dress." Alex nodded before he raised his pistol and blasted the ghoul. The man twitched violently under the bullets before he fell to the ground. The pair of vampires looked at Alex warily but didn't advance.

"I never liked him," said Alex. The pair just nodded. "I'll be right back, I need to get a blade." They nodded again. Katie followed him upstairs and looked at him like he was crazy.

"What are you doing?"

"I'm getting my daughter back. If this bitch wants a fight, then she'll get one." Alex looked through Kara and Mr. Fortune's weapons and frowned. He walked over to the window and looked at the pair.

"Does she want knives or a sword?"

"The lady uses knives," said one. Alex nodded and went back inside. He pulled two knives from his Hunter bag and secured them to his side.

"I can't believe you're doing this," said Katie.

"I'm doing this, you're not." He gave a quick wink and headed out the door. Katie watched him go speechless. It was suicide, but what choice did he have?

They had Ashley.

Alex walked down the street with the pair of vampires at his sides. They were tall, lean men who walked with an arrogant swagger. They kept a pair of long knives in their hands as they walked, but unlike Alex, they didn't watch the road. Alex kept an eye out at all times for approaching vampires, but nobody bothered them. Any vampires they crossed saw them and backed away without a word. They may have wanted Alex, but these vampires showed he was in their care.

Alex didn't know how long the walk would be and took the time to try and understand the situation. He thought about how they'd found out about the secret escape hatch at the Fortunes and how they'd taken Ashley so easily. The attacking vampires must've explored the house top to bottom and perhaps they'd merely stumbled across it. It was a possibility, but he didn't think the right answer.

He remembered the chilling force that had come into the house. It hadn't been directed at him or Katie, but at Ashley. Something out there knew Ashley was there and wanted her outside. The house was too well defended so instead of breaking in, this "lady" had called Ashley out of hiding. It made the best sense to him and also made him worried.

Vampires, like many immortals, became more powerful as they aged. If one here had the power to charm and dominate Ashley without seeing or speaking to her, then she would be the most powerful one present. He had to defeat this vampire to save both his daughter and his town.

A squealing noise drew their attention to an oncoming vampire. This vampire looked mad and recently turned. It probably hadn't even had its first meal yet and was ready to feed. Alex started to draw his knives, but the vampire next to him was ready first. He barely flicked the knife out of his right hand and the attacking vampire went down. It twitched as they approached and reached for Alex.

"I will finish this, keep walking." The one on the right nodded and led Alex on as the other stayed behind to finish the job.

"Not exactly friends with the others, are you?" asked Alex.

"No."

"How much farther is it?" The vampire pointed ahead.

"One left, then a right until the end of the street."

"Left, right, and to the end of the street?" repeated Alex. The vampire nodded. "Good, not far then." The other vampire appeared at Alex's side.

"We will be there soon."

"I heard. So why does Karin want to fight me so bad?"

"We know nothing about Karin," said the one on the right.

"Then Karin was not the one who called me out?" They shook their heads.

Alex thought that was interesting. Karin had been trying to get Ashley for so long he'd assumed it had been her. Now the question was who? Was Karin really the leader of this bunch or was she just a figurehead?

"Has anyone ever told you how beautiful your hair is?" asked Death as she stroked Ashley's hair. Ashley squirmed in her chair, but with Death so close she had nowhere to run. "I love it. As dark as a raven's feather. I'm really quite jealous." Death spun Ashley around and placed her in front of a mirror.

Searing pain shot through Ashley's head and made her scream. It felt like someone had put hot needles through her brain. Death purred and the pain came again. Lances stabbed through her skull and burrowed their way in like snakes. Ashley felt venom behind her eyes and it made her sob. The room started to shake and her head began to blow up like a balloon. She heard screams all around her and blood began to drip up from the floor.

"Open your eyes."

Ashley's eyes opened and she saw only Death behind her. The room was no longer lit, but desolate and cold. The winter air was seeping through the holes in the wall. Death was floating behind her like a demon, her eyes pitch black.

"Realize your greatest fears."

She placed her hands on Ashley's cheeks and the mirror began to move forward. Ashley wanted to scream, but she couldn't find the strength to do so. Her reflection did not shine back in the mirror. Instead, the glass rippled like water. As it advanced it began to grow, and it soon grew big enough to consume her.

Then she was through it. Ashley wasn't sitting in the room anymore, but standing in the street. Her town was on fire and the streets were filled with blood. There were no noises, no people, and no conflict. It was as if the townspeople had suddenly vanished.

"Ashley!" screamed Nathaniel.

Ashley screamed and writhed in her chair. Death ran her hands through Ashley's hair with pride. Every worst fear Ashley had was coming alive in her mind, and she was being forced to relive them time and time again. The more pressure she applied on her sanity, the more the girl panicked. She wasn't hurting the girl and she didn't have to. The body is useless without the mind after all.

After minutes of playing, Ashley's screams became quiet. Her head laid back and she started mumbling incoherently. Death smiled and eased up. The mind is a fragile thing and can only take so much. She played with the girl's mind quietly, forcing her to see nothing but what she wanted. The mirror in front of her only helped reinforce the visions. Death really hoped the girl's father would get here soon. Ashley's mind was already being covered in a dark shroud and she was getting bored.

"My Lady Death!" shouted one of the two vampires. "We have brought the one you desire."

Death rose and stepped through the hole in the wall. What delightful timing. She stepped outside of the house she was using as her base and smiled. Alex did not smile at the sight of her. Faster than she would've expected for a man of his age, two knives were drawn and plunged into her servant's backs. They didn't even get time to scream before they turned to ash and faded away. Alex brought the knives up to Death.

"That wasn't very nice," said Death as she walked out.

"Death knows no pity," said Alex. "Death does not care about your emotions or feelings. It comes when it is supposed to and there is nothing we can do about it." Death smiled and drew her knives.

"Oh I was right about you," she said delightfully. She pressed the blades against her bare flesh and cringed. "You are a man who truly understands the principles of death. You know its cold touch and its inevitable stroke. Yet you walk towards it with fire in your eyes and steel in your hands." Death held her knives out and bowed. "I want no other in this town than you."

"You can have me when I can have my daughter back. Now where is she?" Death nodded to the house.

"She sits inside, waiting for a hero to come and rescue her. Now would you be a dear and throw away the pistol you have." Alex smiled and drew it from underneath his coat.

"You knew I had it?"

"Of course. I would expect nothing less from a man like you." Alex raised his pistol to her. "You don't want to do that."

"Why not?" he asked.

"Because I have only to signal my pawn inside to finish off your daughter. Can you kill me before I tell him to attack?" Alex lowered the pistol.

"And how do I know she's safe then?" asked Alex.

"I promise you this Hunter, if you defeat me, you can have your daughter back. I wouldn't trust any other vampire here tonight with that promise, but I ask you to trust me. Your daughter is not the one I want." Death licked her lips and waved Alex forward.

Alex threw aside his pistol and brought his knife back up. He did believe this one. He could see the look in her eye. This vampire was crazy only for him. Alex took a deep breath as he advanced on Death. He didn't like how she looked at him. This fight would end badly.

He swept his right knife out while keeping his other close. He made his sweeps wide to test Death's defenses. Just as he'd guessed, she was lightning fast and parried each blow only as she needed to. Her eyes didn't even follow the flashing knife around her, but remained on Alex's face. Alex brought his knife around to the right just like before, but just as she parried it, he snapped his leg into hers.

Death grinned as her leg didn't budge. She was more powerful than this small human. When she planted her feet it would take something far greater to move her. She flashed towards him so close her lips were almost on his. "Stop testing the waters," she said seductively, licking her lips. "We're not dating anymore." She lifted her leg and kicked him across the street.

Alex hit the road and kept rolling. He went head over heel and side to side. He groaned painfully and felt his back crack as he rose to his knees. He was getting too old for this. He'd done these kinds of fights before, but those were almost twenty years ago. He wasn't as fast as he remembered or as strong. He stood shakily and was so concerned if he could even stand up that he didn't even think about how his back was turned to a monster.

"I expected better of you," said Death from only a few feet behind him. "So did your daughter."

Death barely managed to finish her sentence as Alex whirled on her. So close was she to him that even with her speed she barely managed to dodge the knife he'd thrown. She watched it sail only an inch above her head and smiled. It was moments like these she swore she had a heartbeat again.

Alex came at her like an angry lion. Death barely had time to recover as he came in swinging. He only had one knife while she had two, but he had the offensive now. Each swing seemed to bring him a little closer to her delicate flesh. She barely blocked a blow coming down towards her when Alex's free hand shot forward. He caught the front of her dress and pulled her and his knife closer.

Death slid her free knife across his arm and Alex recoiled. Even through his jacket, the razor sharp blade had caressed his skin. It was Death's turn to advance and she wasted not a moment. She danced around him, stabbing with both blades. Alex barely turned them away in time and some came through regardless. A line was drawn across his shoulder, his arm, and his side. Death swept up with her left hand and Alex caught her just below the hilt. Blood streaked across her hand and her knife went flying away. Only the foul smile on her face told Alex he'd made the wrong move.

Both the sweep and even Death's hand had been a lure. Her right hand flicked down and cut along Alex's leg. He stumbled in pain and Death shouldered him to the floor. In a flash, she kicked his knife away and knelt on his chest. Her right hand went up and sank back down with the blade. Alex caught her arm with both hands and pushed against her with all his strength. Death licked her bloody hand and smiled.

"You're quite strong for a human," she said. Alex gasped as he put everything against her one arm. He could barely hold her back and she still had one arm free. "Yes, that's it," she whispered. "Fight death with everything you have. Never give in." The knife came up and down in the struggle. Neither side could be budged, but that wasn't a good thing. Alex would get tired, she wouldn't.

"Would you like to know what I showed your daughter?" she said happily. "Let me show you the world outside of this one." Alex suddenly felt cold and Death's eyes became pitch black. "Realize your greatest fears."

Alex's head began to hurt and he shut his eyes to her. This woman was an old vampire for sure. She was trying to force her illusions upon him. He focused only on the knife trying to descend on his chest.

"I will not," he gasped as he pushed. Death smiled and the pain in his head tripled.

"Your will is powerful. You do not fear me at all. It's what I love about you." Alex cringed as the knife began to sink slightly. "Do not worry." She caressed his face gently with her free hand. "I will change that." The push for his mind multiplied and he nearly let go. He could hardly remember that he was holding off the knife and not drowning.

The sound of a rifle echoed and reality returned. Death looked up as her link inside the house disappeared. The other Hunter she'd left behind was here. She was lying on a roof and had found her servant near Ashley. Her leverage was gone.

Alex's hand flexed and Death heard metal clink inside the sleeve. She tried to leap back from him, but she was not faster than a bullet. Alex's sleeve tore open as the round shot out and went through Death's chest. She felt the silver tumble and burn inside of her. She fell backwards and let the ground take her. The wound was fatal and she could see nothing but the stars above her. Alex rose to look at her.

"You cheated," she hissed.

"Death has no rules. It comes when it wants." Death smiled as her chest began to turn to ash.

"You are truly a man worthy to dance with." She blew a kiss to Alex just before she turned to dust completely. "Thank you," she said in a ghostly whisper.

Ignoring the dying monster, Alex ran into the house screaming Ashley's name. He feared the worst when she didn't respond. He found her however in the next room, sitting quietly in a chair. She was alive and tears were running down her cheeks. "Ashley are you alright?" He hugged her tightly and he felt her arms go around him. It occurred to him she wasn't even tied up. She hugged him tightly, but she didn't say anything. He let go of her and looked into her eyes.

"Ashley?" Her eyes were cloudy and haunted. She was mumbling to herself and trying to keep her head down. "Can you hear me Ashley?" She nodded and pressed her head against his chest. Katie came in after them with the rifle over her shoulder and a pistol in her hand.

"Is she alright?"

Alex looked at Katie with scared eyes and shook his head. Katie met Ashley's eyes for only a moment but she could see they were changed. The girl had become torn, her mind frightened. The vampire was dead but Death's touch on her would remain.

"I want to leave..." muttered Ashley. "I want to go home."

"Okay Ashley."

"I want to go home." Alex nodded and led her out of the house.

"We're going home Ashley. We're going home."

Ashley stayed attached to her dad the whole way. He watched her worriedly when Katie put her hand up for them to stop. Alex looked up and saw a small mob of vampires coming down the street. Their eyes were blank as they came.

"They want their master," said Katie. Alex nodded and brought up his reclaimed pistol. Ashley hid behind him and cringed.

"Can she run?" asked Katie. Alex shook his head. Ashley could barely walk on her own. They would have to take care of this here and now.

The vampires suddenly panicked and screamed as the large form of Morgan came barreling through them. Nathaniel appeared two steps behind his dad and began to claim anyone who'd been knocked over. The vampires scattered, leaving Katie and Alex to take the shot at anyone who fled the two wolves. The threat was over in a matter of seconds.

Morgan pursued any who'd escaped, but Nathaniel went to Ashley. He told his father he'd watch them until they got somewhere safe. He stopped in front of Katie and Alex. Both of them looked the worse for wear. Ashley was quivering behind her dad and didn't seem to notice he was there. He looked at Ashley and she barely looked back.

"She's not well Nathaniel," said Alex. Nathaniel looked at him confused and barked at Ashley. Ashley just shook. "The vampire did things to her mind. She needs to rest."

Ashley let go of her father and sat down in front of Nathaniel. She knew this wolf; she knew he was good to her. Nathaniel pawed the ground. Ashley just stared at him confused. Nathaniel struck the ground harder, but Ashley didn't understand. He brought his head low and looked into her eye. All he gained was a glimmer of recognition.

"Nathaniel," started Alex. Nathaniel gave Alex a dark look and looked back to Ashley.

Nathaniel brought his head up suddenly and let loose an ear splitting howl. Alex and Katie covered their ears and cringed at the sudden force. Only Ashley didn't bother to cover her ears. Nathaniel howled once more and gave it even more power than the last. Alex and Katie backed away, but not Ashley. Ashley rose to her feet and came closer to Nathaniel.

This sound. She knew this sound. It cleared her head and filled her with confidence. She didn't have to think about this sound. Something deeper than her thoughts told her this howl was powerful. This noise was powerful for her, and her alone. She gained strength from its high octaves and felt life returning to her. Moments later the skies were filled with dozens of howls. She didn't know if they were real or not, but she took strength in them. For reasons she wasn't sure of, she threw her head back and howled with the wolf.

Alex watched his daughter nervously. He wasn't sure how she wasn't being deafened, but she seemed to be her old self again. Nathaniel's howl rattled all of them, but perhaps it would rattle some things back into the right place for Ashley. He was more curious as to where all the other howling was coming from. It sounded like the forest and town had come alive. Nathaniel stopped howling a moment later and the town went quiet. He and Ashley lowered their heads to look each other in the eyes.

"I know you," said Ashley. She put her arms around the great wolf's head and nuzzled it. Nathaniel sat down and Ashley found herself climbing onto his back. He stood up again and she held onto him like a child would a parent. Nathaniel barked and started walking forward.

"You said it," said Katie and they walked after him. She hoped the worst of the night was finally over.

CHAPTER 28

WAR IS MERCILESS

Mary hurried through the forest with Lidia on her back. Her feet pounded along the hard dirt as she sidestepped the trees. She wasn't too far away from the shelter now. She'd heard her father's call to pull many of the wolves out to the town. There wouldn't be many of them in the den, but they'd gladly welcome Lidia and Mary.

From where they were she couldn't see the town, but she could hear all the terrible things that were happening. Mary was glad Lidia wasn't old enough to change yet. The town was filled with screams and panic. The night sky was dark, but she could see it lit up from the fires raging in town. She hoped everyone would be okay. She understood that somebody had to watch over Lidia, but she desperately wished she could be in town with the others.

"Hello there girls," said a woman gleefully as she stepped into their path.

Mary took a few quick steps back and bared her teeth at this woman. How had she snuck up on them? How had she even known where they were? The woman flashed her white teeth and grinned.

"My name is Karin and I've been looking for you."

Mary paused and considered her options quickly. She knew who this was and she knew she was outmatched. She couldn't fight Karin, but could she get away? She felt Lidia hold her fur tighter.

"Do you know why I came here?" asked Karin. Mary snarled and showed off more of her teeth. Lidia responded.

"Why?" Mary swatted Lidia with her tail and barked at her to be quiet. Lidia just nodded quickly and ducked back down to Mary's back.

"Because I never wanted your town. All I ever wanted was your dad, but I can't have him now. The best revenge on him and that bitch of a mother you have isn't to kill them. The best way I can hurt them is to hurt you." Lidia quivered on Mary's back. Mary barked and clawed the ground before Karin. If Karin wanted to kill them, she wasn't going down without a fight.

"You see these?" Karin pulled out a long pair of knives from her jacket. Lidia shook uncontrollably as Mary growled. Karin smiled and threw both of the knives into the ground. Mary paused and looked at her confused. Karin pulled off her jacket and cracked her knuckles. "The fight would be over way too quick if I used those. Besides, I don't need knives to take on a little girl like you." Mary leaned up and barked for Lidia to get down. Lidia took a moment before she was finally able to shy away from her sister. Karin waved Mary forward. "Let's see how much you know."

Mary knew a lot. She knew she wasn't anywhere near experienced enough to take on a vampire like Karin. She knew Karin would drag out this fight and if she lost, nobody would protect her sister. As she arched her back to drop Lidia she suddenly threw back her head and let loose the most powerful howl she could muster. There were no words in it, only a cry of panic so great she hoped others would hear it. She barely managed to get it off before Karin sped forward and struck her in the chest. Mary felt the wind leave her as she flew back.

"No calls tonight please!" laughed Karin. "This party is already overcrowded." Karin leapt forward again and Mary moved to meet her. She slashed at the woman with her claws, but Karin was like lightning. She blurred left and right so fast Mary wasn't sure where she was. She swung both her arms around to crush anything around her. A young tree went down, but Karin skipped back easily. Karin danced around her laughing before she turned back into a blur.

Mary wasn't sure if she went left or right, but she felt the hit. Karin dashed around and Mary slashed at her again. Karin caught Mary's arm just past the claws and threw her to the side like the child she was. Mary let herself slide and howled once more to the night sky. Karin hissed and leapt at her. Mary brought her claws around to catch her, but Karin was too sly for that. She pushed Mary's arms down and leapt up towards her face. Karin went for Mary's throat, but Mary's large head dropped down and flattened Karin's charge.

Karin hit the ground and immediately rolled to the left. Mary's claws tore up dirt before following after the vampire with her large jaws. She kept Karin rolling as she snapped and clawed after her. If she could just keep Karin from standing, Mary could win this. Karin finished a roll and her slender leg snapped up into Mary's jaw. Mary bit her tongue badly and found herself hitting the ground. How were vampires so strong? She rose to her feet again only to find Karin's foot connecting with the side of her face.

Mary hit the floor and this time she didn't get up as easily. She looked up at Karin and despised how this woman looked at her. It was the same look a person had when they were about to step on a bug. Karin wasn't hitting her again because she wanted her to get back up. She wanted her to scuttle about and attempt to fight back. She was enjoying this.

She feigned injury as she rose to shaky legs. She had to make Karin underestimate her. She snarled as she stepped towards her. Karin just grinned and readied herself for the next attack. Mary let her head droop as she advanced. "Is that all you have?" mocked Karin. Mary grinned. No, no it was not.

Mary leapt up and spread her body to its full length. So close there was no way Karin could escape her. Karin was better in almost every way, but she couldn't match Mary's size. Mary would squish this little woman if she had to. Claws and teeth out, she collapsed herself over Karin.

And immediately found herself gagging. Karin stepped into her embrace and slammed Mary as hard in the chest as she could. Before Mary could move she felt ten more blows just like it hammer home. She stumbled back and sank to a knee. She brought her head back and went for one last howl when Karin's fist crumpled her windpipe.

"What did I tell you?" commanded Karin.

She kicked Mary to the floor and laughed mercilessly. This was just too great. She'd take Mary apart piece by piece and when she was done, there was still the little runt. She looked over to Lidia. The little girl had been shivering next to a tree, frozen by fear. When their eyes met however, something clicked that it was time to go. Lidia bolted into the forest.

"Where do you think you're going?" shouted Karin as she sped after Lidia. Lidia was little and her legs were short, but she was fast. Lidia had always been quick and she had never been faster than she was right then.

Lidia's legs pumped fiercely and her agility rose to new levels. Karin tried to grab her repeatedly, but Lidia dove and twisted just out of reach every time. Lidia's tiny form also gave her leeway to go places Karin could not. She slid through bushes and jumped through the tiniest of gaps in the trees.

"Mommy!" she screamed.

"Your mommy isn't coming for you," laughed Karin.

"Mommy!" Karin landed right in front of her and Lidia went neatly between her legs. Years of avoiding her larger siblings had taught her well. But Lidia never smiled at her speed. Her achievements didn't impress her tonight. Only a single thought went through her head.

Unless someone saved her, she would die tonight.

"Mommy!"

Lidia sprinted through bushes and slid down the hill when she came to it. Karin leapt straight for the bottom and stood there waiting for her. Lidia controlled her slide and kicked off the hill just before the bottom. She sailed just out of reach of Karin's swipes and landed on the other side. She didn't miss a beat and kept running as soon as her feet touched the ground.

Karin growled angrily at the girl. She was growing tired of this chase. It should have never been so hard to catch a little girl, but Lidia was proving more talented than she'd imagined. Still, while the girl was fast, she certainly wasn't smart. She was running blindly in fear.

Karin cracked a small branch off a tree as she chased after Lidia. She spun it in her hand before she sent it flying. Lidia shrieked as the branch swiped out her legs and caused her to falter. She tumbled expertly and rolled to her feet, but slowing down was the last thing she could afford. Karin grabbed her by the arm and lifted her off the ground.

"No more running for you."

"Mommy!"

"I despise your voice. It's far too loud." Karin grabbed her by the throat and Lidia's screams disappeared. "Better. Let's make it permanent!"

Karin threw back her head and screamed in pain as Mary came in from behind her. Mary was bleeding and her body hurt in more places than she could count, but she was on her feet. Nobody touched her sister!

Mary's jaws took Karin around the side and they rolled into the dirt. Lidia was dropped to the ground as Karin suddenly had a much bigger worry. Mary's strength was little, but her teeth were sharp. A wolf near death could still bite and Karin couldn't risk playing around anymore.

She drove her elbow fiercely into Mary's head repeatedly. Mary bit down harder and Karin felt the blood flowing freely out of her side. She smashed harder and harder until Mary's jaws went slack. Her teeth came out and Karin kicked Mary off of her.

Mary rolled a few feet away and didn't get up again. She was still breathing, but she was spent. Lidia came over and held her injured head. Mary tried to bark for Lidia to run again, but she didn't have the strength. Lidia was scared and was holding onto her sister for protection. Mary couldn't protect her anymore.

"Agh! I don't believe this!" shouted Karin. Her side was a bloody mess and she could feel the pain flashing through her body. Despite how injured she'd been, Mary had managed to deal a terrible wound to Karin. It wasn't life threatening, but it was weakening and it hurt. It hurt bad.

Karin turned on the girls with eyes filled with rage. She had toyed with them before. She had wanted to enjoy the deaths of the daughters of her old love. Now the games were over. Now it was time for such a terrible reckoning. She would smash Mary into a pulp and make sure she never got up again. Then she would rip the infernal voice box out of her sister Lidia to make sure she never had to hear that whiny voice again.

"Mommy!"

"Enough!" shouted Karin. "NO MORE!" Karin's anger tripled and she leapt for the girls.

"MOMMY!"

A roar came towards her and she thought for a moment Mary was getting back to her feet. Karin realized very quickly that was impossible. Mary was too badly injured to interfere again. No, this roar was filled with strength and an inexpressible rage. The sound was closer to borderline madness. It all came at Karin as Melissa came bounding over her daughters and straight into her.

Melissa had been coming ever since she'd heard Mary's howl. She'd been running as fast as she could as she realized the evil intent of Karin. The assault on the city had merely been a distraction so the family would get separated. She knew the girls would not come into town and they would be alone.

She was barely back up the mountain when she heard Lidia screaming. Every time she heard her daughter scream for her it felt like a lance through her heart. The fear and terror of what was happening to her children was physically painful. Each scream brought a new level of rage Melissa hadn't imagined possible. Lidia's screams touched her in ways that her other children's cries never would.

If Lidia was screaming for her, that meant Mary no longer could. If Mary no longer could cry out, where was she?

Her other children were werewolves and could defend themselves against some of the worst foes the world had to offer. Lidia wasn't even ten, she couldn't defend herself against anything.

Lidia was just a child. Mary was just a child. They were her children and nothing would ever touch them while she lived.

When Melissa hit Karin, she didn't pounce upon her like a wolf would its prey. Melissa hit Karin like a terrified parent who was about to lose their babies. She rode Karin into the ground and bit deeply into her shoulder. Warm blood spewed out of the open wounds and Karin screamed like a banshee. Melissa drove her sharp claws into Karin's body and raked her repeatedly.

Karin hissed and forgot her pain. She took hold of Melissa and threw her off of her like she was nothing. Karin leapt to her feet and turned on the wife of Morgan. If there was anyone she wanted more than the children, it was Melissa. This was the woman who had stolen her title, her life, and her love. Karin's dying body became filled with limitless strength as she thought of all the ways she hated this woman.

Yet Karin never stood a chance. Melissa was driven by a hatred a million times greater than Karin could ever understand. Even if Karin had been at full strength she still would've lost this charge. Karin had purposely hunted Melissa's children and attempted to kill them. She had beaten her eldest daughter and had meant to kill her youngest. She had endangered her entire family by throwing them into a massive battle for the town that should've never happened.

Melissa charged back at Karin not just as an enemy, but as a mother and a wife. Karin felt light as a feather as she lifted her into the air. Karin felt weaker than a fly and gave just as little resistance. Melissa bit into her neck and collapsed it into a wet mush.

Lidia stayed cuddled up next to her sister as her mom tore at Karin's body. She closed her eyes and held onto Mary. She didn't need to know what her mommy did to the mean monster, she just knew she'd take care of it. That's what mommy did and that was what she would always do.

"Mary! Lidia!" Her mother's arms came around and felt them both. Mary tried to smile, but she just laid there. Lidia crawled into her mom's arms and held her tight.

"I knew you'd come."

"Mommy will always come," said Melissa through her tears. She held Lidia tightly with one arm and felt Mary.

"You did good Mary. I'm so proud of you."

"Is she gonna die?" whispered Lidia fearfully.

"No she won't. Mary will be just fine." Melissa hugged her kids and told them repeatedly how much she loved them. She had come so close to losing them both and she would never let that happen again.

CHAPTER 29

IT'S ALL OVER

Alex didn't know what time it was when they neared his home. It might not have even been ten, but it felt like days had gone by. He was exhausted and his wounds ached terribly. He realized how old he really was with every step he took. His body just didn't take a beating like it used to.

Katie was walking next to him with barely a scratch on her. She'd been the luckiest throughout the night, keeping her enemies at range. There were a few scratches, but nothing life threatening. Alex squeezed his daughter's hand.

Ashley was lying on Nathaniel's back asleep. He wasn't sure if she was asleep, but she wasn't moving or talking anymore. She just clung to Nathaniel's back and stayed there. Whatever that vampire Death had done to her, it was bad. She must've been a very old vampire to be able to touch a person's mind like that. He'd felt her touch too, but he'd been trained to resist such a thing. Plus he'd been in the heat of battle where there was no time to think, only fight.

Ashley hadn't been trained for fighting. She'd been sitting in fear and at the whim of Death's cold touch. He had no idea what she'd done to his daughter's mind, but he could only hope she'd recover soon. He secretly feared the damage done might be permanent. If it was, Death had won their fight, not Alex.

Nathaniel was still walking strong with Ashley on his back despite his injuries. He was cut in several places and his white coat had become darker. He taken the vampires apart easily, but for every one he'd fought, someone had dealt a blow back. Alex could tell his strength was almost to its limit just by his pace. Nathaniel had slowed not because of them, but because he hurt. They were almost home.

The commotion for the most part had died down. Alex wasn't sure what the vampire's plans had been, but the shock force of the werewolves seemed to have halted it. The vampires had come in ill prepared and with no guns. If Alex had to guess, the lead vampires didn't care for the lives of their underlings and had simply gone for a terror campaign. The damage they'd caused to the town would never be fixed and the fear they'd instilled in its people would never leave.

Still, the people had fought back incredibly. Men and women had gathered and taken down their attackers as one. Wild vampires were dangerous, but so were experienced humans with shotguns and rifles. They had to avoid many streets simply because they shot at the mere sight of Nathaniel. It had made their walk home longer, but Alex didn't want Nathaniel going off the path with Ashley on his back. They would all go home together.

They were almost home when Nathaniel's great head rose to the end of the street. Two men were coming around warily with hunting rifles. Nathaniel paused as he saw them and they turned before he could hide.

"There's another one!"

They raised their rifles before Alex and Katie could shout at them to stop. Nathaniel didn't leap aside, but rolled his back away from the shooters, putting Ashley against the street and away from the shooting.

The rifles barked and Alex brought up his pistol and began firing back. Katie purposefully put bullets near their feet. The two men screamed and ran, now shooting wildly and inaccurately. Alex couldn't believe he'd just done that. He'd shot at another human to protect a werewolf. He knew Nathaniel, but he never thought he'd do such a thing. He looked back to Nathaniel stunned and immediately became worried.

Ashley had rolled gently off of Nathaniel as Nathaniel stood. His breathing was ragged now and his white coat was becoming a deep crimson. He'd shielded all of them and was paying the price. His eyes were losing focus as he tried to make it to the house.

"I've got you," said Alex as he came over to Nathaniel. He tried to support him as Nathaniel changed back. He didn't know where Nathaniel had been shot, but it must've been bad. Nathaniel's body shuddered and he stopped walking.

Ashley rose slowly as saw her white wolf limping away from her. She saw his body begin to shrink and fall away. He was turning back into a normal person in front of her eyes. She followed the blood trail and watched his failing form with horror. Images flashed in her mind and she was sitting back in the chair. Death hung behind her and showed her the mirror. She saw her greatest friend, lover, and protector dying. For a moment the tiniest memory returned to her.

"Nath…" she started, but Katie put a hand over her mouth before she could scream his name. Katie shook her head and ran them towards the house. Nathaniel was completely human again and he was unconscious. Alex hoisted him over his shoulder and charged inside. He didn't even bother to open the door, instead he shot the lock with his free hand and kicked it open.

Katie followed him in more cautiously, checking everywhere for hidden attackers. Ashley stayed behind her sobbing as the visions in her mind came true. She couldn't think, she couldn't walk. Katie had to take her by the hand and drag her through the house. They followed her dad down into the basement.

Nathaniel was lying on her dad's worktable as a human. He had the living room blanket draped over most of his body and he was unconscious. Alex limped away to pull out a box and Ashley went to Nathaniel's side. She knew his name.

"Nathaniel? Nathaniel?" She shook him and he didn't respond. "Wake up!"

"We have to get the bullets out so he can heal," said Katie.

"Help him!" shouted Ashley.

Alex took Ashley and pulled her forcefully away. Alex looked into his daughter's terrified eyes and wasn't sure how to direct her. She hardly understood what was going on and she was screaming the name of someone she now hardly knew. The one strong link she'd had in the world was dying in front of her. Her eyes were filled with terror and panic and she needed comfort. Sadly comfort was not a luxury they had right now.

"We will. Stay on the stairs, take this," he forced his pistol into her hands, "and make sure nothing comes down."

"I can't…" she cried.

"Go!" he said as he pushed her towards the stairs. "Don't look back!" Ashley slowly stepped to the stairs as Alex and Katie worked on Nathaniel. "This won't be pleasant."

"Pleasant doesn't matter as long as we get the bullets out. I need your hand here Alex!" Alex turned Ashley around to look at the stairs and went to Nathaniel. Ashley started to turn around only to have Katie yell at her.

"Don't look Ashley!"

Ashley kept her eyes on the stairs and cried. Her head was pounding and the room was shaking. The terrible visions Death had induced were still running through her mind. She saw it unfold no matter where she looked. How was she supposed to not look?

She didn't know whether Nathaniel was awake or not, but she heard him groan audibly. He moaned and cried. Katie kept talking to him, but it only made it worse for Ashley.

"Don't move Nathaniel. It's almost out. Almost out."

Nathaniel cried out in pain and Ashley heard metal hit the ground. Ashley flinched with every cry Nathaniel made. More sounds of metal clinking against the floor and Nathaniel screamed more. Just hearing him made her shake and she had to drop to her knees.

She shut her eyes and put her head against the wall. She didn't need to look back to see what was going on. There was no light coming from above so the shadows of their work danced on the stairs in front of her. She held her ears and cried loudly.

Was this happening? Was Nathaniel really dying behind her or was this just another vision brought on by Death? Was she just imagining that her dad and friends had come to save her? Maybe she was still in the chair being tormented by Death. She banged her head against the wall as the tears came streaming out.

CHAPTER 30

COLLATERAL DAMAGE

 shley was gently shaken awake. She opened bloodshot eyes and looked up to see a woman looking at her.

"Hey kiddo." The woman said lightly.

"Huh?"

"Do you remember me?" Ashley looked at this woman and vaguely remembered her from last night. "My name is Katie."

Katie helped Ashley sit up on the couch. Ashley wasn't sure how she'd suddenly come to be here. She squinted as the sun crossed her eyes and smiled. Katie looked out the window and smiled with her.

"Daylight. It means we're safe now."

"Safe," said Ashley happily.

"Yes it is. How do you feel?" Ashley rubbed her head.

"My head hurts. Is Nathaniel okay?" Ashley felt her head as she said his name. Nathaniel. He was there somewhere in her memories. Every time she tried to focus on his name though, the memories seemed to slip away. Why was he so important again? Katie nodded with a sad smile.

"Yes. We managed to get the bullets out of him."

"Can I see him?" she asked hopefully. Katie shook her head.

"Not right now. He needs time to sleep and heal. Last thing we want to do right now is wake him up." Ashley felt her heart drop. Katie stroked her hair and smiled. "Don't worry, he's very tough. He'll be awake soon."

"Are you sure I can't see him?"

"Yes. We don't want to surprise him. Just give him a little time." Ashley remembered someone else from last night.

"Where's my dad?" she asked suddenly. She couldn't remember his name, but she knew he was her father. There was a deeper connection to him, bound by blood, which not even Lady Death had been able to influence.

"I'm waking him up in a second. I need you to go to your room and pack your bags. Pack everything you need. We're all going away for a little bit."

"Okay." Katie helped her stand up and patted her back.

"Get ready. We want to go as soon as possible."

Ashley nodded and walked upstairs. She wasn't sure how she guided herself into the room that was hers, her feet just remembered the way. Most of the room looked unfamiliar, but some things were normal. The clothes in the drawers felt comfortable to her. She saw pictures of her and the boy Nathaniel on one of the dressers and paused. She ran her fingers along the photos, a smile coming to her face. They must've been good friends or even better. There was another of her and a woman who looked just like her. This must be her mother. Only her mother could be so beautiful.

She pulled the photos out of their frames and put them in a bag. She threw some clothes in next. She found the basics from the bathroom next to her room and stocked up. There were a lot of things here, but she didn't know how to feel about them. Were they important to her? Nothing seemed to have any great importance to her. If it did, she didn't remember it.

Only one thing did seem important to her. There were two small cases next to the window. They looked exactly the same, only one was covered in a fine layer of dust. She opened them each in turn and found beautiful flutes in both. There were pages of musical notes. She didn't know how to read them, but these were hers. She closed the two cases back up and put them in another bag. She filled the second bag with clothing to secure the flute cases. She headed downstairs and put them next to the door. Her dad was awake then.

"Ashley," he said as he hugged her. "How are you feeling?"

"Confused," said Ashley. "Are we okay?"

"Yes. The fighting is over. What do you remember?" Ashley blinked and shuddered. Just behind the darkness of her eyes, she saw the vampire Death looking back at her. Her dad had to shake her before she focused on him again. "Ashley?"

"I remember scary things. Nothing but scary things." He hugged her tightly.

"They're all gone now," he said bitterly. "All the scary things are gone." Alex separated himself from her and stroked her cheek. "Sit down and I'll be right back."

"Okay," said Ashley dully.

"Alex?" asked Katie as she knocked on his door.

"Yeah?"

"I'm going for a bit. I need to see if I still have a place."

"Okay. If you see Morgan or any of them…"

"I'll tell them Nathaniel is here," she finished for him. She came in and gave him a hug. "She'll be okay Alex."

"I hope so," said Alex worriedly. Katie left the room and gave Ashley a hug too. She headed out in the street with her rifle in hand and walked home. She doubted anyone would question her after last night.

Her dad came back into the kitchen and poured her a bowl of cereal. He gave her a spoon to eat with and went back to checking on his things and Nathaniel. She desperately wanted to see her friend, but her dad kept telling her he needed his rest. Ashley wasn't sure what had happened to Nathaniel or why he was in her basement, she just remembered blood everywhere. Her dad said they'd be leaving soon.

Alex went into the basement one last time to check on Nathaniel. After they'd taken out the bullets they'd applied some small bandages and stopped the bleeding. All they could do for him now was let him sleep. His wounds were already healing miraculously, but they'd need more time. He didn't want to leave Nathaniel like this, but they had to leave. Nathaniel's wounds were too dangerous for them to move him. Alex's best bet was to leave him food and water and lock the door to the basement. Then he'd barricade the door and leave Nathaniel down there to heal. He was sure one of his family would come and sniff him out soon. If they didn't, he'd heal and then force his way out. It wasn't nice or perfect, but they'd all survive. After last night, survival was the only thing that mattered.

There was knocking at the door and Ashley perked up. She walked absently over to a nearby window and looked out curiously. Three men in dark clothing stared back at her. She squeaked and disappeared behind the curtain.

"Dad!"

Alex was in the basement and hadn't heard the knock. When he heard his daughter shriek he practically flew up the stairs with his pistol in hand. He found her standing against the wall and nodding towards the window. "Scary people."

Scary people? It was daylight out now; vampires couldn't be out. They could be ghouls, but what kind of ghoul just stood at the door? He peered through the curtain and saw the three men. He didn't recognize any of them. He opened the curtain so they could see him and he pressed the barrel of his pistol against the glass.

"Who are you?" he demanded.

"Alex Jameson?" asked the lead man. Alex narrowed his eyes.

"Yes?" The lead man pulled out something from his coat and held it out to the window. Alex's eyes widened as he saw the Hunter's pendant. The story of the attack had already spread. The Hunters were already here. "May we come in?" Alex closed the blinds and thought hard about what he could do. Refusing them would look bad, but then again, he had Nathaniel just downstairs. He took a deep breath and moved to the door.

"Ashley, stay there," he said.

Ashley nodded and stayed against the wall. Alex opened the door and held up his own Hunter pendant. He made sure they all got a good look at it. The lead Hunter's pendant had only a silver halo on it, meaning he still wasn't too high in the Order. Even though he was retired, Alex wanted to make sure they knew his rank and respected it.

"Come in," he said and put the pendant down. The men came in and Alex closed the door. He frowned as two dogs followed them in. These Hunters were in town with a purpose. "You came faster than I expected."

"Word travels fast," said the lead man. "We were surprised it didn't come from you."

"I was a tad busy last night," said Alex bitterly. "Now what do you want?"

"We need your..." the man paused as he spotted Ashley nearby. She'd crouched down and was holding a hand out to one of the dogs. "This should be done in private."

"After last night I'm not going to be separated from my daughter," said Alex angrily. "She knows everything anyway. You men don't have long because we're leaving town."

"Please then, a few minutes of your time in private is all I'll ask. Any information you can give us could be invaluable." Alex took in a deep breath and sighed.

"Ashley, take your bags and wait in the truck outside. I'll be out in a minute."

Ashley looked out the window terrified. She'd felt safe in the house, but outside. Outside was scary.

"Alone?" she whispered. Alex glared at the Hunters. The lead one nodded and looked back.

"Phillip. Will you stand outside and make sure nothing disturbs her?" Phillip nodded.

"With my life," he said as he led the way outside.

Alex waved Ashley after him. Ashley made her way outside and stopped next to the truck in the driveway. She pulled on the door, but it was locked. She put her bags down next to it and looked around nervously.

The neighborhood was in shambles. Some of the houses were burned down and some were still burning. Perhaps the scariest thing though was the lack of noise. Nobody was sure what had truly transpired last night and they were in hiding. Nobody ventured out of their homes yet or tried to clean up the streets. They stayed hidden as if the open air was poisonous.

"Are you alright?" asked Phillip. Ashley shook her head.

"This place scares me."

"We'll make sure it's safe again. Do you know where you're going to?" Ashley shook her head. "I suppose it doesn't really matter. Home is where the heart is," said Phillip confidently. "As long as you're still alive, you can bring your home with you."

"Until it burns down," said Ashley as she looked at the smoke rising from her town. Phillip followed her gaze and said nothing. He didn't have any comforting words for a situation like this. He doubted anyone did.

Ashley and Phillip both forgot about the town as they heard gunshots from within Ashley's house. Muffled screams came through the walls and dogs barked. Something large started to crash throughout the house. Ashley watched as her home shook and turned into a war zone.

Phillip was already on the move. He'd drawn a pistol from within his coat and kicked the front door open. Ashley ran after him in an attempt to see what was going on. The kitchen table came flying by the front door and both of them had to dive to the ground. A second later a dog came flying past, yelping as it soared through the air. Phillip dove in shooting and Ashley caught a glimpse of the madness.

An enormous white wolf was smashing through Ashley's house. It had to be bigger than a horse and it scared Ashley. Blood was streaming through its white fur and she couldn't be sure if it was its own or someone else's. It was a good guess that it was a mixture of both. When

Phillip started shooting, it bolted for the backyard. It didn't choose the backdoor, but instead went straight through the walls.

Ashley crept in a bit more and saw her kitchen was torn to pieces. She had no idea where the wolf had come from, but it looked like it'd appeared under the house somehow. Most of the floor in the kitchen was torn up as it'd clawed its way through. The house smelled of something strange. Water was pouring into the basement as it'd broken most of the pipes. The hole it'd come through was a decent size, but the damage it'd done to the surrounding area was ten times greater.

Her basement was covered in blood. Ashley covered her mouth as she realized it must've torn the other two Hunters to pieces to make this kind of mess. She didn't see her friend Nathaniel in the basement either. She started to leave when something caught her eye. She moved a little closer and caught her breath. Then the worst and most horrible sound she'd ever produced came out of her mouth.

Amongst the bloodshed of the basement, her father was among the bodies. Ashley was an orphan once more.

Made in the USA
Columbia, SC
30 April 2023

15803177R00219